SPECIAL MESSAGE TO READERS

THE ULVERSCROFT FOUNDATION
(registered UK charity number 264873)

was established in 1972 to provide funds for research, diagnosis and treatment of eye diseases. Examples of major projects funded by the Ulverscroft Foundation are:-

• The Children's Eye Unit at Moorfelds Eye Hospital, London
• The Ulverscroft Children's Eye Unit at Great Ormond Street Hospital for Sick Children
• Funding research into eye diseases and treatment at the Department of Ophthalmology, University of Leicester
• The Ulverscroft Vision Research Group, Institute of Child Health
• Twin operating theatres at the Western Ophthalmic Hospital, London
• The Chair of Ophthalmology at the Royal Australian College of Ophthalmologists

You can help further the work of the Foundation by making a donation or leaving a legacy. Every contribution is gratefully received. If you would like to help support the Foundation or require further information, please contact:

THE ULVERSCROFT FOUNDATION
The Green, Bradgate Road, Anstey
Leicester LE7 7FU, England
Tel: (0116) 236 4325

website: www.ulverscroft-foundation.org.uk

STRAY ANGEL

East London, 1915. While the man she loves is in France fighting for his country, Lily Larkin wakes up at dawn to carry crates of apples to the market stall. Left in charge of Greg's warehouse, she has blossomed from a street urchin into a shrewd tradeswoman. But the market is a man's world and she soon starts attracting some unwanted visitors, including Greg's old rival Scully.

Luckily, Lily recruits her old friends, Margie and Fanny, as helping hands. While the work is hard, it is nothing compared to the drudgery they endured as children of the workhouse.

But Lily has one trouble she must keep secret: before dying, her mother gave birth to a child who was spirited away under the cover of darkness. Searching every corner of the city to find her long-lost sister, Lily soon discovers there is a world of wickedness within London's poorest alleys.

KAY BRELLEND

STRAY ANGEL

Complete and Unabridged

MAGNA
Leicester

First published in Great Britain in 2021 by
Piatkus
London

First Ulverscroft Edition
published 2022
by arrangement with
Piatkus
An imprint of
Little, Brown Book Group
London

A catalogue record for this book is available
from the British Library.

ISBN 978-0-7505-4935-6

Published by
Ulverscroft Limited
Anstey, Leicestershire

Printed and bound in Great Britain by
TJ Books Ltd., Padstow, Cornwall

This book is printed on acid-free paper

For Sandra, with love

Prologue

August 1910

'Is she as scrawny as a newborn should be? The major mustn't suspect a thing or I'll be out on my ear. I'm not stumping up cash for her if she won't pass muster.'

'She's very small and appears to be only hours old, m'm.' The elder of the two women had pulled back an edge of grubby wool to gaze at a tiny, crinkled face still smeared with vernix. The infant was so pale and still she could have been a corpse, but the baby peddler who'd brought her into the house had assured them she wasn't. Vera Priest stroked a minuscule cold hand. She gave a satisfied nod as the scrap of humanity responded to her touch by curling her fragile fingers.

'I'd better have a look at my daughter then.' The younger woman had been carrying on this conversation while styling her long auburn hair at the mirror. She discarded the brush onto the mantelpiece and came to inspect her purchase. Having gazed with faint distaste at the swaddled infant, she drew a finger through its downy hair then wiped the digit on her skirt.

'Well, she is fair like him so that's something. She'll have to do. If you deliver a letter to his club, the major will come by tomorrow for a look at his daughter. He won't part with another penny until he's seen the evidence his bastard's arrived. It's not a boy so he'll be disappointed. But there we are.' She shrugged her silk-clad shoulders.

1

Vera suspected the major would be disappointed thinking his by-blow had drawn breath, but she kept that to herself. The distinguished fellow had not been happy when his mistress had told him she was pregnant. She'd subsequently miscarried but he'd never been advised of that. By then he'd found himself a new fancy piece. His cast-off had been determined to get what she saw as her due. A meal ticket for the foreseeable future was in the offing for as long as he believed he'd fathered a child with her.

He was an honourable man and shouldered his responsibilities, however unwelcome, Major Beresford had assured his ex-paramour through gritted teeth. His hoity-toity wife might contest his good opinion of himself, though, should she discover a regular stop-off point on his way home from chairing the Board of Guardians meetings. He pretended he went to his club in St James's for a nightcap; Cheapside was where he actually headed, because that was where he housed his lady friends.

'Is Mrs Jolley still here?' A noise from beyond the closed door had drawn their attention from the motionless bundle.

'She is, m'm.' Vera knew why the baby peddler had reminded them of her presence by banging the hall chair against the wainscot. 'She insists on being paid before she leaves. I did ask her to meet me tomorrow somewhere away from here, to get rid of her quickly. She wouldn't have it, though, and said she'd wait.'

'I'd rather get the dratted woman settled up now. Her sort can make a nuisance of themselves. I shan't give her an excuse to come back again.'

While her employer went into the hallway, Vera was left holding the baby. She tiptoed closer to the door

2

to peep through an aperture and watch the transaction. Twelve pounds was counted out in one-pound notes and handed over. The recipient, dressed head-to-toe in ugly black garments, and looking for all the world like a poor widow, counted them again with the speedy efficiency of a bank teller. Satisfied none was missing, there was a brief conversation between the two. Vera was about to turn away when she heard Mrs Jolley mention the name of the child's mother. Vera pressed closer to the door, her jaw dropping and her eyes growing round as she listened. Mrs Larkin had been a respectable widow, fallen on hard times, who'd passed away in childbirth in the Whitechapel workhouse infirmary. Mrs Jolley wasn't a workhouse officer. She was a go-between and had decided to stress her credentials and assure her customer she'd only sell a baby of good blood. Not that she needed to go to the trouble. Betsy Finch would've taken a piglet in a blanket if she knew she could pass it off as her lover's illegitimate offspring and continue living comfortably. But even Betsy, mercenary schemer that she was, would have baulked at getting involved with a woman as downright cruel and criminal as Mrs Jolley, had she troubled to delve into the woman's character. Mrs Jolley said her fulsome thanks and a goodbye. A moment later Betsy came back into the room. 'You'll find a wet nurse for the creature, won't you, Vera?'

'I will, m'm,' Vera said, licking her parched lips. 'Did Mrs Jolley say the mother's name was Larkin?'

'I think that was the name she mentioned; poor old stick pegged out having this one.' Betsy shuddered. 'Glad I didn't have to go through that business. Buying a kid is so much easier.' She giggled, starting to brush her hair again, then pinning it up into an

3

elegant bun. 'I'll be bloody glad when I can stop hiding away and go out again now the deed's done.'

'Did Mrs Jolley say if it was *Maude* Larkin in the workhouse?'

'Don't think I heard more than Larkin mentioned.' Betsy turned around, frowning. 'Why, you don't know the poor cow, do you?'

'Just a name from the past,' Vera said. 'It jogged my memory. All forgotten now.' In fact she had never met Maude but, while still working as an office char, Vera had been acquainted with the woman's husband. She'd overheard Charles Larkin speak affectionately about his wife. Vera had felt sorry for Charles when his world fell apart because he fell prey to a vixen, masquerading as a respectable lady. At least Betsy Finch was honest about who she was, even if she did intend pulling the wool over the major's eyes about this pathetic orphan.

'Well, what are we going to call this little perisher?' Betsy sighed, sending the baby an aggravated stare.

Vera uncovered the mite's face again, seeing that her eyes were open, staring at her. She searched the baby's features for a likeness and persuaded herself she'd found it. 'How about Charlotte?' Vera said. 'I think that name would suit.'

January 1915

'Fine sodding New Year this is going to be!'

'What is it, m'm?' Vera called out, having heard her increasingly foul-mouthed mistress ranting in the front parlour. Since she'd been abandoned by her high-born lover, Betsy had let her standards slip.

Not long ago the letter box had chimed as the

4

postman used it. Usually Vera would collect the letters from the mat, but Charlotte had been coughing and she'd been rubbing the little girl's back. Vera took her hand to lead her down the stairs. 'Come and say good morning to your mama, my dear.'

They entered the parlour to find Betsy Finch with a piece of paper shaking in her rigid fingers. 'The bleeding bastard's only gawn and died on me!'

'Mind your tongue! I'll take Charlotte back to her room, then we can talk.' Vera had rebuked her employer before about the language she used in front of the child. At one time Betsy would've slapped her servant down. Now, she couldn't be bothered, having either been at the rum, or be feeling the effects of it. Her first boyfriend had been a sailor and Betsy had developed a taste for his tipple.

When Vera returned, having settled the little girl on her bed with some toys, she found Betsy sitting in an armchair, her elbows dug into her lap and her head in her hands.

Vera retrieved the paper that had been screwed up and hurled to the floor. She already had an idea of the bad news the letter might contain. Having flattened it enough to read it, she felt her heart sink on being proved right. The major had been killed in action in France. At Ypres. Vera was thankful that at least his commanding officer had responded to their enquiry. Perhaps he'd had other such letters from desperate females, petitioning for news of their 'dear close acquaintance Major Beresford', as he'd not been in touch for a long while.

Her mistress could feel satisfied that the unpaid allowance, the long silence, hadn't been an intentional snub as she had suspected. Vera knew men

5

better than the younger woman did, though she'd only had a close relationship with her late husband. Betsy had never sought intimacy with a fellow's mind, just another part of his anatomy and his wallet. Vera had tried to persuade her mistress that the major was a creature of habit and something other than spite had caused his regular payments to suddenly stop.

'Well, you know what this means, don't you?' Betsy scrubbed her eyes with a hanky and pursed her lips. 'We're both out on our arses, and the kid too.'

Vera was getting on in years, but she could get another live-in position as a general domestic and build a small nest egg on which to retire. Her mistress, though decades younger, had only one quality to rely on. When Vera had started working for Betsy Finch five years ago, the girl had been a vivacious good-looker of twenty-four. It had been easy to see how she'd caught the major's eye. Now, though, she was no longer nearly as attractive as once she'd been; she was embittered and appeared older than her years due to heavy drinking and keeping bad company. Betsy had been supplementing her allowance from the major by 'seeing gentlemen', although to give her her due she hadn't started doing that until he had put her off. When too pie-eyed to know what she was doing, she sometimes brought one of the punters home with her. Thankfully it had been a rare occurrence. But Betsy wasn't as discreet as she needed to be — hence her suspecting the major had sussed her out and cut off his funding.

Over the years he had turned up a handful of times to see his 'daughter'. The first time had been just after the child arrived, to satisfy himself there indeed was one. His last visit had been several months ago, when he'd appeared on the doorstep looking smart in his army uniform. He'd patted Charlotte on the head, asked if she could write her name and read some words — both of which she could, courtesy of Vera having spent time teaching the four year old her numbers and letters. Betsy had received scant attention during his brief stay, and she'd brooded on it afterwards. She'd not boasted since that she could lure him back if she really wanted to. He'd always turned up unannounced, convincing his ex-lover that it was a strategy to catch her out in wrongdoing, so he could cut ties with her and remove the child to a foster mother.

'What will you do now, m'm?' Vera asked. Once, the girl had attracted high rollers; now it was spivs on the make. Two had attempted to take her 'under their wings'. She'd resisted, instead letting her regular ponce handle her earnings. Since the major left her she had received several right-handers from violent men. The last had left her with a faint scar across her top lip.

Despite her mistress's deplorable ways, Vera had some loyalty and affection for Betsy. Not as much as she had for Charlotte, though. To all intents and purposes, the child was Betsy's daughter, and Vera feared for the little girl's future now this had happened. She'd not got a reply to her question, so repeated it.

'Dunno . . . thinking . . .' Betsy snapped.

'A proper job, perhaps in a dress shop, might suit you, being as you're so stylish.' Vera tried flattery. 'You've some lovely outfits to wear to interviews.'

'Ain't considering that sort of work,' Betsy snorted. 'I'll barely make rent. I'll have to go and see Mikey.'

'Why? Do you want another punch in the face?'

7

Vera asked dryly.

'Don't need no lectures off you.' Betsy pointed a finger. 'I can't pay you wages now the money's run out, so you might as well start packing. The bailiffs will be on their way soon enough. Rent's due again.'

Vera knew that was true; she'd fielded the tallyman when he'd turned up at the door last week. 'I'll pack Charlotte's things in with yours.' Vera turned towards the door but hesitated in leaving the room. She hated the idea of the child being stuck with a woman who showed her neither care nor attention. In four years, Betsy had barely acknowledged the small person she'd to thank for keeping a roof over her head. She'd only put some effort into the sham of being a mother when the major showed his face. Other than that, Betsy left her servant to attend to Charlotte's needs. Vera had never been able to persuade her mistress to read the little girl a story or tuck her in at night.

'Once I find myself a position, I'll pay a visit and look after her as often as I can to give you a break.' Vera yearned to offer to keep Charlie, as she called her, being as she was turning into quite a tomboy. A female domestic with a child in tow was unemployable, though. Without an income she couldn't even support herself.

'I won't need a break from her.' Betsy got up from her chair with an air of finality. 'She won't be coming with me. It's the kiss of death being saddled with a brat in my line of work. If you can't have her, she'll have to go back where she came from.' Betsy snatched the letter from Vera's hands with a curse and threw it onto the fire. 'That's the end of him, and it's the end of us, Vera. We've been a good team but it's time to go our separate ways.' She went to the sideboard and emptied the depleted bottle of rum into a tumbler. 'I have got one last job for you, though. Pack up the kid's things then take her back to Mrs Jolley. She'll have to find someone else to take the girl. Somebody'll bite at a pretty kid with fair hair.' Betsy despatched the rum in two fast swallows, smacking her lips and slamming down the empty glass. 'Whatever you do, though, don't bring her back here because I'll be gone.'

1

Autumn 1915

'I can't talk business with a woman, ducks!' Rory Scully emphasised the idea was absurd by whacking his flat cap against his thigh and exploding in laughter. 'Especially not one as young as you. Where's your boss? I'll deal with Mr Wilding.'

Scully crossed his arms over his broad chest, eying the girl up and down. She looked about seventeen and had a tumble of chestnut-brown waves framing her lovely face, but his gaze soon shifted to her figure. She might be young but she was luscious and he could understand what that randy hound saw in her. She was no shy pushover, though, to be regarding him with a challenging glint in a pair of gloriously blue eyes.

'Is the gaffer due back soon?' Scully tucked his cap beneath an arm. He'd removed it on entering Wilding's costermonger premises. It was only a token civility; he'd nothing nice in mind.

'In about three weeks' time, with any luck. You'd better take a seat if you're intending to wait for him.'

Lily Larkin's tone was ironic but she gave the fellow a smile. He wasn't the first man to swagger into the warehouse and treat her as the hired help. Just months ago she had been a costermonger's apprentice clerk, taking orders. But not now. Since the man she loved had gone to France to fight, she was running his market business with the help of her friends

10

and colleagues.

Scully turning up and demanding to see Gregory had brought him to the forefront of her mind . . . not that Lily needed much of a reminder. He was constantly in her thoughts despite the problems piling up. Scully wanted to see Gregory Wilding, did he? Well, not as much as she did.

'Where is the skiver then . . . off on his holidays?' Scully put on a good show of seeming surprised. 'Getting idle in his old age, is he?'

'What do you want, Mr Scully?' There was something about him that jarred on Lily; and it wasn't just his assumption that she was too young and dumb to discuss business with him. She sensed he wasn't all he was making out to be. Most people who knew Gregory Wilding were aware by now that he'd enlisted and gone overseas.

'I want to make your boss an offer he can't refuse.' Scully perched on the edge of Lily's desk, forcing her to sit back in the chair to keep at a decent distance. 'And I'd like to make you one at the same time, but I reckon I might get my face slapped if I did.'

'You'll get more than that when the guv'nor gets back and finds out you've been trying it on with his gel.' A young man had just come into the warehouse, unseen by Scully.

Lily stood up, signalling that she was fine, but it didn't stop her workmate eying the visitor with hard suspicion. He knew Scully by sight as a newcomer to his neighbourhood.

He'd not been living there long but already he had a reputation as a man with a big mouth who used his fists. He had the appearance of a successful coster: sturdy rig-out and healthy tan from having been

11

outdoors in summer sun. Aged about mid-twenties, he was auburn-haired, of medium height and muscular. His biceps bulged beneath his shirt as he crossed his arms then cocked his shaggy head in a mocking sort of way.

'So, this is yer sidekick, is it, love?' Scully's calculated condescension turned the younger man red. 'Think I've seen you about, son.'

'Smudger's my right-hand man.' Lily introduced Bobby Smith by the nickname everybody used. 'Now, we've got stocktaking to do, so if you've said all you want to . . .'

'Oh, I haven't even started, ducks.' Scully's tone had changed. He wasn't playing now. 'I'm looking to buy a premises to expand my market business.' He leisurely budged off the desk. 'I've had a nice concern going over the other side of the water, but I want to settle down round here to build my little empire.'

'This place isn't for sale.' Lily cut to the chase to get rid of him.

'Everything's for sale, love.' He gave her a lewd look. 'If the price is right. Your guv'nor understands that. When you're older and more clued up, you will too.' He nodded at the Primus stove on the shelf with some cups set neatly close by. 'Now, how about you make us a nice cup of tea and we can have a chat about things.'

Lily knew he was out to rile her, so she simply put her hands on her hips and gave him an old-fashioned look.

Scully chuckled at her defiance. Her sidekick might be trying to protect her by calling her the boss's girl. Wilding was known for wiping up waifs and strays as his employees. Scully had heard he'd taken on a clerk and had assumed it to be another grateful youth who'd toe the line. Wilding must have lost his wits to volunteer, leaving ragamuffins running his depot . . . or so Scully had thought. But now he'd met them he'd changed his tune. These two weren't timid little wretches. They were strong and confident. But he wasn't giving up on his ambition to make a killing in Gregory Wilding's absence.

'Person could die o' thirst in here,' Scully moaned. 'Come on, rattle them cups 'n' saucers and tell me yer name.'

Smudger took a threatening step forward, getting het up that the man wouldn't take the hint and leave. He would have liked to bash the smirk off Scully's chops. Lily quickly defused the situation. 'I'm Lily Larkin but, like I said, nothing here is for sale. I'm old enough to know that.' She extended a hand for Scully to shake. She might not like him but it was in her nature to be polite even to patronising Jack-the-lads. She jerked her fingers from his tightening grip. 'Sorry, not making tea cos we're too busy to stop. I'll let Mr Wilding know you called when he's back home.'

The planked door of the warehouse swung open and a fair-haired young woman walked in, swinging a shopping bag. 'Got the stuff for tea; they had a few custard creams left . . . ' Margie Blake fell quiet on noticing the visitor.

'Good . . . we'll have those when we get home,' Lily said smoothly before Scully could again invite himself to join the party.

'Custard creams, eh? My favourite.' Scully insolently doffed his cap to her before flipping it onto his head. 'You're all keeping Wilding's open for business then, are you?' He looked Margie over, aware she had shoved a crippled hand out of sight behind her back when he paid attention to her. Apart from that blemish she was another nice-looking girl.

'Unless I can sell you some fruit and veg, or rent you a barrow, I'll say good day.' Lily wasn't giving him tea and biscuits though she was gasping for a cuppa herself.

He sauntered to the door then turned about to assess the trio. Smudger looked the eldest but Lily Larkin was the one with the savvy and would be the nut to crack. The fair-haired girl he dismissed as no trouble whatsoever. Scully gave the warehouse another glance. A place like this in a prime spot in Poplar was just what he wanted, and he wouldn't get a better chance of a crafty strike than while Wilding was off the scene. He stopped his eyes roaming over the stacked equipment with an acquisitive glint. They were all watching him but the smart girl got his foxy smile. The little cow was reading his thoughts about taking it all, lock, stock and barrel . . . including having her into the bargain. 'You remember me to your guv'nor, won't you, now? Let him know I'll be back for that chat.' He sniffed, rubbing a finger beneath his nose. ''Course, if his luck runs out over there and he don't come back, then it'll be me 'n' you having that talk, Lily Larkin. You'll wish you'd offered me that cup o' tea then, love, eh?'

'Oh, he'll be back, and I'll tell him what you said, don't you worry about that.' Lily hated him for playing on her fears for Greg's safety. She bit her tongue on any more back-chat. He was itching for her to give him a reason to hang around a bit longer.

Smudger put a boot against the swinging door, slamming it into the frame to let Scully know he was

14

glad to be shot of him.

'He's full of himself. Didn't like him one little bit. Do you know Rory Scully, Smudger?'

'Never heard his name before. Seen him around though; he's moved into our street with his wife. Guv'nor probably knows him. Ain't many people in this game who've escaped his notice.'

'Said the wrong thing, did I?' Margie started unpacking the shopping bag with her left hand. Her right had deformed fingers that made her clumsy.

''Course not . . . ' Lily lit the Primus and put the kettle on. 'He was just having a nose around and thought he could wangle a cup of tea while he did so.'

Margie Blake was Lily's best friend, a friendship that had been forged when they'd both been inmates of South Grove workhouse in Whitechapel. Margie had started working at Wilding's a few months ago and kept the account books up to date. She could write nicely with her left hand and had received a good schooling in English and arithmetic, as had Lily.

Previously Lily had been the clerk, but now she and Smudger shared the management of the place. They were responsible for the buying of stock at Spitalfields and Billingsgate and operated a market stall, selling produce six days a week. The workforce at Wilding's had halved since the war started. To make up numbers, a neighbour's school-leaver son had been roped in to take out a barrow on street rounds. Joey Robley was a strapping lad of fourteen and had no trouble pushing a loaded barrow. But he was green when it came to dealing with shrewd housewives wanting something for nothing, or when fending off rivals poaching on his patch. Joey did his best, but the business could really do with a mature recruit who'd take no nonsense. And Lily reckoned she knew just the person, if Fanny Miller was willing to give street trading another go.

'I parked our van up round the corner.' Smudger had been indignant to see a horse and cart blocking his way onto Wilding's forecourt. He went to the door to pull it open and watch their unwanted visitor's departure. Scully had jumped onto the cart. He leisurely lit a cigarette, as though aware he was under observation, then, puffing away, flicked the reins over the horse's back. As the vehicle moved off a pile of steaming manure was revealed.

'And you can take your shit with you, 'n' all,' Smudger bawled out.

'Do nicely for the garden, that will,' Lily said calmingly. 'Old girl upstairs uses fertiliser on the roses.'

'You all right, Lil?' Smudger was watching Lily nibbling at her thumbnail. 'Ain't worried about that prat, are you?' He approached to put a comforting arm about her shoulders. 'All gob that one. S'pose you could write and tell the guv'nor though, just in case his leave gets cancelled like it did last time. Guv'nor'll let us know how he wants us to play it if Scully turns up again.'

Smudger had liked Lily from the moment the guv'nor had turned up with his new clerk. Though looking thin and bedraggled and younger than her years in her workhouse uniform, Lily Larkin had soon shown she possessed the spirit of a lioness. In Smudger's eyes her only fault was her tendency to mother her twin brother and tolerate his mistakes — and there had been many. But Davy Larkin was a boy soldier on the Western Front now. Though Smudger reckoned Davy mad to have gone, he also privately thought the separation of brother and sister would do them both good.

'I'm not worried about Scully . . . he's just blowing hot air.' Lily prayed every night for the safety of her boyfriend and her brother. The thought of life without them was unbearable. She wished they'd not enlisted, though she understood why they had, and was immensely proud of them both. They were risking their lives, having volunteered to fight a war on foreign soil that many people believed should be over and done with by now. Lily was proud that Gregory believed in her and trusted her to be capable of running a business he'd built up from scratch and made profitable. She loved being a businesswoman. But not as much as she loved him. She wanted him safely back with her, so she wouldn't write and inform him of Scully's visit when he needed to concentrate on dodging bullets.

'Let's have that tea. Then Marge and me will have a tot-up of the takings when Joey gets back with the barrow. Hope he's sold out and not run into trouble today.' Smudger had had to work the round with the youth for a while to show the interlopers that Wilding's wasn't giving ground. Lily had run the market stall with just one-handed Margie's help, and they'd all pitched in doing the accounts in the evening.

She started spooning tea into the pot. 'It's high time I had a catch-up with Fanny; she's just the person Joey needs to help him out.' Fanny Miller wouldn't take any nonsense off the Burdett Road boys, who were trying to muscle in on Joey's patch. Fanny had been a workhouse inmate too and Lily had liked her from the start, despite the fact she was a few years her senior and hard as nails. Fanny also had a bad reputation, having been a 'working girl' who'd had a baby out of wedlock. But Fanny was now on the straight and narrow and a dedicated, if unmarried, mother. 'D'you reckon Fanny will take the job?'

'Definitely . . . if she's still stuck in that bloody rag shop; you know she hates the work,' Margie piped up. 'I'll come on a visit to Fanny with you. I'd love to see little Ronny again. Wonder how he is?'

'Not so little, I reckon.' Lily smiled, remembering Fanny's sturdy son. 'I expect he's up on his feet and might even be talking by now. Can't wait to see him.'

They gathered round the desk and tucked into their tea and biscuits. Lily had almost forgotten about the unwelcome visitor as she dwelled on seeing Fanny again. But not quite . . . his leering face was still hovering at the back of her mind.

'We could go this Sunday to see Fanny,' Margie suggested.

'Can't do it this weekend . . . already got something planned,' Lily said.

The other two looked expectantly at her.

'There's a place in Bloomsbury that I've not visited yet. It might have a record of my sister.' Lily sounded excited and showed them two sets of crossed fingers before taking a sip of tea. She could hardly wait for Sunday to arrive. She'd go now, this instant, if she could. But her commitment to the man she loved, and to her colleagues, was as strong as that to her little lost half-sister. She couldn't neglect work in favour of family business. Wilding's didn't just provide her livelihood but that of her friends, too. Greg had taken a leap of faith putting an inexperienced workhouse girl in charge of his money and his premises. She'd work her fingers to the bone to be worthy of his trust.

18

Smudger and Margie gave her sympathetic smiles then turned their attention to the plate of biscuits. At intervals they glanced at Lily, immersed now in thoughts of family, not friends.

Both of these friends, in their hearts, believed that Lily should give up chasing a lost cause. Every time she came back from an orphanage none the wiser, she would be down in the dumps for days. But Smudger and Margie adored her too much to upset her by telling her she was wasting her time and prolonging her own agony, looking for a sister who had probably died long ago.

2

'Your half-sister will be fortunate to have survived such early disadvantages, Miss Larkin.' The matron of the Foundling Hospital gazed at her visitor over her clasped, capable-looking hands.

'I imagine so . . . but why did you mention it?' On the opposite side of the desk, Lily sat forward in her chair. The matron had sounded sympathetic, rather too sympathetic. 'Have you come across something worrying in that book? Has my sister died in this place?' Lily's voice had sharpened in anxiety. She cocked her head, trying to read the writing on the page of the open ledger.

'Please don't upset yourself. I have searched entries for the date you gave but not come across a likely girl, living or deceased.' The matron closed the book. 'I'm simply bringing to your attention that infants who have suffered a poor start in life are more susceptible to nasty childhood diseases.'

'Oh . . . of course, I understand.' Lily relaxed slightly, removing her white-knuckled fingers from the edge of the desk. Disappointment, a fruitless visit; they were nothing new and better than crushed dreams. Hearing no record had been found was far preferable to being shown a death certificate. The search could go on; hope could go on.

Lily couldn't deny that this particular infant had suffered bad luck from her first breath. She'd been premature and her mother had passed away giving birth to her, but Lily refused to believe her half-sister was doomed without proof it was so. She was determined to find out what had happened to the little girl, though she had nothing to go on other than a description of her as fair-haired and feeble. Be that as it may, having won the struggle to exist, Lily felt convinced the baby would have battled on, and thrived. They were cut from the same tough cloth, and the love she felt for the sibling she'd never met was overwhelming. Sometimes she would talk to the child in her head, beg her to hold on because her big sister was coming to take her home.

Lily and her twin brother had been inmates of the Whitechapel workhouse when their widowed mother gave birth. The newborn had been spirited away from the infirmary, to be dumped like rubbish and avert a scandal. Since leaving that dismal place, Lily had learned more about their mother's harrowing final hours in labour. She had begun her search months ago at a small local orphanage. No match for her sister had been found. It had been Lily's first disappointment. She'd also felt relief.

Leaving the institution along an echoing corridor, she'd passed half-glazed double doors leading to a classroom. Within she'd glimpsed rows of blank-faced tots seated silently at desks. Only one boy had glanced over at her; a thwack of a cane on a blackboard had soon put a stop to his interest in the visitor. Lily prayed her sister hadn't spent her infancy in an atmosphere as miserable as that. She had been optimistic that things would be nicer at the Foundling Hospital. On walking up the drive earlier, she had stopped to watch children playing chase on a field. Inside it was larger and airier than the grim orphanage, and the atmosphere smelled less sour.

This matron hadn't made her feel that her presence or her questions were a nuisance and she was reluctant to get up and go. 'Would you have another look in the book, please, ma'am?' The request was accompanied by an appealing smile. 'My sister might not be registered under the name of Larkin but Stone.' It was a long shot. The workhouse officer who had smuggled the baby away was unlikely to have allowed another woman's child to bear the name of her lover.

'My sister has a freckled birthmark on her chest and has fair hair and would be five now.' Lily had already supplied this information but wanted to emphasise it. She also added something so far kept back. 'A Miss Fox would have brought the baby here from the Whitechapel workhouse. It's possible she pretended to be the baby's mother so you would take her.' From their conversation, Lily had picked up that a mother had to make a personal application; an impossibility in this case. The moment matron comprehended the child wouldn't have qualified for admission, she had closed the ledger.

Lily itched to reach across the desk, snatch the book, and read it herself to satisfy herself there weren't any clues to her sister's whereabouts concealed within.

'This Miss Fox is surely the best person to approach to trace your sister's whereabouts,' Matron pointed out.

'I can't . . . she's dead now, you see. An accident.' Goosebumps sprouted on Lily's forearms at the memory of that violent incident. 'Unfortunately, Miss Fox didn't tell anybody where she'd taken the baby.'

'Ah, I see . . . ' the matron said in a considering way.

The older woman had cottoned on to there being

nothing straightforward about this missing orphan's story. She was absolutely right to think there was more to it. Lily flinched at the idea of being questioned over why the baby hadn't been put in the Whitechapel workhouse's nursery with similar unfortunates. She shot to her feet, jittery that she might have revealed too much. 'Thank you for your time then, ma'am. I'll try elsewhere.'

'Just before you go, Miss Larkin . . .' Matron pushed herself to her feet. 'Please don't get your hopes up, but there's no harm in taking a look in another journal. You have jogged my memory of something that was mentioned by a colleague many months ago.' She opened a filing cabinet and selected a book, flicking back through the leaves. 'Somebody else did enquire about a female child with fair hair and a birthmark.' She frowned at the entry. 'I didn't immediately think of it, as my deputy conducted that interview. Oh, I am mistaken in any case. This concerns a four-year-old girl, just recently made homeless.' She shook her head. 'We wouldn't have taken a child of four. Only infants below the age of their first birthday are considered. Not everybody is aware of that or, if they are, they believe we might make exceptions. But we cannot, I'm afraid.' She began to close the book with an apologetic smile.

Lily's heart had started to race. Had her sister's father had a change of heart and decided to look for his child after all? He had been lied to, as Lily had, and led to believe Maude Larkin's baby had been stillborn. But unlike Lily, Ben Stone had decided to leave well alone where his illegitimate daughter was concerned. Lily didn't hate him for his view; in fact she had also wondered whether to accept that her sister might be settled with a new family if she'd survived the trauma of her first hours.

'Was the visitor a Mr Stone?' she asked, almost squeaking in excitement.

'Oh, it wasn't a gentleman.' Matron found her place in the book again and this time read more of what was logged. 'A woman came looking for the girl. A Mrs Priest; she once worked for the mother as her house-keeper and became the child's nanny. She had taken it upon herself to try to find out if the girl was settled somewhere.' Matron reached the bottom of the page. Suddenly her expression tightened. Mrs Priest had originally turned the child over to an individual called Mrs Jolley, on the instruction of her employer. The child's father had perished in the war and his widow was no longer in a position to support her daughter, or her housekeeper. The servant now regretted what she'd done and wanted to trace the child to care for her herself. Despite Mrs Priest's efforts to locate the woman, she'd been unable to. Mrs Jolley had vanished.

And well Mrs Priest might rue what she'd done! Mrs Jolley, or whatever other name she went by, was an unscrupulous character. Many innocents handed over to her had disappeared without trace. It wasn't the first time the baby peddler's name had been brought up in Matron's office by mothers searching for children handed over to her. Jolley lured her customers in with lies about finding foster parents who would provide a fresh start in healthy countryside homes. Poor women — abandoned by feckless men and unable to provide for their children — would beg or borrow money to give to Mrs Jolley in return for her worth-less promises. Matron feared that for some of those poor mites, Jolley had been a go-between from mothers to graves, rather than to a better life. Thankfully, the tot Mrs Priest had boarded out to Jolley had a living mother, so that was a glimmer of light that Miss Larkin and the child weren't related.

'What is it?' Lily had witnessed a change in the matron's expression and it greatly disturbed her.

'This child isn't an orphan. Her mother is now an impoverished war widow and unable to care for her daughter. It isn't a match.' Matron returned the book to the cabinet. She didn't want to alarm her visitor with details of a baby farmer's involvement without convincing proof of a connection.

'Have you at least their names and an address? The mother might have adopted her daughter and it is a start . . .'

'There's no mention of an adoption, so it seems unlikely that's the case,' Matron interrupted, clearing her throat.

'Please give me the names,' Lily insisted. 'I need something to go on cos I won't ever stop looking until I find out what happened to her.'

Matron relented a little bit. 'The family lived in Cheapside but have now all moved away. Mrs Priest didn't leave the mother's details or her address. No doubt she was protecting the woman's reputation. Anyway, my colleague would have made it clear to her that we would not have had any dealings with a child of four, so there would be no reason for us to get back in touch.'

'Thank you for telling me, and for seeing me today.' Lily suspected Matron was keeping something confidential back . . . but then so was she. A secret surrounded this search for her sister that even her

25

brother knew nothing about.

'You could always try the Barnardo's home for girls,' Matron suggested. 'The place is in Essex and by all accounts very pleasant. Perhaps your Miss Fox might have taken the child there. Here, I have the details.' Matron picked up a card with the address pre-printed. 'We keep these to hand out to people like you, searching for family members.'

'Thank you.' Lily beamed at the woman and offered her hand to be shaken. She'd learned more today than she had in many months. A four year old with fair hair and a birthmark . . . her sister would still have been four earlier in the year. Lily felt a surge of joyous hope. If it *were* her sister, the brave little thing had outrun her bad luck. She had battled through her first perilous years. Now she would be five. Starting school. A child, not a baby.

Having said her farewells to the matron, Lily walked briskly down the drive, unaware that the older woman was observing her departure from her office window. Lily looked at the address on the card and some of her optimism wilted. The Barnardo's home was quite a distance away. Harriet Fox would never have bothered taking the baby that far. She would have offloaded the newborn quickly, somewhere conveniently local. Lily refused to feel too dejected. Her sister might have been transferred from a City shelter to the Barnardo's home, then adopted from there and brought back to London by her new parents.

Lily knew she could tramp the streets around Cheapside, knocking on doors and making enquiries, but hitting on the right street, or on neighbours who might recall that family who'd moved away, would be like finding a needle in a haystack. Concentrating on

26

finding the housekeeper might be a better way forward. Already she liked Mrs Priest. The woman had been a servant, yet had held the child in such affection that she wanted to check on her welfare and her whereabouts. The housekeeper wouldn't have given up her search. At some point their paths might cross and then Lily would discover whether they were both hunting for the same little girl.

Miss Larkin had stopped to watch the boys playing cricket on the green before passing out of the open gate. Even though the young woman was now gone from sight, Matron continued to gaze into the distance, lost in disturbing memories.

She had been a probationer nurse twenty years ago when a carpet bag pulled from the River Thames was found to contain a baby's corpse. More babies had been found to have died similar disgusting deaths at the hands of an evil, avaricious woman. Amelia Dyer had long since gone to the gallows for her heinous crimes. But there had been other baby farmers hanged since, for taking cash for foster care then disposing of a child they'd had no intention of keeping. Matron sorrowfully shook her head. For as long as desperate women needed homes for children, villains would prey on them for easy money. Ten pounds or thereabouts to foster a child until it was of an age to care for itself. Most of them would have been lucky to attain another birthday once their mothers parted with them.

Mrs Jolley had gone, in all likelihood, to another district, where nobody knew her. London was a maze of backstreets housing poor families and strangers regularly came to stay before melting away again, with nobody taking much notice of them. A woman like

Jolley would continue to duck from view then bob up again somewhere else until the authorities caught up with her. And as for Miss Larkin's sister, what had been her fate?

'Good luck in your search, Lily Larkin,' Matron murmured in a heartfelt way before turning away from the window.

3

'Yes? What can I do for you?'

Lily had taken a step back as that question was barked at her. The hard-faced woman looked a real bruiser. 'Umm . . . we're looking for Fanny Miller. Is she at home?'

'Well, maybe she is. But as she don't live here no more, I wouldn't know. So bugger off, the pair of you.'

Lily and Margie exchanged a look. The dragon looked about to slam the door in their faces so Lily stayed it with a hand.

'Sorry to bother you then, but have you any idea where we might find Fanny?'

'Yeah, try the nearest street corner, and if she's there you can tell that tart from me that if she shows her face round here again I'll punch it for her. This is my place and he's my husband. You tell her that 'n' all.' She stomped inside, crashing the door into its frame.

Ten minutes later, Lily and Margie had settled on a bench in Victoria Park. They'd decided to take a breather after that disappointment and needed to decide what to do next to track down Fanny.

'We could head to the pub. The landlord might know where she is.' Lily gave a quiet sigh, gazing over a peaceful vista. It was a mild autumn day and on a Sunday afternoon in Bethnal Green, families would make the most of their day of rest and take a stroll in the park. The sound of children's enjoyment as they played chase on the grass wafted on the breeze.

'I hope Fanny's all right and hasn't — you know — gone back to her old ways,' Margie said.

Lily did know what Margie meant, and unfortunately suspected there might be something to it. The harridan they'd just encountered had implied Fanny was back on the game. If that were true and she was feeling ashamed of herself, it would explain why she hadn't been in touch to let them know she'd moved on.

Lily and Margie had already been workhouse inmates for many years when Fanny joined them. She had sought refuge there in her late teens when one of her 'gentlemen' got her pregnant and she needed a safe place to give birth. Many workhouses refused prostitutes, believing they'd corrupt the respectable poor, but Fanny had been allowed admission after spinning a yarn about her wicked treatment by a deceitful fellow. She'd told the younger girls that she'd exaggerated her innocence, but wouldn't elaborate more than that, possibly not wanting to shock them. They had taken to brash Fanny from the start, unlike other inmates who'd looked down on her. Lily and Margie had detested the harsh workhouse regime and the staff who enforced it; they had thus understood why some women might prefer selling themselves to avoid the life.

Once she became a mother, Fanny had seemed to turn her life round. She'd discharged herself from South Grove and found a regular job while lodging with an old flame. His wife, he'd said, had left him. Obviously not for good though, and the woman's return might have set Fanny back on a ruinous path. She adored her little boy and would fight tooth and nail to keep a roof over his head. It seemed she'd met her match, though, in the battle-axe who'd re-staked her claim on her husband and her home, sending her younger rival packing.

Lily settled back into the seat and let the sun bathe her face. Her mind wandered to those she loved who were far away from her. She wondered if Greg and her brother Davy were relaxing in a billet on this glorious Indian-summer afternoon. Or were they holed up in trenches, dreading the hours ticking by and the sound of the whistle that would send them over the top at dawn. Whenever she overheard women in shops whispering of gruesome injuries suffered by a neighbour's husband or son, her guts would sickeningly tighten. Rory Scully had meant to be hurtful, saying Gregory's luck might run out in France. There was no denying, though, that the graveyards abroad *were* filling up with Tommies who would never come back.

'Ready for the off, Marge?' Lily shot forward on the seat to snap herself out of the doldrums before they took a hold on her. 'We can't go back not knowing where Fanny's got to.' Lily stood up and stretched, taking in a lungful of sweet, earthy air. 'S'pose our best bet is the pub. Fanny knows loads of people who drink at the Bow Bells. Somebody's sure to know where she's hiding herself.'

As they set off towards the park gates, a child's ball rolled close to their feet. Lily scooped it up then lobbed it back to the little boy waiting shyly a few yards away. He looked about five, the same age as her sister, and had a mop of fair hair. Lily watched him dash back to his mother with his ball secured in both hands.

'I'd like a kid,' Margie suddenly declared out of nowhere as they walked along.

31

'You'd make a good mum,' Lily said, and meant it too, though rather thrown by the turn in conversation.

'Need to find a husband first,' Margie said with a sigh. 'Never even had a sweetheart. And I'd like one of those 'n' all.'

Lily gave her friend a hug, knowing who Margie had in mind to fill that role. But Smudger hadn't so far asked Margie out and Lily wished he would. In her opinion they were two of the nicest people, and made for one another.

★ ★ ★

The pub on the Bow Road was a large, many-windowed affair. Nothing much could be discovered by peering through the glass with a multitude of heads and raised glasses obscuring the view. The popular establishment was teeming with Sunday-dinnertime drinkers. Lily yanked open one of the swing doors and poked her head inside, bobbing up and down to try and spot Fanny's mane of red hair in amongst the throng. The smoky, yeasty atmosphere, rattling with conversation, held an allure that tempted a person to enter. Lily could understand how pubs drew people from cramped lodgings into their cosy aromatic embrace. But alcohol was a false friend. Her father had drunk himself to death by the canal, an empty bottle at his side. By then he'd had no money to buy decent drink and had been stealing spirits from the railway yard where he'd laboured. The impoverished family he'd left behind had ended up in the workhouse.

'All right there, love?' A stocky fellow had seen Lily searching for a face in the saloon bar and had followed her outside. He held a full tankard in one meaty hand and took a swig of beer, eying her craftily. 'What can I do for you then?'

'Nothing, thanks.' Lily backed away as she saw him sway on his feet. 'Just looking for a friend in there.'

'Well, now you've found one.' He gave her a tipsy wink.

'Very funny,' Lily muttered beneath her breath. 'Person I'm after is Fanny Miller. Know her, do you, or where we might find her?' Lily had noticed his heavy-lidded eyes become alert when she mentioned Fanny's name. He'd been about to take another gulp of his drink, but the tankard was dropped to his side so quickly that some beer slopped onto the pavement. 'You two nice gels don't look like you'd be pals with her.' He ogled them with renewed interest.

'Well, we are . . . so do you know where she is?'

'Well, she ain't in there, can tell you that fer nuthin'.' He jerked a nod at the pub. 'Not seen her today. Probably working, if you know what I mean.' A dirty chuckle rumbled in his throat.

Lily linked arms with Margie and started to move on. She wasn't listening to anybody bad-mouthing her friend for what she'd resorted to doing to earn a crust. Men with plenty of beer money in their pockets didn't know of *real* hardship — the sort that left women with few choices in fending for themselves and providing for their kids. Lily's beloved mum had slept with a stranger to protect her ten-year-old twins, and it had been the death of her.

'Oi!' he called. 'If you want that trollop, you'll probably find her where she always is when the boozers are about to turn out: down Sugar House Lane, waiting for a punter.' He approached them and thrust his

33

bristly face closer to Lily's. 'And if you want one, love, you just hang about while I fetch me coat.'

Lily turned scarlet, more from anger than embarrassment, but she wouldn't allow him to see any other sign of having upset her. 'Don't bother . . . I've got better things to do, thanks.'

'I can prove you wrong about that . . . ' He advertised what she was missing by boastfully cupping his groin. 'Ten bob in it for yer 'n' all.'

'Cheeky beggar!' Margie said as his drunken laughter followed them, marching up the street.

'Forget about him.' Lily already had. She'd got used to ribaldry from the customers who'd come in to hire their market equipment from Wilding's. The costermongers had soon acted more respectfully when they realised that her boss had a special interest in her. 'I know where Sugar House Lane is — over by the factories and the Abbey Mills sewage works.' Lily pulled a face at the prospect of breathing in that air. 'Looks like you were right then; Fanny is back streetwalking.'

'No point going to find her, is there? She won't want a job selling fruit and veg. If she did, she'd have come over to Poplar to ask for one, rather than do what she's doing.'

Lily thought about that as they walked along. She reckoned something worse than losing her boyfriend and her lodging had happened to Fanny. She had said that she never would go back on the game, and that she was determined to make Ronny proud of his mum. 'I want to go and find her.' Lily sounded quietly determined. She came to a halt and turned to Margie. 'I reckon she's got trouble of some sort. Perhaps she's got herself badly into debt.' Lily knew how easily that could happen. Her childhood had been blighted by

34

her father's debts that in turn had led to her family's disintegration. 'If you want to go home, Margie, I'll understand, honest.'

'Don't be daft,' Margie said. ''Course I'll come with you. Wish I'd brought a peg for me nose, though. Gas works are over that way 'n' all.'

'Wasn't that long ago we had more pegs than we knew what to do with. Shifted quite a few of those on Mondays.'

'Cos Monday is washday . . . ' Margie lilted.

Lily reflected on when they had all worked together, selling door to door after they'd left the workhouse. They'd enthusiastically thrown themselves into it, but their business had floundered due to their inexperience and lack of cash to invest. They had sold all sorts of household goods from their barrow: soap and soda, washing lines and pegs and every type of polish.

'We had a lark all of us, didn't we?' Margie gave Lily a cheeky nudge. 'Good times, they were, looking back.'

'Yeah . . . didn't always seem so at the time, though, when we was getting drenched through,' Lily reminded her. 'Let's find Fanny before she gets herself in worse trouble. Nicholson's gin distillery's down Sugar House Lane. She likes a drop of their Lamplighter.'

★ ★ ★

Lily and Margie had reached their destination, but even before they'd spoken to Fanny their optimism about making her see sense had dwindled. They'd spotted her, dressed in a fancy maroon costume and feathered hat, idling by some factory railings. Delighted surprise had animated her face when she

35

heard a chorus of familiar female voices hailing her. She'd almost waved . . . then the reality of accounting for her behaviour had dawned on her and she'd beat a retreat to avoid them.

'Fanny! Wait!' Lily puffed out, having charged down the road. She was determined to have it out with the older woman even if things didn't go well. But Lily was banking on the friendship they all shared being stronger than Fanny's shame at being caught soliciting. Lily and Margie had always been aware of her past, and that she could be ousted by her boyfriend's jealous wife. Something other than those mishaps must have occurred for Fanny to want to shun them.

'What's up, Fanny? Why won't you talk to us?' Lily grabbed her friend's arm to halt her. Margie was bringing up the rear at a slower pace, her skirt gathered away from her trotting feet in one set of sturdy fingers.

'Nothing's up. Clear off, the pair of you.' Fanny jerked her elbow free. 'Go on, clear off; you two don't want to be seen hanging about with the likes of me.'

'That's where you're wrong, see.' Lily renewed her grip on her friend. 'We've just come here specially to find you, Fanny Miller. And we knew very well what you'd be up to when we did. What's happened? You had a decent job in the rag shop. Did you get sacked?'

'Decent job?' Fanny snorted. 'You call sorting through stinky old clothes a decent job?'

'Compared to this I do; you thought the same thing not so long ago.' Lily sighed. 'Look, what's happened to set you back on this road? Let's go to a caff and have a cup of tea and a chinwag to sort things out, like we used to do, eh?'

'Nothing to sort out, and ain't going to no caff. I'm

36

skint. I'm already in trouble with the landlord for not paying me rent.' Fanny's eyes were darting to and fro to spot a punter. 'Who told you I'd be here, anyway?' She turned to Lily and cocked her head, waiting for an answer.

Lily felt her heart go out to Fanny. Behind the defiance she could see a glitter of tears in her friend's eyes. 'Don't know his name. Some bloke in the Bow Bells told us where to head.'

'He fancied Lil: said if she wanted a customer he'd fetch his coat, and give her ten bob,' Margie chipped in, looking scandalously amused.

'Should've brought him along . . . I'd've seen to him fer five bob. Ain't had a sniff of business yet,' Fanny said with a coarse drollery the other two remembered from their months spent pounding the streets together, pushing a barrow.

They had tramped for miles during the course of a working day, wending their way up and down the backstreets of Whitechapel and Bethnal Green, clattering a bell to bring out the housewives to inspect their merchandise. By midday, when they'd sold off some of it, and space was available, they'd take a turn having a ride on the cart and tuck into sandwiches and a flask of tea. Margie had had a go pushing the barrow one-handed to give a colleague a chance to rest her weary legs. The enterprise had brought little financial reward but they'd been happy enough, rising when it was still dark to load up at the wholesaler's, knowing that a hard slog was in front of them. They'd sing songs to drive out the sleep as the sun came up, and constantly reminded one another how marvellous it was to be free of the workhouse. Had Fanny easily forgotten that all she'd wanted a year ago was to be a respectable woman and a good mother? She'd vowed to take any regular employment she could get to start a new life.

A donkey-jacketed fellow who'd been about to bowl into Sugar House Lane had hesitated at the corner instead. For several minutes he'd been furtively watching the trio of young women as they exchanged heated words. Fanny suddenly spotted him peeping from under the brim of his cap and hurried in his direction, waving him closer. He decided not to and turned tail.

Fanny whipped off her hat in frustration, thrusting her fingers through her shaggy coppery locks. 'He's one of me regulars 'n' all.' She trudged back towards Lily and Margie.

'What's happened to you, Fanny?' Lily demanded. 'I can't believe you've gone off the rails because your boyfriend's wife turfed you out. You knew she might turn up. You said you wouldn't be too bothered if she did.'

'Don't give a toss about him, or her,' Fanny answered hoarsely, avoiding her friends' eyes.

Lily suspected that wasn't the case; she could see Fanny's lower lip wobbling. She also reckoned something other than that bust-up had brought Fanny back into this murky business, conducted in alleyways or neighbourhoods where a stench of factory and human effluent hung in the air. Lily couldn't bear seeing her upset while not knowing the cause of it. She stalked Fanny, who tried to evade her outstretched arms. But Lily doggedly persevered. Finally she had Fanny trapped against the railings. Then she gave her a hug . . . the sort of fiercely protective embrace they would share, unseen by the workhouse

38

officers, who didn't approve of conversation or displays of affection. 'It'll be all right . . . whatever it is that's happened, Fanny, it'll be all right. Look, we're here to help now.'

'Won't be all right . . . can't be.' Fanny choked, starting to gulp and to shake. 'It's too late for me. Just got what I deserved, I suppose. Never deserved having nobody to love who loved me back, not someone bad like me.'

'Don't talk daft. You can do better than him,' Lily said loyally, planting a kiss on Fanny's forehead. 'He was a wrong 'un, telling you his wife had gone for good. And what a rude old cow she is. Good riddance to both of 'em, I say.' Lily tried to make Fanny smile, but failed.

'She's welcome to him. Only one person I ever really loved: me baby.' Fanny howled, and broke free of Lily's hold to fold over at the middle in anguish.

A quick glance at Margie's whitening face was enough for Lily to know the same dreadful suspicion was in both their minds. When Fanny's sobs had died away to hiccoughs, Lily gently cupped her friend's wet cheeks. 'What's happened to Ronny?' she whispered. 'Did you take him back to the workhouse when you had nowhere to stay?'

Fanny violently shook her head. 'Would never have let me little boy go back inside that place on his own. Never!'

Lily took out her hanky and cleaned her friend's face of tears and snot. Margie, eyes widening in apprehension, had come closer and was hovering to add her comfort when the time was right.

'After his wife chucked us out I managed to get us a lodging, sharing rent with a girl I used to know from me bad old days.' Fanny started a faltering explanation. 'She was working up West most nights, so me and Ronny had the place to ourselves at bedtime. I was still doing a shift at the rag shop. Me old neighbour helped me out, minding Ronny even though I couldn't pay her more than coppers.' Fanny sniffed and rubbed her face. 'The room was damp . . . a real dirty hole, but I couldn't afford to get a better place on rag-shop wages. It was that or back to the workhouse.' Her features became pinched. 'I knew if I went back there they'd separate us. Ronny would be taken to the nursery and I'd never see him again. So I saved every farthing to try and get us a better lodging, but Ronny got sick.' Fanny's voice faded into a croak. 'Diarrhoea . . . poor little mite was so poorly . . . but he didn't suffer long. Thank the Lord for at least one small mercy.' She squeezed her eyes shut and inhaled. 'I couldn't even be a good mother and bury him decent,' she burst out. 'Didn't have enough money, so he's in a pauper's grave. Before I let them take him away I swore to him I'd get him a proper marker. A cross . . . and I will. Even if this is what I have to do to get it.' She blinked at Lily through bloodshot eyes.

Lily hadn't realised she'd started crying until she found she couldn't utter a word of comfort. She attempted to speak but sobs emerged. Margie's bowed head and quivering shoulders indicated she was also weeping for the little boy they'd come to love. When they'd been street hawkers, Fanny would bring her son along when she'd nobody to mind him. A lot of the manual work had been beyond Margie's dexterity, but she could change a nappy and fasten a safety pin one handed as fast as the other two. Fanny had called her a natural, and joked that Margie could take her fractious baby home when Ronny's teeth were bothering him.

Humbled by their grief, Fanny drew her friends into a cuddle. After a few minutes, when the sound of their mingling choked murmurings had died away, the girls' arms sagged back to their sides.

'Lost me job cos I was too upset to turn in for a week,' Fanny sniffed. 'I went back to Roger and begged him to help me lay me baby to rest properly, but his wife interfered. Right ding-dong it should've been, but I couldn't stop bawling and he just stood looking like he didn't know what to do. He'd been like a dad to Ronny and promised me he'd tell his wife he was divorcing her so we could be a proper family. When it came to it he didn't have the gumption for anything like that.'

'You've seen him in his true colours then,' Lily said gruffly, wiping her eyes. 'I'll chip in for the cross. I want to, please let me,' she added when Fanny refused the offer with a headshake.

'Ain't told you about all of this to get you to give me your money.'

'I know that,' Lily said gently. 'Ronny was dear to me . . . like a little nephew. That's how I thought of him. You and Margie are like me sisters . . . we're family of sorts, that's how I see it.' Lily hugged Fanny again to impress on her she meant it.

'I want to as well,' Margie said. 'Cos what Lily said is right. I'm closer to you two than I am to my lot. When I turned up on me mother's doorstep after I got out of the workhouse, she just opened up the bedroom window and shouted at me to sling me hook. Didn't even bother coming downstairs to speak to me after five years.' That rejection had hurt Margie more

41

than the first time she'd been abandoned. Mrs Blake had taken her eleven-year-old eldest girl to the workhouse, telling her she'd come back for her. She never did. A cripple who in all likelihood might never find work and contribute to the household kitty was too much of a burden in Mrs Blake's eyes.

Her friends' spontaneous generosity had made Fanny sniffle. 'Don't deserve pals like you two,' she croaked. 'You don't know the half of how disgraceful I am. Couldn't ever tell you about it neither.' She dried her face on her sleeve.

'S'pect we've all done things we're ashamed of and keep to ourselves.' It was certainly true in Lily's case. They'd all known and despised Miss Fox when at the workhouse. But of the three of them, only Lily knew the whole truth behind the officer's death. Gregory knew; he was more than a best friend. He was the person Lily loved and trusted the most in this world.

'Shall we go for a bite to eat and talk about things?' Lily suggested, now they all seemed calmer. 'My treat,' she added, as Fanny sheepishly reminded her she was broke. 'Next time we go to a caff you can pay out of your wages from your new job.'

'What new job?' Fanny said glumly.

'Ah . . . that's something else we should talk about, Fanny Miller . . . ' Lily's words tailed off as she noticed two men dressed in khaki swaggering down the road. They were meandering over the pavement, bumping into one another, obviously having been drinking until closing time. From their sly smiles Lily could guess what they were after. She boldly went to meet them. 'Sorry . . . shop's closed,' she said politely, and turned her back on them. 'Ready for the off?' she asked her friends. Having received nods, she linked arms with them and the trio set off up the lane, leaving the baffled privates behind.

An indignant voice bawled after them, "'Ere, ain't you 'eard? Women are supposed to be showing us Tommies a good time when we get back on leave.'

'Thass right . . . official line, that is . . . ' The other soldier added his slurred two penn'orth.

Once Fanny would have given them some riotous back-chat and made her friends blush. But she didn't today. The girls proceeded sedately towards the High Street, lost in their own private memories of little Ronny. It was to be a bittersweet reunion.

4

'What does Greg Wilding say about me joining the firm?' Fanny put down the teacup that had been hovering by her mouth and gave a disappointed sigh. 'Oh, Gawd! You haven't told him about this, have you, Lily?'

The girls had settled in the caff and ordered a pot of tea and currant buns. The moment the waitress had finished putting down the crockery, Lily had launched into offering Fanny a job at Wilding's.

'He doesn't know cos he's not back on leave yet. He won't mind though,' Lily reassured her.

'You sure about that?' Fanny replied dubiously.

'What makes you think he will mind?' Lily had picked up on something in Fanny's comment and it niggled at her. 'Have you seen him at some time?'

'Yeah, I have . . . no need to worry,' Fanny tacked on. 'He's never been interested in me.' She looked awkward before blurting, 'I paid a visit to the warehouse months ago to tell you about losing me home and Ronny. I was hoping there might be a job in it for me, but you weren't about that afternoon, so I spoke to him. Not for long though.' Fanny paused, fiddling with her teaspoon. 'When you didn't follow it up, I thought you probably didn't want to stay friends after all. You've moved up in the world since you hooked up with him, and good luck to you.'

Lily swallowed a mouthful of bun in a gulp. ''Course I want to stay friends! Greg never told me you'd come over.'

'It doesn't matter, Lil. He was entitled to tell me to stay away.'

'He did what?' Lily was so shocked she almost jumped to her feet. She couldn't believe Greg would've been cruel enough to treat a grieving mother that way. He could be a hard-nosed wheeler-dealer, but his heart was definitely in the right place in Lily's opinion. He'd shown her kindness and patience, even when she'd not always deserved it. But she knew he didn't like Fanny. On the day he'd freed Lily from the workhouse, he'd warned her to steer clear of Fanny Miller. It had been one of their first clashes, and they'd had many a fiery skirmish since. 'Did you tell him you wanted to speak to me about losing your baby?'

Fanny shook her head. 'I couldn't speak to anybody about it . . . only wanted to talk to you and Margie at the time. I felt so rotten I just wanted to die.'

'I should've come over to see you sooner. I always intended to but so much was going on with my brother signing up then Greg enlisting. Loads of arrangements had to be made with suppliers and with the bank for me to keep things running smoothly while he's away.' Lily sighed. 'It's no excuse, though; and I don't know why Greg treated you like that. He knows we're friends and always will be. I am sorry, Fanny. I've let you down.'

'No need to be sorry,' Fanny replied gruffly. 'Don't go sayin' nuthin' to him about this, will you?' She sounded earnest. 'Can't blame him for wanting me out of the way.

He was just looking out for you. Men don't want their wives or girlfriends knocking around with my sort. Those Tommies thought you and Margie were tarts just cos you were standing with me. It'll be my fault if people start talking about you.'

'Don't care what anybody says; won't change anything between us.' Lily wasn't just being kind; she meant every word. Fanny's warning was valid, though. The fellow in the pub had assumed she must be a prostitute just because she'd called Fanny Miller a friend. Hypocrites like him, willing to buy women they despised, could think what they liked. These three workhouse girls had been through too much together to turn their backs on one another. 'I'm not ashamed of being seen in a caff with you, or working with you or anything else we decide to do. And that's that.'

Margie nodded vigorous agreement while picking up stray currants from her plate and popping them into her mouth.

'Anyway, if you fancy having another go at selling door to door, there's a job for you for as long as you want it. And if you get a yen for starting up on your own account when you've saved a bit, then that's all right by me.' Lily smiled. 'I'm not saying it to get rid of you before you've even started. It's just that I know you always wanted your own little business, didn't you?' Lily finished her tea and sat back in the chair. 'Anyhow, whatever us lot get up to, I reckon we'll be pals for life.' She held out her hands for her friends to take and gave them a firm shake before letting them go.

'I've done some bad things, as you both know.' Margie tapped her nose and gave a wink, reminding them of when she'd lived in a brothel after scarpering from the workhouse. Shunned by her mother, she'd been destitute when a madam offered her a lodging and a job writing some blackmail letters to well-to-do clients. 'Glad I got away from that cathouse.' Margie

46

gave a shiver. 'I was always frightened the Old Bill would turn up and arrest me, even though none of it was my idea. I just did as I was told to keep a roof over me head.'

'Thank heavens writing letters was all that woman expected you to do when you lived there.' Lily rolled her eyes.

Margie gave a vigorous nod. It was the one time that having a deformity had worked in her favour. The madam had told her it would put men off.

'Couldn't believe me luck when you came over that day and said you wanted me to be a clerk at Wilding's.' Margie had almost exploded with pride when offered her first proper job. She'd become resigned to being turned away by employers who averted their eyes in disgust from her crippled hand. They wouldn't even give her a fair chance to prove herself at interviews. Several times her application letter had been praised as being the best the firm had received, but none of that counted in her favour once the gloves were off.

'You're a good bookkeeper. You're faster than me at mental arithmetic.' Lily wasn't lavishing false praise: it was true. 'Anyway, you're me friend, and us three have to look out for one another.' Lily glanced from one to the other of them.

'Thanks, Lil. I'll take the job,' Fanny eased back into the conversation with a rather bashful smile. 'When can I start?'

'Monday morning, first thing. You know the drill. Up with the lark.'

Despite her light tone, Lily was still bothered to know Greg hadn't told her about Fanny's visit months ago. Lily knew she'd have to challenge him over it when he got home, to ease her conscience. Then no

47

doubt they'd end up arguing. 'You can lodge with me and Margie at our flat. The firm pays for a couple of places for staff to use. Smudger and Joey Robley share a lodging. You'll be teaming up with Joey. He's a nice lad but gets bullied by some youths who are trying to nab his round.'

Fanny crossed her arms, mouth pursed. 'Are they now? We'll see about that.'

Lily chuckled. 'Just the reaction I was hoping for, Fanny Miller.'

They sat in amicable quiet, gazing through the caff window into a mellow afternoon, lost in their own thoughts. Fanny broke the peaceful mood with a confession.

'When I fell pregnant I wanted to get rid of me baby cos I knew I'd have to pack up working. The idea of entering a spike terrified me. A pal lent me some money and told me about a nurse who moonlights as an abortionist. In the end I couldn't go through with it, though.' Fanny dropped her gaze. 'When the little love passed away, I was so mad with grief that I screamed at meself for not having that abortion. I shouldn't have done it. I've been tormenting meself in case Ronny knows I said I wished he'd never been born. I believe in heaven and angels, see. I've told him over and over I didn't mean it . . . but what if he's not listening to me now?'

'Before Mum took me to the workhouse, she told me she wished I'd never been born,' Margie said. 'I know she didn't really mean it. Just everything getting on top of her. That's all it was.'

'We all say and do daft things when we're het up,' said Lily. 'I've done loads of things I regret.' She settled her elbows on the table and cupped her face with

48

her hands.

'I like to dream that Mum and Dad are back together in Paradise. I like to think they're looking out for me and Davy. And our little sister too. I'm going to find her eventually. Perhaps they'll help me from up there . . .'

Margie and Fanny exchanged a sceptical look. It upset Margie especially to think that the fruitless searching for her little sister might eventually embitter Lily. 'Ronny was like a little cherub with his rosy cheeks.' She brought the conversation back to the baby whose sad fate they knew.

'Teething gave him red cheeks, Marge,' Fanny said ruefully. 'Oh, he was the best little boy and I'm glad I had him just for a short while. His dad must've been one of the nicer blokes I hooked up with, cos Ronny didn't get his sweet nature from me.' Fanny pulled a face, making her friends ruefully smile.

'Talking of angels 'n' spirits 'n' things: d'you remember Nora Clarke's friend who went mad as a hatter and killed herself by drinking disinfectant?' Margie nudged Lily. 'A week later Nora said she saw her ghost in the dormitory.'

'Nora didn't say it again though.' Lily sounded grave. 'Not after the master told her she'd been hallucinating and he'd transfer her to an asylum if she repeated it.'

'It sounds daft, but I'm glad we all ended up as workhouse girls. Wouldn't be friends otherwise, would we?' Fanny said.

'Like finding gold rings in the gutter, meeting up with you two in there.' Margie echoed the sentiment.

Lily smiled but wouldn't lie and say she saw anything good in the place where her mother had died.

As far as she could, she avoided dwelling on the work-house to prevent a redolence of soiled humanity and boiled cabbage swirling in her nostrils, making her feel she wanted to retch. 'Right, let's cheer up and stop talking about that dump.' She looked from one to the other of her friends. 'Shall we start a savings jar for Ronny's cross?'

That suggestion received enthusiastic agreement.

'Bet you can't wait for Greg to come home, can you, Lil?' Margie had noticed her friend's sombre expression.

'Longing to see him . . . wish he'd never gone,' Lily said softly. 'Or Davy, for that matter. This damned war was never meant to drag on so long.'

'It'd solve everything if the blokes poaching on our patch got into khaki,' Fanny pointed out.

'Cowards like them won't go and fight,' Margie remarked.

Lily wouldn't wish that sort of danger on anybody, even the Burdett Road boys. But it wasn't just those troublemakers playing on her mind. Rory Scully's visit still niggled away at her. She hated the idea of bringing all of this up with Greg when he got home, spoiling his leave, but knew she must.

'Are we all finished?' Lily got out her purse to pay the bill, counting out the coins and giving the waitress a couple of coppers as a tip.

Fanny rubbed her palms together. 'Frosty mornings now the leaves are starting to fall.' She poked a fancy shoe out from beneath the hem of her skirt. 'I'll have to swap this working gear for new working gear. I'll need a nice warm coat and a pair of boots off a stall in Chrisp Street market.'

'We could collect your stuff from your lodging now,

if you like. If you move in with us today, you'll be closer to work and have a few extra minutes in bed in the morning.'

'A flit in the middle of a Sunday afternoon?' Fanny pushed her hat to a jaunty angle and chuckled. It was the first time that day her friends had heard her properly laugh; it was a wonderfully welcome sound that started them off too. 'That's a bloody good idea.' Fanny shoved back her chair and stood up. 'Me land-lord can whistle for his rent. Diabolical liberty what he was charging on the poxy hole anyhow.' She looked at her friends with unembarrassed affection. 'Thanks for coming over today. I feel happier than I have in ages, being with you two.'

'I hope it's the start of better times for you, Fan,' Lily said gruffly. 'I really do.'

★ ★ ★

When they got back to the basement flat in Poplar, Lily walked from one bedroom to the other, assessing the space and the furniture. She knew they'd need to have a change-around now there were three of them to house. While the other two discussed sleeping arrangements, the newcomer stood diffidently in the corridor, looking up and down and all around. Fanny couldn't believe her luck. Never in her life had she been offered such spacious accommodation. Roger had only had a spartanly furnished bed-sitting room with a hob grate to keep the place warm and to cook on. They'd had no furniture other than an armchair and two stick-backed chairs, plus a metal-topped table that he had fashioned out of an old Singer sewing-machine stand and a sheet of zinc, purloined from his workplace. The double bed had accommodated them all at night: the couple one end and Fanny's baby tucked beneath the sheets at their feet.

Eager to explore her new home, Fanny went into the kitchenette, gasping in delight at the sight of an inside tap and a sink. Those things were a novelty for her too, as was a proper cooker. Lily followed Fanny into the kitchen and found her friend turning the squeaky brass tap on and off, like a child with a new toy.

It was hard to imagine the agony Fanny had been through in losing her son. But what really got Lily down was knowing she could have offered condolences months ago. Greg had disappointed her rather than angered her, keeping her in the dark. 'Get that kettle on, shall we, and have a cup of tea?' Lily smiled at Fanny and opened a cupboard, finding some cups and saucers.

'This is a smashing place, Lil,' Fanny burst out. 'Two rooms! And a proper kitchen!' she marvelled. 'You've really fallen on your feet, you lucky so and so.' She gave Lily a spontaneous hug. 'Thanks for letting me move in.' She pulled open the oven door to peer inside.

'Well, it's not quite two rooms,' Lily pointed out. 'The boxroom used to be the coal bunker.' She wrinkled her nose as she spooned tea into the pot. 'Still smells a bit in there but it's nice and clean and cosy now. When I got out of the workhouse, that was where I slept. I'll go back in there, and you and Margie can share the big room.' Lily poured boiling water into the teapot. 'All right by you, Marge, if we swap around and you bunk down with Fanny?' she asked as the youngest girl joined them in the kitchen.

'S'long as she don't snore,' Margie said with a grin.

'What about when Greg comes back on leave?' Fanny crossed her arms. 'If he's paying for it all, he won't want to bed down with you in the small room, Lil.' She pulled a face. 'Don't reckon he'll want me here at all, giving the place a bad name.'

'He's got his own place. It's nicer than this,' Lily said, handing round teas then finding the biscuit tin. She prised off the lid and left it open on the kitchen table so they could help themselves.

Fanny took a Bourbon, looking thoughtful. 'Hasn't he asked you to move in with him then?'

'He gave me the keys to his flat when he left for France, but I preferred having Margie's company, so I've stopped where I am.' Lily glanced around at her home. The ceilings throughout the flat were low and grubby. The distempered walls also needed a fresh coat of paint. But it was clean and cosy. Lily was fond of this basement home, and not even the echo of Jane Wright's abrasive voice could spoil precious memories of her first joyous days of freedom. She'd started her life as an adult, and a working woman, right here.

Back then Jane had been Gregory's girlfriend, and she hadn't been happy to have Lily dumped on her. 'A workhouse ragbag,' Jane had called her unwanted flatmate. But over the months they had come to tolerate one another, and at times Jane had been kind. She had given Lily her first set of clothes so she could take off her detested workhouse uniform.

'You ought to keep tabs on Greg and move in with him.' Fanny gave Lily a significant look, helping herself to another biscuit from the tin.

'I trust him . . . '

'I trusted Roger.' Fanny grimaced. 'More fool me.

53

And he didn't have what your feller's got.'

'What's that mean?' Lily prompted.

Fanny gestured with her half-eaten Bourbon. 'He's doing all right for himself, and he's good looking. Can't blame me for noticing. Every woman does.'

'I know he's handsome,' Lily said. 'Still trust him.'

Fanny exchanged an ironic look with Margie, who was leaning on the doorjamb. 'Wish I was still that naïve.'

Lily felt a slight niggle of irritation but let it go. Fanny was abrupt and spoke her mind plainly. It was one of the things Lily had liked about her . . . admired about her. And she was grieving for her son and was bound to be feeling raw and perhaps a bit resentful. It was understandable.

Having finished her tea, Fanny started exploring again. She opened the larder and peered in at neat stacks of crockery and rows of tins and packets. She lifted a tin of Bird's custard powder. 'Blimey . . . ain't seen one of these in ages. Me mum had one once . . . Christmas, think it was.' Fanny was usually careful not to mention her family and if her friends brought up her early life she'd change the subject. As she did now. 'Right, if you show me where I can put my stuff I'll start to unpack.' She jiggled her hips. 'First, though, you'd better show me where the privy is. That tea's gone straight through me.'

5

Lily both longed for and dreaded the sight of envelopes on the doormat. A glimpse of familiar handwriting was always thrilling, but she'd only allow herself to open letters from France once she'd scanned the rest of the post. Concealed amongst mundane bills and news from loved ones could be something stamped 'Whitehall' that had arrived more speedily than Western Front mail. Within would be a paragraph of kind words destined to rip her life to bits.

Scooping up the envelopes, Lily shuffled them, bated breath burning her throat. There was nothing that looked suspect, so she relaxed and tore open the letter bearing her brother's scrawl. He would like some cigarettes and some biscuits and Bovril if she could manage to send them, she read, in amongst the complaints of being hungry and having lice. She smiled; he was still her Davy. Being a boy soldier hadn't stopped him moaning or scrounging, and that indicated to Lily her twin was doing well enough. It was hard to believe that he'd gone to war as a sixteen year old, ten long months ago. He'd joined up in the expectation of soon being back home for good. No such luck; it hadn't all been over by Christmas as promised.

The letter bearing Greg's writing was slipped into Lily's pocket, to be lingered over at bedtime. She loved dropping off to sleep imagining his gruff voice telling her the news she had devoured with her eyes.

That morning Lily had been working at Chrisp

Street market, and had just arrived home for her dinner break, impatient to see if word had arrived about Greg's travel arrangements. On the day he got back she planned to meet him at the station with a hug and a kiss then welcome him home to a celebration tea.

Feeling blessed to have received letters from the two most important people in her life, Lily started humming as she went into the kitchen to put the kettle on. Usually, she would have a hearty meal at midday, but she felt too excited to bother cooking and settled for making toast. In between dipping a knife into the jam pot, she re-read Davy's letter more slowly, chuckling at the cartoonish sketch he'd done of his sergeant. The moustachioed character looked suitably bellicose, with teeth bared and steam jetting from his ears. She imagined Davy and his youthful pals jumped to when their sergeant ordered them to.

The moment she'd finished bolting her food, she put the dirty crockery into the bowl and washed up. A few minutes later she was locking the front door, then hurrying back along the lane to relieve Smudger on the stall. He claimed he had hollow legs and was always peckish.

His mother lived in the lane and, as Lily drew closer to the spot, she saw Eunice Smith with some of her neighbours. The woman broke away from the group and came over to Lily.

'Everything all right?' Lily asked, doubting it was. The elderly widow who lived in the ground-floor back room was howling into her hands.

'Mary's just heard that her grandson's been killed at Loos. She more or less brought the boy up after his mother passed on.' Eunice sorrowfully shook her head. 'Poor lad had just turned eighteen.'

'Oh, I'm so sorry,' Lily whispered, taking a step towards the distraught woman to express her condolences.

Eunice caught her arm. 'I know you mean well, love, but I wouldn't speak to her . . . not now. She's not herself.' As though to prove Eunice's point, the woman started cursing. 'I'll stay with her this afternoon, get her a drop of brandy. It might help.' Eunice glanced over her shoulder at the gaggle of women. 'We said we'd all chip in a few coppers to try and calm the poor love with a drink. This bloody war.' She let out a long sigh. 'It scares the life outta me.'

'Your Smudger's still safe at home,' Lily soothed. She knew Eunice idolised her only child.

'How long's he safe for, though? They'll be calling up soon, mark my words. We all knew things were getting bad after that big ship was sunk in the spring. And every night now I'm looking up at the sky for one of those Zeppelin things. The Hun'll be back to bomb us . . . damn them,' Eunice said with a shiver.

Lily gave her neighbour's arm a comforting pat. Eunice was getting into a state with her imaginings, though Lily had to admit she and many others shared similar fears of where this was heading. The ship Eunice had referred to was the Lusitania, which had gone down in May, with women and children on board. The Zeppelin raids over England were becoming more frequent, leading people to the terrifying conclusion that the war wasn't just being fought on foreign soil, and civilians were targets as well as Allied troops.

'My Bobby's the same age as Mary's grandson.' Eunice used her cuff to dry her moist eyes. 'They used to be good pals before the lad moved away to live with his stepfather. When they was schoolkids they'd race up and down this lane on a cart they'd made out of pram wheels and old boxes.' She sniffed, squaring her shoulders. 'I got nothing to cry about. Poor Mary . . . she only had the one grandchild.'

Lily dug in her purse. 'Here, I want to put something in the pot for the brandy.' She handed over some coins. 'I remember her grandson coming over to see her every so often.' The freckle-faced lad had looked younger than eighteen; he'd been a friendly sort and would always raise a hand and call a greeting as Lily passed by.

'Won't be coming over to see her no more,' Eunice concluded bleakly.

Lily said a subdued goodbye and hurried on towards Chrisp Street market. Glancing over her shoulder she saw the neighbours standing in a protective circle around the bereaved grandmother. With a pang Lily realised that the same postman who had delivered her longed-for letters must have delivered Mary's heart-breaking news.

★ ★ ★

'Apples just up from Kent . . . Cox's, Russets — who wants 'em? Juicy and ripe. Won't find no better prices. Spuds, carrots, cabbages, fresh from the Fens. Don't hang abaht, gels . . . selling out over 'ere . . . ' Smudger had been bawling out his sales patter at the top of his voice, but as a customer approached he toned down his spiel. 'There y'are, love . . . all that lot fer a tanner cos I like the look o' you. Make you a couple o' pies, those will. Can't go wrong.' Smudger had taken the brass scoop from a set of scales and filled it to the brim with firm, autumn-coloured apples. The young housewife opened her shopping bag for him to shoot the fruit inside. He gave her a wink as she handed over the coin. 'See you soon then; bring us a bit o' that pie and I'll slip you a nice big cucumber in exchange. Marrow if yer good.' The woman started to flirt back but he'd already pocketed the cash and forgotten about her, having noticed Lily on her way.

Smudger used less bawdy repartee when she was around. Lily didn't mind his sauciness, in fact she welcomed it boosting their profits. The housewives enjoyed a bit of banter. There was no sisterly solidarity in market trading; the women preferred being served by a man, and the dirtier his teasing, the better they liked it, and came back again. Smudger was a good salesman and always shifted more stock than she did. On a mellow autumn day, browsing the stalls for bargains and being chatted up by a good-looking barrow boy was a welcome break for a careworn housewife.

'Sorry I'm a bit late, Smudger. I stopped to talk to your mum on the way back.' Lily didn't tell him why. Eunice would be the best person to break the bad news about his childhood friend. 'Bet you're hungry, aren't you? You can nip off now.' He preferred going to the caff for his dinner whereas Lily scooted home as it wasn't far. She served a customer with loamy King Edwards and onions as large as her palms, while Smudger took off his leather apron and emptied its money pouch into the tin.

'Almost sold out, haven't we?' Lily pulled on her overall and happily assessed the dribs and drabs of produce. When they'd opened up in the early-morning light, the sides of the rig had been piled almost as high as the awning. They could pack up and get back to the

59

warehouse early. Smudger was teaching Lily to drive in spare moments and she'd love to surprise Greg by driving herself to Charing Cross to fetch him home. Keen to find out when that would be, she rubbed together her earthy hands, then made to retrieve his precious letter from her pocket. But something was niggling at her. She withdrew her fingers and cocked her head at her workmate. Since getting back from her dinner break he'd not spoken, and was avoiding looking at her. 'Something up, Smudger?' She shifted her position and noticed the bruise on his cheek. 'Oh, what's happened?' Lily cried. 'I've not even been gone an hour. Has there been trouble?'

''S'nothing . . .' he said gruffly, pulling the brim of his cap down. 'He come off worst, anyhow.'

'Who?' Lily demanded.

'Nobody . . .' He gave up on being illogical and started again. 'Some prat started chucking our cabbages about so I clumped him.' Smudger made a dismissive gesture. 'He was just showing off in front of a gel from the pub. He was trying to wind me up.'

'Looks like he succeeded,' Lily dryly observed.

Barmaids from the local pub would often dash over the road to buy vegetables if they had a rush on at dinner time and had run out of spuds. Lily had noticed that one of them had a crush on Smudger. Though he laughed and joked with her, as he did with everybody, Lily had never seen him pay her enough attention to fight over her.

'Be all right on yer own, will you, if I go and get meself pie 'n' mash?' He shrugged into his waistcoat and rolled down his sleeves. 'Won't be long. Market's quietening down now anyhow.' He straightened his spotted neckerchief then screwed his cap more firmly onto his forehead with a flick of the wrist.

''Course I'll be all right. When you get back we'll start packing up early.' Lily watched him walk away, head down, as he fiddled with the lid of his tobacco tin. He didn't swagger as some of the costermongers did, believing themselves cock of the walk. Lily had known Smudger for over a year now and he wasn't arrogant or easily geed up. She reckoned there had been more to him getting into a fight than cabbages being chucked about in front of a barmaid.

Lily started tidying things away in readiness to get going on his return. She was strong from the years of hard graft at the workhouse. Long hours in the laundry room, mangling thick wedges of soaking cotton and hoisting heavy airers loaded with bed sheets up to the ceiling, had prepared Lily for a hard outdoor life. Even in the winter, with her fingers stiff and icy, she loved every minute of costermongering. It was a nicer cold, a different weariness to that she'd endured for five years at South Grove workhouse.

Now the pallets were mostly empty and easier to lift, she stacked them quickly and efficiently by the side of the van ready for Smudger to load them later.

While she worked, her mind was racing ahead to meeting up with the others at the depot. She wondered if Fanny and Joey had met trouble on their round today. Perhaps one of the Burdett Road gang was responsible for Smudger's injury. He might be reluctant to elaborate in case of worrying her. From the corner of an eye, Lily saw a customer approaching and stirred herself into action. The middle-aged woman approached to squeeze the two Savoy cabbages left on the stall. 'Still got dew on 'em.' Lily unfurled crisp curly leaves to reveal glistening droplets. 'Be fresh tomorrow, those will, Mrs Grundy.' The woman always did her shopping as the market was winding down to drive a hard bargain. 'You can have the two and pay for one,' Lily said as the woman continued squeezing and poking the greens. Lily knew she'd make a loss but wanted to clear the scraps rather than pack them up to take back to the depot. The woman had a brood of seven kids to feed, all under fourteen, but Lily wasn't simply being kind-hearted. Regular customers liked to think they were getting preferential treatment and something extra. There were plenty of costermongers in Chrisp Street market to choose from, and Lily didn't want housewives switching allegiance.

'Oh, all right. I'll take them though they ain't got much heart to 'em.' The woman sounded as though she were the one doing a favour. 'And I'll have a full scoop of them apples for a tanner, same as he gave to the other woman.' Mrs Grundy crossed her arms as though anticipating an argument. 'Knocked off early, has he, your feller?'

'Smudger's gone for a late dinner.' Lily smiled to herself, piling apples onto the brass dish. Mrs Grundy certainly never missed a trick. Her eyes and ears were straining all the time to discover if somebody else might be getting a better deal than she was.

'Saw your Smudger fighting with Claudette's old man a little while ago. What's that all about then?' The woman hiked an inquisitive eyebrow.

'Claudette?' Lily repeated the name, mystified, while tipping the apples into the woman's bag.

'Oh . . . so you didn't know. Ain't gossipin', you understand.' Mrs Grundy dropped some silver and copper onto Lily's outstretched palm. 'Just thought I was doing the right thing, bringing it up, like. Could be you should know about it, if you get my drift.' She gave Lily an old-fashioned look before picking up her cabbages and marching off.

It didn't matter how many times Lily explained to inquisitive folk that she and Smudger were just colleagues, they would assume there must be more to their relationship. Mrs Grundy seemed to believe she was tipping Lily the wink about him cheating on her with a married woman.

The market was always alive with wild tales spread by bored housewives. Lily had to admit she enjoyed listening, bug-eyed, to a lot of them, along with everybody else. The gossip rarely held much truth. Smudger had been in a scrap, though, and if he had been giving the eye to someone's wife, that would explain why he'd not wanted to talk about it. Though he was a good friend, it wasn't really any of her business what he got up to after work; but if it spilled over and affected the business . . . Lily sighed. Greg would be home soon, and she didn't want him coming back to a heap of trouble. She supposed she ought to tackle Smudger over it, just in case there was a serious bust-up brewing.

She turned back to hefting boxes and fitting them expertly together. Her slender build and pretty face, framed by thick chestnut waves, belied an impressive strength. She dumped the last one on top then heard a child cough to gain her attention.

'Why aren't you at school, Annie?' Lily asked, though she could guess the answer to that. 'School-board man'll be after you, you know, if you keep bunking off.'

The girl cuffed her nose and gave a diffident shrug.

'Mum kept me 'ome again. Sent me out to do the shopping.'

Lily knew the girl's mother and what the woman expected her daughter to do when she sent her out 'shopping'. Pol Skipman was a drinker and a thief. She'd been caught stealing numerous times. Her tactic now was to send her kids out to do her hoisting for her. They were faster on their toes and would be dealt with more leniently if caught in the act. In particular Mrs Skipman used Annie to fetch home some produce, so they had something for tea. The girl wasn't the eldest of Pol Skipman's four kids; Annie's older brother was now working full time. As soon as he became the family's main provider, Annie took over as pilferer-in-chief, backed up by a younger brother who had been spotted grabbing stuff then running off. Annie had tried to steal from Wilding's in the past, but Lily had caught her and threatened to turn her in if she did it again. Now, the girl presented herself at the stall.

'Anything spare for us today, miss?' Annie glanced around nervously. She usually waited until Smudger had disappeared before approaching. He'd send her off with a flea in her ear, which was better than the other costers, who'd despatch her with a boot aimed at her backside if she sidled too close.

Annie was used to other people's contempt; she'd grown up being jeered and spat at because of who her mother was. 'If I could have a few spuds and onions I can make a potato pie before me big brother gets in for his tea.' Annie sniffed and eyed a pile of carrots. 'Some of them would help to fill us up, miss.'

'Well, we're packing up early so I've got stuff over. If you don't mind taking it you'll save me the bother of chucking it away.' It was a game they played: Lily pretending she wasn't an easy touch and the girl making out she wasn't really begging.

Lily knew if she turned Annie away, the girl only had two choices: she could go back home with nothing and risk getting walloped, or try thieving from a different stall and risk being collared. Lily regularly stowed a few vegetables in a box under the stall so she'd have something to give to Annie if she turned up. Smudger knew what went on and would simply shake his head when he stubbed his foot on the pallet by his feet. He'd told her she was encouraging the girl to keep coming back. Lily knew he was right; still, she would carry on putting stuff by. She knew how it felt to be that age with your belly rolling in hunger. And at least in their own way the family were managing to stay outside a workhouse.

'Thanks, miss.' Annie gave a bright smile as her bag was loaded with vegetables.

'Here . . . you might as well have the last of these apples. Bruised, most of them.' Lily tipped a scoop of shiny perfect fruit on top. 'Saved me the job of carting it all back, you have.'

Annie dropped her chin, letting her tangled mousy hair cover her face. 'Could I take that pear as well, miss?'

Lily glanced at the solitary pear at the back of the stall. That really was bruised and had been put aside to go into the gutter. 'You like a pear, do you?' Lily said, rolling it over the boards towards the girl. 'So do I.'

'Me little friend Charlie does.' Annie put the pear carefully into her bag then set off.

Lily watched the child lugging the full shopping bag in both hands, then turned her attention back

65

to clearing up. After a few minutes she sensed she was under observation, then a strong waft of tobacco smoke reached her nostrils making her whip around. Rory Scully was lounging against the stall, roll-up hanging off his lower lip. He doffed his cap and she noticed he'd made an effort to slick down his springy auburn hair. She hoped it wasn't for her benefit.

'Ain't gonna make your gaffer rich, givin' away stuff to ragamuffins, are you now?' He tutted mockingly. 'If you worked for me, I'd have to put you over me knee and give you a spankin' for what you just done, Lily Larkin.'

'Well, I don't work for you, and never would, so you're out of luck.' She grabbed a broom and started sweeping cabbage stalks into the gutter. Though she'd sounded admirably insouciant, she was blushing, and her hands were shaking. He'd startled her, materialising like that and staring at her as though he'd lunge across the stall and rip her clothes off. 'We're packing up so don't bother hanging around. Can't sell you anything.' She slung that over a shoulder, praying he'd clear off now he'd had a dig and embarrassed her.

'Where's your sidekick? Left you to do all the donkey work, has he?' Scully blew a sigh. 'Bad manners, some fellers.'

Lily leaned on the broom and cocked her head at him. 'Takes one to know one. Thought I'd made it clear I'd nothing more to say to you.'

'That's all right. I'll have it out with Smudger. Where is he?'

'Gone home early.' Lily lied instinctively. This man was trouble and she didn't want him loitering until Smudger returned. 'Anyway, he's not got time for you either.'

'We'll see about that when I catch up with the toerag.' Scully took a leisurely drag on his cigarette. 'Gone off home and left you to drive that, has he?' He smirked in disbelief while jerking a nod at the van.

'Yeah . . . I can drive it, and shortly me boyfriend will be getting home on leave, and I'll be picking him up from the station in it.'

'Clever gel, ain't you? Know what happens to gels who're too sharp for their own good?' He leaned across the stall, lustfully eying her up and down. 'They get more'n a spanking . . . ' He glanced at the open back of the van where ropes were visible, then darted looks to left and right.

Instantly Lily was hit with a wave of dread and disbelief. He appeared on the point of vaulting the stall to bundle her into the vehicle. She dropped the broom with a clatter and banged the doors shut.

The noise seemed to bring him out of a trance. He sniffed, straightened up, puffing out his chest. 'So you watch yer step, Lily Larkin,' he said. 'And tell Smudger I'll be back.' He dropped the cigarette stub and put a boot on it. 'I'll be watching out for when Wilding's got leave . . . if he's still alive . . . ' He left that nasty comment hanging in the air for a moment before insolently doffing his cap again and sauntering off.

Lily waited until he'd disappeared from sight before sinking down to sit on an upturned box. She took a deep, calming breath. After a few seconds her heart stopped racing and she shot to her feet. She wasn't going to let Scully intimidate her. He hadn't wanted to speak to Smudger; he'd come by to remind her that he was still around and was a force to be reckoned with. The only way to deal with people like that was

67

to ignore them rather than give them the attention they craved. She'd promised Greg she could cope with whatever came her way in his absence, and she would. She was used to being bullied and threatened, she'd been a workhouse girl.

* * *

'Know anybody called Claudette?' Lily asked as she and Smudger were folding up the tarpaulin between them about half an hour later.

Smudger didn't turn a hair. 'Why d'you ask?' He chucked the oilskin into the back of the van.

'Mrs Grundy was having a stir as she paid for her stuff. She reckons you were fighting with Claudette's husband.'

'I was.'

Lily gave him a moment to enlighten her further, but he didn't and continued coiling up ropes. 'Anything I should know about?' she prodded.

He retrieved a half-smoked cigarette from behind his ear and relit it. 'They're me neighbours and he knocks her about. Since they moved into the lane I can't hardly get a wink of sleep for the row they make. I went over and had it out with him last night. Now he's sobered up, he's come by to make something of it. Ask Joey if you don't believe me. He heard what went on last night.' Smudger turned his attention back to clearing equipment off the stall.

''Course I believe you.' Lily was taken aback by how shirty he sounded.

'Could've fooled me,' he muttered, throwing the ropes on top of the tarpaulin. He slammed the back doors of the van. 'Ready for the off?'

68

'No . . . not yet.' She caught his arm, miffed by his attitude. 'Look, I'm not being nosy; I was worried. If Mrs Grundy saw you having a scrap, I expect others did too. Don't want to get a reputation for being a roughhouse, do we?'

'Never bothered the guv'nor being thought a villain.'

Lily had to smile at that. 'Greg's gone respectable since he employed me to keep his records straight. He even pays his income tax.'

'Yeah . . . you've settled him down, no doubt about it.'

'Well, don't sound so disappointed!' Lily jokingly complained.

'Maybe I am . . . ' Smudger flicked away his cigarette butt.

'You're in a funny mood this afternoon, Smudger.' Lily gave him a penetrative look. 'You like this Claudette, don't you?'

He gave a self-conscious shrug. 'I feel sorry for her. Her husband's a wrong 'un.'

'Why on earth did she get shackled to him then?' It was a daft question, and one she could answer herself. Her own brother had nearly been forced to marry a girl, thinking he'd got her in the family way. Afterwards, when learning it'd been a false alarm, Davy had realised he'd had a lucky escape. A single slip-up, and a pregnancy, could lead to a bad marriage and a lifetime of regret for a mismatched couple.

'Claudette didn't have no choice. She come over from Belgium with her folks at the start of the war. Whole boatload of other Belgian refugees was with them when they docked at Folkestone. Her parents married her off to the first bloke that showed an interest in her. In their minds, having an English son-in-law gives the family a permanent foot in the door over here.'

Lily could see that Smudger was getting angrier the more he spoke about it. She couldn't deny it was a horribly selfish thing for Claudette's parents to have done. 'How old is she?'

'Seventeen,' Smudger replied. 'She only went along with it for the sake of the younger kids. She regrets it now.' Smudger rolled his eyes and gave a defeated sigh. 'All right, might as well tell you. She's married to Rory Scully. I didn't keep all this from you when he came to the warehouse all them weeks ago. I thought he looked familiar, but hadn't ever spoken to him or his wife back then. I know 'em now, though,' he dryly concluded.

'Oh, no. Not him,' Lily groaned. 'We could have done without you being mixed up in his affairs, you know. Why didn't you say sooner?'

'Didn't want to worry you. But I ain't turning a blind eye to him laying into her,' he said through gritted teeth. 'Scully's a wrong 'un. Reckon you already worked that out for yourself.' Smudger scowled, wagging a finger. 'If he shows his face round our yard again when I'm not there, you make sure to tell me, won't you? I'll go after him and have it out with him properly.'

'It's good of you to stick up for Claudette.' Lily decided not to mention that the wife-beater had been right here, just fifteen minutes ago. She didn't want Smudger dashing off to find him. Another fight was the last thing they needed. Scully had obviously been loitering about to resume hostilities. Thankfully the two men had missed one another by about ten minutes.

She sighed. Her happiness on receiving her letters a short while ago had all but disappeared. 'Greg's due home soon and will deserve a rest. Don't make things any worse for him, Smudger, will you?' she said.

'Things have got worse for Claudette. She thinks she's up the spout,' Smudger muttered, almost to himself.

'Oh, the poor thing. That won't help her,' said Lily.

'Last thing she needs is a kid round her ankles with a husband like that. She wishes he'd enlist and go away and leave her in peace.'

'Perhaps he will . . . ' Lily attempted to sound optimistic.

'Claudette thinks he'll play at being a family man to stay in civvies. Bachelors'll be drafted first.' Smudger climbed into the van.

Usually he would courteously open the door for her first. His forgetfulness indicated that he was brooding deeply on it. Lily got in beside him, glancing at his profile as they made slow progress past traders dismantling stalls, and scavengers poking through the detritus in the gutters to find something edible. Smudger was still frowning and so was Lily. He was showing more than just a decent man's sympathy for an abused woman. He was getting involved with another man's wife and that was bad news in any circumstances. In this case, with Rory Scully in the picture, Lily reckoned Smudger couldn't have picked a worse set of people to tangle with.

She had never considered Smudger a coward for holding back when one by one his colleagues joined up. He was an only child, and she'd imagined he felt a duty to support his widowed mother for as long as possible.

But perhaps Claudette rather than Eunice was behind his decision to stay put until he had no other choice in the matter and was sent to fight.

72

6

Nearly two months later

Lily's second home was a barn-like wooden building, with large double doors situated on the left side and windows studded at intervals along its considerable frontage facing the road. Inside, the beamed, vaulted ceiling was strung with hurricane lamps, and screwed-in hooks abounded, to string up stuff. The walls had been racked out to take equipment that needed stacking and storing. Lily had adored the warehouse from the moment she set foot in it. Greg had brought her back to his depot on the day he'd rescued her from South Grove. Within minutes of entering the planked building, scented with ripe apples and tobacco smoke, she'd eagerly begun exploring all the trappings of a costermonger. She'd been surprised and impressed by how tidy everything was. Barrows, poles, sets of scales and tarpaulins all neatly arranged. She'd soon learned that her guv'nor ran a tight ship and expected his workforce to be as effective as the equipment he kept in tip-top condition. A roguish East Ender, maybe, but Gregory Wilding was a diamond in the rough nonetheless. He had the nous to understand that a self-made man, running a successful company, required a professional approach. And he demanded his workforce shared his attitude so he could continue to build the business up.

Today, Lily took little notice of her surroundings; she'd barely waited for the van to pass through the open iron gates and come to a halt on the concrete forecourt before jumping down. Leaving Smudger unloading the tarpaulins and pallets, to be barrowed inside, she hurried towards the warehouse. The Burdett Road boys hadn't been behind the trouble at the market but the day could get worse if Fanny and Joey had been under attack. Problems tended to cluster together.

She found Margie filling in the ledger, sipping at a mug of tea. But there was no sign of the others having returned early. 'Any problems today, Margie?' she asked breezily, not wanting to worry her friend unduly. 'Anybody called in for any reason?'

'Only him.' Margie nodded at somebody standing in the shadows, then started chuckling.

Lily twisted about and her dumbfounded amazement soon transformed into a squeak of joyous disbelief. 'Greg . . . ' She launched herself into his arms, spilling his tea, and was spun about. He kissed her long and hard on the mouth then put her back on her feet, still wrapped in his embrace.

'Just been to the flat to find you. Margie said you were going home dinnertime. I hoped I'd catch you there. Didn't you go after all?'

Lily found she couldn't answer now an overwhelming rush of relief and happiness had stolen her voice. He was actually here, in the flesh, with her. She buried her face against his shoulder, gulping back sobs.

'Hey, don't be sad . . . ' Greg cupped her bowed head. He'd yearned to touch her again, thread his fingers through her silky hair and glory at the stroke of it soothing his rifle-roughened palms. 'I've missed you,' he whispered.

'Missed you . . . so much . . . ' she choked. After a

74

moment she sniffed a giggle. 'Sorry, not much of a welcome home for you. Didn't mean to blub when I saw you. Came as such a surprise . . . a lovely, wonderful surprise.'

'I know,' he said gently. 'Feel quite emotional myself.' He sounded self-mocking, but his tawny eyes appeared brighter than usual.

'I did go home.' Lily answered him at last and went onto tiptoe to press her lips against his. 'We just missed one another.'

'Is Smudger with you?'

'He's unloading outside.'

'Anything up?' Greg asked, tilting up her chin. 'You came in like a rocket.'

She shook her head, her eyes locked with his. The desire in his gaze was exciting her and their small talk seemed superfluous. He wanted to kiss her — properly kiss and caress her — and she wanted it too. But they both knew it wasn't the time or place with the others around.

'Sold out early, eh?' Greg gave a nod of approval and teasingly tickled her cheek. 'That's my girl.'

Lily couldn't stop gazing at him or touching his handsome face with her restless fingertips. The foreign summer had bronzed his complexion and his fringe of fair hair was tipped with silver lights. He'd always had a lean and athletic physique, but the rigours of army life had put more breadth and definition into his torso. Her palms traced the sides of his neck and settled on the epaulettes on his shoulders.

'Uniform suits you. You look the part . . . I wouldn't mess with you.'

'Shame . . . I was hoping you would,' he murmured against her cheek.

75

Lily blushed but continued to rub her knuckles on his lean jaw. His early return was a blessing, yet she wished she'd had warning of it. She had wanted to do so much to welcome him home on his first leave. All her plans to drive to collect him from the station and bring him back to a special tea had gone to pot.

'I didn't expect you for another week, Greg.' She tidied a straggling chestnut curl behind an ear, aware she wasn't looking at her best, in her rough cotton work clothes.

'As soon as I heard we were getting relieved early I wrote and told you.'

Lily pulled the letter from her pocket with a groan. 'It turned up today. I was saving it for later. I usually read yours in bed.'

'Do you?' A wicked glint entered his eyes and he leaned closer to say, 'That's when I read yours . . . if we get a decent billet in a village. Other than that, it's propped up in a dugout in a trench.'

'It's been dreadful over there, hasn't it?' A mention of the war had tempered the thrilling chemistry between them. Lily cupped his bristly chin, insisting on having some details of what dangers he'd faced.

'Time enough later for all of that.' He brushed a thumb over her lips. 'Let me hold you some more so I know you're real and I'm not just dreaming about you again.' He nuzzled her cheek, rocking her in his arms.

'If I'd known you were back today I would've made myself presentable.' She'd bought a new outfit and had even splashed out on her first lipstick. Instead of being dolled up to the nines, here she was welcoming him home in a beetroot-stained blouse with fingers dirty from handling potatoes. Lily felt a little shy

76

now they were alone. When they'd kissed and whispered lovingly, Margie had diplomatically abandoned her post and gone outside to warn Smudger that the guv'nor was back.

'You smell of lavender and look beautiful to me,' Greg said solemnly. 'You broke my heart wearing a workhouse uniform, after all.' He held her at arm's length, looking over her curvaceous figure beneath the serviceable outfit. 'Not a waif now though, are you?' He pulled her back into his embrace, closing his eyes and tilting his head up. 'Have I told you I've missed you, Lily Larkin?'

'I've missed you.' She slid her arms about his neck. 'I was going to do a lovely tea with jelly and cake and all that sort of thing.'

'Never mind . . . we'll go out and have a slap-up meal in a fancy restaurant. Can we afford it?'

Private Wilding was still her Gregory then. He was keen to hear if they were making money and that contented Lily. His appearance might have subtly changed but underneath he was just the same. 'We're doing all right; profits are a little bit down since you went. I've taken on somebody else so the street round should soon pick up.'

'Good. Clever gel . . . knew I could rely on you to look after things for me.'

'Couldn't do it without Smudger though,' Lily said fairly. 'Or the others. We're a good team.' Mentioning Smudger had reminded her of the fight, and of Rory Scully sniffing around to get his hands on the warehouse. But she wasn't bringing any of that up to spoil this blissful reunion.

'Any rival firms been giving you grief?' Greg asked. She shrugged, wishing he wasn't quite so adept at reading her thoughts. 'Who would dare to when they know you'll sort them out the moment you're back.'

He moved a shoulder, as though his muscles ached, but his eyes were on her and narrowing.

'You asked me a question before you went.' Lily distracted him.

'I know I did.'

'D'you want my answer?'

'I do ... later, when we're properly alone.' The unmistakable clatter of wooden pallets hitting concrete had been in the background while they'd been talking. 'Got lots to say to you when it's just us and no interruption.'

'Same here ... ' Lily said, hiding her misgivings behind a sunny smile. There were thoughts haunting the back of her mind that could spoil this happiness before it had properly begun. They only had a short time together and then he'd be gone again. She was tempted to forget about every other person and problem and just concentrate on the two of them. But taking the coward's way out wouldn't wash with either of them.

★ ★ ★

'Ta, love; could just do with a breather.' With a smile, Smudger took the mug of tea Margie held out to him.

The back doors of the van stood open and the interior was virtually empty now that most of the equipment had been hauled out and dumped on the ground. He sat down on the metal coachwork, then shifted to one side so there was room for Margie to perch beside him. They rested together quietly, enjoying what was left of the afternoon. The late autumn sun was slanting low on the horizon and the breeze held the caramel musk of fallen leaves. She had told him about the guv'nor turning up unexpectedly, and he'd taken the news in the subdued way she had anticipated. Margie understood Smudger because she thought about him a lot; she knew she probably never crossed his mind once out of his sight, though.

'Guv'nor's in the dark about Fanny Miller starting work here,' Margie said. 'He'll get a surprise in a minute when she turns up with Joey after he told her to stay away. D'you reckon fireworks will start?' She took a sip of tea. 'I've made meself scarce in case Lily breaks the news when they've finished canoodling.'

'Lily can twist the guv'nor round her little finger. Always could, right from the start.' Smudger continued rolling tobacco. 'Whatever she wants, she'll get.'

He sounded sour and Margie gave him a sideways glance from beneath her lashes. She often looked at him when he wasn't watching, wondering how it would feel to be kissed by him. No man had ever tried to kiss her, and she knew why. But at least Smudger didn't avert his eyes in disgust from her as others did. When she filled out their hire chitties, some of the customers walked off, pretending to examine the tarpaulins they didn't need. She'd tuck the stumps of her fingers inside her palm, then use the fist to keep the paper still while writing left-handed. She didn't have to hide anything with Smudger, though, because he took no notice of her deformity. When they'd first been introduced he'd asked what had happened to her, assuming she'd tell him about an accident. But he hadn't looked revolted to discover she'd been born a cripple.

'Want a fag?' He licked the Rizla then offered her the finished smoke.

She nodded, glancing around for somewhere to stow her mug to take the cigarette. He saved her the bother by sticking it between her lips then striking a match for her.

'Wonder if Davy'll be back for Christmas?' she mused, exhaling smoke.

'It'll make Lily's year if he is. Sun shines out of his arse where she's concerned.' Smudger finished fashioning himself a cigarette and lit it.

Though it hurt Margie to know he had a crush on Lily, she could understand why. Margie adored Lily too, in a different sort of way, and knew she always would, just as Lily would always love her back. They'd endured purgatory together, and supporting one another through it had bound them for life.

Margie knew that Smudger was blind to her as far as romance went, just as Lily would never view him in that way. He had the resigned air of somebody who had grown used to disappointment, and Margie knew how that felt. She recognised in Smudger a kindred spirit and, just to tighten the screws, found him good looking in a comfortable sort of way too.

'What happened to your face, Smudger?' Margie had leaned forward to tap ash onto the ground and noticed the mark on his opposite profile. He'd not had that when leaving the depot at first light to load the van at Spitalfields.

He idly rubbed some knuckles over the mark. 'Nothing worth mentioning.' He stood up and jerked a nod. 'Here comes trouble. Better go and say hello to the guv'nor. Then when I've shifted this lot inside, I'm off home. Leave 'em all to it.'

Margie had also spotted Fanny and Joey in the distance, pushing the barrow between them.

Smudger grabbed an armful of equipment but didn't make it inside the warehouse. The door creaked open and the couple came out, hand in hand. Greg did a double-take at his employee's bruised face but — rather than remarking on it — he just raised a quizzical eyebrow.

A careless shrug was Smudger's response to that unspoken question, yet he'd turned hot under the collar. Dropping the tarpaulins and ropes, he held out a hand. 'Good to see you back in one piece, guv'nor.'

'Good to be back, Smudger. Have a pint later, and catch up on things, eh?' Greg said.

His boss's tone wasn't as inconsequential as it sounded. There'd been punishing strength in Greg Wilding's fingers just now. Smudger knew he was in for a grilling. He'd promised this man he could take care of business, and of Lily, in his absence. Looking bashed up was making Greg doubt the wisdom of putting trust in him.

'Meet you in the Manor Arms about six o'clock and we'll have a talk.' Greg had been distracted by the unmistakable sight of Fanny Miller on her way down the road, coppery hair in a frizz about her face. 'Now there's somebody I recognise,' he said dryly. 'But who I wasn't expecting to see pushing one of me barrows.'

'I said I had lots to tell you later.' Lily gave him a twinkling smile. 'I'll say this now though: Fanny's been a godsend.' The new recruit had been on the team for almost two months and so far there had been no more violent clashes. Judging from the casual way they were ambling along, it seemed Lily's hunch about them running into difficulties today was unfounded.

Fanny had boasted that she gave back better than she got when the Burdett Road boys slung insults from an opposite pavement. Lily could remember the choice remarks her friend had dished out when they'd pushed a barrow together, so knew Fanny was capable of getting the last laugh. Inwardly she breathed a sigh of relief that they'd not been inundated with trouble on the very day Greg came home.

'Looks like they've sold out; that's something in her favour.' Greg's mild tone didn't fool Lily. He was annoyed about Fanny but so was she: he should've told her about her friend's visit months ago. When they were on their own later, sparks might fly. But that was nothing new. They'd always aired their differences; even as his workhouse waif she'd never been too timid to challenge him over things she believed were unfair.

With the business of stowing barrows and equipment all completed, and accounting for the takings to the boss finished too, the others had gone home. Greg had been civil to the newest recruit and she, looking wary despite Lily's reassuring smile, had been uncharacteristically subdued. Lily had been expecting him to bring up the subject of Fanny's employment straight away once they were alone, but he didn't.

'Fancy a trip to the West End for something to eat later?' he asked, settling down on an upturned orange box and lighting a cigarette.

'I'd rather stay right here and make our own feast.' Lily gave him an appealing smile. She didn't want to go to a noisy restaurant or a crowded pub. She wanted to do what they used to do when he'd first brought her here to work. At dinner breaks they would brew up tea or Bovril on the Primus stove and eat hot beef and onion pies bought from the corner bakery. She was nostalgic for those early days, getting to know one another, even though their relationship had been fiery as she'd sought to establish herself in his eyes as an independent young woman rather than a wilful kid.

When she first knew him, Greg had had girlfriends and Lily had been his apprentice clerk. Those pretty blondes who'd hung on his arm did pique her jealousy now, if she thought about them. At the time it hadn't mattered a bit . . . she'd just seen him as her guv'nor. Her twin brother had been the only man capable of breaking her heart back then.

'While you catch up with Smudger in the pub, I'm going to go home and smarten meself up,' Lily said. 'Want to look gorgeous for you.' She gave him a flirtatious wink. 'I'll buy some pies and meet you back here at about seven o'clock, if that'll give you and Smudger enough time for a chinwag.'

'Why don't you come to the pub with us? We could eat afterwards.'

She wrinkled her nose. 'I'd sooner get our supper ready for when you get back.' She didn't want to tag along and give Smudger an excuse to duck a man-to-man talk. This wouldn't be the finish of hostilities, so he might as well own up to the fight with Rory Scully. Smudger's interference in another man's marriage might be rooted in good intentions, but it could only end badly. He might listen to his guv'nor's — or his mother's — blunt advice whereas Lily imagined she'd get told — quite fairly — that she didn't know anything about such things.

'Penny for 'em . . .'

'Can't believe me luck that you're really home again,

guv'nor.' Lily had slipped back into an old familiar way of addressing him, making him chuckle.

'You can show me how pleased you are to see me later.

For now, though, s'pose we'd better lock up and I'll take you home to make yourself look nice.'

'Thought you said I always look beautiful, even in workhouse rags,' Lily teased.

'So I did . . . ' He smiled ruefully. The memory of finding her half-naked and humiliated, even now had the power to infuriate him. He felt like going back to South Grove to have it out with the master, and he didn't care if years had passed. Mr and Mrs Stone had presented Lily for discharge barefoot, and in the dress she'd worn when admitted as a child. Five years on it hadn't gone round her fifteen-year-old body, so the back had been ripped open, exposing her buttocks. They'd been content to make a spectacle of her to be mocked on the streets. But Greg had cared, far more than he'd realised at the time. He had paid for the workhouse uniform so that Lily would be allowed to put it back on.

Lily was also dwelling on that day when, unbeknown to her at the time, he'd won her heart. Now, overcome with feelings of love and tenderness, she rushed at him and slipped her arms about his neck. 'I know I've told you already but I've missed you like mad. We'll have the best time while you're home, darling. The Wood Green Empire's got a show on and a special price for servicemen. And we could see a film at the Hippodrome.'

He lifted her up and instinctively she wound her legs about him. 'I'm glad I'm back 'n' all, Lily. You don't know how much.'

There was a weariness to his tone she'd not heard before. But he returned the kiss she'd given him, with such passion that she was feeling languid and weak-kneed when he set her back down. A certain resigned look was hooding his eyes; he knew there were issues to be discussed that kisses and cuddles couldn't remedy. As did she. To delay the inevitable, she turned her thoughts to her brother.

'Have you seen Davy recently? I just got a letter from him. It turned up with yours. He seems all right but I'm worried he's making light of things.'

'He was fine last time I saw him,' Greg reassured her. 'Cocky as ever.'

'That sounds like Davy.' Lily sounded rueful and relieved.

They walked outside and, while Lily locked up, he lit the flares by the gate for their return later. The evening was drawing in and it would be dark by the time they had supper. She'd watched him carry out this routine a thousand times before and wished with all her heart that she could do so for more than just another seven days.

'Is it going well for us over there, Greg? How have you really been?' She carefully observed his reaction. She wasn't a fool and knew the letters the men sent were intentionally cosy to avoid worrying loved ones back home.

Flames were colouring his profile, highlighting his fatigue and the deeper lines on his face.

'It's war, Lily . . . nothing much good about it. But I'm home for now. And Davy's holding his own, honest.' He came over to her and opened the van door, helping her in. Then he got in beside her. 'How have you been doing here?' His penetrating look equalled

85

hers for astuteness. 'What's going on with Smudger?'

'He'll explain later, I expect.' Lily gave him an appealing look. 'Don't make me tell tales, Greg.'

'Have you had any luck finding your little sister?'

Lily grimaced and sorrowfully shook her head.

'We'll keep looking while I'm home. I want to,' he reassured her, anticipating her saying he should rest.

'If you don't mind, there is a place I'd like to go and visit in Essex. We could make a day of it — have a bite to eat in a country pub.'

He squeezed her fingers, clasped in her lap, before returning his hand to the steering wheel. 'Sounds good to me.'

'Do you think I'm just wasting my time, carrying on with this?' Lily knew her friends were at pains to hide their scepticism about her search.

'If you give up too soon you'll never forgive yourself,' he said simply.

'It's just a feeling I have . . . in here.' She placed a fist against her heart. 'I'm sure she didn't die. She's out there. I know it.'

'We'll find her then, Lily.'

7

'What did he say?' Fanny had burst out with a question before allowing Lily a chance to shut the street door. 'I'm sacked, aren't I? Knew me luck couldn't last. He's gone nuts about you giving me a job, hasn't he?' She continued pacing agitatedly to and fro in the narrow corridor.

''Course not.' Lily gave Fanny's arm a reassuring shake. 'I told him you'd been a great help, and I meant it. After that, we talked about other things.' Lily unlaced her work boots, easing them off.

'Does he know you hired me to keep the Burdett Road gang off our patch?'

'Not yet. I will bring it up, though. Not that I want to waste a second of our time together worrying about those damnable troublemakers.'

'Smudger might beat you to it when he and the guv'nor have a drink in the pub,' Margie called from the kitchen, having overheard her friends' conversation.

Fanny gave a relieved smile, then padded off in her stockinged feet to join Margie. A pot was simmering on the stove, a wooden spoon stuck upright in it. She started stirring the bubbling contents.

Margie was sitting at the small table, sawing some doorsteps off a loaf. 'D'you want some of this macaroni cheese and bread and butter, Lil?' she asked.

Lily stopped in the doorway, watching her friends preparing their teas. 'Smell of it is making me mouth water; but I'm only back to wash and change. I'm having supper with Greg so I'd better hurry and get tidied up.'

'What're you going to wear?' Margie put down the knife, eager to discuss her friend's plans.

'Wear those new glad rags you got off Cyril, won't yer, Lil?' Fanny was also interested in seeing Lily dolled up for her big date.

Lily nodded, carrying on their conversation as she went into her room. 'I was going to give the blouse a press, but won't have time. It'll have to do as it is.'

Just last week Lily had shopped for a lovely set of clothes to wear to welcome Greg home. The blue wool crepe skirt and frilled paler blue blouse studded with pearly buttons had Harrods on the inside labels. They'd been a bargain at nineteen and six the pair, off a second-hand stall in Chrisp Street. Lily had grown adept at driving a hard bargain. Cyril wouldn't throw in the elegant navy blue hat she'd wanted as part of the deal, but he'd let her have a pair of dainty leather shoes half-price, at five bob. Lily had known she was pushing her luck wanting the velvet hat, but she'd learned that bartering down to the last farthing was the essence of market trading. She was chivvied to sell fruit and veg at a discount, so expected to get a deal in her turn. If Cyril had stuck to his word and put it by for her, she'd go back and pay for it when she'd saved up enough cash.

'Be a dear and heat me up some water for a wash, Fanny?'

Lily called out as she started unbuttoning her beetroot-stained blouse.

Fanny stopped stirring to fill a large saucepan and put it on the hob next to the macaroni.

'I'll fetch your clothes in from the hall cupboard,'

88

Margie offered. She'd followed Lily into her bedroom. This was a special occasion and she wanted to be part of it.

'Thanks,' Lily smiled gratefully as she stepped out of her old clothes. 'I want to get going as soon as I can. Need to stop off and buy some meat pies for supper.'

'You'll be lucky.' Fanny had come in carrying a bowl of lukewarm water with a flannel and towel under her arm. 'Bakers will all be sold out by now.' She nudged Lily. 'If it was me I'd make him take us out for a champagne supper.'

'He suggested going up the West End, but . . . ' Lily shrugged. 'Rather just have a quiet night together.'

'Yeah, don't blame you,' Fanny said, putting the bowl down on the floor. 'You want to keep it nice 'n' cosy, just the two of you.' She dropped the flannel into the bowl. 'Macaroni's ready, Marge, when you are.'

'Take it off so it doesn't burn. We can have it in a minute when Lil's gone.' Margie had returned and laid her best friend's new outfit carefully on the bed. 'You've got loads of snarls in your hair, Lil. Looks like you've been dragged through a hedge backwards.' She picked up a hairbrush. 'I'll soon sort 'em out for you.'

'Quite a breeze this morning — me hair was flying all over the place till I tied it back. Then it came loose . . . ' Lily started unhooking her underclothes. 'Crikey! Go easy, Marge,' she said as her friend went to work with the brush held in a strong left hand.

'Here, you'd better have this back.' Fanny came into the room with a bar of Yardley's lavender soap she'd borrowed yesterday.

'Thanks . . . ' Lily liberally applied the soap to the wet flannel and started washing her face and naked torso, then one by one plunged her feet into the bowl on the floor. Usually she'd give them a scrub and a soak to ease the aches in them, but there wasn't time this evening, and she didn't dare bend too low or she would be scalped, with Margie still attacking her tangles. 'I haven't got a decent pair of stockings,' she groaned. 'Mine have got holes in.'

'You can borrow mine — only rinsed them through yesterday. They should be dry.' Margie lobbed the brush onto Lily's mattress and disappeared from the room.

'You staying over at his place tonight?' Fanny asked, propping herself on the doorframe.

'No . . . I'll be coming home. Won't be too late either. Work tomorrow.'

'You're bringing Greg back here?' Fanny's eyebrows shot up in surprise. 'He knows that me and Marge'll be here, does he?'

'He won't stay overnight. He's courting me, Fanny.' Lily smiled. 'He never takes liberties.' She'd sometimes wondered whether she wanted him to . . . until she remembered where that could lead. They weren't actually engaged yet and, with Greg going back overseas, the prospect of rocking a baby in her arms was the last thing she needed right now. Courting was lovely . . . kissing and caressing was exciting, yet without the risk of any ghastly problems that existed for unmarried women who got 'in the family way'. Lily prayed she'd never know the desperate unhappiness of feeling backed into a corner and with no option left but to hand a beloved son or daughter over to an institution like the Foundling Hospital.

Fanny closed her dropped jaw to snort a laugh. 'Blimey . . . who'd have believed it? Greg Wilding's a proper gent, keeping his trousers buttoned cos he's fallen in love.'

'That's what he tells me.' Lily spoke lightly, though feeling peeved by Fanny's attitude. 'Greg's not as bad as people think, you know. He's had to build a reputation as a bit of a villain to keep the likes of Rory Scully and the Burdett Road gang off his back.' She continued doing up pearl buttons on her blouse. 'I trust him. He says he really loves me . . .'

'Yeah, I know, Lil.' Fanny looked apologetic. 'Don't mind me. Just jealous. Only bloke who ever treated me decent was Roger, when we was schoolkids and first started walking out. Then I went and ruined it and he married somebody else.' She smiled sourly. 'Good fer you, wanting an engagement ring on yer finger first. Then get him to wear a French letter. They don't always do the job. My little Ronny was proof of that. But they're better than nothing, though, in stopping the babies. Cos they break yer heart 'n' all.' Fanny abruptly turned away and headed for the kitchen.

Lily had picked up on Fanny's resentment but still wanted to comfort her. She was pining for her baby, and her childhood sweetheart. But Lily sensed something else was responsible for making the older woman bitter about life. Fanny rarely spoke about the people in her past, changing the subject if questions were asked. Lily had secrets, concerning her half-sister. Margie was happy to tell anyone about her history. Of them all, the least was known about Fanny's childhood. Her father had died when she was small and Fanny and her big sister had lived with their mother until the oldest girl married. Fanny mostly glossed over her brother-in-law's existence, simply calling him

91

a swine. Lily had often wondered what had first set Fanny on the path to ruin, or why she had returned to prostitution when she yearned for a respectable life with a husband and a family. Saving up her ill-gotten gains for a wooden cross to mark her dead baby's grave didn't seem to be the whole answer.

'Did you see Roger when you went over to Whitechapel at the weekend?' Lily provided an opening for a chat, in case Fanny wanted to get something off her chest.

'Saw me old neighbour. We keep in touch. She grew fond of Ronny, babysitting him all the time like she did.' Fanny spoke without turning around and continued stirring the macaroni.

'Would've thought you'd bump into Roger or that dragon he's married to, being as they live next door.'

'Well, you'd've thought wrong then.' Fanny swung about, pointing the wooden spoon. 'Why're you poking yer nose in anyhow? Nuthin' to do with you if I see him or not. We all know he prefers being married to an old cow to being with me, so don't bother rubbing me nose in it. We can't all have your luck with yer perfect businessman boyfriend, can we?'

Lily was momentarily left speechless by Fanny's explosion. 'I'm not prying, or rubbing your nose in it,' she spluttered. 'I'm just worried about you, Fan. You look sad . . . and I'm sorry if . . . ' Lily gave up clumsily trying to explain and apologise.

'I am fucking sad! Lost me little boy, didn't I!' Fanny pushed past Lily in the doorway and stormed into her bedroom, almost knocking Margie out of the way as she came out, clutching some stockings.

'Don't mind her,' Margie said kindly. 'She has been mooning over Roger again. She thinks I don't know she's been trying to write him a letter. I offered to help her cos she's no scholar, our Fanny. She went mad, told me not to spy on her and shut the letter in a drawer.' Margie rolled her eyes. 'Heard her crying again last night.'

'Shall I go and say sorry again?' Lily felt confused as to how to put things right because she wasn't sure what she'd done wrong. She sincerely wanted to impress on Fanny that she'd never knowingly upset her. 'I haven't forgotten about Ronny. I think about the little dear all the time.' And that was the truth. Lily's missing sister was never far from her thoughts, day or night. Ronny's sweet face would come to mind too, reminding Lily how fragile life could be for vulnerable infants, even those as loved as Ronny had been. A feeble, fair-haired workhouse orphan might never have had anybody to rock her tenderly and ease her pains. But those type of thoughts had to be sent packing. Her sister was well and waiting to be found. And now Greg was home, she had somebody to help her in her search.

'Leave her be.' Margie steered Lily away into her own bedroom. 'Her clouds'll pass over . . . they usually do. She'll be back in with us in a minute to see you all dolled up.' Margie cupped Lily's miserable face. 'She's just jealous, and I can't blame her. I am too. But I'm glad for you, Lily, honest. You deserve to be happy more'n any of us. Without you we'd have drifted apart. And we wouldn't be having macaroni cheese and bread and butter for our teas, that's for sure. More likely me 'n' her would be facing a bowl of workhouse skilly.' Margie jerked a nod at Fanny's door. 'She needs to think about that.' Her speech done, Margie added, 'Right, I can try and help you pin this up if you want.' She lifted a hank of Lily's thick wavy hair.

'I'll wear it loose . . . that'll be fine.' Lily sat down on her chair. She rolled on her borrowed stockings and eased her feet into her shiny new shoes. She barely acknowledged the pleasure of supple calf leather slipping over toes, still throbbing from her work boots. Her euphoria had evaporated, leaving her puzzled by feelings of guilt. Had her joy at having Greg home, safe and well, made her seem too full of herself? She'd never consciously gloat; the idea of it made her squirm inside. She'd sooner have Margie's friendship than her gratitude. In the workhouse they'd been equals: dressed in similar rags and eating the same slop. When one of them had been subjected to punishment, the other would creep from her dormitory bed at night to whisper comforting words or rub the sting from beaten limbs, risking yet more chastisement. Lily had been most in need of succour, as she'd broken the rules more often.

'Look a picture, you do. Blue's your colour.' Fanny had sidled into the room to break the ice with a compliment. Lily jumped to her feet and opened her arms in truce. Fanny eagerly rushed over. They embraced but nothing was said, and Lily sensed it was probably best to leave it that way.

'A sophisticated do is called for, being as you're togged out like a classy lady.' Fanny turned her attention to Lily's hair, looping it up and winding it into a glossy, rich brown chignon. 'Looks lovely like that. Take a gander at yourself.'

Lily stepped to the mirror and inspected her reflection, Fanny's boisterous red curls a background halo to her own crowning glory. 'Pin it up then would you,

94

please?' Lily smiled, not daring to risk hurting Fanny's feelings again by saying she didn't think the style suited her.

Margie fetched the hairgrips and Fanny set to work with surprising speed and skill. Finally she teased a few tendrils free to drape on Lily's cheeks and soften the sleek do.

'Smashing, thanks . . .' Lily said, and found her new lipstick. She was in a rush to get finished here and get going.

She wanted to be on her own, or with Greg. And she'd never felt that way before when with her friends. Normally she'd only ever reluctantly leave them.

'I'd go easy with that,' Fanny said. She and Margie had stood back to watch Lily inexpertly applying her new scarlet lipstick.

'You don't 'arf look glamorous, Lil,' Margie sighed.

'Perhaps a bit too glamorous, if you get me drift,' Fanny cautioned. 'He might think you're wearing make-up cos of me.'

Lily felt tempted to ask why Fanny imagined she was on Greg's mind so much. She dropped the lipstick onto the dressing table, annoyed with herself for being as touchy as Fanny had previously been. 'He gave up trying to tell me what to do a long time ago. I'll wear whatever I like. Anyway, his previous girlfriends wore lipstick.' Lily rubbed her lips together, assessing her reflection. She wasn't happy with her hairstyle or her lipstick. But she wasn't changing either. Perhaps something different was what she needed. She turned around with a smile. 'Will I do?'

She received twin grins and nods of approval.

Lily splashed herself with lavender water, then studied her reflection one final time. She certainly appeared older than her seventeen years. And more worldly. Perhaps in time it might be a look she preferred, because every trace of a workhouse waif was gone now.

Lily hugged her friends, collected her coat and bag, and was soon hurrying up the stone steps that led from the flat.

'He'll wipe that off her mouth,' Fanny said, the moment she heard the door shut. 'Blokes are funny about marrying gels who paint their faces.'

'Lily said his other girls wore lipstick.'

'Wasn't courting them, was he?' Fanny smirked. 'Lily wants to watch it. He's been used to having a woman on the go who can wear all the lipstick she likes.'

'Got anybody in mind for that vacancy then?' Margie asked dryly. She'd absconded from the workhouse as an innocent fifteen year old, but soon had her eyes opened wide when she'd stayed at that brothel. She'd observed the girls competing for male attention. They'd all had favourite clients, and poaching a colleague's regular had led to fights, in the same way as the costermongers scrapped to protect their patches. Margie knew that Fanny was hurting and that was making her irritable in her turn, but the older woman shouldn't be taking it out on her true friends. In Margie's opinion she should remember that and show Lily more support and respect. 'Tell you this fer nothing, Fanny Miller, you ain't amongst good-time gals now. Tell you something else: I think Greg Wilding knows he's lucky to have Lily.' Margie sent her roommate a cautionary glower. 'And so are we. You could do with remembering that next time you feel like blowing your top.'

Fanny wasn't used to meek-and-mild Margie spouting off. 'Who d'you think you're talking to, you bleedin' cheeky mare?' she spluttered, once she'd conquered her surprise.

'You . . . ' Margie crossed her arms. 'You want to go back to streetwalking, and your cathouse pals, be my guest. But if you're stopping here, you can snap out of it. I'm sorry about what happened to Ronny, but taking it out on others won't bring him back,' she rattled off. 'Lily might put up with your moods, but he won't if he finds out you've upset her. He'll sling you out.'

'Don't care if he does,' Fanny bawled. 'I can make me own way. Always have . . . always will.'

'Yeah . . . seen how you do it, 'n' all,' Margie said flatly. She relented a bit when she saw the spark of tears in her friend's eyes. And she was a friend, even if she drove Margie up the wall at times. 'Look, if you still want Roger, perhaps you should go back over Whitechapel and fight for him. I've seen you in a dust-up and would put money on you coming off best with that fat old cow.' With that parting shot, Margie left Fanny in the corridor and went into the kitchen. 'Bloody hell! The macaroni's stuck to the bottom of the pot.'

Fanny stomped into the kitchen, about to defend herself for forgetting to take the pan off the heat, but instead she shrugged, pulling a face.

'Bread and dripping then.' Margie gave Fanny a conciliatory wink. 'Ain't the end of the world.'

8

'Any meat pies left, please? I'm making a special supper for me and Mr Wilding.'

Lily had spotted the baker pulling down the blinds at his windows and had put on a spurt to burst into his shop before he locked up.

'Pies? No, ducks. Too late. All gone.' He grimaced an apology. Wilding's employees were regular customers and he didn't like upsetting any of them.

'My, you look a treat, dear. Off out somewhere nice?' His wife had come out of the back room, wiping her sugary hands on her apron. She'd been washing off trays glazed with residue from sticky buns but now stood transfixed, admiring Lily's new clothes. The girl had an enviable figure to show them off: slender but curvy where it mattered. And the blue of her outfit matched the colour of her large, sparkling eyes.

'I'm welcoming Gregory home today,' Lily explained a little breathlessly, still recovering from her dash. 'He's back on his first leave.'

'Is he now?' The woman gave her a beam. 'Lucky you . . . and lucky him. I can see you've made a big effort.' She tried not to stare at the girl's scarlet mouth. She was more used to seeing Lily togged out in her plain old work clothes; even then there was something enchantingly pretty about her. She didn't need artifice but she was young, she'd learn. No doubt quite soon . . . when her worldly-wise boyfriend caught sight of her painted like a tart. 'So what're you after, dear?' The woman turned to the virtually empty racking.

A few solitary loaves of varying shapes and sizes were dotted here and there. She usually made bread puddings with those turning stale. 'The big tins'll still be springy and they'll do you for toast tomorrow . . .'

'Miss Larkin was after a couple of meat pies for supper, but I told her we've sold out.'

'Nonsense. We can always rustle up something tasty for a brave Tommy back on leave.' Her husband received a quelling look. 'Steak-and-kidney do you, Lily?' She tempted, 'They're the round ones . . . packed with meat, cooked in onion gravy. And I've got a couple of custard tarts for your afters. I know Mr Wilding likes those; he used to come in and buy a bag of them . . . or send that flashy blonde to fetch them when she was still around.' The woman gave a disapproving sniff.

The flashy blonde referred to was Jane Wright, Lily's first flatmate after escaping the workhouse. Jane had always been as stylishly turned out as a fashion model. But she hadn't been the easiest person to live with, or to like. Lily experienced a pang at this reminder of Greg's sophisticated girlfriend. She refused to dwell on past rivals, now of no consequence. She wanted to buy their supper and get going so she could make the warehouse cosy for them to settle down and eat in. 'If you've got some pies left out the back, I'd be grateful to have them.'

'You're very welcome to whatever I can find.' The woman gave an emphatic nod.

'I put those by for our supper,' hissed her husband.

'Well, you can have toast and jam because Mr Wilding's back home and he deserves a steak-and-kidney pie and a custard tart more than you do,' she spat back.

Lily had heard the whispered exchange between husband and wife. 'It doesn't matter if you've put them by for yourselves.' She didn't want to cause any bad feeling. She'd had her fill of that earlier, with Fanny.

'Oh, it does matter, and you will have them, dear. Tommies on leave deserve a good feeding and a bit of razzle-dazzle before they're sent back over there.' Her head did a little jig. 'What the poor lads must go through in those trenches . . . then up they go over the top. And all the while you poor lasses are trying to be just as brave at home, waiting for news of your sweethearts.' The woman clucked her tongue. 'The least people like us can do is show some gratitude and make a few sacrifices in our turn.' She gave her husband a pointed stare before disappearing out the back.

Lily avoided the baker's eyes, despite sensing he was avoiding hers too; trying to stop himself glaring at her, she imagined. Judging by his girth, the loss of a steak-and-kidney pie and a custard tart wasn't going to harm him.

'There, still nice and warm.' The woman handed over two neatly wrapped parcels. 'Now you enjoy your special supper.'

'Thanks very much . . . do appreciate it . . . ' Lily quickly found her purse, keen to escape.

The woman held up a flat palm. 'Our treat. A little welcome-home present for Mr Wilding. And remember me to him, won't you? He's always been a good customer and such a handsome lad. 'Course he's not a lad now, but he was when he started up his place over the road . . . ooh, must be six or seven years ago now . . . '

100

'Thanks so much . . . from both of us.' Lily quickly backed out of the door before the woman did any more reminiscing and infuriated her husband into exploding. He appeared no better pleased at giving stuff away free than at losing his supper; his face was florid with temper.

Lily closed the door and rushed off in the direction of the warehouse, happily clutching her aromatic booty.

★ ★ ★

Greg patted his stomach and pushed his empty plate away. 'Well done for coming up with that meal, darling. It wasn't half bad.'

Lily felt immensely pleased by his praise for her scraped-together feast. The baker's wife had been right about the pies being packed with meat and oozing with gravy. Lily reckoned they must bake two special ones for themselves as she'd never tasted anything as good from there before.

He had turned up at the warehouse shortly after Lily's arrival. By then she'd cleared the desktop for them to use as a table and had placed some lighted candles on it. The crockery and cutlery were serviceable rather than special. Greg had brought in a few brown ales for himself and a small bottle of port for Lily so they could toast his safe return. She wasn't a keen drinker but she would've felt mean turning down raising a glass on such a fine occasion.

'Don't think I can eat all of this — I'm almost full.' Lily cut her custard tart in two and transferred the larger bit to his plate. She'd watched him wolf down his own so she knew the pastry wouldn't go to waste.

101

'Well, if you're sure.' He grinned and despatched it in seconds, then picked up the brown ale, gazing at her through candle flame.

'Don't look at me like that.' She felt herself blush beneath his slumberous eyes.

'Why not? You've made yourself gorgeous for me. And you weren't kidding about that either, were you?' he said huskily, then took a swig of beer.

'We women are supposed to show you men a good time when you're back on leave . . . official line, that is . . . ' Her words tailed off. She regretted repeating a phrase she'd heard from another soldier. The private had thrown the taunt at her and her friends on the day of the reunion with Fanny. Lily was feeling warm and mellow from the port but perhaps it hadn't been wise to down a whole cupful and let it oil her tongue. Greg was looking thoughtful.

'Where d'you hear that little gem? Fanny Miller?'

'The baker's wife told me you Tommies deserve a good feed and some razzle-dazzle on leave,' Lily neatly sidestepped. 'She was full of praise, and asked to be remembered to you.'

'Do you want to go up West then, and see a show for some razzle-dazzle?'

Lily gave him a smile. 'I'd honestly rather stay here . . . just the two of us.'

'You're dressed for a night out . . . you look different.'

'Classy?'

'Alluring . . . '

Lily sensed a hint of irony and tilted her chin. 'I think I look different too. Older.' She waited for a comment. None came so she didn't tell him that she'd decided lipstick and pinned-up hair didn't suit her. Perhaps in a year or so they would, when she was really older than seventeen instead of pretending to be. But as he'd mentioned Fanny, Lily reckoned she might as well follow that lead to get something off her chest. 'Why did you think I was repeating something Fanny had come out with?'

'All the soldiers say it to girls they fancy.'

'You've not said it. Don't you fancy me?'

'Is that a trick question?'

'No . . .'

'I don't need to say it. I can show you how much I fancy you.' He smiled. 'D'you want me to?' He put down the bottle and held her gaze with his. The way she challengingly cocked her head at him made his smile deepen. There had been friction between them from the start . . . some of it good; the sort that kept her on his mind day and night.

She tutted a reprimand in a way that drew from him a dry chuckle. He'd really have liked a different signal now she was seventeen. But he could wait. 'I love you, Lily. When you're ready to do more than kiss and flirt, we'll both know.'

'And I love you, I do, and always will, and if you're fed up with just kissing and flirting all the time, then say.' A seriousness had crept into her tone. She was remembering Fanny's genuine astonishment that Greg Wilding was keeping his trousers buttoned because he was in love. She knew what Fanny had been thinking — hinting — and now a seed of doubt had been sown in Lily's mind that wouldn't budge.

'I like kissing and flirting with you, so now we've finished eating . . . ' he said suggestively, pushing back his chair.

'There's something I've got to bring up about

103

Fanny.' Lily realised there wasn't any good way to lay this blame at his door, so she might as well spit it out. And do it before they started kissing. 'I wish you'd told me Fanny had come over to see me months ago. She thought I'd been ignoring her when I didn't get in touch. I'd never have done that. She's me friend and that won't change.' It was a convincing declaration, though Lily doubted it was completely true. A crack had appeared in their relationship, and as much as she wanted to mend it, she wasn't sure that was possible.

'I've never pretended to like Fanny Miller,' Greg said. 'I don't think you should be as pally with her as you are. She's got a bad reputation, and with good cause.' He prised the top off another beer. 'Now we're on that subject, I don't want her working for Wilding's and getting the place a bad name.'

'Well, while I'm here, she's staying right where she is for as long as she wants to. Fanny's lost so much recently. I'm not taking away her job as well.' Lily knew a further explanation was called for, so launched into, 'Her baby died; the poor little mite got ill and died. That's what she came to tell me and cos I never knew about it she thought I'd turned me back on her when she needed a friend.'

Greg massaged his face and expelled a regretful sigh through his fingers. 'That's a real shame. I didn't know. She never said a word about her kid . . . swear it.'

'She told me she didn't mention it to you. Perhaps she didn't get a chance before you told her to clear off and not come back.'

He pushed himself to his feet and walked off to idly inspect the equipment stacked from floor to ceiling.

Tarpaulins, ropes and poles to fashion market rigs, everything clean and stowed in its place. Now she was in charge she kept everything as he had. He might understand her but she knew him too. She'd become accustomed to all his moods and his habits, even before that first kiss that'd changed their relationship and forced her to acknowledge he'd become the most important person in her life. Her workhouse friends . . . even her twin brother hadn't meant as much after that. Within minutes of first meeting Gregory Wilding in the master's office, there had been an unspoken pact between them. He'd looked at her with his sly golden eyes and, though he'd been a stranger, not her cousin as he'd claimed to be, she'd gone with him willingly. Her intuition about him had allowed her to stand up for herself, challenge him, and still believe the invisible bond they had would hold through fights and arguments. She'd trusted him to always treat her well. And he'd never let her down.

'Did Fanny Miller tell you anything else about the day she came over?' he eventually said, breaking an expectant quiet.

Lily thought about that, while an unpleasant sensation stirred in her belly. 'What d'you mean?' She stood up and took a few steps towards him. 'What else should she have told me?'

'Nothing . . . forget it.' He came to meet her. 'Let's get out of here for a while . . . go for a walk . . .'

'No, I won't forget it.' She knocked his hand away as he reached for her. 'Did something happen?'

'Yeah . . . she asked where you were and I told her to clear off and not come back. I'd've chosen me words more carefully if I'd known she'd recently been grieving for her son. I'm sorry about that.'

He was telling her what she already knew. What she'd told him she knew. 'Don't treat me like a fool. I know there's more to it. What else happened?'

'What d'you think?' He sounded exasperated as he cupped her face in his hands. 'She's your friend but she's also a working girl, always on the lookout for a punter.'

Lily jerked free, licking her lips. 'She's a costermonger now. Same as me. And she wouldn't do that, not to me. We're friends.'

'She wasn't a costermonger back then. Maybe she wouldn't do it to you, but she didn't know about us. I put her wise and told her not to bother either of us again. I told you from the start she's bad news.'

'She tried to kiss you?' Lily demanded.

'Yeah, that sort of thing . . . ' Greg shrugged it off with a version of the truth. Fanny hadn't bothered with preliminaries — she'd gone straight for his trouser buttons.

Lily was shocked to hear her friend had come on to him, but at the back of her mind perhaps had had an inkling of it. Fanny had mockingly called him a perfect boyfriend as though she knew something Lily didn't.

He swore beneath his breath. 'Look, I don't want secrets between us, Lily. But I wish I'd not told you now.'

'Don't ever lie to me.' She turned away. 'I won't say anything to Fanny about this. She was in a dreadful state just after losing Ronny. She probably wishes she'd not acted daft with you now.' Lily sat back down in her chair. 'Can't even begin to know what she went through, burying the dear little soul. He was only a year old.'

In the ensuing quiet she remembered there were

106

other problems that needed airing. He had met Smudger in the pub earlier; whatever had been discussed would still be on his mind. She'd rather they didn't get bogged down in that too. She regretted bringing up Fanny and creating an atmosphere that could worsen. It was his first evening home and they should be relishing every minute of it. But, if Fanny had shown more persistence, what might have happened then? Lily slid him a glance that he seemed to have been waiting for, and had interpreted.

'She's not my type. But if you think I'm lying, and something went on, say so.'

'I don't. It's just a shame I wasn't about that day when she turned up.'

'Yeah . . . then you'd have proof I was telling the truth,' he drawled in defeat. ' . . . So, were you going to let me know about the Burdett Road boys trying to muscle in on us? And Rory Scully's been in here looking the place over, hasn't he, and you too by the sound of it?'

''Course I was going to mention it.' Lily toyed with her fork. 'Just thought we should have a nice supper and a quiet evening on your first day back.' She sounded hypocritical after grilling him over Fanny. From his ironic expression, she gathered he thought so too. 'Rory Scully's just a bloody nuisance and I can deal with him.'

'Fanny Miller's a bloody nuisance and I can deal with her.' He sat down opposite, and stretched across to take her hand. 'I'm sorry about her son, I really am. I know you were fond of him.'

'I was,' Lily said croakily. 'He was the sweetest little boy.' She curled her fingers around his, accepting a truce.

Greg stood up, pulling her to her feet. 'Let's not bicker; I've not even been back a full day yet.'

'I know.' She lay her cheek on his chest, hugging him around the waist. She was content to stay just like that, feeling comfortable and warm in his arms, but he eased his position, shifting her to rest against his other shoulder. She'd noticed before that he'd seemed to favour one side of his chest.

'What's the matter?' She gingerly pressed the spot that seemed to trouble him. 'Does that hurt?'

'It's nothing. Just a scratch,' he said, easing away from her prodding.

'What? Oh, you're not wounded, Greg? What happened? Show me!' Lily frantically tried to unbutton his jacket.

'It's nothing. It's healing.' He caught her hands, holding her back.

'Let me see.'

'You're not going to make me take me kit off and catch me death,' he teased her. 'I caught a bit of shrapnel. It's been stitched.' She'd not give up trying to undress him, so he took over, easing his shoulder free of his jacket then his shirt to show her a patch of inflamed skin . . . for a second. Then he was shrugging back into his clothes. 'See, nothing to it.'

'Didn't look like nothing to me!' Lily differed. 'Looked like you ought to be in hospital.' She felt dread roll in her belly. This was his reality and hers now: wounds and stitches and constant fretting that next time it could be worse, far worse. Her eyes started to prickle and she lowered her face so he wouldn't see her tears. Sweethearts needed to be brave. That's what the baker's wife had said. And she was right.

'I didn't need hospital. If I'd got stuck in one, I

108

wouldn't have made it home on leave. Dressing station sorted me out in no time.' He chuckled. 'Guess who was on duty there and patched me up?'

Lily started to shake her head then her eyes widened in wonder. 'Not Adam Reeve? You've seen Adam?'

Greg nodded. 'Yep. And when I told him I was coming back to see you, he made sure he sorted the dockets so I got discharged as fit to travel. Good bloke, he is.'

'Oh, he is,' Lily said with passion. Adam had been the workhouse's medical officer, and a godsend to Lily in that diabolical place. He'd been her champion, educating her and employing her as his office clerk so she got a rest from toiling in the laundry for a day or two a week. He'd joined the Royal Army Medical Corps and had been serving on the Western Front for almost a year.

'Adam gave me a letter to give to you. It's in my kitbag. I'll dig it out tomorrow.'

Lily beamed and hugged Greg in thanks, making him wince again. 'At least promise you'll see a doctor while you're home.'

'No time to waste on that. Got lots to do.' He planted a kiss on her forehead. 'We've got a trip to Essex in a couple of days.'

He was trying to distract her by mentioning resuming the search for her sister at the Dr Barnardo's home. Even that had lessened in importance, now she was anxious about him bursting open his stitches. 'You won't go after Rory Scully and start fighting, will you? There's no need for any trouble. He only came here once. If Smudger made a meal of telling you, it's probably because he's got a beef of his own with that family.' Lily kept back that Scully had hung about in

109

the market, making snide remarks and threatening to spank her.

'Smudger admitted what's been going on.' Greg exasperatedly shook his head. 'Fred Jenkins or your sod of a brother . . . now, I could believe them chasing after a married woman.' Fred Jenkins had been the oldest of Wilding's apprentices and the first to join up. Greg hadn't been that sorry to see him go as Fred had started getting too big for his boots. 'But I thought Smudger had more sense than those two,' Greg continued. 'I left him with strict instructions not to invite trouble while I was away. Smudger couldn't have picked a nastier bloke to antagonise.' Greg had every intention of paying Rory Scully a visit before returning to France, to warn him off.

'Smudger's kind-hearted and feels sorry for Claudette. After what he told me about her background, I feel sorry for her as well.' Lily sighed. 'She's married to a brute and I think Smudger's brave to stand up for her.'

'So do I, but he's not helping; he's making things worse, sniffing around.'

'She's got nobody else. Her parents won't protect her. They married her off in the first place. Smudger's the only friend she's got.'

'There's more to it than being friends. Scully's got a grievance all right.'

'You don't reckon Smudger's having an affair with her?' Lily gasped.

'I know he is.' Greg gave a bleak laugh. 'He told me the baby she's carrying could be his. The pair of them will have a lot more to worry about if her husband ever twigs about that.'

Lily covered her gaping mouth with a hand.

'Smudger certainly kept that bit to himself!' she spluttered. 'Oh, Gawd. His mother will flay him if she finds out about this.' Lily knew she'd also like to knock some sense into Smudger for stirring up this hornet's nest. 'Margie really likes him, too,' she added as an afterthought.

'Bit of a mess all round then,' Greg said. 'He's promised to steer clear of Scully's wife now, for her sake. Her husband doesn't suspect about the adultery yet.'

'Are you sure?' Lily bit her lip. 'They've had a fight.'

'According to Smudger, that was just for poking his nose in where it's not wanted.' Greg dropped his head back and groaned a laugh. 'Could have done without all this.' He moved towards his chair, pulling Lily with him and urging her down onto his lap.

He stroked her face, drawing her attention from her frantic thoughts to him. 'How about that flirting and kissing now and we forget about the lot of 'em for a while. I'm back on leave and you're supposed to be showing me a good time.'

'And you're supposed to be down on one knee, Gregory Wilding, and begging my answer to a special question. Or perhaps you've changed your mind about asking it.'

'I haven't. Just wasn't sure whether it was the right time to bring it up and risk getting the wrong answer.' He eased himself from the chair to the floor with her still balanced on one of his knees.

'I love you, Lily Larkin. Will you do me the honour of marrying me and making me the luckiest and happiest I've ever been?'

'I will . . . cos then I'll be the luckiest and happiest I've ever been.' She hugged him, then placed her lips on his, nibbling and teasing them open with her tongue. She sighed when the playfulness was past and he took over, kissing her with a passion that forced her head into his supporting hands.

'We're engaged then — unofficially until I can get you a ring. Do you want to choose it or have a surprise?' He brought them both to their feet, still holding her tight to his body.

'I'd like a surprise; doesn't need to be expensive . . . but a sapphire would be nice.' She'd already looked in jewellers' shop windows and had preferred the deep blue stones she'd seen. She wiped a thumb over his lipstick-smudged mouth, biting her lip to stop herself laughing.

He used a khaki sleeve to scrub off the rest. 'Messed your hair up as well,' he said, attempting to pin up a long loose curl trailing on her flushed cheek.

'Doesn't matter.' She reached up and pulled the pins out of her bun, letting waves of glossy chestnut-brown hair cascade to her shoulders. 'Didn't like it much anyway — the girls did it for me.' She left it there; enough had already been said about Fanny.

9

'Oh, I wasn't expecting anything as good as this!'

Greg had helped Lily alight from the van and they stood close together, gazing at the tranquil setting of the Dr Barnardo's village home for girls. The London orphanages she'd visited had been miserable places, stark in architecture and atmosphere. Even the Foundling Hospital in Bloomsbury — though nicer than the rest — lacked the appeal of this little countryside community. The fresh scent of mown grass and the sound of children's laughter drifted on the air. What drew Lily's eyes again and again, though, were a host of beamed and gabled cottages, so simple yet sweet in style that she wouldn't have been surprised to learn they'd been modelled on a child's doll's house.

They had driven onto the Mossford Lodge estate past the porter's gatehouse, taking a meandering narrow road towards the main buildings. Lily had continually swung her head to left and right, determined not to miss any aspect of this wonderland. There were verdant lawns, flower beds, fountains sprinkling and glittering in the autumn sunshine. She recalled the matron at the Foundling Hospital telling her that Mossford Lodge was a pleasant place, but Lily hadn't been prepared for anything quite as charming as what was unfolding before her.

She pivoted on the spot to watch a group of children in pristine pinafores playing with a bat and ball. More uniformed girls were seated on a bench situated on a large green, around which were a semicircle of detached cottages. 'I wouldn't have minded ending up here when I was ten.' It was a rueful understatement. Anything less like the grim workhouse in which she'd been incarcerated for five years, she couldn't imagine. Yet she hadn't actually spoken the truth: she would have endured anything to stay close to her mother and brother in Whitechapel. But they'd gone soon enough, leaving her to carry on alone.

Greg was also looking reflective as he took in a scene that would gladden the heart of any destitute child told it was their new home. 'Beats the St Pancras industrial school into a cocked hat.'

Lily hugged him. She knew his back bore the permanent scars of his time as a pupil at that place. The scars she had were in her mind.

'How wonderful it would be if I found my sister here. Living with other girls — like sisters — in one of those lovely houses.'

Greg murmured agreement, then straightened his tie, snapping to. He gave Lily a smile and offered her a hand. 'You never know, Lily, and if we don't go in, we won't find out. Are you ready?' he asked.

She nodded, placing her fingers in his.

★ ★ ★

A short while ago, a couple had been seated opposite Lily and Greg in the quiet hallway. She had discreetly watched them conversing in murmurs, while a gemstone brooch had winked at her from the woman's lapel. When Lily and Greg had taken their seats, the strangers had smiled and exchanged a few friendly words about the mild November weather. They seemed cultured, but not uppity people, and had put

114

Lily in mind of the philanthropists who would visit the workhouse. They'd turn up on sale days to purchase crafts made by elderly inmates, raising funds for the Whitechapel Union.

'A girl would be lucky to have them as her mum and dad.' Lily sounded wistful as she watched the people walking towards the exit, their interview over. 'I wouldn't interfere if my sister were settled with folk like that. I'd leave her right where she was and just stay in the shadows, in case she ever needed me.'

'Can't just go by appearances.' Greg had his elbows on his knees and was studying his polished shoes, planted on the parquet floor. 'Good looks and good character don't always go hand in hand. Thought you'd learned that lesson the first day you met me.' His teasing was accompanied by a wink slanted up at her.

Lily chuckled. She knew he was trying to ease her nerves with a joke while they waited for their turn to see the matron. But what he'd said about appearances being deceptive was nonetheless true. The couple in charge of the workhouse had put on a good show of being upright citizens, and had succeeded in hoodwinking people into believing it. Mr and Mrs Stone were actually corrupt and horrible. Yet they were still ruling the roost at South Grove. Lily would cheer to see them toppled, even though they shared a relative in her half-sister. Their first grandchild had been nothing to them; they had been more interested in protecting their reputations than their son's newborn daughter.

She turned her thoughts back to the people who'd just left; she assumed they'd come to offer an orphan a home. Perhaps they had no children of their own

115

or wanted a playmate for an only child. They had seemed in good spirits when departing arm in arm. Lily hoped they'd had a successful meeting. She hoped the same was in store for her. She wasn't expecting a miracle. She'd accepted there was only a slim chance of finding her sister in one of those quaint houses. Gaining another snippet of information today would be enough to keep her dreams alive, though. Knowing her sister's fate, good or bad, was the most important thing. She wouldn't give up until she did.

Fantasising about the lovely cosy home the little girl might have — a soft bed with dolls and teddies on the pillows; plenty to eat and clean clothes to wear — was all very well. But a loving mother to guide her and soothe away her pains was more important than toys. Her customers in the market were all housewives scraping by on their husbands' wages, but Lily had watched them wiping noses and rubbing scraped knees and balancing tots in their arms when little legs got too tired to walk. Those careworn women would carry their kids home while also weighed down with a shopping bag.

'Matron will see you now.' A woman had approached to beckon them along the corridor.

Lily took a deep breath. Her heart had started to race, as it did every time she entered an orphanage and was uncertain whether in fifteen minutes' time she would leave feeling dejected. She took Greg's arm and he immediately covered her unsteady fingers, giving them a squeeze. Behind her back she had a set of crossed fingers. The name that she had memorised from her visit to the Foundling Hospital buzzed about in her head, as they followed the clerk towards an office at the end of the corridor. She would ask about Mrs Priest. It was the only lead she had to go on.

* ★ ★ ★ *

'How did it go?' Margie had come out of the kitchen the moment she heard the street door being opened.

Lily shook her head. 'They couldn't help.' Lily unpinned her new velvet hat. Cyril had put it by for her as promised and she'd worn it for the first time to go to Essex. She'd hoped it would be her lucky charm.

'Well, never mind . . . ' Margie gave her friend a consolatory hug.

'I did find out Mrs Priest's name is Vera. She had been there, searching for a Charlotte. The matron wouldn't tell me more and I suppose it's a good thing it's all kept confidential to protect the children. She confirmed they had no records of a girl named Larkin or Stone who fitted the bill, or of a Harriet Fox having ever taken a foundling there during 1910. So that's it. Seems I'm following Mrs Priest around. I can't go and ask her about Charlotte as she didn't leave an address. I doubt Matron would have given that to me anyway.' Lily injected some brightness into her voice. But I've had such a smashing day.' She started unbuttoning her coat. 'I was catching flies when we drove onto the estate, Marge.' Lily exaggerated the dropped-jawed and goggle-eyed look she'd worn on first clapping eyes on the girls' village home. 'It's such a wonderfully different sort of orphanage. There are trees and fountains and a whole load of pretty cottages for the girls to live in with a house mother. The matron told us there's a school and a church and an infirmary on the grounds. I saw some of the children outside; they

117

actually looked glad to be there. Not miserable as sin like we used to be. They're given good clothes and get proper training for jobs. Some even travel overseas to fresh starts if they want. You know what else? Every cottage has a pretty name: Rose and Myrtle and Daisy and so on. When I heard there was a Lily Cottage, just for a moment I thought: this is it. My sister must be living there.' Having rattled off her account, Lily took a breath, reflecting on her long conversation in the matron's office. The woman had been very keen to praise the gentleman who had started it all, though Dr Barnardo had passed away some ten years previously.

Once the meeting was over, Lily had felt able to relax and properly enjoy the rest of the day, despite the anti-climax. 'On the way home we stopped and had a blow-out in a pub: roast beef and Yorkshire puds. The sun was still out and it was warm enough to sit in the beer garden for a while to let our food go down. Then time was up, worst luck.' She grimaced. 'And we headed back to London.'

Margie cuddled Lily again, knowing her friend was putting a brave face on her disappointment. 'You've had a real treat then, Lil. Glad you're back though. How about we put the kettle on?'

Lily nodded an agreement. 'Has Fanny gone out?'

'She's visiting her old neighbour over in Whitechapel.' Margie filled the kettle. 'She asked if I reckoned you'd mind her taking what was left of our veg to give to the woman. I said you'd probably be eating out with Greg today. I'm off out as well, so it would only have gone to waste.'

'She's welcome to have it; we'll have fresh tomorrow after Greg's been to Spitalfields.' Lily knew that usually

Fanny wouldn't have directed a question through Margie. But little conversation passed between the two older girls now, although they kept up a pretence that everything was back to normal. There'd been no more cross words. No mention had been made of Fanny making a pass at Greg. But Lily sensed Fanny knew that embarrassing incident had reared its ugly head. Since losing Ronny, she'd become sour at life. Lily could understand why and made allowances for it.

'Where are you off to later then, Marge?' Lily set out two cups and saucers.

'Going to the pictures with Smudger. New film's showing at the Hippodrome.'

That came as a big surprise, until Lily gave it more thought. If Rory Scully did accuse his wife of adultery, it would be handy for Smudger to claim to have a girlfriend. 'Smudger's asked you to walk out with him then, has he?' Lily asked lightly.

'No . . . nothing like that.' Margie had the teapot in her good hand, and flicked dismissively with the other. 'We walked home together the other day. He said he's fed up spending evenings indoors or down the pub.' Margie smiled. 'It was me suggested going to the pictures for a change. He just went along with it.' Margie handed Lily her cup. 'If you don't ask, you don't get.' She smiled wryly. 'I know his heart's not in it, but who knows what might happen in the future.'

'Smudger's nice but there's other blokes out there, Margie. Someone else might come along and you might like him even better.'

'It's all right, you don't have to be kind. I know Smudger's fallen in love. He told me.'

Lily put down her tea. 'He told you?'

Margie nodded. 'I know about Claudette. He talks to me about things. He says I'm a good pal.'

'I reckon you are too,' Lily said pithily. 'You deserve better than hanging around in the background, waiting for him.'

'Would you have told me he was involved with this Claudette, Lil?'

Lily sighed, having been put on the spot. 'I honestly didn't know he was until yesterday. Greg discovered they were more than friends. I would've told you if it seemed Smudger was leading you on. Did he tell you she's expecting?'

Margie nodded. 'They only slept together the once, so he reckons it's more likely to be her husband's.'

'He really has confided in you, hasn't he?'

'I'm glad. Being his pal is fine by me for now. I can wait till he comes to his senses.' Margie's smile was almost serene. 'He can't marry her, she's got a husband. And even if he is horrible, she's stuck being Mrs Scully.'

Lily knew that was true, but it wouldn't stop Margie getting hurt, watching Smudger mooning over another woman. Lily was also worried that Greg could get hurt due to the embroilment of Wilding's and the Scullys. He had taken Rory Scully's interest in muscling in on his business with too large a pinch of salt for Lily's taste. She guessed he hadn't forgotten about it, but was playing it down to ease her mind. She'd not brought the subject up again, wanting Greg to relax now he was home rather than be bombarded with problems. While they'd been out, enjoying their trip, she'd banned all thought from her mind of the horrible man. Scully shouldn't be allowed to interrupt Greg's precious leave, or her vital search for her sister. But while his troublemaking ambitions went unresolved, Lily could sense his shadow on their shoulders. She inwardly made herself a promise to speak about it tomorrow when she and Greg had a quiet moment at work.

The noise of the door being slammed jerked her out of brooding on it. Fanny came in bringing a scent of frosty air with her. She rubbed together her gloved palms. 'Gettin' nippy out there now it's drawing in,' she said by way of greeting.

'Tea in the pot if you want one.' Lily gave her a smile and set another cup. 'Had a good afternoon over in Whitechapel?' she asked conversationally.

'Yeah . . . and thanks, but don't want no tea. Me friend's been brewing up all afternoon. I'm getting me head down.'

Lily told herself not to take it as a snub. Perhaps Fanny wasn't slurring her words or giving off a whiff of booze and fags. Lily reckoned it was none of her business if Fanny had been to the pub with her old boyfriend behind his wife's back, rather than drinking tea with her one-time neighbour. Fanny had been propped against the door jamb but let go of her support to head unsteadily towards her room. Lily felt sad that the older woman might have just lied about something rather than confide in her friends as she once would have done. Lily felt sad too that Fanny hadn't bothered asking how her long-awaited trip to Essex in search of her sister had gone.

* * *

'Didn't know you were back home. Nice to see you, son. You look well . . . all things considered.'

121

'Wish I could say the same about you, Walter,' Greg said, giving the haggard-faced man a grin. 'You been overdoing it on the turps, mate? Heavy night in the pub, was it?' Greg wheeled the particular barrow Walter favoured over to him. He knew the man liked a pint and a whisky chaser. Greg had joined him for a drinking session on many an occasion in the past.

'Wish a hangover was all of me problems,' Walter said. 'Left the missus at home, crying her eyes out. Had a notification from the War Office. Our eldest boy . . . ' Walter's gruff voice tailed off. 'Well, he didn't make it, see. Just found out yesterday. None of us got a wink of kip.'

Greg dropped the tarpaulin he'd unhooked onto the barrow and thrust his fingers through his hair. 'Aw . . . dammit! So sorry, Walter. Wouldn't have made a joke if — '

'You weren't to know, son.' The older man took pity on him. 'Bleedin' war's not your fault. Turning real nasty, out there, ain't it? We had a letter just days ago off our Jack. We thought he was doing all right, but that letter got delayed, see. Time it turned up . . . well, he was already buried by then.' Walter sniffed, turning his attention to the working day ahead. 'I'd better take a set of scales 'n' all, and a rope. Then that'll do me; I'll divvy up with young Margie.'

By now the others in the warehouse had got wind of Walter's tragedy. Such stories were becoming commonplace but people always rallied around in sympathy. The other costers left the carts they were piling with equipment to mooch over. They thumped Walter's shoulder, grunting their condolences. Lily and Margie had been by the desk, preparing paperwork. Lily came to give the grieving father a spontaneous hug.

122

He was a longstanding customer, and always pleasant and polite. Some of the younger fellows might be a bit too familiar with her and Margie when Greg and Smudger weren't about. But Walter never was. 'Don't know how you've dragged yourself out of the house after what you've been through.'

'Got three at school to feed, love,' replied Walter with a shrug. He approached Margie with a handful of copper and silver on his palm, already counting out his money.

'You put that back in your pocket,' Greg quietly said. 'And keep hold of the barrow for as long as you need it. I know you won't take liberties. We go back a long way.' Walter had been one of Greg's first customers when he started up the business.

At sixteen he'd had a fire in his belly and nothing in his pockets but a wad of IOUs. Now he didn't owe anybody a penny. But he owed loyal customers like Walter, and he never let himself forget it.

'Yeah, we do go back some years, son.' Walter gave a weary nod. 'Better years than these, they were. You keep your head down when you get back over there. And shoot a few of them Hun for me for what they did to Jack.'

After all the customers had gone, they all looked at one another.

'That was a good start to the day,' said Greg with a regretful whistle through his teeth.

Lily put her arms around him. He felt bad for having made that comment. But there had been no malice in it.

'He's a good old boy,' Smudger said. 'He won't take it to heart.'

'Make sure he gets preferential treatment for a

while,' Greg said. 'They'll miss Jack's pay.' He glanced at Smudger. 'Let's get to the market and see if I can remember how to do a deal there without upsetting anybody.'

★ ★ ★

'So you're back, are you, Gregory Wilding?' A jaunty young woman had come right up to the stall to lean across and pat Greg's cheek. 'Missed you, I have,' she said with a wink. 'You always used to promise me a bit extra. Never got it though. Still waiting.'

A few passing women had heard the exchange and approached to listen, and laugh.

'You out to get me into trouble, missus?' Greg said, piling carrots onto the scoop for another customer. 'Go on then: tell me what you're after and I'll see if I can oblige.' He glanced at Lily and gave her a wink to let her know it was a game she was in on.

'I'll 'ave a pound of yer best tomatoes to start. Still thinking about the rest. Let you know in a minute, what else is on me mind.'

Greg had the tomatoes in a bag in seconds. 'Right . . . well, as I'm just off to have me dinner, I'll leave you with Smudger. He'll be better at guessing what a sauce-pot like you's after.'

'Spoilsport . . . ' the woman called after him as he moved away.

He jerked his head at Lily. 'Come on, Smudger can hold the fort while we get something to eat.'

'You're still popular, I see.' She gave him a warning dig in the ribs, then slipped her arm through his as they started off through the crowds towards the caff. It had been a busy morning and she was parched.

124

She could just do with a cup of tea and a bun. She felt proud of the way people greeted him, genuinely pleased to see him back in one piece.

Lily didn't mind the women acting up with him, or him responding in kind. She'd cut her costermonger's teeth listening to Greg and Smudger — and the other vendors — using masculine charm to open customers' purses. Market trading was a carousel of earthy innuendo.

'Gawd bless you, Mr Wilding, and keep you safe.' An elderly woman thumped his arm then continued on by, swinging her shopping bag.

In her mind Lily fervently echoed those kind words, and hugged herself more tightly to his side.

★ ★ ★

It was dark when the men returned to the warehouse. At mid-afternoon they had almost sold out, so Lily had walked back early to give Margie a hand with the accounts, leaving Greg and Smudger to dismantle the stall and pack up. She heard the van's engine and saw a sweep of headlights flash against the windows. She was just on her way outside to help them unload, when an almighty crash made her whip to the door and yank it open.

It appeared that Smudger had pulled forward in a jerk without shutting the back doors properly. The stacked pallets in the back had tumbled out onto concrete. It was a stupid thing for Smudger to have done.

Greg had been closing the gates but at the unexpected bang he'd ducked down to the ground and thrown his arms up to protect his skull.

Lily shrank back, feeling anguished. She knew he

125

was no longer with her in Poplar but back in a trench in Ypres. She closed the door, not wanting him to know what she'd seen, and how it had affected her. She was aware of Greg yelling at Smudger for what he'd done, smashing the pallets to bits. He deserved a bawling out. He'd seemed preoccupied most of the day. And they could all guess why: Claudette Scully was on his mind.

Lily waited until things seemed quieter, then stepped outside as though nothing was amiss. 'Well, that's a bloody mess,' she declared, pointing at the splintered wood. 'When you've cleared it up there's a pot of tea brewing, if you're interested in a cuppa before we knock off.'

She had considered bringing up the problem Scully presented, but decided against it. If she appeared anxious about the situation, Greg would make a point of having it out with Scully to ram home that Wilding's warehouse wasn't for sale and he should keep his distance. In a short while Greg would be returning to the Western Front, and a far more deadly enemy than Scully. He was just a schemer and a coward who beat his wife. Nevertheless, Lily didn't want the two men clashing. She could deal with Scully herself.

10

'You took yer time. Where the bleedin' hell have you been? Give us that here.' The woman snatched the half-bottle of gin from the girl's hand and uncorked it with shaking fingers. After she'd taken a swig she gave a sniff and eyed her breathless daughter. 'Well . . . what kept you, Annie?'

'She wouldn't give me the gin at first and shut the door on me.' The girl was panting, having run home. 'I had to hang about on her step till she'd open up again.' Annie had known she'd get set about if she returned empty-handed. She'd crouched down and pleaded through the letter box for ages before the door was finally reopened. 'She said you didn't settle up with her for the last lot. I promised her you would, and you'd pay for this bottle 'n' all. She let me have it after that but warned me not to go round there troubling her no more.'

'Said I didn't pay her?' Pol Skipman snorted in outrage. 'She had the whole bleedin' lot of fruit and veg you brought in from the market.' Pol's greyish complexion coloured up in temper. 'Don't you go promising her nuthin', you hear?' Annie was used to dodging cuffs so avoided the worst of her mother's slap. 'I'll have that crafty cow for tellin' lies and fer palming me off with watered-down gin.' She had a right to be narked: she had handed over every last spud and apple that Annie had brought back from Chrisp Street last week. In exchange she'd been given some gin, and to disguise the fact the bottle wasn't full, it had been topped up with water. Pol hadn't twigged about that until she'd got home and tasted it or she'd have thrown it back at the cheat. She'd let the woman get away with it and now she'd suffered having the trick played on her twice. Pol looked in disgust at the bottle her daughter had given her but gulped from it again anyway.

Annie had believed her mother would allow her to cook up a potato pie and stewed apple for their teas after she'd lugged home the market stuff that Lily Larkin had given her. She should have known better. Anything worth swapping or pawning never stopped long in their house. Pol had taken the packed bag off her and peered inside. On that occasion, Annie had received a pat on the shoulder rather than a clump. She'd ducked anyway, just in case. The shopping bag had been put aside with a promise from Pol that they'd enjoy a hot meal the next day and use up the loaf and pot of jam first. By the following morning the bag full of begged-for food had disappeared.

'Can I get going now, Mum?' Annie asked. On rising, she'd put on her best pinafore in the hope of slipping off to school with her brother and sister. But Pol had collared her while pushing the younger kids out of the door. 'Afternoon lessons haven't started yet. I'll just say I had the bellyache this morning and that's why I'm late turning up.'

'What d'you want to keep bothering with school for?' Pol scoffed. 'Learnin's no use to people like us. The younger ones can go but you know how to read and write now. What you need, miss, is a full-time job like your brother.'

Annie rolled her eyes. She heard this line all the time. 'Nobody'll give me a job,' she pointed out for what seemed like the thousandth time. 'They're not allowed to when I'm not even turned thirteen yet.'

'Odd jobs here and there'll do you fer now.' Pol expressively danced her hand about. 'I know you do your doorsteps weekends, but there's more out there if you go looking. There's kitchen work, and munitions factories are taking on all the time. Tea-gel job in one of those would suit you.' Pol was irritated to know it'd be a far stretch for Annie to make out she was an adolescent when she hadn't started developing. She was flat as a pancake from top to toe, yet a neighbour's daughter had a bosom at twelve and had told the factory foreman she'd turned fourteen to start work. Pol was impatient for Annie to sprout so she could also tell some lies, and start putting proper wages in the kitty.

On Saturdays Annie visited better neighbourhoods and knocked on doors, asking people for tuppence to do their step. She had built up a few regular customers and sometimes could earn over a florin working from daylight until noon. She would have carried on into the afternoon, but housewives weren't interested in hiring her later in the day; steps needed to be finished first thing. Annie rarely got to squirrel away the cash she made. Pol would be out searching for the girl while she was still working, and would collect every penny in her pocket to stop her spending it on her way home.

'School-board man will be round to see you, Mum, if I don't go in this afternoon. Teacher said I can't play truant no more. She's gonna report me.' Annie pushed a strand of lank hair behind her ear.

'Did she now?' The gin was uncorked again and Pol took a hefty swallow. 'Well, you tell that nosy bitch to mind her own business. Or I'll come up the school and explain things with this.' She raised a fist.

Annie knew it was no idle boast; when her mother wasn't too tipsy to stay on her feet, she was often to be seen scrapping in the street, sleeves rolled up and hairpins clenched between her knuckles to gain an advantage on somebody who'd crossed her.

Annie tried a different tack to escape her mother's clutches. 'You off charring today, Mum?' Like most slum dwellers, Pol never lifted a finger to clean her own home, just other people's. She certainly never scrubbed her own front step. But the spinster on the top floor would get in the way of neighbours' kids clattering along the passage on their way to school. She'd rear back on her heels and roar at them to hop across and not put their dirty boots on the spotless stone. Annie wondered why the woman bothered when she lived in a wreck like the rest of them.

'I can brush your hair and help you get ready to go out, if yer like?' Annie guessed her mum was hungover and needed persuading to leave the house. Not that she looked fit to present herself to the outside world. If Pol cleared off, though, Annie could nip to school. There was another reason to get her going: if her mother worked she might filch something for tea later. Annie's belly was grumbling. All she'd had so far was a cup of weak tea and it was after midday. 'I'll find the comb and the hairpins for you, Mum. You sit down.'

'Suppose I'd better turn in or me lady'll put me off.' Pol gave a heavy sigh. 'Make yerself useful then.' She settled on a chair to have her hair styled.

Pol preferred being a char to a laundress as it provided benefits. She wished her lady's husband liked a tipple so she could filch a livener at work. Unfortunately, the couple were teetotal. But Pol usually managed to help herself to something from her client's larder while wiping down the shelves. She took a few empty jars to work in her bag to siphon off some tea or sugar without leaving an obvious trace of what she'd done. If she was asked to throw the stale bread to the garden birds, she'd allow them a slice then slip the rest into her bag. The jewellery boxes were left alone since she'd been up in court for theft of a brooch. She'd learned her lesson about being too greedy, having been threatened with a sentence of hard labour if brought before the magistrate again. But linens and victuals were fair game as far as Pol Skipman was concerned, since richer pickings were out of bounds.

Annie painstakingly continued plaiting her mother's tangled rats'-tails then coiled and pinned the greying roll on her crown. It was an improvement, but nothing else about Mrs Skipman looked nice. Her worn cardigan had a hole in the elbow and a grimy apron sat over an equally dirty brown drill skirt and sludge-coloured blouse. Luckily the dark materials didn't betray all the stains. But they reeked of body odour and her hands and fingernails were tanned with ingrained dirt. She had nothing on her feet other than her late husband's darned woollen socks that stood in for slippers. Six years had passed since he went, but she still cursed him daily for succumbing to pneumonia and leaving her to bring up his four kids. The youngest had still been in her belly when he was buried.

'Get me shoes from under the table then, Annie,' Pol ordered testily. The hair of the dog had perked her up, easing her headache. She started undoing the pinafore, casting it onto the bed. 'I'll put something on

131

the table teatime, though you don't deserve it. But the others do, I suppose.' She sounded martyred. 'While I'm out skivvying, you go and knock at number ten and number twelve. Them old girls might want some coal fetched in now the weather's on the turn. They always hand over a copper or two when you run errands.' Pol prodded her daughter's shoulder. 'And make sure you skim a good few lumps off the top 'fore you hand over the buckets. And don't bring back no slack.' She ferreted in a pocket for a coin. 'There, I'll treat you to a ha'porth of chips fer yer dinner.'

Annie didn't take the bribe. 'I'm going to school, Mum.' She knew if she didn't get going soon she'd be too late for registration. She backed out of the door, infuriating her mother with her defiance.

'You'll do as you're bleedin' told and earn some money, same as me. Put on that pinny over yer clothes, you lazy little cow.' Pol pointed at the soiled rag she'd taken off.

Annie turned and bolted down the damp passageway and out into a cold autumn sun, only glancing back once at the ugly tenement with its crumbling brickwork and wonky window frames. She didn't really believe her mother would find the energy to give chase, though she could still hear Pol bawling threats.

They had two ground-floor rooms in the three-storey house in Poplar. Their front room was used as a bedsit, where Pol slept on an iron-framed bed with her two youngest. There wasn't much else in the way of furniture: a pine table with a split in the top and three mismatched stick-back chairs. There was no sofa; everybody sat or sprawled on the sagging mattress if a hard stool got too uncomfortable. There was a hob grate for cooking — not that much was ever put near it, other than toasting forks and kettles for tea. A hot dinner was a treat for them all, and Annie would be the one to cook it. Mostly they existed on hunks of bread spread with marge — or jam, if Pol had foraged successfully in her lady's cupboard. If Annie managed to secrete a few of her doorstep coppers, she'd buy herself a bun from the bakery and gulp it down on the way to school. Her mother sent the little 'uns off with a breakfast of bread and marge and weak tea inside them. But Pol's attitude was that her eldest daughter had received enough assistance at coming up thirteen years old and should learn to fend for herself.

Annie was aware she'd get a hiding later for disobedience. The prospect of a beating didn't curb her enthusiasm to get to the playground before the afternoon bell was rung, neither did it tempt her to turn back. She liked her teacher and her lessons and would attend school every day, given half a chance.

Annie whipped around the corner then settled into a walk as a stitch niggled beneath her ribs. She'd already been this way once today, to fetch her mother's gin. It was a slightly better area: some houses even had small front gardens with Michaelmas daisies straggling in narrow borders. Where Annie lived, there was nothing fronting the slum but a ditch overflowing with foul mess.

Suddenly Annie brightened up. She'd caught sight of her little friend swinging to and fro on a wooden gate. Annie had asked after her earlier when she'd knocked at the house and received a curt reply about Charlotte having gone to school. That had been a lie then, but it didn't surprise Annie. Ma Jolley was dishonest. The woman had ordered Annie to stay on the step but she'd crept into the hallway, drawn inside

133

by a baby squealing in the back room. On peeking through a crack in a door, Annie had glimpsed the woman topping up the gin bottle with water from a jug. She'd also observed two tiny tots wrapped in shawls lying on the armchair. It'd been impossible to tell if the infants were boys or girls. Then Ma Jolley had turned around, muttering at them to shut up and Annie had fled silently back outside in case she got caught out spying.

Charlotte had seen her and was waving. Annie raised her hand and put on another spurt. 'I come over here a little while ago but your mum said you'd gone to school.' Charlotte was only half her age but Annie liked her and felt sorry for her. Ma Jolley was horrible and definitely didn't suit her name. A more miserable sort of woman would be hard to imagine. In Annie's eyes she was far worse than her own mother, who could at least be nice when sober.

'Not allowed school.' Charlotte had rarely been to the local infants' class. 'I got sent to my room when she saw you outside.' The child continued using a foot on concrete to swing herself to and fro on the gate, resting her chin on the arched timber rail.

Annie grinned. 'I'm not allowed school neither but I'm going anyway. You can come with me, if you like. Want to?' She had spoken on the spur of the moment and knew this could get her into trouble. She darted a glance at the door. It was ajar, allowing her a glimpse of the shadowy hallway. She could hear the babies still wailing. 'Your mother's busy with the little 'uns.' Annie held out a hand, tempting the little girl, but she knew why Charlotte hesitated. Annie had seen bruises on her in the past. Last week, when she'd taught her to play hopscotch on the pavement, Ma Jolley had come out of the house and dragged her in. Annie had heard the sound of wallops and the girl crying. But she was a similar character to Annie and remained defiant despite threats and punishments.

Charlotte looked over a shoulder at the house she hated. 'Mother said she's going out later to take a baby where it should be.' She hadn't actually been told that, she'd overheard the woman gabbling to herself, as she often did, about what she'd just done or what she'd yet to do. Charlotte never went along with Ma Jolley when the babies were taken away; she was always locked in her room.

'Perhaps she's taking it home cos it's unhappy. It's always crying. I've heard it.'

'The babies always cry. They're lucky though. I want to go back to my other home. Don't like it here. Don't like her.' Charlotte had cried a lot when she first came to live with Mrs Jolley. She'd pleaded to be allowed to go home but it hadn't got her anywhere and she'd been shaken and told to shut up.

'You'll like it at school today.' Annie noticed tears brightening the little girl's blue eyes and held out her hand again.

Still the child hesitated, though she longed to go with Annie.

'You frightened of yer mum whacking you?' Annie sounded sympathetic.

Charlotte nodded. 'She's not my mum. My real mum's pretty and smells nice.'

The child used to watch from the bedroom doorway as Betsy Finch got ready to go out. After she'd put on a silky dress and used her powder and lipstick, the woman would pick up a fox fur from the eiderdown and wrap it about her shoulders. Then she'd brush

135

past her adopted daughter as though she didn't exist. Charlotte would trail in her wake, mesmerised by a sharp snout and a pair of amber eyes. Betsy would call out her goodbyes then be gone from the house in a cloud of scent. Charlotte had liked it best of all then, when it was just her and Mrs Priest. There would be bedtime stories and glasses of warm milk and biscuits before being tucked in. Then everything had changed. Charlotte didn't like Vera now. She'd told a lie and that was why the woman who'd always been nice to her had been crying when she'd said goodbye. She'd promised Charlotte that she would have a nice new family, but it hadn't been true.

Annie had been thinking about what Charlotte had said. 'Who is Ma Jolley then, if not yer mum?'

'She told me to call her Mother and said I have to live with her like the little ones cos our mums don't want us any more.' Charlotte hung her head. 'I want to go home. Don't even remember being naughty.'

'Don't have to be naughty for mums to turn against you,' Annie said. 'My mum says she wishes she could get rid of all of us lot. Then she's different the next day and brings us in a bit of fish 'n' chips to share.' Annie tried to cheer the child up. 'I bet your mum does want you. She might've got ill though, so can't have you back yet.' She lowered her voice, frowning at the door. 'You don't want to believe her. Ma Jolley tells lies.'

Charlotte nodded solemn agreement to that. She'd heard the woman promising Vera that children loved being in her care and she found them nice new parents, living in the countryside. Charlotte had only lived in drab, dirty places similar to the one she was in now. She had been dragged from one London district to another with her new mother. They never remained long in one house before the bags were packed and they were off again. But always more babies would arrive to be looked after, wherever they lived.

'My mum might be ill, I suppose . . . ' Charlotte was looking thoughtful. Betsy had quite often sprawled on the settee, calling Vera to fetch her headache powders.

'What about your real dad? Can't he have you?'

'He's dead. He was a soldier in the war.'

'You're a foster kid then, poor thing.' Annie ruffled the little girl's fair hair. She knew some children at school had been boarded out after they'd been orphaned, but they seemed to be happy. 'Shame you got stuck with old Ma Jolley.'

Charlotte nodded. She felt sad most of the time, but was quick-witted and had picked up that she could take advantage when Mother was busy with the babies. She hated being cooped up indoors with the smell of mess and sickliness. Sometimes she'd sneak out of the kitchen door and spend hours sitting in the washhouse out the back, watching the birds pulling worms in the flower bed, or the cats sunning themselves on the shed roof. Mother had banned her from playing in the street and she was punished if discovered out there, waiting for Annie. But having heard her friend at the door earlier, she'd been tempted to slip outside, hoping Annie might come back. And her hunch had paid off. Charlotte wasn't bothered about going to school; if she were to risk punishment she'd sooner use the adventure to find her old home. Whatever it was she'd done, she'd say sorry and promise never to do it again if they'd just let her stay with them. She'd had nice food there and a fruit bowl had always been on the table. Mrs Jolley had laughed at her when she'd asked for a pear to eat. Best of all, at that other house her daddy had come to visit her in his soldier's uniform. The last time Charlotte had seen him he'd given her a sherbet dab. But Vera had said her daddy wouldn't ever be coming back again. And Mother had told her the same, with a nasty laugh.

'After we've been to school, can we look for my other house?'

'If you want.'

'I'll come with you then.' Charlotte got off the gate and trotted to pull the door closed to delay discovery of her absence. She'd told Mother she was going upstairs to her room before quietly opening the front door to nip outside.

Annie grabbed the child's hand and hurried them both up the street, glancing over her shoulder for any sign of pursuit. The area was quiet, with no gossiping neighbours standing around. It was a Monday, and housewives would be occupied out the back in the washhouses. Sometimes Pol kept Annie off school on a Monday specifically to light the copper and do the family's washing.

By the time they reached the corner, Annie's conscience was niggling at her. But she knew if she'd asked permission it wouldn't have been given and Charlotte would get a beating. The little girl had started to skip at her side and was smiling up at her, enjoying the escapade. Annie couldn't turn back.

'Did you get me a pear from Lily in the market?' Charlotte's blue eyes widened optimistically.

'Me mum gave all the fruit and veg we had to Mrs Jolley. You never saw the pear then?'

Charlotte thrust out her lower lip, shaking her head. She'd seen Mother exchange things with neighbours.

They were never let further into the house than the hallway. Neither were the strangers who visited for just a few minutes to leave babies to be cared for. Once the women had gone, the babies would stop being cooed over and be dumped on the armchair and ignored. But the money collected from their mothers was looked after. Charlotte knew where it was hidden. She'd seen the tin box that was kept behind a loose brick in the kitchen wall. She understood that it was a secret. Somebody had banged on the door once while the cash was piled on the kitchen table. Charlotte had watched Mother stuffing all the notes into the tin and hiding it again before she opened up to a neighbour who was wanting to sell a blanket. Charlotte had kept quiet about what she'd witnessed. She'd learned to be secretive, for fear of being locked in her room. Young as she was, she instinctively knew she must see what was going on.

'Why did you knock on our door this morning?' Her friend wouldn't have come over especially to play. Charlotte wasn't allowed friends to play with. The girls only bumped into one another by accident. After Mother had taken her medicine, she'd sometimes fall asleep, then Charlotte would go out the front and loiter by the gate, longing to see Annie.

'Come for some gin. Ma Jolley doesn't drink all of hers and my mum swaps her for it.'

'Mother drinks the medicine as well as the gin.'

Annie tightened her hand on Charlotte's as they approached the road, hurrying her across when a horse and cart had passed. 'Medicine? What's up with her?' The woman looked all right to Annie, just peculiar.

'Babies getting on her nerves.' Charlotte parroted

139

what she'd heard Mother jabber when whipping the brown bottle from her apron pocket. She would give it to the babies to make them sleep. Mother had tried to give her some of the sickly syrup when she wouldn't stop crying and asking to go home, but Charlotte had spat it out. It was the first time Charlotte had ever received a smack, months ago, on the day Vera left her behind. Charlotte had felt Mother's hand plenty of times since.

Up ahead, Annie could see the school gates and hear the bell being rung. But Charlotte started to drag back.

'You'll like it,' Annie persuaded, seeing the child looked apprehensive. 'If you don't go to school regular, you won't ever learn to read and write, and that ain't fair.'

'I can read and write my name,' Charlotte said proudly, squinting up at her friend. 'Vera taught me.'

'Who's Vera?'

'She's Mrs Priest and she lives at my nice house. When we go there, you'll see her.'

'What road's that house in?'

Charlotte frowned; it hadn't occurred to her that they might not know which way to go to get there. 'Don't remember. It's by a big shop on the corner. If we can't find it after school, can I come and live with you, Annie?' Charlotte raised pleading eyes.

'I'll ask me mum,' Annie promised, then urged her young friend into a trot.

11

'Who the bloody hell is this?'

So surprised was Pol to see Annie sidling in, pulling a child behind her, that she forgot her disobedient daughter deserved punishment. Pol gawped at the little visitor, thinking she looked vaguely familiar. Pol knew she ought to have been able to place such an angelic-looking kid with hair the colour of butter and eyes big and blue. Even the fact that she was thin and pale didn't detract from her prettiness.

'Her name's Charlotte . . . Can she come and live with us, Mum?' Annie pleaded. 'We can't find her other house to take her home and she hates it with Ma Jolley cos she's not her real mum. She gets whacked and locked in her room there. Ain't that right, Charlotte?'

The little girl gave a slow, solemn nod.

Pol clacked shut her dropped jaw. 'Live with us?' she spluttered, throwing down the toasting fork in incredulity. 'And talking of getting whacks, what have you brought in today, apart from a bleedin' stray? I told you to go out and earn, not offer other people's kids board and lodging when us lot ain't got enough to go round. Live here, indeed!' Pol plonked her hands onto her shapeless hips. 'So, have you got a few coppers for me, cos if not I'll pay you, my girl.' She glared threateningly as Annie shook her head. But Pol's eyes kept returning to the quiet child. She recognised her now; the girl would peer at her from the shadows when she went round to collect gin from Ma Jolley's

141

place. The poor kid hadn't looked happy then and she didn't now; her shoulders had slumped and her chin had dropped to her chest. She looked defeated and Pol knew how that felt.

She could understand why the little lamb didn't want to go back to Ma Jolley. She was a weird and unpleasant character. When seen out, she'd stride along in her big black coat and her fancy black hat, with her head down and eyes fixed on the ground. She'd never pass the time of day or grunt a greeting. Unless she was doing business with you, she ignored you. Once Pol had seen her carrying a carpet bag as though she were off on holiday, and had jokingly remarked on it as they'd passed in the street. She hadn't got a reply, and if the woman had gone to the seaside, she hadn't stayed long, worse luck.

'Saw you at school this afternoon. You didn't look very happy. Don't you like it? Is that why you don't go much? How old are you?' There were two children on the bed shoved against the wall. The youngest, a girl, was curled up on her side, snoring. The boy had fired out the questions. He was sitting cross-legged, watching proceedings. Suddenly he jumped off the sagging mattress and approached Charlotte.

'I'm five . . . do like school . . . not allowed to go,' Charlotte whispered.

'Why's that then?' Pol barked, turning around. 'Ain't been sick with a sore throat, have yer?' Pol had heard just yesterday that diphtheria was going round and she was scared stiff that her youngest's sore throat might be something worse than tonsillitis. All the mothers at the school gates were looking suspiciously at other people's kids to spot one who looked paler than usual and might be the culprit spreading germs.

142

As far as the neighbours were concerned, all Pol Skipman's kids were as right as rain, thanks for asking.

Charlotte shook her head. She'd just run quite a long way so she knew she must be quite well. Whenever she didn't feel well, she felt sleepy. And she was wide awake and enjoying herself. 'Not been ill,' she confirmed as Mrs Skipman continued looking at her.

'Hmmm . . .' Pol said, and opened a cupboard to find the teapot.

'I'm nine and me name's George.' The boy jerked a nod at the sleeping girl. 'That's Clare and she's five and she ain't feeling well. Want to get up on here, Charlotte?'

She nodded and allowed the boy to lift her up onto the bed, then he sat beside her. George had the same mousy-brown hair and friendly eyes as Annie, and Charlotte returned him a smile, shyly, her teeth nipping at her lower lip.

'Don't get too comfortable. You ain't stoppin'.' Pol pointed a finger at the little girl, who gave another solemn nod to indicate she understood. 'And I ain't got nuthin' for you to eat, neither, so don't go lookin' at me with them big sad peepers.'

'She can have some of my food,' Annie said quickly. 'You like toast, don't you, Charlie?' That afternoon she'd learned why the little girl liked friends to call her by that pet name: Vera had used it, and Annie could tell that her little friend had been closer to Vera than to her real mother.

'Yes . . . like toast.'

'Right, you can have a bit of Annie's toast and a sup of her tea then she can take you back home. No, I will.' Pol changed her mind. 'I've got a bone to pick with your mother, and no better time to do it than today, I

143

reckon.' As well as having it out with Jolley about the diluted gin, Pol was going to tell the woman she'd fed her foster kid her tea. As far as Pol was concerned, they'd then be quits, and she didn't owe anything for a second lot of watered-down gin that'd only been fit to tip down the privy.

Annie sawed at the stale loaf and stuck the hunk of bread on the toasting fork while her mother shook the kettle. Satisfied there was enough in it to make their teas, Pol put it on the hob and turned her attention to the little girl. 'So, Charlotte . . . where's your real mum then?'

Charlotte gave a bashful shrug.

'She might've died,' Annie spoke up for her little friend, who seemed intimidated by Pol's brusqueness. 'Charlie's real dad got killed in a battle. She's an orphan.' Annie hoped that news might prick at her mother's sympathy. She was always saying how sorry she felt for the women who'd lost husbands and sons to the war. It was one reason why Annie's elder brother Eric kept quiet about his plans.

'Gawd awmighty! Who's she?' A filthy-faced youth had arrived home, unheard above the noise of raised voices and clattering crockery. His alien appearance and barked question had startled Charlotte. She shot back on the mattress in fright at the sight of him.

'Got yer wages for me?' The teapot was forgotten the moment Pol spotted her eldest. She came out from behind the battered table and held out a hand.

Muttering beneath his breath, the lad brought a handful of silver and copper from his pocket and dropped the mucky coins into his mother's palm.

'This is me friend, Charlotte . . . or Charlie, I call her.' Annie introduced the child as soon as Pol had

144

retreated to the teapot. Charlotte was sitting with her knees drawn up to her chin, blinking as she took in the wonderful family chaos. 'He's me big brother called Eric and he looks all black cos he's a coalman.'

'Charlie's a boy's name and she's a bit young to be your friend, ain't she?' Eric had soon forgotten about the visitor. He started his evening routine of stripping off his sooty clothes, leaving them where they fell at his feet. Finally, he eased off his boots, and stood in just his socks and grimy underwear. Then he helped himself to warm water from the kettle and filled a tin bowl to wash in.

'Oi! That's fer making tea,' his mother complained. 'You sod! You should've waited.'

'No time . . . off out.' Eric had found a bit of soap in a cupboard and was speaking from behind a film of greyish lather on his face.

'Off out?' Pol was immediately suspicious. She grabbed his wet chin, yanking his face to hers. 'You got more money on yer?'

'No, I ain't.' He jerked himself free, thumbing his smarting eyes. 'Me pal said he'd treat me to a bit of nosh later in the caff. He feels sorry for me; he knows I never got a penny once you've been down me pockets.'

Pol backed off. 'George, go and fill this so we can get a pot o' tea made 'fore the fire goes out.'

The boy jumped off the bed and took the kettle his mother held out. There was a tap and a sink on the first-floor landing for all the tenants to share.

Slowly Eric's features emerged as he scrubbed his face dry with a towel. He was fifteen, and skinny, but had the world-weariness and drawn complexion of a man twice his age. He'd started full-time work at twelve, and hard graft and malnutrition had stripped the child out of him. He finished sluicing his forearms then kicked his work clothes into a corner. A moment later he'd padded through into the back bedroom.

Annie spread jam on some toast for her and Charlotte to share. 'George won't be long.' She settled on the bed beside the girl and offered her the plate of toast. 'We'll get a hot drink in a minute.'

'You will if the heat's still there to boil it,' Pol said darkly. 'I was relyin' on that coal you was supposed to bring us in.' Now Eric had gone from the room, Pol turned her attention to rummaging in her eldest boy's trouser pockets. A disappointed sigh proved there was nothing left. The oily clothing was dropped back on the floor and she brushed together her gritty fingers.

Annie watched Charlotte enjoying every scrap of her toast spread with plum jam. The child licked her index finger and captured crumbs to nibble. 'Come on. I'll show you where I sleep.' Annie hoped that removing her friend from under her mother's nose might cause Pol to forget about taking the girl home. For a while at least. Annie put the empty plate on the table and made an escape while Pol was busy relieving George of the filled iron kettle he'd just lugged in.

Annie quietly shut the door of the boxroom, where Eric was pulling on a pair of corduroy trousers that were too big for him. They had been his late father's, as had the belt he was using to keep them up. He jutted his chin at Annie.

'You make sure you divvy up for what Charlotte just had. Mum ain't screwin' the cost of the kid's grub out of me.'

'She had half of mine so nothing extra got eaten.' The two elder children knew their mother might

146

conveniently forget that Annie had shared her tea and demand some money or errands were her due in return for feeding an uninvited friend's mouth. The Skipman kids rarely brought school pals home, ashamed of the reception they'd get. The unexpected appearance of this little girl had come as a novelty to the family, even to Eric, who was studying her. 'Ain't seen her about. Where's she live then?'

'Round the corner with Ma Jolley. They only moved in a few months back.' It never took Pol long to sniff out newcomers in the neighbourhood, open to a bit of bartering. Apart from that, nothing much was known about Ma Jolley's background. 'Poor little Charlie's an orphan and she ain't allowed out to school or to play. You managed to give her the slip today, though, eh, Charlie?'

The girl gave a nod.

'You're in trouble then.' Eric wagged his finger at the child. 'You 'n' all, if the old gel finds out you took her,' he warned his sister.

Annie didn't want to think about that, or that it didn't seem to have occurred to Pol that she'd run into more trouble than she was bargaining for later, when taking Charlotte home. It was too late to put any of it right now, so Annie mentally shrugged off those problems and sank down onto her flock mattress on the floorboards. In this bedroom there was just enough space for a chest of drawers and a bunk. The pallet Annie used had been squashed up under the draughty window. Eric had been given the proper bed, as in Pol's opinion he deserved a good night's sleep to be fit to work and act as man of the house. Eric had told Annie she'd get the bunk soon, anyhow, as he'd had enough and was leaving. She patted the space beside her. 'This is where I sleep, Charlie. Bet your bedroom's nicer, ain't it?'

'I've got a proper bed like that one.' She pointed to the bunk. 'But I like this house.' Charlotte was smiling as she knelt beside Annie and glanced around at the cramped space. Away from Pol's sharp tongue, she felt more relaxed and talkative.

Eric hooted a laugh. 'You're welcome to have my place then, gel.' He continued fastening the buttons on a checked shirt that swamped his wiry torso. 'Cos I'm not hanging around a minute longer than I have to.'

Annie put her finger to her lips to warn him to tone it down. Their mother was known to snoop, and if she got wind of what Eric intended to do she'd go into hysterics.

'You ain't really going to the recruiting office?' Annie whispered, eyes bulging in disbelief.

'I am. Me pal too.' He glanced at the door and lowered his voice, just in case his mother had her ear against it. 'That's why we're going to the caff later. We need to work out what to say to make 'em think we're old enough to join up. He's had enough of humping coal sacks for our guv'nor, same as me.'

'Don't want you to go, Eric,' Annie hissed. 'Just stay a bit longer. Please.' She swallowed the lump in her throat.

He grimly shook his head. 'I've promised me pal we'll do it together, and I ain't lettin' him down. Anyhow, I'm done with knockin' me guts out and having nuthin' to show for it. If I'm gonna use a shovel all day long, then I might as well dig trenches as shift coal. In the army you get regular pay and meals. Might even get a medal. At least Mum can't turn me pockets out every day.'

'What about us though?' Annie was fretting about how they'd cope without him. She and her mother would need to step up to full-time work, and even then they would struggle to live and pay the rent without Eric's wages. 'You're being bloody selfish not thinking of the younger ones. George and Clare both need their shoes soling 'fore winter gets here.' Hand-me-down shoes reached the family's youngest with little wear left in them. 'And Clare needs some jollop for her sore throat.'

'I've just handed over fer that.' He yanked tight on his belt in irritation. 'I'll send home some of me army pay,' he snapped, aware his sister was still glowering at him. 'I've got a bit of bunce stashed away too. I'll hand it over before I go.'

Pol had constantly nagged at Eric to thieve coal. She'd shut up after he'd told her he'd had to plead to keep his job after getting caught at it. Pol hadn't brought it up again. Having his wages was more important than keeping the fire alight. In fact, Eric's boss turned a blind eye to his apprentices filling their pockets with coal each day. Eric would hide his booty in a hole he'd dug. When he'd got enough lumps to fill a bucket, he'd sell it for fag money and a night out with his pal. It was his sole luxury.

'No sense giving your savings to Mum. She'll spend it on booze then be flaked out on the bed for days; then we'll get evicted,' Annie flatly pointed out.

'You can look after it then. Ain't a fortune, anyhow. About eleven bob . . . that's all.'

Eleven bob was almost three weeks' rent on the hovel they lived in. Annie was amazed, and envious, that he'd amassed so much. She'd never had more than a shilling for herself. And she'd had to move that from place to place to prevent her mother finding it. Pol had been known to prise up floorboards looking for odd coppers.

Eric had noticed his sister's eyes spark at the mention of his nest egg. 'But don't ask me where the cash is, cos I ain't tellin' you yet.' He pulled on his jacket, then jauntily flipped a tweed cap onto his crown. He was now dressed head to toe in his dead father's clothes. Dejectedly, Annie realised he could pass muster as older than his years when presenting himself to a recruiting sergeant.

''Ere's yer tea then.' Pol had barged in carrying two cups. 'Fire's gone out so kettle didn't boil. It ain't that hot. You'll need to drink it up quick.'

Eric took his and despatched it in two gulps. Annie sprang up and took her cup, handing it to Charlotte, who promptly spilled some down her front.

'Just as well it weren't too hot then,' Pol said gamely as the little girl looked at her with wide, apologetic eyes. 'Let's have that pinafore off you.' With no more ado she started taking off the child's wet clothes: pinafore and plain, grey dress. 'I'll dry these on the stove while it's still warm so yer mum don't know what's happened.' She tested Charlotte's vest, pulling it up to see if the girl was damp underneath. She paused, noticing a fading bruise on the child's hip. She also saw freckles on the child's ribs. 'Got a birthmark, eh, Charlotte? So's Annie. Show her your mark, Annie.' Pol smoothed the vest back down over the shivering child. 'You can keep that on cos it's dry enough.' Pol chafed the little girl's arms. 'You nip under that cover and keep warm.'

Annie pulled down a saggy sock to display a large

150

white skin patch by her ankle. 'Me dad had one just like it,' she boasted.

'Right, I'll dry this lot off and see if there's any more left in the pot. If not, you're out of luck fer your tea, Annie.'

While his mother had been occupied with the others, Eric had slipped out with a sly goodbye. Annie had kept one eye on him, knowing he was off to find his pal and talk about enlisting. She hated the idea of her big brother going overseas but understood why he wanted to. She wished she could do the same. In fact, she'd be jealous if he managed to escape and go to war. She was pinning her hopes on his hopes coming to nothing. She felt mean about that.

* * *

'Why can't she ever do as she's told?' the woman screeched, her fist banging the table top in frustration. 'I've told her to keep inside or she'll feel my hand. The disobedient wretch is really in for it this time. I'll get rid of her and concentrate on the little ones.' Ma Jolley's stout figure began traversing her foul-smelling back parlour. While marching, she brutally whittled away at a thumbnail with a set of brown teeth. There was nobody there capable of conversing with her, but the baby on the settee was responding to her rising voice. The patchwork blanket covering him undulated as he wriggled his thin limbs, but she paid his whimpers no heed.

'Charlotte's pretty face would attract attention on the streets. Has she been kidnapped?' Ma continued her monologue. 'No . . . she'll be around here somewhere. The little nuisance has wandered off and got lost. And good riddance. I'll leave this rotten place, and her. It's time to go and settle elsewhere.' She dug a hand into her apron pocket and brought out the Godfrey's cordial she kept there. Normally she would measure out drops onto a spoon but this time didn't bother and swigged from the bottle. In fact, her threats to abandon Charlotte were empty. The child was too valuable to be offloaded. If Ma's plans eventually bore fruit she would reap more reward from Charlotte than from the rest of the foundlings she'd taken in put together. So, wretch that she was, the girl had to be kept in safe custody for now. She'd caused trouble, though, and deserved a lesson she wouldn't forget. Ma's fists tightened as she enacted her thoughts.

Prone to laudanum-induced forgetfulness, Ma Jolley had rushed out of the house that afternoon, carrying the carpet bag, in the belief she'd already locked Charlotte in her room. She'd returned, empty-handed, to silence. The one remaining baby on the settee had been dosed up and was still asleep. After a while, the absence of any noise had drawn Ma upstairs, only to find the bedroom empty. In a panic she had scoured the back yard and the street for the girl, but hadn't banged on doors to ask if anybody had seen her foster daughter. Ma hated interference, and so was loath to bring her business to anybody's attention. The last thing she wanted was somebody reporting a missing child behind her back. If a policeman turned up, making investigations about the children in her care, she'd be in trouble. But it was possible a patrolling Bobby had come across Charlotte and taken her to the station. That vexing idea set the woman off babbling to herself again. 'How can I go and find out if that's where she is? Questions and more damnable questions will be asked.' She swigged from the brown bottle, then used the back of her hand on her sticky mouth. 'The major's family must be found. His widow won't pay up without evidence of his fornication.' Ma held on to the table as the drug took hold, making her light-headed. But it had calmed her. 'Charlotte's as bright as a button and will find her way home. I'll take her to visit Mrs Beresford. The girl will speak up and say Major Beresford's her father and that he regularly visited her and the Finch woman.' Ma started wobbling her head up and down in satisfaction. 'His widow will accuse me of lies and insolence. But Charlotte is my ace in the pack.' Ma sank down on the sofa beside the mewling tot. 'A workhouse baby, maybe, but that girl is as delicate and pretty as any of good stock. Mrs Beresford will take her in to save face and protect her dead hero. People like that never let their dirty washing be done in public.' As the baby's wailing jangled her nerves, Ma tipped the bottle onto her index finger then inserted the syrupy digit between the infant's pale lips. 'I'll retire from the babies when it's done and have that cottage by the sea. Devon is the place for me.'

For years she'd been fantasising about an early retirement to an idyllic spot. She never acted upon it. She'd not retire, or stop baby farming, while the easy money continued to roll in and her nest egg was growing. Her husband and two sons were gone now: he to meet his maker, and they, ungrateful wretches, to wives she thoroughly disliked. Initially, the babies had been company for her, and a living. Soon she'd liked the ten pounds paid better than the demanding infants. There were only so many she could take and, if she were to make a profit, some had to go to make

153

room for more ten pounds to arrive. There was no use in squeamishness; some had to be helped on their way to heaven.

Ma found the bottle again, unstoppering it just as a loud rat-a-tat-tat on the door made her jump in alarm. Her quivering fingers dropped the laudanum onto the floor. In an instant she was on her knees, scrabbling to recover it before its contents were lost, soaked up into the mouldy rug.

* * *

'I expect your mother's been worried, so better say sorry, Charlotte, love.'

Pol shook the child's hand to make her raise her head. She knew Charlotte was weeping. As they'd walked along in the twilight, she'd heard the child snuffling and had seen her using her sleeve to dry her eyes. Pol wasn't a sentimental sort, but the moment the little girl had wriggled her fingers into hers, her heart had melted. She had tightened her grip on that small cold hand in comfort. A person couldn't help but be swayed by the sweet little thing's quiet, polite ways. She hadn't got her manners from old Ma Jolley, that was for sure. She felt bad returning the child to Ma, when Charlotte was obviously frightened of her. Pol had enough on her plate, though, and couldn't make ends meet with her own four kids under her feet and no husband bringing in. She couldn't have another mouth to feed, no matter her eldest daughter's promises about sharing her bed and her food. And Clare was worrying the life out of Pol, running a temperature and off her food. It was unlike any of the kids to go without their teas. But her youngest hadn't wanted her toast as her throat was too sore to swallow. A diphtheria epidemic had broken out in a school in Stepney a few weeks back. Pol was hoping it hadn't spread . . .

A muffled sob drew her eyes downwards. 'Come on now . . . no waterworks,' Pol said gruffly. Finding a grimy hanky stuffed up her sleeve, she wiped Charlotte's eyes. 'You'll get a telling off . . . but you deserve it, don't you?' Pol had her faults but couldn't be a hypocrite. In Ma Jolley's place she'd feel tempted to dish out a hiding too, if her Clare had disappeared for hours on end without a by-your-leave.

'Mother will smack me . . . ' Charlotte whimpered.

'She might not. You say sorry and I'll make up a yarn about why you went off to school.' Pol wasn't yet sure how that was going to work, but she'd have to put on her thinking cap quickly, now she'd made the boast. She gave the child a reassuring wink then frowned at the door she'd banged on several minutes ago. She could see a yellowish lamplight through the half-drawn curtains, and hear a baby crying. She was sure Ma Jolley was in there. The woman was taking her time, though, opening up. Pol didn't want Charlotte getting her hopes up of going back home with her.

The door creaked open an inch and Ma Jolley's droopy jowls appeared around the edge of it. Her suspicious eyes dropped to the child she held responsible for the accident with the Godfrey's cordial. She'd managed to save very little of it. But for fretting over Charlotte's whereabouts, her bottle of solace would still be safe in her apron pocket. 'Where in damnation have you been? You know you're not allowed out, you little pest.' Ma's lips were drawn back tight against

155

her teeth in temper. She opened the door wider, snaking out a hand to drag the girl inside.

'Oi! Just you wait a minute there.' Pol knocked away the woman's spiteful fingers before they could fasten on Charlotte's shoulder. 'Now . . . I've got something to say to you and you'd better listen cos I'm on to you, Ma.'

A nervous tic caused Jolley's nose and mouth to move in opposite directions when she was agitated, pulling her face into a grimace for a second or two. And she certainly was agitated now. She was the one entitled to a grievance, and was tempted to say so to this infernal busybody. Instead she shot a sharp look at Charlotte, wondering what tales she'd been telling. The girl was like a wraith . . . turn round and she'd be hovering in a doorway, silently watching and listening to what went on.

'You might be her foster mother but you can't go around whacking her like you do. I've seen the bruises on her.'

'She's chastised when she needs to be. I'm on to you, Mrs Skipman,' Ma hissed. 'You've got that daughter of yours to take Charlotte away so you could pretend to find her. Don't dare ask for a reward. I haven't forgotten you owe me for gin.'

'Take her?' Pol snorted. 'Your foster daughter don't need kidnapping. She'd run a mile from here and stop with anybody who'd have her.' Pol jabbed a heavy finger against her opponent's chest. 'So you listen to me. You go hitting her again and I'll have the cruelty man on to yer. Don't think I won't.'

Ma noticed the curtains next door twitching as her neighbour was disturbed by Pol's raucous voice. She made another lunge for Charlotte, but Pol wedged her body between the two of them.

'Ain't done saying me piece yet.' Pol jutted her chin.

'Inside then.' Ma suffocated her anger and stepped aside. She'd sooner have the bigmouth in the hallway than on the step, drawing attention to them all.

Pol marched over the threshold, wrinkling her nose against the stench. The only other time she'd been in this passage was to swap vegetables for gin. On that occasion the reek of mildew and soiled nappies hadn't been quite so stomach-turning. 'Your Charlotte's been to school today then had her tea round at ours . . . but no charge fer feeding her and minding her for you.' Pol continued to position herself between Ma and the little girl. 'We're even now, in respect of that gnat's piss you passed off as gin. Twice you've caught me like that; it won't happen again.'

Ma was barely listening to the complaint; she was digesting what she'd just heard while battling her astonishment. Charlotte was half hidden behind Mrs Skipman's skirts, beyond the reach of a thorough shaking. Ma knew who to blame for abetting the child in attending school and staying out late. She was too young to have come up with such a deceitful plan on her own. The Skipmans were behind it.

The children in her custody came and went quickly and quietly, which suited Ma, as she was at pains to prevent records being kept of their stays. Charlotte was different, though; she'd remained longer than the others. Ma had overheard some neighbours discussing seeing her foster daughter often gazing out of a bedroom window when all the other kids her age were in a classroom. Ma had kept Charlotte's curtains closed from then on and had enrolled her at the infants' school, allowing her to attend a handful of

157

times in the hope the gossips would shut up before they attracted the interest of a school inspector who decided to pay a visit.

'You know we've done you a favour, don't you?' Pol had been watching the older woman mulling it all over, now on the back foot. She pressed home her advantage. 'My Annie's teacher told her the truancy man's doing his visits round this neck o' the woods.' Pol almost smirked at the look of alarm jiggling Ma's ugly features. 'Annie was off to her afternoon lessons and saw your Charlotte . . . who should've been at school. Me daughter took the kid with her in case the fellow turned up. You wouldn't have wanted strangers knockin' 'ere while you was out and she was on her own, would you now?' Pol had been aware of a baby whimpering all the while she'd been talking. 'Got yer hands full, eh? Sounds hungry, poor little mite.'

'Upstairs to your room and stay there,' Jolley snapped at Charlotte, ignoring the comment about the crying baby.

'Just wait a minute, Charlotte; we've forgotten to tell yer foster mother about the policeman, haven't we?' Pol loudly clucked her tongue for good measure. 'Sorry, Ma . . . better fill you in on this. We passed a copper on his beat a moment ago.' Pol barged past to put an encouraging arm round Charlotte's trembling shoulders. The girl had turned about close to the foot of the stairs, her chin touching her chest. 'I told him if a woman called Mrs Jolley had been out searching for a missing kid, no need to panic as I was taking her home. I give him your address and he said he'd come by next time he was passing to make sure everything was all right. So you expect his call, Ma. Nice chap, he was, fer a copper, eh, Charlotte?' Pol gave the little

158

girl a squeeze.

Charlotte looked up and faintly smiled, nodding agreement to her part in the ruse.

'He said he'd make a note of all of it at the station, in case you turned up to report it.' Pol smothered a smile as Ma recommenced twitching. 'I'll get my Annie to come round and walk to school with her tomorrow, if you like. We've all taken a shine to Charlotte so don't mind watching out for her and making sure she's all right.' Satisfied that her warning had got through, that there would be consequences if Charlotte took a beating, Pol reckoned it was time to quit while she was ahead.

'See to your own business, Mrs Skipman. Charlotte's my concern, not yours,' Ma spat through her teeth. 'If she's going to school, I'll take her.'

The baby wailed again and Pol stepped uninvited into the back parlour. The sight, and stronger stench, shocked her into a standstill just a yard into the room. She lived in squalor herself, but this woman had a superior house in a better road. In Pol's view Ma Jolley was a worse slattern than any slum dweller, because she had a choice in the matter; and she could afford a fancy black hat. Pol approached the settee and picked up the baby before Ma could stop her. Its thin little frame was barely palpable beneath the patchwork quilt. 'This kid needs feeding up and changing. She stinks.'

'It's a little boy,' Charlotte said quietly. She was standing in the doorway. 'He's Billy.' She looked at Ma Jolley. 'Has Edward gone home this afternoon?'

'Did you take him home?' Pol asked, when in the dim lamplight she saw Ma Jolley's cheeks jumping like the clappers.

'You impertinent woman.' Ma snatched the baby and rocked it, cooed to it as though it were dear to her. 'Get out of my house now.'

Pol knew her time was up. She had just one more trick up her sleeve to help protect Charlotte. This was no idle boast either; she intended to follow through on it. 'I'll be going up the school meself tomorrow as me youngest ain't at all well and won't be going in. Talk is there's a diphtheria epidemic going round, so I'm worried sick and want to find out if any other kids are off with sore throats. Anyway, while I'm there I'll tell the teacher I had a word with you about things.' She pointed a finger. 'Can't say I didn't warn you if the school-board man turns up.' Pol brushed past and left the house with a final encouraging pat on the shoulder for Charlotte. Outside she loitered on the step, listening. If she heard Charlotte's cries she'd bang on the door again. If not let in, she'd speak to a real copper rather than an imaginary one, and tell him a child was being ill-treated. All kids deserved punishment for misbehaviour; Pol had no high horse to get on over that. She loved her kids, even though they, and life, got her down and made her do and say things she later regretted.

Ma Jolley didn't look as if she had any love in her. She adored making money though. Pol had seen the way she snatched at whatever was being bartered, determined to come out top dog in a deal. Something was wrong in this house and it was niggling at Pol's guts that perhaps she should go and find that policeman anyway. She peered through the window but the light had gone out. She put her ear close to the door panel, but everything was quiet; even the baby had stopped crying.

160

12

'Heard you wanted to speak to me.' Greg propped a hand on the bar, avoiding beer slops.

Rory Scully jerked away from his pal and gulped at his ale, feeling unprepared for this surprise meeting. His gut instinct was to go for an early punch, but he'd sunk a few pints and didn't want to risk going down like a sack of spuds in front of an audience. 'That's right. Got a business proposition for you.' A fist was flexing at his side, preparing for action if his subtle approach failed. Greg Wilding wasn't here to have a friendly chat, however casual his manner. 'Nice to see you back though, mate. How was it over there?'

Greg nodded in sardonic thoughtfulness. 'Not too bad. Guns and shellin' and stinking latrines . . . all that sort o' stuff. Get into khaki and find out for yourself, eh?'

'Married man, me. Can't join up and leave me wife now a nipper's on the way. Poor cow needs lookin' after.'

'Right, yeah . . . that's something else we need to speak about. Do it outside, eh?'

'Fog's come down out there.' Rory rubbed his hands together. 'Here in the warm's fine by me.' His heels were elevating in his boots to add an inch to his height. Wilding was taller than he was, if not as broad. That, plus the fact the man was stone-cold sober, heightened Rory's sense of being at a disadvantage. He'd regularly stop off at the Prospect of Whitby pub for a good drink after work to delay returning to a dump

161

of a room and his wife's miserable phizog. Tonight Claudette had gone to Bermondsey to see her folks. Rory kept her on a tight leash but didn't mind her doing that. She always came back with the money for her keep that he'd threatened her to get. He'd done her and her family a favour by marrying her, and she should learn to appreciate it instead of nagging at him for spending money on booze. He wished he'd gone straight home to an empty place now, though. Rory didn't like surprises, and it hadn't occurred to him that Wilding might track him down to confront him in public.

'Buy you a drink, mate? I'll make out it's for me.' Rory winked. Breaking the law might essentially improve his chances in a fight with a man who should've looked battle-weary but instead seemed depressingly strong and healthy. Besides, most landlords turned a blind eye for regulars treating pals — even if they weren't pals. The government's ruling that landlords must reduce hours and ensure patrons only bought alcohol for themselves was a diabolical liberty in a seasoned pub-goer's books.

'I'll take a drink with you. Bitter. Pint.' Greg wasn't fooled by Scully's old-pal's act. Before they parted, somebody was bound to get hurt. He knew Lily would be furious about this meeting. She'd been keeping tabs on him, asking where he'd been and who he'd seen. It made him smile; other women had demanded explanations, suspecting him of cheating . . . often with just cause in the past. Lily's suspicions concerned a navvy with a vicious streak. Greg felt guilty breaking her trust, but his conscience wouldn't allow him to walk away from this. He knew Scully better than she did and he couldn't return to France without first having

162

done his utmost to protect her. He'd visited several watering holes that Scully was known to haunt before hitting on the right one. He wanted to get this done and get going. He'd been out too long and Lily would be fretting.

'What you offering then?' Greg shoved his hands in his pockets.

'Eh?' Rory swiped beer froth from his lips.

'You told my fiancée you wanted to buy me out. What've you got to put on the table?' Greg watched cunning creeping over the other man's features. There wasn't a hint in that coarse-stubbled face that marriage and impending fatherhood had reformed Scully. He was the same thug from years ago. Then he'd been based over the other side of the water. Now he was settled in the East End, a stone's throw from where Lily lived. Far too close for comfort.

'Well . . . this ain't the time or place,' Scully growled. 'I'll come over to your depot and we can sit down and have a natter about it.' He had not foreseen a demand to put his money where his mouth was; he'd been certain Wilding would warn him off. Rory had next to nothing to put on the table, and he didn't intend to part with his few quid, in any case. His deal would be done behind Wilding's back. Once he'd found out who the landlord was, he'd offer the man a tempting profit-share investment in the business. After snatching the lease from under Wilding's nose, he'd barge in. He wasn't getting put on the spot in front of witnesses, or being sniggered at by Wilding, or any of them for coming up short.

'Won't be another opportunity to talk about this; I'm back to France shortly. So we'll settle it now. If you come up with five grand before I leave, we'll do

163

a deal. Other than that, we won't. So don't bother my fiancée or any of my people again, or there'll be a reckoning.'

'Five thousand pounds for a lease on a poxy shed?' Scully started guffawing, looking around for others to scoff along. He'd tried to extort the lease to the warehouse site when Wilding was starting out. The seventeen-year-old youth would be a pushover, so Rory had thought, until he had come off worst. He had a scar on his shoulder to show for that humiliation. He'd believed it was the perfect moment to try again with just the hired help in the way. But Wilding was back, and he wasn't a kid now with murder in his eyes and a market pole in his hands. He was a man with a cooler head, and the more unpredictable for it.

Greg waited for him to stop laughing. 'It's a freehold, on an acre of land. I bought it off the landlord a year ago. That's my price so either put up or shut up.' The worth of his business was closer to a few hundred than five thousand pounds. But he wanted to make a point that he wasn't selling to anybody because the place was too valuable to him. 'My lawyer knows the price I'm after, and he knows about you. So no need for you to go back and bother my fiancée ever again about this, or anything else. Take your bullshit to Westwoods in Cheapside. That plain enough for you?'

Rory knew he was being treated like a kid with his nose up against a sweetshop window, wanting things he couldn't afford. He'd left it too late to nip in and do a deal with the previous landlord. 'Lease, freehold . . . whatever you've got, it ain't worth that ridiculous amount of money,' he snarled.

'It is to me. That's why I'll be keeping it.' Greg took

164

a mouthful from the beer the barman had quickly put down before retreating to a safe distance. 'Now that's out of the way, let's turn our attention to domestics, shall we?' Greg glanced about, aware they were drawing sly glances. Everybody was waiting, sensing trouble was about to erupt. Even those with no intention of refilling empty glasses were loitering, anticipating some entertainment.

Rory also knew they were under observation. He guessed his dirty washing was about to be aired and he wasn't having that. A couple of costermongers at the other end of the bar had their heads together, smirking. And the pal he'd been drinking with had done a disappearing act when things started getting heated. 'Best we move outside if women are being brought into this,' he muttered. Crashing down his empty glass, he swaggered towards the exit, his fingers curling around the hilt of the switchblade in his pocket. He never went anywhere without it and was always happy to use it on men who tried to make a monkey out of him.

Greg picked up his tankard and followed, noticing that the spectators weren't far behind, elbowing one another for a space at the windows to observe what happened next. Outside the pub he walked straight past Scully, stationed with his stout legs akimbo, close to the double doors. 'Don't reckon you want an audience any more than I do.' He jerked a nod to the faces behind frosted glass.

Greg halted at the mouth of an alley and turned about, but received a hefty shove that sent him staggering further into a misty gloom that was scented by the Thames river just yards away.

'Not that pleased to see me back after all then?'

Greg complained, wiping spilled beer from his donkey jacket.

Scully ignored the taunt. 'I don't mind an audience meself,' he crowed. 'People don't mess with me when they see how I deal with trouble. But if you don't want that lot to watch you get a whipping, son, that's all right by me.'

'Got something to back that up, have you?' Greg guessed Scully had a weapon. His right hand had disappeared into his jacket pocket a while back and had stayed out of sight. Greg understood he was dealing with a villain but had stupidly reckoned on a fair fight. Scully hadn't been able to disguise the fact that this meeting had come as an unpleasant surprise. Nevertheless he was tooled up and ready for action on his way home from work. The man obviously had enemies aplenty.

'Yeah, got this . . . ' Scully displayed the knife, tossing it repeatedly in his hand so faint gaslight from the streetlamps bloomed on the steel as he caught the hilt.

'Pretty smart with a blade, eh? That'll come in handy fixing bayonets.'

'Think you're smart, don't you, Wilding?' The knife was steadied, pointed at Greg's chest. Rory was getting fired up by his opponent's nonchalance. The damp freezing fog had sobered him up to a degree that any thoughts of finishing this another time had vanished. He was envious of everything Wilding had and wanted it. Being resentful wasn't enough; he owed the upstart a lesson from last time. But he'd not done riling him yet. 'I'll have your business. I'll have your gel too. Sweet she is, but needs taming.'

'Good luck with that,' Greg said, taking another

gulp of beer.

'She'll be eating out of my hand, once she's been over me knee and had the spankin' I promised her.' He growled a dirty laugh. 'Bet she's cold and lonely at nights. I'll keep her warm while you're away, pal. Time I'm done with that workhouse kid, she'll do anything I tell her to.' He'd wound himself up thinking of the little beauty squirming under him. His wife lay like a log of wood and there wasn't much fun in that. An image in his mind of Lily naked was sending his blood surging through him in a burst of heat, geeing him up. He lunged forward. 'That's fer starters, Wilding.' He'd heard the younger man's grunt of pain as the knife sliced his flesh. 'Couple of stripes on yer pretty-boy face and perhaps the gel won't want you anyhow.'

A short silence was punctuated by Rory's panting breaths and shuffling boots. He had been expecting Wilding to charge closer to throw a punch, but he was retreating out of reach and out of sight in the dense atmosphere. Scully could just make out that he was drinking the pint in long, continual gulps.

'Thirsty, was yer?' Scully mocked as he heard the unmistakable sound of smacking lips.

'Didn't like to waste it.' Greg emerged from the fog, bending to place the empty tankard down and enter the fray. Instead he suddenly leapt forward and swung the heavy glass up into Scully's chin, sending him reeling. Greg went after him, kneeing him in the groin then swiping his legs from under him with a booted foot.

He dropped down, ramming his full weight on his adversary's right arm, immobilising the weapon. 'Don't go near my fiancée again or speak to her or

167

even look her way or that knife'll end up in your guts.' He wrested it from Scully's fingers, stabbing the blade up to its hilt in the rocky earth by his scalp before springing up.

'You've broken my fuckin' jaw.' Scully groaned, struggling to his knees and nursing his throbbing face. He suddenly spat out a piece of tooth.

'Ain't stopped you gabbing, has it? You'll live. And you'll lose more than your teeth next time. So keep your distance from me and mine.' Greg started back towards the street.

Rory was determined to save face by having the last word. 'You tell your sidekick to stay away from my missus or I'll 'ave him,' he flung after Greg. 'Tell Smudger if he comes round interferin' again I'll take good care of him.'

'Take good care of your wife and he won't need to stick his oar in. He only does cos you keep beating the living daylights out of her.' Greg swung around. 'Big man, ain't you, eh, knocking a pregnant woman about?'

Rory wiped dribbling blood off his mouth with his sleeve. 'She's my wife and she's my business. Not his. My wife ain't interested in a kid like him hanging around anyway. Tell him to stay away from Claudette.' He jabbed a finger into the fog.

'I've told him. Smudger's his own man, but if he has bowed out, someone'll take his place. A woman screaming for help brings decent people running. Old Bill'll be hammering on your door next.' From this exchange Greg was optimistic Scully didn't suspect the baby might not be his. If he did, he was protecting his pride by pretending ignorance of his wife's adultery.

168

Through the shifting mist he could just glimpse Scully yanking at the knife to free it. Greg had felt the tremor up his arm as the blade hit rock. He'd felt a jolt of pain at the same time and the sticky warmth of blood soaking his shirt from where he'd been stabbed. With any luck the blade would have buckled. He wasn't hanging around to find out and risk a knife in the back. He fished in his pocket for a cigarette and emerged into the street, striking a match while shouldering through the spectators who'd quit the pub to be nosy.

Having recovered his swagger and his weapon, Rory followed a few seconds later. The blade was useless but back in his pocket. He spotted his pal, hanging about with the others at the foot of the alley. Rory hoped the fog had prevented them all watching him being knocked down or seeing the damage to his face. But they weren't deaf and would have heard him bawling out his threats. He was thankful he'd kept his mouth shut about the baby. He'd be a laughing stock if rumours started circulating about his wife having an affair and being knocked up by a youth.

For the time being, Rory was keeping his suspicions to himself. If he alerted his wife she'd warn Smudger to scarper before his day of reckoning came. Rory intended to get revenge on the whole lot of them.

'All right, mate? Would've had yer back just now but needed the bog. Guts are playin' me up something chronic.'

Rory shoved his spineless pal aside and ignored the rest of them as well. He carried on strutting towards home.

13

'Ain't the guv'nor back yet?' Joey Robley had mooched into the warehouse to stand with his hands in his pockets, looking sheepish.

'Don't know where he's got to.' Lily closed the ledger she'd been flicking through and dredged up a smile. 'I was expecting to see him over an hour ago.'

'He won't still be packing up the stall in Chrisp Street,' Joey pointed out. 'Smudger's been home ages. He told me the guv'nor was all loaded and ready to set off so I come back cos I've something to tell him.'

'Well, you can tell me, you know.' Lily had been sitting at the desk but stood up, encouraging the lad with a smile. It wasn't like him to return once he'd finished his shift. If it couldn't wait until the morning, he'd something important on his mind.

'Me mum said I should talk to Mr Wilding before he goes back,' Joey mumbled. It was no use speaking to Lily about getting a reference, his mother had warned him, being as she was friends with the tart.

'Heaven knows when he'll turn up. I'm thinking of clearing off meself in a minute cos I'm fed up of waiting for him.'

Lily's anxiety was making her irritable. And she was feeling cross that Greg seemed less aware than she did that every second of this, his last evening at home, was precious and should be spent together. 'You might as well let me pass a message on, Joey.'

The boy didn't need much persuading. He was hungry and wanted his tea. He knew he wouldn't get it until this job was done to his mother's satisfaction. 'Me mum says I'm to quit me job with Wilding's, and move back in with her instead of bunking with Smudger.'

That caught Lily's attention; she'd been peering out into the night for a sign of the van's headlights emerging through the fog, but now turned away from the door. 'You want to quit? Why?'

'Don't want to. Got to.' He rubbed a finger under his nose. 'Sorry, but me mum's on the warpath.'

'She thinks you can get a better-paid job?' Lily knew he got a fair rather than a generous wage, but his weekly perks of free accommodation and a cotchel of fruit and veg were bonuses. The buckshee produce had always gone down well with Mrs Robley. With her eldest living away from home, there was more space for the younger kids to spread out at home, too.

'She reckons I should work elsewhere. She's got me an interview at Hobson's, making bike deliveries to customers while I do me apprenticeship. I'd rather stay here, though. I like working for Wilding's, and bunking with Smudger's been a good laugh. He's all right.' Joey morosely shuffled his feet. He'd felt grown up living with a man of eighteen. He'd been able to have a crafty fag and a few beers away from his mother's beady eyes.

'D'you want me to have a word with her then?' Lily was bewildered as to what the problem could be. Hobson's was a big general store on the High Street that sold everything from children's clothes to crockery.

'No, don't do that,' he said quickly. 'I told her I'd deal with it meself.' His mother had pulled on her coat, threatening to do battle on his behalf when he'd

171

seemed reluctant to carry out her orders. 'I don't want her starting on you. And it ain't Fanny's fault either.'

Lily's ears pricked up. Whenever Fanny's name cropped up, it seemed complaints weren't far behind. 'What's not Fanny's fault?'

The boy blushed, darting glances at the door, as though he might bolt out of it rather than explain, but he rattled off, 'A busybody's told me mum that I'm walking the streets with a trollop.' He sank down onto an upturned crate used as a makeshift stool. 'I never hid from Mum I was doing the round with a woman called Fanny Miller. Mum was none the wiser to that name. But our neighbour went by on the bus the other day and recognised Fanny when we was pushing the barrow together. The old cow's wound me mother up. Now I'm getting it in the neck cos the whole street's gossiping about us.'

Lily rolled her eyes, sighing. 'Look . . . whatever Fanny's done in the past she's just trying to earn an honest living now. But I'm sorry if you've got into trouble over it. Fanny will be too. I know the two of you get on.'

'We do; I always stick up for her when the Burdett Road boys sling insults at her. And she does the same for me when they try pushing me around. One of 'em landed on his backside in the gutter yesterday when she tripped him up.' Joey grinned, but his amusement soon waned. 'Thing is, me little brothers have been getting the rough end of it at school from other kids. They've been trying to stick up for me, see.' Joey wearily stood up. 'Can't have that. So I'm packin' it in. Sorry . . .'

'You're a good lad putting your family first. And you're a hard worker, so I hate to lose you. I understand, though; I expect your mum needs you back living with her while your dad's away.' Lily made it easier on the lad as he was looking embarrassed about it all.

'Yeah . . . that's it. Still no news of him coming back on leave.' He grimaced disappointment.

Mr Robley was a merchant seaman away on lengthy spells of duty. Now the war was dragging on, people had given up talking about early victories and husbands and fathers soon returning home. Women soldiering on alone with kids' mouths to feed had to plan accordingly.

'I'll supply a reference if you want one.' Lily patted his shoulder.

'Yes, please . . . thanks.' Joey gave a grateful smile. 'Anyway, I'll be in until me new job starts next week — if I get it, that is. Mum's banking on it cos she knows old man Mason gives employees a clothes voucher and me little brother needs kitting out to start school in the New Year.' He rolled his eyes. 'The others have started on at me to get them new togs too, but they'll have to do with hand-me-downs and second-hand market stuff. Mum says if I start taking liberties I'll lose me new job before I've had it a week.'

Lily chuckled. 'Once you're serving behind the counter, I'll come in and buy something, then praise you to the skies to Mr Mason. How's that?'

'Thanks,' he said, smiling bashfully. 'Best be off now . . .'

'Oh, one last thing, Joey.' Lily stopped him sloping off into the evening mist. 'Would you keep quiet about the trouble with your mum and let me break the news to Fanny in my own way?'

''Course . . . won't say nuthin' and we'll carry on as

173

normal fer now.' The boy looked relieved to have that burden lifted off him.

Once he'd gone, Lily sat down at the desk again, but instead of opening the ledger she settled her chin on a fist, gazing glumly into space.

She wondered how Fanny would take this news. It wouldn't be an easy conversation. Their closeness had never fully recovered from the previous bust-up. Fanny's flatmates no longer asked where she'd been when she came in late in the evening, looking the worse for wear. The younger girls had guessed Fanny was again having an affair with Roger, but they'd learned their lesson about asking after him. And nobody with a heart could blame Fanny for numbing the pain of losing her baby with a drink.

Greg had rightly predicted Fanny's employment at the firm might have repercussions. But Lily still believed people were entitled to a second chance without their pasts holding them back. Despite her faults, Fanny was a conscientious worker and she'd been a good friend.

Lily sighed, wondering whether to light the Primus and make a cup of tea while she waited. She was hungry too. Since Greg had been back on leave they'd usually eaten their suppers in a Corner House after watching a film or seeing a show. This was their last evening together. Tomorrow he'd be packing up to catch the evening train to Dover, then onward to Calais on a troop ship. They had planned to repeat their warehouse supper. Just the two of them, wringing happiness from every second of these final hours together. Would it be a happy farewell, though, after she'd discovered what was delaying him?

A simple explanation might be forthcoming; she

didn't want to be a nagging shrew if he'd had a fare-well drink with a pal. During his leave they'd worked together most days. Other traders would whistle to get Greg's attention in the market then shout out their offers to meet up for a jar in the rub-a-dub. He was well known and well liked by a lot of people. The housewives who'd asked after him while he'd been away had all made a point of patting his arm in a motherly fashion. Rory Scully hadn't put in an appearance at the market or the warehouse. Lily was starting to allow herself to hope Scully had come out with empty bluster and had given up on it now.

'You look as though you've got the world on your shoulders.'

Lost in her thoughts, Lily hadn't heard the door open and close quietly. She shot to her feet, curbing her instinct to run and give him a hug. 'Maybe I have. Where've you been?'

'With another woman.'

Lily gave him an old-fashioned look. 'Very funny.'

'No, really I have . . . ' He came closer, took her in his arms, pursuing her evasive face until she allowed him to capture her lips and kiss her with innocent sweetness.

'That doesn't make up for anything. Where've you been?'

'Getting you this.' He drew a jeweller's box out of his pocket. 'The assistant was closing up but she let me in when I told her it was urgent. I just hope you like it and it fits. I chose it earlier in the week but asked them to make it smaller . . . it seemed too big before.'

Lily took the tiny casket, feeling rotten now for suspecting him of having forgotten about her, and about

175

the ring he'd promised to get to seal their engagement. She opened the lid. A sapphire stone flanked by diamonds glittered up at her. Even in the weak lamplight Lily could see the gems were big and beautiful. 'Oh, it's lovely, Greg! But you shouldn't have spent so much. It looks very expensive.'

'I wanted you to have the one I thought you'd like best.' He took the ring out of its velvet nest and slipped it onto her slender finger, rotating it to and fro to test it. 'Look at that . . . perfect.'

She went onto tiptoes and tenderly kissed him on the lips. 'Thank you . . . I love it so much . . . and I love you. You should have let me know you'd be late though.'

She'd recognised the name on the jewellery box. The family business was on the High Street. When window-shopping for a ring, she'd glimpsed through the display of gold and silver a young woman she'd taken to be the proprietor's daughter, busy behind the counter. 'I thought you'd gone to find bloody Rory Scully and I was starting to worry . . . and get angry.' She rested her cheek on the coarse cloth of his donkey jacket.

Lily raised her head when he didn't laugh off her accusation. She gazed searchingly into his tawny eyes but he didn't flinch. 'You have seen him, haven't you?'

'Yeah, in the pub . . . had a beer . . . wasn't with him more than twenty minutes. I wanted to make sure he got the message to stay away from you, and that nothing of mine's for sale.' No lies in that but he could see the warmth in her eyes fading.

'And that was it?' Lily slowly freed herself from his embrace and stepped back.

'More or less . . . '

She pursed her lips, assessing his appearance. His face and hands looked undamaged ... more or less ... 'You've had a fight, haven't you?'

'Nothing drastic happened, Lily. Look ...' He spread his hands.

'What about him?'

'What about him? He got what was coming to him.'

'You bloody fool! Don't you see he'll just come back now when you're gone? He'll take it out on Smudger,' Lily cried, spinning about in agitation.

Greg captured her shoulders, holding her still. 'No, he won't. Smudger's staying out of it now. It would be better if he moved to another part of town though. He lives too close for comfort to Claudette. Now Joey's jacked it in, Smudger can find somewhere just for himself.'

'You've spoken to Joey?'

'Just ran into him outside. He told me why he's leaving.'

Lily considered that, wishing she'd been the one to bring the subject up. 'I suppose you'll say I told you so.'

'I won't make an issue of it. If you return the favour over Scully getting what he deserved.'

'Fanny's not stirring up the same sort of trouble as him. It's not her fault nasty people gossip and bring up her past.'

'I know ... but having her around isn't good for business, is it?'

Lily started fiddling with the ring on her finger, slipping it to her knuckle and back.

'You're not going to take it off and throw it at me, are you?' he asked ironically.

'You can have it back if you've been deceitful. I

177

don't want a husband like that.'

'When have I been deceitful?'

'If I hadn't brought up about Rory Scully, would you have owned up about what happened this evening?'

He walked off a few paces before pivoting back, thrusting his hands into his pockets. 'Were you going to own up that he said he'd put you over his knee and spank you?'

Lily could feel her cheeks burning. She'd had no intention of ever mentioning that. But obviously Scully had boasted about it. 'Don't try to wriggle out of this — '

'Says the girl who wouldn't have told her fiancé that a man threatened to rape her!' he shouted. 'If I'd known that sooner I would have gone after him sooner, and for far better reason than to tell him his eyes are bigger than his wallet.'

'It wasn't that bad; he was just showing off. He wouldn't have done anything in the market with people around.' Lily's attempt to smooth it over was in itself deceitful. Scully hadn't been larking. His eyes had held a rapacious glint as they'd stripped her naked. She recalled having felt panicky afterwards, aware he could have overpowered her and bundled her into the back of the van. Once out of sight, bound and gagged, she'd have been at his mercy. Her uneasiness had lingered long after he'd gone. She'd kept it all to herself, fearing Greg would do what he had done in reprisal.

'You don't know him, Lily. Scully's not a rascal, he's a thug who carries a knife. He says anything like that to you ever again, you let me know straight away.'

She licked her lips, alarmed by his fury. 'There's no need to worry, Greg.' She forced a sweet smile to her lips. 'I can take care of myself.'

'No, you can't,' he said coolly. 'I can. And you have to let me, or he'll try again. Next time he might hurt you. It won't be punch-ups then, it'll be murders.' He paused. 'Promise me you'll let Smudger deal with Scully if he comes back while I'm gone. Smudger's wise to him and his tricks. And he hates him as much as I do.' He noticed tears brightening her eyes. 'Look, I'm not blaming you, sweetheart. You're not long out of the workhouse. You're still naïve about how dangerous life outside can be. You're a tough girl but this is different cruelty to what you knew in there.'

Lily couldn't deny wanting to believe folk outside were kinder than the workhouse staff. And she knew she was still learning about the ways of the world. In those early days of freedom, she'd felt reborn. She'd delighted in every sight and smell, staring at people and things. Basic acts such as going to the shops and markets, earning money, spending money; every single thing had been new and exciting. After five years' incarceration, dressed in rags, eating slop, she'd started to find her feet and be normal again. She'd blossomed from a workhouse child into a business-woman, thanks to Gregory Wilding who'd given her the chance in the first place. Without him she'd still be there, getting older and lonelier, browbeaten by a regime that was careless about whether inmates lived or died.

'It's my fault. I shouldn't have enlisted.' Greg enclosed her in a strong embrace that drew her to her toes. 'I should have stayed with you. I'm a bloody idiot.'

'You're not!' she said fiercely. 'I'm proud of you. All you soldiers are protecting us here at home.' She banged her forehead on his chest in frustration. 'I can't stand that Scully is making us argue and feel afraid for one another. He shouldn't have power over us. I had enough of being bullied in the workhouse.'

'I know. Don't worry about him. He'll keep his distance now anyway.' Greg hoped his threats of retribution were enough to make that true. But Scully was arrogant and bore grudges. A man like that might suffer any consequences to defend his ego and hard-man reputation. Greg was beginning to resent Smudger too for having made things worse than they needed to be, messing about with Claudette and giving her husband a genuine grievance and a reason to come back.

'I didn't want our last evening to be spoiled like this,' Lily said.

'We can't let it be spoiled,' he said simply, and tilted up her chin. 'No more talk about any of them. Agreed?'

She nodded, slipping her arms around his neck.

'Your stitches?'

'Still holding up. He gave me a stripe on my arm but I've bound it up.'

'Bad enough to keep you in England?' She seized on that possibility.

''Fraid not. I'd be more likely to get a stint in chokey than a hospital. Fighting on leave, Private Wilding . . . tut, tut, letting the side down.'

'You'd better let me look at it; it might need a proper bandage.' They kept a small medical kit on a shelf in the warehouse for cuts and grazes got from dropping boxes on toes, or getting splinters in fingers.

Greg hesitated.

'Let me see,' she insisted.

He took off his jacket and rolled up his stained shirtsleeve to display the bloodied rag wound tightly

180

about his arm.

'Don't need to go back over there to be in the wars, do you?' Her voice had trembled as she saw the amount of blood he'd lost. He was trying not to show he was in pain, but she'd noticed him wince as he'd manoeuvred out of his clothes. 'You should see a doctor and get it stitched.' Lily had unwound the rag and exposed the gaping wound.

He shook his head. 'Doctors ask questions — coppers might get involved. I'll do it myself when I get home later.'

Lily gawped at him, uncertain she understood his meaning. 'What? You'll stitch it?'

He smiled wryly. 'Not the first time I've patched meself up like that, Lily,' he mildly informed her, rolling down his sleeve. 'Shame your doctor friend Adam's not on leave. I'd pay him a visit.'

Lily knew Adam would help too, no questions asked. 'Well, he's in France and you can't do it left-handed.'

'I'll manage,' Greg said, despite knowing she had a point.

Lily hurried to the desk and took from the top drawer a small sewing kit kept there for hem and button repairs. 'Black or white?' She held up two cotton reels, trying to inject some levity into her voice to quell the nausea rolling in her belly.

'I'm not doing it now. It'll wait till later. Let's go and celebrate our engagement with a nice dinner.'

'I'll do it.' Lily sounded calm though her teeth were chattering. She chose the black cotton, the better to see it against his flesh.

'You don't need to do it . . . ' Her suggestion had taken him aback.

181

'I do, unless you're double-jointed.' She poured hot water from the kettle into a bowl and washed her hands with the carbolic soap they cleaned up with after work. 'Sit down,' she ordered, holding a needle and a length of cotton up closer to the hurricane lamp suspended from the central timber beam directly overhead. The light was weak but she threaded it on the second attempt. She lit the Primus and held the needle in the flame to sterilise it.

'You look as though you know the drill, but I don't want you to do this, Lily. It's not a nice job. You'll upset yourself . . . '

'I'm a workhouse kid; I'm used to being upset. Sit down.' She sounded bossier, manoeuvring the crate beneath the light with a foot. Her legs were shaking as she approached, dragging him over to the crate and pushing his shoulder until he was in a seated position. She inspected the wound while holding the needle out at an angle to keep it clean. 'You hold the edges together till I get going,' she said. 'Be brave . . . ' She gave him a wobbly smile.

'Lily . . . don't . . . '

'Shush, or I won't be able to concentrate . . . Blanket stitch, I think . . . ' she muttered. She saw him tense and turn his head, his teeth gritted as the needle entered his flesh. She swallowed the bile rising in her throat and carried on, glancing at him every time in mute apology as the muscles in his jaw tightened in pain. When she'd made four puncture marks either side of the wound, she gave him the needle to hold and went to get the scissors to snip the cotton. She bent, kissed the crown of his head, then bolted outside to be sick.

'Sorry . . . ' she said sheepishly, having returned and

182

found him still seated, resting forward with his elbows on his knees and his head in his hands. 'Couldn't hold it in.'

'You're a marvel, know that, Lily?' he said without looking at her, his voice husky with emotion. 'That's a bloody good job.' He glanced at the neat stitches then at her. 'I'm sorry — really sorry — that I didn't get out of the way of that knife. You shouldn't have had to do that.'

'Wasn't so bad.' She tried to ease his anguish. The lamp above was sparking on the water on his lashes. 'If we weren't mangling sheets or scrubbing floors, we were mending stuff.' She used her hanky on her lips to clear the taste of vomit from them. She busied herself pouring fresh warm water into the bowl and found a clean hanky in the desk drawer. She carried the bowl beneath the light and started to dab away the dried blood on his skin, avoiding the stitches.

'Could do with you over there as a nurse, y'know.'

'I used to read Adam's medical books when I was in his office, working as his clerk. Got more schooling than I should've, thanks to him. He was always on my side.' She helped Greg manoeuvre back into his shirt. 'You'll need to get some antiseptic and keep the area clean.' She took his chin to make him nod an acknowledgement of her advice. 'Then when you get back to France, go and find Adam, and let him look at it for you.'

'Yeah . . . I will.' He stood up wearily and gazed at her with such tender adoration that Lily felt she'd melt.

'Wish this wasn't your last night at home,' she said wistfully. 'Seven days wasn't nearly long enough.'

'I know, love. Shall we go out for an engagement

dinner? Can you stomach food?'

Lily gave a vigorous nod. ''Course. I'll go home and change then you can pick me up in about an hour and we'll have a Corner House feast.' She'd lost interest in a cosy little last supper in the warehouse. It'd be too late to catch the baker's open now, anyway. It was her engagement day. It should have been one of the happiest, most memorable of her life. And it was. But she knew she'd remember this evening for all the wrong reasons. 'You'll be busy packing up to leave tomorrow.'

'Yeah, got to report for duty by midday. Wish I could pack you in me kitbag, Mrs Wilding.'

She chuckled, loving the way he could make her laugh even when her heart felt it might split in two. 'Mrs Wilding . . . That's a bit premature.'

'Next time I come back we'll make it real, shall we?'

Lily nodded, kissed his lips. 'Yes . . . I want to.' She rested her head on his chest, glad that the collywobbles in her guts were finally settling. She could do justice to a good dinner. Apart from that there was something she had to say later, when they were alone and relaxed, that would make this a wonderful night for them after all. She wanted to go home with him so they could wake up together for the first time.

184

14

'Cheer up, Lil,' Fanny said. 'Joey's done me a favour. I've kept quiet about this cos I didn't want to let you or him down. But the time's right to tell you I want to quit as well.'

Lily did crack a relieved smile then. She hadn't expected a positive reaction from Fanny.

After Greg had brought her home in the van, Lily had let herself into the flat then hesitated in the hall-way, weighing up whether to break this news right away or wait until the morning. She'd still felt woozy but rather invincible from the trauma of sewing up her future husband's arm. She'd burst into her flat-mates' bedroom, even though she could hear the girls laughing and feared she was about to sour the mood.

'Blimey. All change soon at Wilding's then.' Margie was perched on the edge of the bed and had been interestedly listening to proceedings. 'So why're you leaving us in the lurch, Fanny Miller?' She resumed rolling down her stockings.

'Got some news of me own.' A secretive smile played over Fanny's lips.

'Go on then, spit it out.' Lily started to chuckle. 'Reckon I could guess at it though.'

'Me too,' Margie said, tossing her stockings to hang over the headboard.

'I'm moving in with Roger. He's told his wife he's leaving her and she can keep the room. He's found us another place to live . . . better place cos he's got a new job. He's started in a munitions factory and he

185

reckons he'll be able to get me a job there too. Good wages and they're crying out for workers.'

Lily and Margie got in a tangle rushing to give Fanny a congratulatory hug. After their cuddles, Fanny resumed her tale. 'Won't be working there long. I'll be packing up for good.' There was a dramatic pause before she announced, 'I'm in the family way again. Roger's always wanted kids but he and his wife never had any. She told him it was his fault. Can't be though. I've not been near another man and that's the honest truth.' Having rattled that lot off, she gave a beam of self-conscious happiness.

Lily exchanged a joyful look with Margie before doing a jig on the spot. 'That's the best bloody news I've heard in ages,' she exclaimed, collapsing onto the bed. 'I'm so happy for you, Fan.'

'Second that,' Margie said emphatically.

'Wasn't sure at first when me monthlies didn't come,' Fanny explained. 'But I am sure now. I had to tell him first, before I told you two. That's why I was late back yesterday. I didn't know how he'd take it. But he's pleased as punch.' She frowned. 'Sorry I've been a cow sometimes. Just it's all been getting on top of me. Will he, won't he leave her . . . and all that sort of thing going on up here.' Fanny whirled a finger close to her springy copper locks.

'We didn't take no notice cos we're used to you by now, Fanny Miller,' Margie quipped.

'He's asked me to marry him once he's got the money to get divorced. I don't care if we carry on as we are, though. I trust him when he says he won't leave me again and wants us to have more kids.'

'Sounds like you'll have a brood round your ankles in no time.' Lily chuckled. 'You'll be knocking on me door asking for a job on a barrow so you can have a breather.'

'I will, too . . .' Fanny said huskily. 'Anyway, I'll pack up me things at the weekend if that's all right.'

'I'll help you,' Margie said breezily. 'Soon as you're off, I can have the bed to meself. Could do with a good night's kip without you keeping me awake with yer snoring.'

'Do not!'

'Bleedin' do!'

'Celebration's called for. I'll get us a drink.' Lily had brought back to the flat the unfinished bottle of port from Greg's welcome-home candlelit supper. The bottle had been in the kitchen cupboard, but Fanny hadn't touched it, preferring to do her drinking in pubs with her boyfriend.

Lily carried in a tray holding three cups and the port. She settled the tray on the bed once Margie had shifted over and smoothed out a patch of quilt.

'How far gone are you, Fanny?' Margie asked.

'About three months.' The expectant mum held down her skirt so they could see the tiny bump. 'Won't ever forget my Ronny,' she said. 'I'm still getting him his mahogany cross.'

'Don't forget to pack the savings jar in your trunk.' Lily handed round the drinks she'd poured. They had all steadily been donating to the jar on the shelf in the kitchen. The silver and copper almost reached the top.

'I reckon a toast is called for.' Lily raised her cup. 'Here's to Fanny and Roger and the baby, and their new jobs and new life. Good luck!'

The other two rowdily echoed that sentiment before glugging the port.

'And here's to Greg Wilding and you and your luck, Lily,' Fanny said simply.

'Thanks. We got engaged today,' Lily burst out. She drew from her pocket the jewellery box. She'd taken the ring off and replaced it in its nest. She'd not wanted soap getting into it when she washed herself. Also, it would have been mean to flash it about when reporting bad news about Joey and the gossip. Things might have got heated, had Mrs Robley's hand in Joey's defection not been skimmed over; Lily had concentrated on highlighting the lad's improved prospects. An apprenticeship at Hobson's was a definite step up from pushing a costermonger's barrow for a living. In the end everything had turned out far better than Lily had dared hope. She opened the casket to display her ring.

'Phew . . .' Fanny whistled. 'Look at that beauty. You take good care of it, gel.'

'I'm worried to wear it in case something happens to it,' Lily said, and she wasn't joking.

'Reckon I would be too.' Margie delicately touched the gleaming gems with her left hand. 'Better not put it on for work, Lil, you might knock out the stones, loading boxes.'

'I'd never take it off. Make a show of it, I would,' Fanny giggled, wafting her left hand under their noses in demonstration.

Lily had anticipated that of her two friends Fanny would act the most withdrawn by her good fortune. But Margie wore the wistful expression. She had no joyous news to share about boyfriends or babies on the way.

'We've not toasted your luck yet, Margie,' Lily said, snapping shut the lid and returning the box to her

188

pocket. 'Here's to you and to your future.' She raised her cup.

'Nothing to drink to there, have we?' Margie shrugged her shoulders and turned away.

'Well, here's to Smudger coming to his senses then,' Fanny said bluntly, swigging port then swiping the back of a hand over her mouth. 'He needs a kick up the backside. Damn fool wouldn't know a good thing if he tripped over it.'

'He can't help who he's fallen in love with,' Margie retorted. 'You of all people should understand that, being as you're hooked up with a married man.' Margie finished her drink in a gulp and thumped the cup onto the tray. 'Don't need no more toasts. Need the privy,' she said and marched out.

Lily and Fanny exchanged a pained glance.

'Wish I'd not mentioned toasting her luck. It was bloody thoughtless of me.' Lily gave a regretful shake of her head.

'Smudger's the one should be feeling guilty, not you,' Fanny said flatly. 'You're trying to do the right thing; he ain't. I reckon he knows Margie's soft on him. He should stop taking her to the pictures and to the caff; it's just prolonging the agony.'

'She likes going out with him.' Lily knew there was truth in what Fanny had said. The longer it went on, the more Margie would hope he was treating her as though she were his girlfriend because that's what she'd eventually be. Lily hadn't given up on hoping the same thing. 'One day, maybe things'll come right for both of them,' she sighed.

'Smudger needs to be careful. That Rory Scully is a nutter. Never spoken to him meself but I heard on the grapevine that he set about a bloke for accidentally

189

spilling his drink in the pub.'

Lily's guts lurched, even though she'd no need of further proof of Scully's brutality. Less than an hour ago she'd done her best to put right the damage he had inflicted on the man she loved. But she wouldn't tell her friends what had happened; it was too grave an episode to drop into a conversation. She imagined Greg would also rather keep those details private. Anyway, Scully didn't deserve such attention. He'd be gleeful if he knew she was tormenting herself over him.

Lily's sudden pallor hadn't escaped Fanny's notice; she changed the subject. 'When are you two getting hitched, Lily?'

'Next time Greg's back on leave. Won't be a fancy do: just you two as me bridesmaids, and perhaps Smudger will be asked to be best man.' Smudger had fallen in Greg's estimation because of his embroilment with Claudette, but Lily reckoned her right-hand man had been a loyal friend and employee.

'Just let me know when, cos I wouldn't miss it for the world.' Fanny gripped Lily's hands, giving them a playful shake. 'You deserve all this happiness, Lil.'

'Can't believe it's really happening,' Lily said solemnly. 'Without him I'd still be mouldering away in the workhouse.'

'He's lucky to have a gel as good as you in his life.' Fanny squeezed her friend's fingers before letting them go. 'So am I, and should have said so before. Won't ever forget what you've done for me. You've been a true pal, Lily Larkin.'

''S'what friends do for one another.'

'You've been a better friend. I'd still be on the game down Sugar House Lane if you'd not given me a job

190

and a place to live. Roger wouldn't have taken me back. He told me that straight. Now he's proud of me, doing decent work, living with nice people.' She paused. 'He was my first and only sweetheart. Odd, that, when you think of all the men I've had . . . ' She sniffed. 'Anyhow, he says I'm back to being the girl he fell for when we was schoolkids. Seems so long ago; can hardly remember way back when. Before I turned bad.'

'You're not bad, Fanny,' Lily said softly. 'What happened all those years ago?' She had never asked such a direct question before about Fanny's troubled past. If she had it would have been ignored, or she would have been told in no uncertain terms to mind her own business.

'Me no-good brother-in-law happened,' Fanny answered after a short silence. 'He was me sister's boyfriend when he raped me. She was sixteen, quite the young lady, out to work then. I was thirteen . . . schoolgirl still. Didn't have no bosom to speak of, and to this day I don't know what he saw in me.' She glanced at her hands, polished her nails with a thumb. 'Never told me mum or me sister what he did. I was going to, but he give me a black eye and half a crown to keep quiet. I told Mum a kid from another school bashed me for laughing at him, then I bought me first decent skirt off a second-hand stall down Ridley Road market.' Fanny gnawed her lip. 'When he did it again he didn't offer me that.' She clicked her fingers. 'So I told him to give me half a crown, or I'd blab. He paid up and I didn't get a clump that time either. Bought meself leather boots with that half-crown. Me mother was suspicious but she never said much. Think she was just glad I was saving her the job of clothing me.

191

It went on like that till he got me sister up the spout. They got married and moved to Lambeth, and I missed the half-crowns.' Fanny tilted her chin, defiantly meeting Lily's eyes. 'And that's how it started.'

After a quiet few moments Lily said gruffly, 'All done with now, though, Fan.' She emptied the bottle into their two cups. 'Fresh start and love and happiness for you . . . for us all, Margie included, please God.' She raised her cup, waited for Fanny to join her. In unison they finished the port.

15

'Have I told you, you brush up well, Lily Larkin?'

'You have, guv'nor, but thanks again for the compliment,' Lily cheekily replied.

She was again wearing her elegant blue outfit and had styled her glossy chestnut-brown hair into loose curls. The lavender water had been liberally sprinkled and the sapphire was back on her finger. A few wonderful hours were stretching in front of them and anticipation was making her heart race.

Beneath the excitement, though, she felt rather subdued. When all dolled up, with the van's horn tooting outside, she'd done a twirl for Fanny and had been given the thumbs up. But no approval from Margie who had already gone out. While Lily had been having a wash, Margie had left with barely a farewell and no indication of where she was off to. Fanny had said to pay her no mind. Lily did mind, and ached inside for the melancholy girl who was her best friend. But she didn't know how to help Margie mend her breaking heart. How hard it must be for her to smile and congratulate them, while yearning for it to be her turn to be the one celebrating good news.

Lily bucked herself up. Greg deserved her full attention and some light-hearted fun on this of all evenings. She'd been aware of him taking his eyes off the road at intervals to direct more admiring glances her way. She returned the compliment.

'You don't look too bad yourself, you know.' She cocked her head, studied him, dressed in his suit and tie with neatly combed hair and his lean jaw freshly shaven. He'd looked like this the first time she'd seen him, arranging her discharge from the workhouse into his custody. No donkey-jacketed barrow boy on that occasion either; he'd appeared sophisticated and every inch the successful businessman when confronting the master in his office. She'd been fifteen and had thought the blond stranger wonderfully handsome with his bright shiny hair and tigerish eyes. Back then, the only men Lily saw were the master and his son. And Adam Reeve, the medical officer who had become her dearest adult friend. The segregation of the sexes had been the harshest rule to bear: husbands separated from wives, and brothers from sisters. Whole families were split up on admission, some never to be reunited. At ten years old she'd been too young to join her mother in the women's quarter and had never seen Maude Larkin again.

Gregory Wilding's arrival had been a momentous event, destined to change her life; she'd not stopped thinking about him, or longing for him to return for her. He'd promised to give her a job, and reunite her with her twin brother. Back then Davy, rather than her new guv'nor, had been her whole world. Her twin had been the only relative she had left, so she'd believed. Only later had she learned her mother had had a baby in the workhouse and the sire's identity was being kept secret to avert a scandal.

Lily could see her reflection in the night-dark glass of the van's side window. She examined her features, wondering if that little girl resembled her, just a little bit. Or perhaps she had her father's face. She had his fair hair, by all accounts. And, strangely, Ben Stone was similar to Gregory Wilding in looks, though not as tall or handsome . . .

'Where will you go next to search for your lost sister?' He seemed to have a knack of knowing what was up when she was quiet and thoughtful. 'It's a shame we didn't have more luck at the Dr Barnardo's home.'

'If Davy gets leave at Christmas, perhaps he'll have some fresh ideas about where to go to look. I won't ever give up until I know what happened. Good or bad.' She paused. 'I wonder if Mrs Priest is still looking for Charlotte? I think she is. I reckon she's like a dog with a bone, same as me.'

'You might be after different kids, Lily,' Greg gently pointed out.

'I know; but I'd love to run into her, even if it's just to find out if she's succeeded in her search. I feel as though I know that woman and like her. I want her to succeed. Perhaps she's heard about me too, while going from place to place; the two of us, looking and looking for a little fair-haired girl with a birthmark . . . ' Lily felt tears prickle her eyes. She didn't want to spoil this special evening with sorrowful thoughts. 'Let's cheer up. It's your last night in civvies for a while so where do you want to go? To a dance, or to see a show?'

'How about both? It's still early.'

'There's a magician topping the bill at the Wood Green Empire; Margie and Smudger really enjoyed it last week. We could eat first in the Lyons place on the High Street.'

They started to head north and Lily settled back into the seat. She noticed Greg flexing his fingers on the steering wheel; her handiwork was mere inches away from that wrist of his. 'Your wound's giving you gyp, isn't it?'

'Just throbs a bit every so often.' He glanced at her.

'You got over it well. I thought you might pass out: you turned white as a sheet.'

'I'm fine now.' She started to chuckle softly. 'Just another string to me bow. Clerk, costermonger, quack nurse . . .'

'I reckon you could do or be anything you wanted,' he said. 'Helps that you're a little brainbox.' His amusement faded into seriousness. 'I'm the luckiest man alive to have you.'

Lily laced her fingers into his, idle on the steering wheel. 'I'm lucky too. Never thought I'd ever feel this way . . . like I do about you,' she said shyly.

He raised their clasped hands, sweeping his lips over her knuckles, then drew her closer so he could lean and kiss her mouth.

'Better watch the road, you know,' she said, squinting at oncoming headlights. His praise reminded her of her talk with her flatmates. It had been wonderful to see Fanny so happy, with a new life beckoning. 'Just now, I let the girls know about Joey quitting.'

'Did you need Dutch courage first?' Greg asked.

'What?'

'You taste of port.' He licked his lips, savouring the sweetness.

'We toasted my engagement. Fanny had some lovely news as well, and because of it she wasn't bothered a bit about Joey moving on.' Lily paused. 'You'll be pleased to hear that she's given in her notice too.'

'That's handy, makes things easier.'

Lily rolled her eyes at his dry response. 'She's moving in with her boyfriend and getting married as soon as he's divorced. Best of all, she's expecting another baby and they're both overjoyed about it.'

'That is good news,' Greg said. 'I did genuinely feel

196

very sorry for her, losing her son, you know.'

'I pray things will finally go right for her this time.' Lily raised two sets of crossed fingers as she always did when wishing and hoping out loud.

They turned towards Turnpike Lane and the bright lights of Wood Green High Street. At the far end was the theatre, but Greg slowed down before reaching it and parked opposite the Lyons teashop. 'Right, let's eat.' He pulled on the handbrake. 'I'm ready for this. Me poor old belly thinks me throat's been cut.' He got out and came round to help her down. Then, arm in arm, they crossed the road.

★ ★ ★

Margie was feeling increasingly nervous. It was not yet seven o'clock but dusk had long ago darkened into a moonless November night. The gas lamp at the end of the street barely illuminated the misty spot where she was standing, which in one way was a good thing. She didn't want to be seen hanging about close to Smudger's lodging. She knew he wasn't at home but even so loathed the idea of him ever finding out she'd been here this evening. She was banking on her rival feeling exactly the same way about that, and keeping her mouth shut too.

Families lived in this neighbourhood, but it wasn't a friendly place, and it wasn't sensible for a lone young woman to hang about in dark East End alleys. Scurrying sounds were an accompaniment to the thump of blood in her ears. Cats and rats would be foraging just out of sight, but human vermin would be about too. Margie knew that at any moment she could have an undesirable encounter if she stayed here too long.

197

Still she stayed put, hopping from foot to foot, unwilling to give in to timidity and hurry off home. If she went ahead with it, she risked being told to mind her own business. But she couldn't stop hoping Smudger would one day be her business, even though he didn't yet see it that way.

She was getting annoyed with herself for dithering and gave herself a talking-to. Either go and knock on the bloody door or forget about your big ideas and clear off before you get into bad trouble. Her deformity made her vulnerable, and usually Margie avoided situations where she might be at a dangerous disadvantage. She could punch left-handed and had come off best in the past scrapping with a workhouse bully. The girl would purposely wait until Lily was in solitary confinement, being punished for misbehaving, before cornering Margie. Lily had been her guardian angel, and the staunchest of friends. She still was, but Margie was putting a stop to being a burden. If she'd announced where she was off to this evening, Lily would have warned her to steer clear, or would have insisted on coming too. But Margie was done with letting others fight her battles. She'd known her dearest friend since she was eleven years old, but they had both turned seventeen now and were young women, not kids. From now on she was showing them all she was standing on her own two feet. Lily would then have the future she deserved as a wife and mother without thinking Margie still needed her apron strings to cling to.

Margie jerked back into the shadows as an arguing couple barged along the pavement. They passed by without noticing her, but somebody else had. She nearly jumped out of her skin as a curtain in the terrace of houses was hiked up and a woman banged on her windowpane.

'Piss off, you tart, or I'll come out there . . .' was just audible through the glass. The woman demonstrated with a jerking thumb that Margie had better get going, or else.

The likelihood of the battle-axe acting on her threats had given Margie the kick up the backside she'd needed. She'd get scant sympathy from anybody if she was mistaken for a soliciting prossie. Pulling up her coat collar she marched across the road. A glimmer of light at the first-floor window reassured her this wouldn't be a wasted journey, in any event. Margie entered through the portal and went straight up the bare timber stairs. It was pitch black, and she held on to the rickety handrail for dear life. But she knew where she was heading and, without hesitation, crossed the landing and rapped smartly on the door.

The knock was immediately answered by somebody Margie hadn't expected or wanted to see. Such an unpleasant shock caused her gaping mouth to ruin her confident expression. In a past conversation Smudger had told her that Claudette's old man regularly stopped off at the pub on a work night and was rarely home before eight o'clock. Tonight of all nights he had changed his routine! Margie was tempted to turn around and flee down the stairs, but that would really arouse his suspicion and make things worse, not better, for Smudger. Lamplight leaked from the lodging onto the landing, giving her a good enough look at him. He didn't appear drunk, but he did look to be furiously brooding on something. Margie guessed it might have a lot to do with the fact his face was bashed up. She forced her eyes away from the ragged tear on his chin. 'W . . . want to speak to your wife. Is . . . is she in?' she eventually stammered, having found her tongue.

'Who are you?' He ignored her question, barking out one of his own. He settled a beefy shoulder against the door frame while sizing Margie up. There was something familiar about her fair hair and pretty face but he couldn't quite recall where he'd seen her before.

'Don't matter if she's not in,' Margie muttered hoarsely, starting to shuffle away. 'Sorry for bothering you.'

'You ain't bothering me, darlin',' he drawled. 'Thought you wanted to come in and speak to me wife?'

Margie, already jittery, was startled by a noise from across the hallway. She darted a glance over her shoulder. A woman was silhouetted in her doorway, making a show of sweeping dirt out onto the landing to cover the fact she was spying on them.

'All right, ducks?' Scully jibed. 'Had a good look at me lady friend, have yer? Eyeful, ain't she?'

'You dirty bleeder. I'll tell Claudette what I seen you up to when her back's turned.' The woman shook the broom bristles at him then slammed her door.

Rory grinned. 'Don't take no notice of that old bag, love,' he cooed. 'She's just being nosy.' The unexpected novelty of a luscious fly approaching his web had cheered him up, transforming his scowl into a crafty smile. He bowed mockingly, sweeping an arm in a welcoming gesture. 'No need to be standoffish. We're friendly enough folk on the whole. Step inside so we can talk in private.' He knocked the door wide open with a foot, keeping his eyes glued to the jumpy girl.

200

The last thing Margie was prepared to do was tear Claudette Scully off a strip in front of her husband. In Margie's eyes the selfish cow was endangering Smudger, encouraging him to stick around in the vain hope that one day they could be a couple. For his own good, Claudette should set him free by telling him it was over between them. His workmates were turning against him because of her. Everybody was conscious of the trouble he was drawing them into, knocking around with a woman who was married to Rory Scully. Fanny had openly mocked Smudger as a fool, but Margie knew that Lily and the guv'nor were losing patience with him too. Margie didn't want Smudger to suffer when deep down he was a good man with a good heart.

She had come here to talk woman to woman, and if Mrs Scully had a scrap of decency in her she would be persuaded to do the right thing. That would have been the gist of Margie's argument had she had the opportunity to air it.

Things hadn't gone to plan, though, and now she was regretting this escapade. Scully had been in a recent fight and Margie wanted to know who with. Yet she daren't ask about it. Smudger didn't have this man's brawn or his vicious streak and would have come off worst in a scrap. Claudette could be inside licking her wounds if her husband had let fly at her too. Margie knew there would be no keeping her inter-ference quiet now. She couldn't bear the thought of Smudger turning his back on her, of not even allow-ing her the comfort of his friendship because she'd poked her nose in.

She was shivering with dread and every instinct was urging Margie to turn and belt down the stairs.

Yet she owed it to Smudger to try to smooth things over now she'd stirred them up; she could tell Scully was joining dots together in his head, and not liking the pictures he was drawing.

'Look, I just wanted a chat with Claudette about a job coming up on a costermonger's barrow.' Margie blurted out the first useful thing dredged from her memory. Fanny was leaving and they were a woman down. 'I've been asking around after housewives who might want a job, see. It wasn't important though. Sorry to have bothered you with it. You can tell her it'll keep until another day.'

Scully took a furtive look around the dim landing. A medley of thuds was coming from the other rooms as people went about their lives, barging about and crashing pots and pans. But all the doors were shut and likely to stay that way on a cold and foggy night. 'I'm interested in hearing about it, love. In yer come to tell me more.' He stretched out, gripped Margie's forearm, and yanked her out of sight.

He put his back against the closed door and crossed his arms. She'd steadied herself against the wall following his rough handling, which had knocked the hat off her head and messed up her hair. The misshapen fingers splayed on dirty distemper cast ugly shadows, jogging his memory. He remembered her now all right, even without the clue about costermongers' barrows that she'd given him.

She was one of Greg Wilding's employees. The thought of that man caused his mouth to stretch, bringing blood back to the surface of his split lip. The cut stung enough to revive the humiliation he'd felt on walking past a crowd of men who'd witnessed him get it. Rory was in the mood to take it out on

202

somebody, and his wife wasn't about to be his whipping dog right now. Scully had assumed Claudette would be with her parents this evening. He'd been impatient to buy tobacco and brown ales to soothe his battered ego, so had gone to Bermondsey to relieve her of the money they gave her. The Belgian couple hadn't seen their daughter, they'd said, and had shut the door on him before he could hold his hand out. With nothing in his pocket to spend, he'd gone home. While waiting for his wife to put in an appearance, he had driven himself into a frenzy, plotting retribution. Rory had hammered on Smudger's door earlier, looking for her, but the place had been dark and silent. Now the pair of them were forgotten, as was the cash Rory had been obsessing about having. Whenever a woman looked at him in half-light with big, frightened eyes it made him horny . . . and she was one of Wilding's workhouse kids to boot. This one might not be as attractive as Lily Larkin but she'd a pretty face: full lips and nice blonde hair. She'd do. He could use his imagination.

'Where's your wife then?' Her guts were tied in knots, the palms of her hands felt ice-cold and clammy as Margie darted about an anxious look for Claudette. There were no other doors leading off from the room; nowhere else she could be. The lodging was home to a few sticks of battered furniture, an unmade bed dominating the wall space. The smell was sour: ash from the grate and unwashed sheets overlaid with the kerosene burning in the solitary table lamp. 'She's not even in, is she?' Margie was controlling her voice, though she was close enough to him to see lust in his hooded eyes as they slipped over her figure and locked onto her hips.

'I reckon you just told me a lie, little Margie. If I remember correctly, that is your name, ain't it?' he purred. 'I don't reckon you come here to offer me wife a job; I've got a costermonger's barrow she can push so don't need one of Wilding's.' He started towards Margie. 'Who sent you? Smudger, was it? Using you to pass messages to her, is he?'

Margie vigorously shook her head. 'He don't even know I'm here. So leave Smudger out of it.' Though terrified, Margie instinctively protected him.

'Jumped to his defence pretty quick, didn't yer, little Margie. Like him, eh, is that it?'

'He's me boyfriend,' Margie declared proudly. 'And he's waiting for me. We're going out to the pictures tonight,' she lied. 'So I've got to get going or he'll come looking for me.' Margie took some bold steps forward as though to shove Scully out of the way to reach the door. It was a bad move, bringing her too close to him to escape.

He fastened a brutal hand on Margie's trembling jaw, closing her chattering teeth. 'Your boyfriend's been messing around with my wife. I reckon you know that, and that's why you've come here. You was after giving Claudette what's for, weren't you?' He chuckled deep in his throat in a way that made Margie's skin crawl. 'Nice-lookin' gel like you needs something better to do than talk to my wife. Ain't got nothing interesting to say, that one. You'll like it better passing the time with me, promise you that.'

Margie had spent many months in that brothel, writing blackmail letters for the madam. The expressions men wore when anticipating fornication were all the same, and easily recognisable. 'Let me out of here,' she croaked, jigging on the spot in fear. 'Or I'll

204

scream the place down.'

'That ain't very nice, is it? You come here, bangin' on me door, disturbing me neighbours. The old gel saw you; she knows what your game was, turning up after dark while me wife was out.' Scully started to move, forcing Margie backwards with him. 'Now you're here, love, only polite to be nice to me.' He had her cheeks pinched together tightly, preventing her uttering another word, let alone screaming. And those wild blue eyes were driving him crazy, sparking with tears. He felt as though he might burst out of his trousers at any minute. 'What you got under that coat . . . sweet li'l figure, I bet.' He fumbled at her buttons, leaning to grunt in her ear. 'What's good for Smudger and my missus is good for us too, eh? Only fair in my book I get a crack at you. We can all play at that game, eh, love?' With a flat palm he suddenly shoved Margie backwards onto the crumpled bed, knocking the breath out of her. In a second he'd followed her down and was smothering her terrified howl with a calloused hand.

16

'I didn't know you could dance, Lily.'

'Reckon you still don't.' She managed to get out a wry reply before being whirled around in Greg's arms. The pianist was pounding out a flourish of closing chords, then he sat back on his stool, arms aloft, as the assembly burst into applause. Lily was clinging on to her partner, too giddy to join in with the others showing their appreciation. 'Don't think I'll be putting a Tiller girl out of work, do you?' she said on a breathless giggle.

Greg put an arm about her waist and led her back to their table after their hit-and-miss attempt at a foxtrot.

'I'm more of a waltz girl.' Lily sounded rueful. She knew she'd trodden on his toes numerous times while attempting to keep up with the speed of the music. She'd done better when waltzing. He was a competent all-rounder and she supposed he'd had plenty of practice when taking his previous girls out on the town.

'You didn't learn to waltz in the workhouse, that's for sure.' He pulled out her chair then sat down opposite.

'Fanny showed Margie and me how to do a basic one, two, three.' She smiled at the memory of them bumping into furniture in the basement's cramped bedroom space, cackling with laughter as they got in a jumble of elbows and knees after setting off on the wrong feet. The three of them had become friends

206

in a place where nobody ever danced or sang. But despairing souls capering dementedly had been a common sight in South Grove workhouse.

Having refreshed himself from the tankard on top of the instrument, the pianist commenced tinkling another introduction on the keys, drawing couples back to the dance floor. Greg gave her a challenging smile. 'Ready for another go, twinkle-toes?'

She rolled her eyes, shaking her head. 'Need a breather after that or I'll bring up me supper.'

Greg took a sip of beer. 'Do you want to head off towards the theatre so we don't miss the start of the show?' He glanced at his pocket watch.

'S'pose we ought to. It's lovely here but we should see the magician.' She wanted to fit in every possible pleasure on this, their last evening together for heaven-only-knew how long.

After parking on the High Street, they'd tucked into a pie-and-mash meal in the Lyons tearoom then had set out on the short stroll towards the theatre. The sound of a lusty sing-song in progress had lured them into an avenue off the main road. They'd followed the hoots of merriment to a community hall, bustling with activity. Inside a dance was in full swing. A banner strung above a table, laden with plates of sandwiches, cakes and drink bottles, proclaimed that the local branch of the Red Cross was fundraising for the Voluntary Aid Detachment. Greg had bought the entry tickets, and had donated a generous amount on top.

Lily had worked up a thirst from her exertion and helped herself to a sip from his beer, pulling a face at the bitter taste.

'Do you want to stop off at a pub for a port and

lemon?' he asked.

'You villain; you'll get me into trouble, drinking at seventeen.'

'There's worse trouble this villain could get you into, my love,' he drawled with a subtle smile.

'Don't I know it!' Lily clucked her tongue, blushing but matching him for sauce.

He sat back in his chair, gazing at her with tender mockery. 'It's easy to forget you're young when you're so damn gorgeous. Capable little thing as well, aren't you?'

'Apart from when attempting a foxtrot, you mean.' She arched an eyebrow.

He grimaced, rubbing an instep through shoe leather.

'I don't want a drink; let's head straight to the theatre when we're done here.' Lily glanced about at laughing faces. 'There's a smashing atmosphere. It's hard to believe such trouble's going on in the world when everybody's so happy and relaxed.'

The tape on the window glass, and the blackout curtains, were the only concessions to an enemy at large capable of blowing them all to smithereens. The Zeppelin raids had first hit London back in the spring. Many more bombs had been dropped since, putting paid to anybody's hope that the airships wouldn't be able to travel inland as far as the capital. Hundreds of civilians had perished, children amongst them. Pockmarked streets throughout the East End and elsewhere bore testament to the raging fires that had resulted from the barrage. The hit on Smithfield Market just months ago had resulted in fatalities and had brought things particularly close to home. Spitalfields or Billingsgate could be next. If the attacks were at dawn, when teeming with traders, casualties would be disastrously high. In addition, costermongers and their families living hand-to-mouth could face terrible hardship if unable to buy stock.

The pianist took another beer-break and the dancers drifted away. After a few minutes he picked out a tune it seemed many of the fellows present knew the words to. 'Mademoiselle from Armentières, parl-ey-voo ... ' began a rousing chorus; it was repeated just once before an authoritative-looking fellow with pips on his arm waved a hand in the air. 'Ladies present, old chap,' he called to the pianist, but gave a wink and a roar of laughter. The warning was a clear ban on risqué versions being aired. It was a song for men in the trenches. The pianist gave a mock salute and instead played a rendition of 'Pack Up Your Troubles', which had the choir back in fine form. Greg and Lily joined in, Greg beating time with a palm tapping the table top.

'Quite a stroke of luck stumbling across this shindig,' Greg said as the song finished. He glanced around the hall. It was a basic hut, basic grub, nothing fancy at all, yet he knew this evening would be a memory to cherish. Top brass in braided uniforms were mingling with the lower orders in khaki and hospital blues and a host of civilians. Nobody was standing on ceremony, just making the most of enjoying themselves while they could. 'The Voluntary Aid Detachment's worth rattling a tin for.' Greg took another swallow of beer. 'VADs are a godsend over there. Not enough regular medics to go round all the aid posts and hospital trains and so on. Last time I saw Adam Reeve he was worried they'd struggle to get staff and equipment for new dressing stations springing up close to the front lines.

Christ knows they're needed. Canal barges are

being used as well to get the casualties away. Damn good idea, don't you think, using waterways?'

Lily nodded and sat forward in her chair, propping her elbows on the table and listening intently. This was the most he'd volunteered to tell her about what he'd experienced in France. She'd been eager to talk about it from the moment he'd got back, but had given up asking questions he avoided answering. She'd not pestered him to relive for her benefit what he'd done and seen. Greg was no different to any other soldier, wanting to plunge back into normality the moment he stepped on home soil. When her twin brother had been on leave, he'd told her outright he'd discuss anything but the war. He wanted to forget about the bloody Hun for a week or so, was how Davy had put it. But for Greg the hours and minutes had started ticking down and cruel reality was niggling close to the surface. She knew he regretted enlisting; she also suspected his conscience would prod him to do exactly the same again. The majority of men accepted that they had little option but to go and fight if the hateful conflict was ever to be brought to an end.

Over recent days he'd appeared unusually sombre at times when he believed himself to be unobserved. At the back of his mind would be thoughts of the next manoeuvre, the next billet, the next whistle-blow sending him over the top. Playing on Lily's mind was the early-morning incident in the warehouse when they'd learned that Walter's son, Jack, had paid the ultimate price. The memory of Smudger's carelessness, making Greg instinctively duck for cover, as only an alert soldier would, still brought a lump to her throat, too.

'I've written letters for Davy and Adam. Would you take them back with you and deliver them, Greg?'

''Course I will, be glad to,' he said.

'I've seen the recruiting posters for the VAD.' Lily was keen to keep the subject alive. 'I'm going to offer to enrol. Not sure what use I can be, but there must be some way of helping for a few hours a week. Us girls have started knitting for the troops. It's not easy for Margie to get to grips with the needles, but she's almost finished a scarf, and it's not a bad job either. There must be more I can turn me hand to than just making woollies.' She tapped her fingers on the table as an idea sprung to mind. 'Now I can drive, perhaps I could deliver supplies for the Red Cross or something like that. They've got depots all over the place and must be crying out for volunteers to take stuff from A to B. The van's spare on Sundays and I've got the free time.'

Her enthusiasm made him smile. 'You're not a bad driver either.' He stroked his chin, deliberately sceptical. 'Mind you, there was that time you stalled the thing in the middle of Chrisp Street and we couldn't get it going again.'

'That wasn't my fault.' She tutted. 'You'd forgotten to fill it up with fuel, as I recall.'

He put up his hands in surrender. 'Guilty as charged.' He leaned across the table, sliding his palms either side of her face. 'This leave hasn't been nearly long enough. Promise you won't forget to see me off at midday?' He wasn't being facetious now . . . his golden gaze was solemnly moving over her features, imprinting them on his mind. 'God, I'm gonna miss you, Lily,' he groaned. 'One of our platoon's gone on the missing list over there. Talk is he's done a runner to make his own way home. We all understand how he feels . . . '

211

'Don't you dare even think it!' she whispered, casting a wary glance at a loud-voiced chap with a thick moustache.

She imagined he was a brigadier or similar. He had been moving closer, giving her admiring glances. 'Deserters get shot, you know that,' she hissed. 'Everything will be fine here and, don't you worry, I'll be at Charing Cross to kiss you goodbye tomorrow. In fact . . . ' She took a deep breath, removing his hands from her cheeks to squeeze them tightly. 'In fact, you can wake me up in the morning to make sure I'm not late.' She blurted out what had been on her mind for hours. 'I'm coming home with you tonight.'

He gazed at her and smiled wryly. 'I'm not going to do anything stupid, Lily; I don't need persuasion to behave.'

'Good. That's not what it's about. It's about me as much as you. About what I want, as well,' she said quietly.

'Are you sure?' His voice sounded gruff, desperately hopeful. 'You are, aren't you?'

She nodded. 'I know what I'm doing, Greg. I am ready, and I want to . . . so no need to be gallant.'

His mouth quirked. 'Wasn't going to be, darling . . . don't think I've got that sort of strength any more. Since I've been back, all I've wanted to do is love you.'

A pounding heart was making her feel light-headed. Had she expected him to still be gallant? It didn't matter if he'd weakened; she was ready and wanted to love him back. She longed to understand the market housewives' dirty chortles and winks when the subject of husbands and bedtime cropped up together. 'Best get going now or we'll miss the last performance at

212

the Empire.' She pushed back her chair, fanning her flushed face with a hand. 'I'm ready for some fresh air.'

He stood up, helping her into her coat. 'This magician, Lily . . . are you sure you want to bother with him? I don't reckon his tricks'll be up to much,' he said with such a poker-face that she erupted in giggles. She adored the way he could calm and amuse her at the same time.

'Compared to yours, I suppose you mean,' she teased, giving him a hug. 'Oh, all right. Straight back to Poplar then.' She took his outstretched hand and was led towards the door.

Little conversation had passed between them as they drove towards the East End. He was smoking, she gazing out of the side window up at the heavens, searching for a shining star peeping through the thick ether. It had seemed appropriate that their first time sharing a bed should be marked by a magical celestial display. But no, not even a glimmer of moonlight broke through the haze to romanticise this special night. The glow in the pit of her belly had increased, though; she felt warm from top to toe despite the murky chill outside. Occasionally she glanced at his handsome profile, and the feelings she had for him overwhelmed her. Yet there was something she had to bring up, even if it did dampen the mood. French letters were a help in stopping a woman getting pregnant, so Fanny had assured her. The older woman had also said that they didn't always work, and she'd had her beloved Ronny to show for it. Fanny had been glad of that failure from the moment she'd held her little boy in her arms; but Lily wasn't ready to have a baby. In fact, the idea of it terrified her. She'd seen how local women — widows in particular — struggled to bring up their children without a husband's assistance. For an unmarried woman it was harder: there were insults to cope with. People could say what they liked about her, but she couldn't bear the thought of one of her children being taunted as a bastard. Her little sister had been branded so by Harriet Fox. Much as she'd hated that spiteful cow, Lily wished the workhouse officer were alive to be interrogated over the child's whereabouts.

Harking back to that episode had stirred old familiar yearnings for her birth family. Soon they were dominating her mind, making her feel melancholy. She made a determined effort to stop thinking of the Larkins' tragedies. Tonight she would concentrate on the man she would soon be marrying. He was her family now, and of course she still had her beloved Davy. And the promise of her sister. For the time being, no more family than that was needed, bringing her back to the question of French letters. Greg was a man of the world, she'd known that from the beginning when she'd met his glamorous girlfriend. Jane Wright had made no secret of the fact she regularly slept with her boyfriend. While living as Jane's flatmate, Lily — fresh from the workhouse and as green as cabbage — had been enlightened by Jane, whether she wanted to be or not, on the subject of randy men.

Greg would know where to get French letters, and in addition Lily would keep her fingers tightly crossed at the crucial moment. She inwardly smiled; she could almost hear Fanny hooting that keeping her legs crossed was the only sure way to avoid rocking a baby in nine months' time. She knew he'd not blame her if she went back on her word because of baby fears; he'd be kind and say he understood. It would be mean of her to do it, though; teasing and unfair. Lily had decided on it. Besides, on his next leave they'd be husband and wife. She'd start making plans straight away for a small wedding. A register office affair would do. She'd no need of white dresses and hymns being sung. Afterwards, a cosy reception in the local pub, with their friends, would be fine by her. She was wondering whether Davy might be granted leave for her big day when it suddenly hit her that they'd just driven past people who'd seemed familiar. She swivelled on the seat in an attempt to peer back through the gloom.

'Oh, stop a minute, would you?' The van was brought to such an abrupt halt that Lily nearly slid off the seat into the footwell. Her velvet hat had tipped forward and she pushed it out of her eyes. 'I think we just passed Smudger back there.' She jerked a thumb over her shoulder.

'Do you need to speak to him?' Greg frowned.

'No ... but he's with a girl. I think it's probably Margie, though I didn't get a good look at her. She went out earlier in a bit of a huff.' Lily sighed. 'We were talking about boyfriends and Fanny took a swipe at Smudger. You know Margie, she always defends him. But I've a feeling she's out of patience over the Claudette business. I hope she's tearing him off a strip, actually. He deserves it.'

'I know he does. But he's said it's done with and no more messing about with married women from now on.'

'I won't get involved if they're in the middle of a ding-dong. I'll leave them to it. But I should let Margie know I won't be back tonight so she doesn't fret about where I've got to. She'll be home alone if Fanny stays out too.'

Greg pushed the gearstick into reverse.

'Thanks . . . ' She leaned to peck his cheek as they slowly moved backwards. 'Won't take a moment, promise.' She already had her fingers on the door handle, ready to jump down.

'It's Smudger, all right.' Greg had stared for a moment to correctly identify his employee's stocky figure hunched into his donkey jacket. The vehicle had come to a halt parallel to two people on the opposite pavement, half hidden behind a shifting mist. They appeared engrossed in conversation, unaware they were under observation. The woman started gesticulating and walked off a few yards, as though they were bickering.

'It's not Margie.' Lily sounded disappointed now she'd had a better look at Smudger's companion. She was of similar height and slenderness to Margie but had very dark hair, not fair. 'I've never seen Claudette but no prizes for guessing who that might be,' Lily said grimly.

Greg cursed, furious that Smudger had let him down again. There was little time left for having it out with the love-sick fool, and this bad business looked set to carry on affecting everybody. 'He could be telling her it's over.' Greg took Woodbines from the dashboard and jammed a cigarette in his mouth before hurling the pack back to its resting place.

From that frustrated gesture, Lily deduced he didn't honestly believe what he'd said. He was thinking about going over and starting on Smudger. What was the point, though, if more promises of future good behaviour were worthless? Greg would return over-

216

seas, fretting about Rory Scully taking revenge. And she'd torment herself that her future husband wasn't concentrating on keeping himself safe in France but was worrying about her being dragged into the mess. Greg could be ruthless and had prospered in a hard world by defying convention, being his own boss. She was fretting now that he might follow his fellow rifle-man onto the missing list. The consequences of that were terrifying.

'I should've sacked him and found a new manager to take his place while I had the chance.' Greg struck a match to the cigarette, took a hefty drag, then glared at the couple across the road. 'I've left you with a hin-drance in him, not a help. He's giving Scully all the reason he needs to start a riot. Well, it's not too late to do something right now.' Greg started to open the door.

Lily quickly grabbed his wrist with two hands to stop him getting out. 'I can sort this out with Smudger later in the week. Don't let's waste what time we have left on those two. Anyway, you might be right. She's acting browned off. If it is Scully's wife, perhaps he's just telling her he can't see her again.'

'Don't think so, Lily.' Greg had an arm propped on the steering wheel, a look of defeat on his face. Push-ing himself upright, he jerked a nod at the embracing couple. Whatever tiff they'd been having hadn't lasted long. He'd been relying on Smudger being the loyal and trustworthy employee he'd always been. The youth had promised he would do the right thing where Claudette Scully was concerned. But Greg could see now that, from Smudger's point of view, it meant sticking by the woman he loved, even if she was married to somebody else. 'It's no good, Lily. I've got to speak to him . . . and her.' Greg took a savage drag on his cigarette before pitching it out of the window. 'And knock their damn stupid heads together if I have to.' He jerked the door open and leapt down. 'Stay where you are. I'll just have a quick word and be right back.'

Lily wasn't staying where she was. She got out and trotted after him, the night's icy atmosphere abrading her throat. If a fight started, he'd damage the wound she'd stitched. And she wasn't having that after what it had taken out of her to do it in the first place.

Smudger noticed company had arrived and removed the woman's arms from around his neck. He shielded her from the coming confrontation by positioning himself in front of her petite figure.

'Want to tell me what's going on?' Greg demanded.

'Nothing to tell,' Smudger snapped back. 'I'm finished work for the day so it ain't none of your business what I get up to.'

'That's where you're wrong, see. Thought we had an understanding about this. There'd be no more risking trouble with Scully, you said. That's the only reason you've still got your job.'

'I can handle Scully.' Smudger nervously swivelled his flat cap on his scalp.

'You think so? You're prepared for him to stab you then? Cleverer than me, I'll give you that. He pulled a knife on me earlier and I got a stripe on me arm to show for it.' Greg jabbed a finger close to Smudger's face. 'Scully knows about you two. I told him you'd walked away from her now to calm him down. When he finds out she's still playing about behind his back, he'll go berserk. And can't say I blame him.'

From the corner of an eye Lily saw Claudette shrink

218

back and cover her mouth with her gloved hands. So she hadn't realised her husband knew Smudger's interest in her went beyond that of a concerned friend and neighbour. Neither had Smudger cottoned on that Rory Scully thought of him as a rival rather than a nuisance. He was gawping in disbelief at Greg. Blinkered by passion, the lovebirds no doubt believed they'd been successful in keeping things secret. Lily felt her heart go out to Claudette. She obviously had a nightmarish life with Scully. Nobody could blame her for daring to hope a decent fellow like Smudger might be a knight in shining armour.

Lily left the men arguing and approached the other woman. She had retreated against a brick wall and was trying to conceal her face with her hat brim. The streetlamp close to the kerb shed enough light to give Lily a tantalising glimpse of Claudette's features: small nose and thin lips above a sharp chin. Lily cocked her head to try and catch the girl's eyes but she refused to look up. She had hair far darker than Lily's own; almost black and secured into a roll at her nape. Having accepted that Lily wasn't going away, she raised her head. Her eyes were very dark, thickly fringed with black lashes, and her complexion clear and quite pale. Overall she was a pleasant-looking woman rather than a beauty. But Lily could see why Smudger was smitten. Claudette oozed fragility and that would appeal to his caring nature.

'I'm Lily Larkin and I am pleased to meet you, Claudette.' Lily extended her hands in friendship. 'It would have been nice to get to know you under different circumstances, though.'

The young woman attempted a smile and briefly touched Lily's hands. She was soon glancing

219

anxiously at Smudger. But the two men were again going at it hammer and tongs. Her saviour wasn't about to come over and speak for her.

'Did Rory really stab him?' Claudette spoke in accented English, indicating Greg with a jerk of her chin.

''Fraid so.' It suddenly occurred to Lily that Claudette, like any wife, would know what her husband kept in his pockets; but she'd clearly not told Smudger about the knife. The news of a weapon being involved had come as a huge shock to him. 'I know your husband's a brute. Smudger might get badly injured if you two continue to carry on like this.' Lily kept her tone even, though her sympathy for Claudette had withered a bit. If she cared for Smudger she should have warned him of the dangers. If she loved Smudger she would have stopped seeing him to keep him safe. 'You wouldn't want him hurt like that, would you?'

'No! But he is my only friend in Poplar. I need him. Rory's a devil. I wish I'd never agreed to marry him.' Claudette burrowed her chin against her shoulder and started to cry.

'Won't your parents help you to leave him? Can't you go and live with them?' Lily put a comforting arm around the weeping girl. 'Haven't you told them he's beating you?' If she kept asking questions she might eventually get a response.

'Oh, they know,' Claudette said bitterly. 'They've seen the marks on me. But they don't help. In their eyes I'm his responsibility now and England is better than Belgium. Here they have somewhere to live . . . some work and some food. There they have nothing. Our village was burning when we left. I would go back tomorrow; for me it was better there than here, even with the Boche everywhere.'

'Does Smudger know you want to return there?' Lily learned something from the girl's silence and evasive eyes. Poor Smudger was being kept in the dark about that as well. Lily concluded that Claudette might class Smudger as her only friend in Poplar, but she hadn't fallen in love with the man risking so much for her.

'I must go home now ... my husband will expect me soon. He gets in a bad mood if I'm late.' Claudette didn't explain further but tears were again dripping down her cheeks as she started to move past Lily.

'Where does he think you are on a filthy night like this?' Lily had been wondering how the girl had managed to slip away to be with Smudger.

'He lets me fetch money from my parents. If they don't have it to pay, Rory goes himself and is a pig to them. They made an agreement so he'd marry me and help Papa get work. Two florins a week, Papa pays.' Claudette pulled a hanky from a pocket and dried her face. 'He can't afford it all the time; they have my little sisters at home to feed and are poorer than he is.' Her eyes settled on Smudger again. 'Sometimes I meet him instead of going on the bus to see them.'

'Smudger gives you four shillings so your husband won't get suspicious about where you've been,' Lily summed up for herself. Claudette had some strategies worked out and Lily admired her for it. But the fact that Smudger seemed to be a patsy — endangering himself for unrequited love — was making her feel sad ... and rather angry. 'Your husband's bound to find out you've not been honest,' Lily warned. 'S'pose he bumps into your parents? Do they know to lie for you?'

221

'They will try to protect me, but they are frightened of their own shadows. I've told them to hide if they see him in the street.' Claudette shrugged acceptance of the risk she was taking. 'Every day I pray something bad will happen to him and he won't come home ever again. Or I think I will run away to somewhere he won't ever find me. But now I am . . . up the spout, Smudger calls it, there is more trouble for me than before. Something must be done quickly. We were talking of it just now. I can't stand to live like this . . . '

She'd been constantly darting glances to and fro as though expecting the brute to appear. Suddenly her eyes became fixed on a spot close to the parked van and she gulped in despair. Lily whipped around, squinting into the mist. It took her a second longer than Claudette to recognise Rory Scully's burly figure jogging across the road towards them. His wife suddenly dashed off without uttering another word to anybody.

The quarrelling men didn't immediately notice Scully's arrival on the scene. By the time they did Claudette was being hauled back along the pavement by her husband, a hand nursing her slapped cheek.

Greg swore vociferously when he saw things had taken a turn for the worse. 'Use this, fer fuck's sake!' He forcefully tapped his employee's forehead, restraining Smudger as he would have rushed to defend Claudette. 'Go stormin' in and you'll make it ten times worse for her. She's his wife, not yours. And there's nothing you can do about that.' Following his warning, Greg shoved Smudger against the wall, virtually standing on his toes in an attempt to keep him out of further trouble.

'Been looking all around for you.' Scully thrust his

face close to his wife's lowered countenance. 'Had a feeling if I found him, you'd be close by, you no-good whore.' He turned his attention to Smudger. 'So, what you doing out with my wife, you little runt?' Scully snarled. 'Come on, let's have it . . . I'm waiting.'

'Smudger's with us, been down the pub together,' Lily burst out. 'We spotted Claudette walking along in the fog and offered her a lift home in the van. Something wrong in that?'

'See what I mean about your gel, Wilding?' Scully began banging his thumb rapidly against a set of fingers. 'Too much to say for herself. She needs bringin' in line, pal.' He shook his head, feigning amusement. 'Offering me missus a lift, was yer? Ha ha . . . I like it . . .'

Greg's hands formed fists. He knew Lily was giving him a speaking look, pleading with him to ignore the taunts.

'Now you're here, Scully, you can take your wife home yourself, save me the trip.'

Scully dragged Claudette by the wrist, forcing her to stand in front of Smudger. 'Say g'night to yer fancy man then, dear,' he told his cowed wife, giving her arm a shake. But he wasn't looking at her, he was leering into Smudger's face. 'Fair dos, mate . . . I've already said g'night to your tart.' He clicked his tongue in approval. 'Nice-looking gel you've got there — obligin', ain't she? Shame about that claw, but makes up fer it with her other hand.' He made a lewd gesture. 'You tell Li'l Margie to come back 'n' see me, any time she needs a real man instead of a kid.'

'Eh? What's that mean? What you saying?' Smudger spluttered, blinking in bafflement.

Greg was also struggling to make sense of what he'd

just heard and Smudger managed to break free of his slackening restraint.

'Why've you brought Margie into this?' Smudger roared. 'You liar! You ain't seen her. What's your game, saying something like that?' He would have chased after Scully who was already swaggering up the road, pulling his wife behind him. Claudette peeped over her shoulder and this time Lily made a grab for Smudger. She didn't need to; he stayed where he was, rubbing a hand over his shell-shocked expression as the fog swallowed up the couple.

'What did he mean? What's happened to Margie?' Lily swung an anxious look between the two men, her face as ghostly white as the atmosphere.

Greg took her in his arms to soothe her. He had a feeling something far worse had occurred this evening than Smudger and Claudette getting caught out. Lily had said her friend had gone out earlier . . . to find Smudger. Margie would have headed to the neighbourhood where Rory Scully also had a lodging. Greg knew the man would have arrived home from the pub in a foul mood after taking a drubbing. Had he bumped into Margie and something happened between them? Greg hoped it wasn't what he believed Scully capable of.

'I must go and speak to Margie,' Lily babbled. 'Straight away. I have to find out if she's all right.'

'I know.' Greg put an arm about her shoulders, urging her towards the van. 'Come on . . . I'll take you home.'

17

To avoid trips and falls at night, the three girls had a habit of leaving the passage light burning for a late-returning flatmate. But the place was in total darkness and the lack of noise seemed odd too. A sense of foreboding was giving Lily the shakes. She'd always loved this little sanctuary but it seemed to have taken on a sinister air, as though its quiet black cloak protected a dreadful secret. The gas mantle was situated yards away opposite the kitchen. For quickness she fumbled for the matches and a candle kept on a shelf close to the bedroom shared by her friends. Opening the door, she hesitated on the threshold. 'Margie . . . Fanny, anybody home?' she croaked, holding the burning sconce aloft.

All seemed silent, then a soft snuffling sound penetrated the thump of blood in her ears. She rushed forward, making out the slight body huddling beneath the eiderdown. 'Margie?' She dropped to her knees by the iron bed, causing the candle flame to elongate and waver.

Margie's head emerged from the covers then she burrowed her face into the pillow, away from the light. But not before Lily had caught a glimpse of the mess she was in. 'Oh, Marge, what's he done to you?' she moaned. The candle was clumsily discarded onto the floorboards where it extinguished.

Margie dragged her arms out of her cocoon and put them around Lily who was trying to hug her through the bedding. 'Don't cry. It's me own fault. Shouldn't

225

have gone there.'

'Sit up, Margie . . . come on, love. I know something's gone on with Scully. Sit up and tell me what he's done,' Lily hoarsely pleaded. She'd been hoping against hope that the swine had just been out to goad them with his innuendoes. But in her heart she'd known there was more than boasting involved.

The girl shook her head, curling up on her side with her knees drawn tight to her chest. 'Don't matter what he did . . . serves me right for being so stupid.'

Lily pushed herself onto her feet and groped her way, in the dark, to find the oil lamp on the dressing table. She lit the wick, turning it up until a muted glow bathed the room in yellow. 'I'm not going away, Marge. I'm staying right here with you, so you might as well tell me what's happened. I know you've seen Scully — he bragged about it, the vile bast — ' Lily swallowed the abuse teetering on her tongue-tip. Intuition was warning her to remain calm for Margie's sake, even if inside she was raging. 'We saw him along the road just now. He hinted at things . . . ' Lily kept quiet about Smudger and Claudette. Margie had suffered enough already without having that extra hurt.

'What did he say?' Margie had struggled upright, squinting through eyelids made red and puffy from violent weeping. 'Whatever he said, I'll say it's not true,' she cried. 'I'll say he never touched me. I'll say he's a fucking liar!'

Lily crouched by the bed again, a trickle of nervous sweat beneath her collar despite the chilly feel to the room. Margie had dropped her forehead to her raised knees and her tangled fair hair was coating her profile. Lily brushed away some strands with her fingers to get a better look at her friend. Beneath a glistening of shed tears, a bruise was sprouting on her cheek, and the corner of her mouth was grazed. 'Has Scully raped you, Margie? You have to tell me. We'll get the police on to him tonight; he won't get away with it, promise.' Lily tried to turn her friend's face towards her, but Margie jerked herself free and fell backwards onto the pillows. She'd lost her grip on the eiderdown and a dark stain on the sheet and a stale coppery smell was exposed. Lily drew back the covers to see Margie shivering in bloody underclothes.

'Ain't much. Looks worse than it is. It'll stop soon,' Margie said, yanking the eiderdown back over her.

'You're hurt! How bad is it? Oh, let me see!' Lily let Margie win the tug of war to keep hold of the bedding.

'Leave me alone! I've had a look down there; ain't much to worry about,' Margie shrilly insisted. 'Was me own fault, knocking on his door like that. Woman across the corridor saw me. She thought I was a tart visiting him 'n' all.' Margie's chest was pumping hard in distress. 'Just keep quiet about this, you hear? Don't want no fuss.'

Lily sank down to the floor again, swallowing, and trying to find something sensible to say that would get through to Margie. Scully should be arrested tonight for what he'd done. She cleared her throat. 'Be all right, Marge, it will, honest. Nobody'll blame you; but Scully should get everything that's coming to him for doing this to you. Greg'll fetch a policeman . . . he's waiting outside in the van.'

'No!' Margie yelled, rearing up and pushing Lily so hard that she tipped her onto her posterior. 'Just leave me alone, Lil.' She curled up again, hugging a pillow to her belly. 'Don't want no police. Don't want nuthin'. Just leave me alone . . . please!'

Lily got onto her hands and knees, and crawled back to the bed. 'Won't leave you alone ever. You know that. Best friends us.' She rested her forehead on the mattress to stop Margie seeing her fright and distress. She drew in a deep breath to control herself. 'Why you letting him get away with it, Marge, after what he's done?'

'Ain't doin' it for him . . . doin' it for me. Don't want no one to know,' Margie said. 'Don't even want Fanny to know. Glad she's gone out and ain't due back.'

'Yeah, just as well she's out and don't know about this,' Lily murmured. 'She'd've been round his place and ripped his head off by now.'

That brought a glimmer of a smile to Margie's bruised lips. It was soon gone. 'Fanny's got her good luck at last,' she murmured. 'Ain't spoiling that for her. Don't want nobody getting in trouble cos of me being a stupid fool. When Fan gets back in the morning I'll be more meself. I'll be able to help her pack her stuff up, like I promised.'

'Me too . . . ' Lily said. There was quiet for a moment; Lily released her grip on the edge of the mattress and sat back on her heels. 'Fanny can borrow a cart to take her cases to Islington. Make a day out of it, shall we? All take turns pushing. Be like the old days when we was doing our street round, selling bloody soap and soda.'

Margie murmured agreement and her tiny smile was back.

'Fancy a cup of tea, Marge?'

'Don't want no tea . . . ' Margie lay back, her forearm over her eyes.

'Well, gonna put the kettle on anyhow, cos you need a clean-up, love. I'll find me nice soap and talc and you can have a nice wash.' Lily rubbed Margie's arm with gentle, comforting fingers. 'Then, after that, see how you feel. Might want some tea then.' She got to her feet and went to the tallboy, searching for Margie's nightdress.

'Needs darning,' Margie said, knowing what Lily was after in the drawers. 'It's in the sewing box. It'll have to do me though to change into . . . if you'd fetch it.'

'I'll just get that kettle on the go then I'll pop outside and say goodnight to Greg. He's waiting in the van. He wanted to know there's nothing to worry about and you were back home, see. You're all right then, are you, Marge? I'll tell him that, shall I?'

Margie sat up, drawing her knees up to her chest and settling her chin on them. 'Yeah . . . I'm all right. Just tell him that.'

Lily went into the kitchen and filled the kettle then put it onto the stove. She stared at it for a moment before folding over at the middle and letting out a long, silent howl. She did it again, backing against the wall, her face a contorted mask of anguish. She rolled again, gripping the edge of the sink to stop herself sagging to the floor. The pitted china slicing into her palms helped her slowly straighten up. She turned on the brass tap, let the spots of blood on her hands trickle away into the plughole. She dried them off on her blue skirt then unbuttoned her coat and hooked it, and her hat, up behind the door. She checked the kettle for heat and then headed back to Margie.

Lily settled on the edge of the bed and began taking the pins out of her friend's hair, running her fingers through it to ease the knots. She pushed it back behind Margie's ears. 'Give that a brush 'n' all while we're tidying you up.'

'Used to do me hair for me in the workhouse, remember, Lil?'

'Yeah, and you'd do mine . . . when the old cows weren't watching.' She gave Margie a playful nudge. 'Full of grit most of the time, wasn't it?'

'Yeah, grit, or nits . . . ' Margie snorted. 'Weren't even worth using pins to style it, even if we could've got our hands on some. Reckon they thought we'd go nuts and stab each other if they let us have hairpins. Silly sods give us needles for sewing though.' Margie laid her head on Lily's shoulder. 'You'd tie my hair up for me in darning-wool bows — remember, Lil?'

Lily nodded. 'That bloody awful soap. Never forget that. Felt like rubbing Vim on your face.' Lily put both arms about Margie, hugging her, planting a kiss on her hair. She smelled different, of him . . . male sweat and tobacco and something else that turned her stomach. 'Right, I can hear the kettle starting to sing. I'll just take it off and let the water cool down then find you some things. Only be a few minutes.'

Lily came back, carrying the bowl of warm water with towels under her arms and the lavender soap and talc in her pockets. She carefully arranged the washing things on the floor by the bed then laid a nightgown on the mattress.

Margie frowned at the lace-frilled linen. 'That's yours, Lil. You bought it for your bottom drawer.'

'Don't matter, you can have it to keep cos I spotted one on Ridley Road that I like even better for me honeymoon.' She gave Margie a smile. 'Right, you sort yourself out then while I go and speak to Greg.

230

Won't be long. Then we'll make the bed up again with clean stuff.'

Margie nodded and slowly started to push the eiderdown off to get up.

'That's it, get cracking,' Lily encouraged her. 'Don't let the water get cold, love.' Lily turned for the door.

'You won't tell Greg, will you? I don't want you to. Don't want Smudger ever to find out about this.'

'Greg wouldn't say anything if I told him not to, but I'll keep quiet, if that's what you want. Swear it.'

'Thanks, Lil,' Margie said. 'He must be freezing out there.'

'He'll be all right. Probably left the engine running . . .'

Lily used the iron railings to help her reach the street. She felt drained, her legs wobbly, but with her skirts in her fists she trotted the yards to where Greg had parked. The lane got too narrow for any vehicle other than a handcart to reach the very end where the basement flat was situated, down steps worn thin in the middle from centuries of feet pounding up and down.

He'd been watching for her; the moment she emerged through the mist he got out of the van to catch her in a strong embrace. 'What's happened?'

'It's all right. Margie's home now,' Lily said, burying her face against his shoulder.

Greg shifted her back to get a look at her pale features. 'What's happened, Lily?' he urgently demanded. 'Is she all right?'

'She says she is. Don't ask any more.' She put her hand across his mouth, dropping her chin to avoid his compelling stare. 'I can't tell you any more. I've given my word and won't break it.'

He tilted her face up, saw the depth of sorrow in her soulful eyes. He shook his head, his lips drawn tight against his teeth. 'That bastard shouldn't get away with it,' he exploded. 'Scully needs a good kicking and a stretch inside at least. I'd like to see him swing.'

'I know. So would I.' Lily gazed off down the lane. 'Margie won't have it. No fuss, she said. Don't go after him or she'll think I've betrayed her. Promise you'll go straight home and get ready for tomorrow.'

'That sounds as though you're not coming with me . . . are you?' He urged her back into his arms and they clung together for several minutes, their breath steaming into the night air. 'You coming home with me now, Lily?' he repeated.

'I can't. I can't leave her. Margie's got nobody with her . . . she needs me with her.'

'I need you.'

'I know . . . I'm sorry.' Lily disentangled herself. 'But we've got other nights, lots of them. I'm going to start planning our wedding so that next time you're back everything's arranged and we can be married.'

He half smiled, sighing up at the sky. 'Good . . . write and let me know all about it. Will you still come to see me off tomorrow?'

She nodded vigorously, hugging him tightly and laying her head against his chest. 'I'll be there, pacing about at the station before you even turn up, I expect.' She cupped his jaw in her hands, touching their lips together. 'You're a good man. I'm lucky.'

'Thought I was tonight . . . ' he said wryly.

She gave him a wistful smile, a love-filled kiss. 'You will go straight home?'

He nodded.

232

'You won't go to find Smudger to knock sense into him?' After the commotion, Smudger had walked off alone, looking dejected. Much as she'd not wanted to feel sorry for him, she had. But not now.

Greg shook his head. 'He won't be at home. He'll be drowning his sorrows somewhere, and I'm done trawling pubs looking for prats this evening.'

'It's probably best if he's left alone right now.'

'Margie shouldn't have to work with him after this. Neither should you. I'll leave it to you to sack him,' Greg said. 'He knows it's coming.'

'Margie loves him. That hasn't changed . . . can tell that clear as anything.' Lily sighed. 'We'll see . . . ' She pushed a hand through her hair and glanced back the way she'd come. 'I'd better get going; Margie reckons she'll be back to herself tomorrow. I hope so . . . really hope so, but don't see how she can be . . . ' Lily choked.

Greg held her, comforting her by rocking her in his arms. 'See you at Charing Cross then. Don't be late. Be waiting for you.'

She nodded, wriggled her fingers in his when he seemed reluctant to let her go. She stepped away a few paces then rushed back to give him another swift kiss. Seconds later she was hurrying back along the lane, eyes on the ground to avoid potholes and debris likely to trip her. Before descending the steps to the basement, she turned around to wave. His figure was indistinguishable in the mist but she could detect the van's heavy outline and a faint red pinprick of light as he smoked a cigarette. She felt a selfish urge to race back and tell him to wait . . . that after she'd said goodnight to Margie she'd be with him. She raised a hand, wondering if he could see her; then carefully she descended the damp stone steps and closed the

233

door, locking it.

'Made some tea . . . fancied a cup after all,' Margie announced as Lily came into the kitchen, rubbing her hands together. The kitchen table had been neatly set with crockery and a plate of custard creams.

'Smashing; could just do with a hot drink. Cor . . . it's freezing out there.' Lily shivered. 'Shouldn't have taken me coat off. Don't know why I did that when I knew I had to go back out again.'

'Sit down by the stove.' Margie pulled a chair away from the table and closer to the warmth. 'I'm feeling better now I've had a wash,' she said, aware of her friend's concerned gaze on her. 'Stopped bleeding now.' She poured the tea and handed Lily a cup.

'That's good . . . ' Lily said quietly and sipped at the burning brew. In her pretty nightie and with her cheeks rosy from vigorous towelling, Margie did look brighter. Lily took another swallow of tea to stop all her anger and loathing for Scully tumbling out like bile. Margie didn't want a fuss. So that's how it would have to be.

'Didn't go over that way to talk to Smudger tonight.' Out of the blue Margie volunteered an explanation. She pulled the other chair close to the stove, a fragrance of lavender wafting off her as she settled opposite, balancing her cup and saucer on her lap. 'Went after Claudette, to tell her to leave him alone before she got him into big trouble.' Margie took a mouthful of tea. 'Would never have banged on that door if I'd known she'd be out. Saw the light on, see. Thought she was in. Muggins here thought that her rotten husband would still be in the pub.' Margie finished her tea in two gulps and sat staring into the grouts at the bottom of the cup. 'Just my bleedin' luck, eh?' A tear dropped onto Margie's lap, a spot of grey on the pristine white cotton.

Lily clasped one of Margie's hands. 'He's just scum, Marge. Not worth spit. He's certainly not deserving of those.' She used their laced knuckles to wipe away the wet on Margie's face then found a hanky in her pocket and handed it over.

'Not crying cos of him. Feel ashamed. All I've done is caused more trouble, instead of making it right.' Margie dabbed at her eyes.

'No need to feel ashamed cos none of it's your fault.' Lily leaned closer to Margie. 'You'll put this behind you, I know you will,' she said earnestly. 'You won't let him get this one over on you, oh, no! Not you, cos you're strong and he's nothing.'

Margie grimaced. 'You're right. Ain't letting him keep me indoors, hiding away. Nothing happened, cos he's nothing. And that's that.' She gingerly touched the sore spot on her cheek. 'Got this when I had an accident in the dark out there.' She jerked a thumb towards the steps outside. 'Fanny won't need no per-suading on it. She nearly broke her ankle that night she took a tumble coming in.' Margie's lips quirked. 'She'd had a skinful, mind you.'

Lily smiled and helped herself to a custard cream then offered the plate to Margie. They sat back, munching their biscuits. 'Better get that bed changed,' Lily said and stood up.

They soon had the clean sheet on the mattress and the dirty one, and Margie's stained underclothes, soak-ing in soda water in the sink. Margie made another pot of tea while Lily took off her engagement ring and put it carefully back in its box. Then she rolled up her sleeves and finished dunking and rinsing and

235

wringing the washing with fingers made numb by icy water. She put on her coat then pegged it all out on the line although it was dark and the fog wouldn't help it dry. But Margie wanted it out of the way in case Fanny turned up early and asked questions about the sink being full of bloodstained linen.

'Feel cold tonight . . . will you bunk in with me, Lil?' Margie asked when Lily was inside again, locking the back door and rolling down her sleeves.

'Yeah, snuggle up . . . like we used to when we was kids, eh?'

They carried the tea tray into the bedroom and Lily quickly got undressed and into her nightie, then dived under the eiderdown next to Margie. She'd no energy or inclination to wash her face or hang up her best clothes. She left the blue outfit where it fell, for sorting out tomorrow.

They sat up in bed finishing the tea and custard creams. Then Lily used the hairbrush on Margie's rats'-tails. 'That's better,' she said, cocking her head.

'Gonna get it cut in one of them new short styles.' Margie gathered her long fair hair up to frame her cheeks.

'Suit you, that will.' Lily took out her own hairpins and gave her locks a cursory shake. She placed their used crockery on the tray by leaning over the edge of the mattress. 'Don't know about you, but I'm ready for shut-eye,' she said, reaching to turn out the lamp.

They wriggled down and cuddled up together, as they used to in the workhouse, when the dormitory warder wasn't looking. If girls were spotted comforting one another after upsets or punishments, they'd be separated and sent back to their lonely bunks.

Lily could feel Margie's heartbeat thudding into

her arm, slowing down as her friend warmed up and relaxed. Lily gazed into the blackness. She knew that after this she was going to find it difficult to be around Smudger. Rory Scully's rampage hadn't been Smudger's fault, but that wouldn't stop her blaming him. To keep faith, she'd keep quiet, though, and let Margie take the lead in how the aftermath of this monstrous tragedy played out.

'Night, Lil . . . ' Margie rolled away with a sleepy sigh.

'Night, Margie . . . ' After a while, Lily heard soft snuffling: the good sort that told her Margie was dropping off. Lily longed to fall asleep too but doubted she would be able to. She tried to concentrate on the lovely time she'd had tonight — joyful memories to be treasured and revisited, to see her through the loneliness after Greg had gone.

Yet it seemed to her that she'd no right to such happiness. One of the people she loved had been enduring the worst sort of hurt while she'd been dancing and singing, laughing and eating well. Margie's memories of tonight had been forced on her and there'd be no escape from them for as long as she lived.

Was it down to her that Margie had gone out in a huff on the spur of the moment? It had been Lily's suggestion to get out the port to toast good luck. She'd got engaged and had been feeling elated, showing off her ring while Fanny showed off her baby bump.

Lily turned onto her side, dreading the hours of darkness she had to get through, tormenting herself, before she could get up and go and see Greg. To say goodbye.

18

A battalion of fresh-faced soldiers was jamming the entrance to the station platform. Some of the kitbags that had been dumped on the ground by their booted feet had parcels of food balanced on top. Greaseproof paper done up with string held meals prepared for beloved sons rather than husbands, Lily guessed. Those middle-aged mothers were here too. All being sensibly brave while straightening collars and handing over clean handkerchiefs to boys off to war for the first time, judging by their youthful excitement. When — if — they returned to stand here in uniform again, they'd be different.

Lily had her own food offering in the bag clutched to her chest and was hoping the pastry wasn't already crushed into crumbs. She continued along as fast as she could, stepping over trunks and skirting round embracing couples, all the while searching for Greg. From time to time she jumped on the spot in an attempt to catch a glimpse of a familiar blond head in a sea of caps. Whistles and appreciative glances followed her as she elbowed a path past a group of navy ratings.

'Thought you were going to be here before me. I've been going crazy searching for you.'

Lily had felt a warm weight on her shoulder seconds before Greg whispered teasingly in her ear. With an arm around her waist, he ushered her away from the rail track towards the back of the station where it was quieter. He lifted her up so their faces were level.

'I was getting worried you might have decided against a last-minute goodbye.'

'Well, you bloody well thought wrong, then.' She could see panic fading from his eyes and pressed her cheek to his as she calmed down too. After last night's calamity she'd been fretting that he might have deserted in order to stay close to her and protect her from the monstrous Scully. She yearned for Greg to be able to stay. But not like that. Not in a way that would necessitate him constantly looking over his shoulder. Gregory Wilding had never had a craven side. It wouldn't suit him, or her, for him to be that way. Yet she mourned for their lost night of passionate love that had turned to ashes. It couldn't be reclaimed. It would be a long, long wait now before they could fall asleep in one another's arms. Or wake up together in the morning . . . to a new day's kiss and a first pot of tea to drive out the sleep. There was so much she had wanted to experience as a proper lover. Thrilling things and simple things that couples everywhere took for granted as part of their shared love and contentment.

'Don't cry, Lily . . .'

She hadn't realised she was. She scrubbed her eyes dry on his khaki shoulder, forcing herself to be cheerful for him. 'Oh, don't mind me,' she said. 'Just . . . I'm annoyed the bloody van wouldn't start and made me late. Smudger got it going in the end. Then I put my foot down, I can tell you. I was in such a rush to get in here, I almost jumped out and left it running.'

That made him chuckle and he let her slowly slip down onto her feet. 'Smudger is handy for a bit of mechanics. I've been thinking about business, Lily.' He started off quickly, knowing he had an awful lot to say to her in a short space of time. 'I'm leaving you with too many problems, and I wish to God I didn't have to.' He shook his head, his expression mingling regret and frustration. 'Let the street round go now. Don't bother finding people to take over Joey and Fanny's barrow.'

'But . . . the Burdett Road boys will move in on that patch,' Lily warned.

'So what?' He shrugged. 'I don't care if takings go down. I don't want you to struggle to cope with it all. Just concentrate on the market stall, then when I'm home for good we can build things up again.' He frowned, cupping her cheeks. 'Sorry . . . went steaming ahead without asking about Margie. How's she doing today?'

'I told her to have a lie-in. She was still in bed when I left. She's tired . . . more tired than I've ever known her to be.' Lily paused, remembering fetching Margie her breakfast cup of tea then smoothing her face with her fingertips, as though she were a sick child in need of nursing. But the practicalities of earning a living for them all wouldn't go away because of personal tragedies. They needed addressing. 'We're short-staffed; it'll be just me and Smudger now Fanny and Joey are finished. If Margie stays at home, I'll do the books then I'm finishing early. We're helping Fanny pack up her stuff. She'll be gone from the flat tomorrow. Starting her new life.'

'I wish her all the best.'

'Oh, so do I,' said Lily fervently. 'But you were right: it was a risk taking her on when she's such a rebel. I'd do it again though. She's me friend. Always will be.'

'You're loyal to a fault.' He sounded rueful. 'That brings me to Smudger. You've always got on with him, and it seems Margie'll back him to the hilt whatever he does, but sack him. I don't want him drawing Scully back like a magnet while I'm not there to deal with him.' Greg moved his forehead against her soft, smooth brow. 'What damnable luck that it all kicked off on my last night at home. We were having such a good time as well. I missed you last night,' he murmured, kissing the pulse at her temple. 'Wish I could walk out of here with you and sort this out.'

'Well, you can't!' She tugged on his lapels and spoke firmly to make him listen, and to quieten that siren voice in her own head, tempting her to encourage him to run away with her, somewhere they would never be found. 'It's all under control, honest,' she blurted. 'Margie's ready for Smudger's questions.' Lily paused. 'I didn't tell her at first that we'd seen him and Claudette together last night. But she knows now that Scully's caught them out.' She frowned. 'In a way, I hope Eunice gets wind of what he's been up to; she'll knock Smudger into kingdom come.' Lily wasn't joking. Eunice Smith adored her son, but she was a plain-speaking, clean-living woman who'd brought him up to do right. Until recently Smudger had been a credit to his mum, and Lily was banking on him being so again. If he'd listen to anybody's lecture, it would be to his mother's.

'They're not my main concern, Lily. I've seen the way Scully looks at you. He'll be waiting for a chance to ambush Smudger and give him a pasting. He might get you on your own instead. If Smudger's gone, that thug won't have a reason to hang around the warehouse or the market stall.'

It was a valid argument, but came with consequences. 'If I sack him it'll just be Margie and me on

241

the payroll. We'll never manage.'

'You'll need to recruit somebody quickly to take Smudger's place. Make sure he's strong and savvy enough to buy stock that's cheap and best quality, and able to run the market stall with you.' Greg was talking faster, squinting into the distance.

She'd heard it too: a faint hooting whistle that had torn a hole in her heart. The train was coming.

'He'll have to know a bit about mechanics to keep the vehicle and the carts on the road. Honest and hardworking too. Pay whatever you need to, to get the right person . . .'

'Sounds like Smudger's the right person,' she said forlornly. For all his faults, Smudger had been the best, most versatile employee a boss could hope for. She sighed. 'I'll write . . . let you know what happens.' She took his face between her hands. 'Keep safe, my love. Don't fret about any of this . . . please.'

He kissed her fiercely. 'I'll write and let you know as soon as I get the date of my next leave. You can make wedding plans then. I want to marry you more than anything, Lily. Hope it'll be next spring . . . I'll have an Easter bride.'

She nodded, unable to speak now her throat had a huge lump in it. She'd vowed she wouldn't cry, but felt the hot water trailing down her cheeks for the second time.

He wiped the tears away with his thumbs, looking over a shoulder as the train rattled and wheezed into the station. Pandemonium soon started. All around kitbags were being lifted and farewells were being yelled, while guards and porters rushed about shouting.

'Here . . . got you some of the meat pies you like from the bakery. There's a custard tart in there too.'

242

She'd almost forgotten to give him his food.

'Thanks, love.' He took the package, got from her bag, and slowly they turned about arm in arm, walking towards the train. There was a bustle around the doors as servicemen trooped on, leaning out of windows to clasp hands with loved ones for a few more minutes. A little boy in his mother's arms refused to let go of his daddy's fingers, holding up the queue waiting to board. Lily and Greg gladly dallied right at the back, eking out every second left as they watched the family.

'Where will you go next to look for her?'

'I don't know.' Lily glanced up at him. He knew her so well that he had realised that a sad-faced tot with fair colouring would make her think of her sister. 'But I will start again next week.'

'Wish we'd had time to go together to more places.' He sighed.

'So do I . . . ' She pressed together her quivering lips, watching the little lad's fingers being unhooked from his father's by the woman holding him. She was crying, but bouncing the boy in an attempt to make him cheer up as she walked away.

The queue of men had almost all boarded now and Greg knew he couldn't hang back much longer. 'Write straight away if Scully causes any more trouble.' He gave her a little shake to impress on her that she must do it, then pulled her into an embrace. 'You won't forget, will you?'

'I'll write . . . twice a week, promise.'

He gave her a last kiss. 'Go on, get going now,' he said huskily. 'Don't want you to see me turning on the waterworks. If I keep looking at you, I'll blub.'

She nodded, smiling while simultaneously inhaling

243

a shuddering sob. She turned and walked away, stopping at the entrance, and concealing herself behind a pillar. She watched him boarding the train as guards started slamming doors and waving flags, peep-peeping on whistles. Lily sank to her haunches, resting her forehead on her knees as the train groaned and shuddered then started to pick up speed. The chugs grew fainter and fainter and she knew it would be almost from view. She straightened up, pushing locks of untidy chestnut-brown hair out of her eyes. She stared until the last carriage disappeared. Then the tension left her and her shoulders slumped. She didn't want to go back to the warehouse, or join Smudger on the market stall. She'd always eagerly set about her work, but that spirited girl had gone.

She'd kept from Greg that she felt unequal to the faith he'd put in her to carry on without him. She wanted to hide away in bed and not emerge until that train was again heading into the station and he was on it. Would she run up to him then, welcome him home and admit that she was a coward and a failure? Wives and mothers all over the land had far more to cope with.

On the day she'd left the workhouse in her rags and worn boots she'd felt invincible — ready to take on the world, and win. She'd believed then that nothing could be as bad, and everything would be hers to grab. She'd been warned to steer clear of Gregory Wilding or she'd be sorry. But she'd liked him from the start, challenged him from the start. She'd not felt frightened of life then: she'd pelted towards it, chin up, arms outstretched.

She'd need to reclaim that fifteen-year-old orphan's attitude . . . or she'd be sorry.

'All right, Margie?' Margie raised a hand to Smudger's mum. The woman was in the process of clearing debris that had blown onto her step into the gutter, with the aid of a bald-looking broom.

Eunice Smith leaned the broom handle against brickwork then crossed her arms, preparing to have a natter. 'Glad that bleedin' fog's lifted today,' said Eunice, oblivious to the fact Margie seemed keen to edge past. 'Could hardly see me hand in front of me face. And it's given the old gel upstairs her bronchitis back.' Eunice jerked her head at the first-floor casement. 'Poor old stick, she is, coughin' and splutterin' all the while.'

Though Margie had positioned herself hoping she wouldn't, Eunice caught a glimpse of the bruise on her cheekbone.

'Gawd-love-us! You been in the wars, ducks? That looks painful.'

'Fell over in the fog. Clumsy cow, I am; I went straight down the basement steps on me backside last night. Soon fade, it will.' Margie gave a shrug.

Eunice sucked her teeth. 'Death trap round here at night. Could do with a few more streetlights. We should get on to the council, eh? Not that they'll do anything for the likes of us folk livin' here.'

'Yeah . . . anyway, can't stop. Off to work for a few hours now me headache's gone.'

'Righto, let you get cracking then. Oh, do us a favour, would you, love, and tell Bobby to bring his old mum in some spuds? Run right out, I have, and fancied doing meself a shepherd's pie for tea tonight.' Nobody used Smudger's real name apart from his mum.

245

'I'll pass it on, if I see him,' Margie promised.

'Thanks . . . ' Eunice gave Margie's arm a pat. 'And you take care. No more tripping over.' She gave a wink. 'You sure you hadn't been . . . ?' She used a hand to mimic upending a glass.

'Oh, all right, I'll own up. I did take a port with the girls yesterday evening. Lily and Greg got engaged. Celebrating, weren't we . . . ' Margie rolled her eyes before walking off with a smile that tugged painfully at her grazed lip, making her eyes smart.

'Good on her! Wish her all the luck! You tell Lily that from me.' Eunice went off chuckling. She liked Lily. In fact, she liked all those girls, even the brass-faced redhead.

But she was no fool. Her late husband had been a violent man. She knew what a woman looked like after taking a smack in the mouth.

* * *

'You're late.'

'You're early. Wasn't expecting you to be back yet. Sold out already, Smudger?'

'Didn't buy as much stock this morning; intended having an early day.'

''S'all right . . . won't tell Lily,' said Margie jokily. 'I'm only doing a couple of hours meself, then off home. Helping Fanny pack her stuff when Lily gets back from the station later. She's bound to be in bits for a day or two with him gone.'

'Why've you had the morning off?' Smudger ignored the reference to their bosses' sad parting. He walked closer to Margie. For all her casualness he sensed tension between them, and saw that she was deliberately

246

concealing her profile while hanging up her coat.

Margie knew he was trying to get a good look at her. She took a deep breath then launched into the lie for the second time. 'Fell down the steps in the fog. Bashed me face.

Couldn't get no sleep cos it was aching so much.' She turned about and jutted out a cheek to give him a clear view of the damage. 'Lily said to have a lie-in and take a headache pill. Did the trick. I'm more meself now.'

'Fell over, did yer? Fancy that.' He went to the Primus and lit it, putting the kettle on. 'Just making meself a cup of tea, want one?'

'Yeah, ta . . . ' said Margie, though she'd heard the sarcasm in his voice. She didn't care if he believed her or not, she was sticking to her story. She got out her books and pencils then sat down at her desk. Opening the ledger she wrote in the day's date. 'Got your Spitalfield chitties for me to log?'

He stepped over, dropping the folded invoices he'd taken from his pocket. They fluttered onto her deformed fingers. The claw, Scully had called it, and the memory set Smudger's back teeth grinding again. 'S'pose Lily told you about the bust-up last night with Rory Scully, did she?' he burst out.

'Yeah . . . had to come, didn't it?' Margie was keeping her tone light. 'You must've known he'd catch you two out eventually.'

'What did Lily say happened?'

'No point telling you. You was there, so you already know.' Margie nodded at the Primus. 'Kettle's boiling.'

'Right, answer me this.' Smudger gave in and cut to the chase. He leaned closer, his large hand smothering

247

both of hers to force her to stop writing and pay attention. 'Scully bragged he was with you last night. Really with you. Did he attack you 'n' give you that?' He stared at the bruise.

'Ain't surprised he stooped to tellin' lies.' Margie pulled her hands from under his. Yet she hadn't wanted to. Most people couldn't even bring themselves to look at the stumps, let alone touch them. Yet Smudger had, as though it were the most natural thing in the world to hold her hand. 'That low life'll come out with anything to wind you up and get back at you for sleeping with his wife.' She gave Smudger a blameful stare then sedately picked up her pencil and carried on with her work.

'So you never saw Scully then? He never touched you or give you that bruise then?'

'Saw him all right; went over your place to ask if you fancied going to the caff or the pictures.' Margie knew she had to admit to being in the vicinity. She'd intended to visit unobserved but had been spotted by his neighbours. 'Scully was hanging about. Looking for his wife, I expect. You was out, with her, so I went home.' Margie started unfolding the bills, shaking them with her left hand to remove the creases. 'Stupid of me bothering looking for you; weren't a night to be out gallivanting.' Margie started copying the figures into the ledger.

'And that's it?'

She nodded.

'If you reckon I believe that, you must think I'm stupid as well.' Smudger straightened up and marched to the Primus, turning it out under the whistling kettle.

'Yeah, I do, as it happens,' Margie exploded, unable to hold her temper. 'Perhaps if what went on last night

248

has taught you a lesson, it'll all be worth it. Scully's no good, and neither's she. One day, you'll see that. And I ain't got nuthin' else to say, so just shut up and make us a brew or clear off. I'm busy.'

'Don't want no bleedin' tea, and yeah, I'll clear off. Got something to do,' Smudger grimly said, and stormed out.

Margie sat there for a moment with her eyes closed and her chin dropped to her chest. Then alarm set in and she raced to the door to call him back and calm him down before he made things worse. She caught sight of him just as he sprinted round the corner; it was then she realised she'd forgotten to tell him his mother wanted some potatoes taken in.

19

By the time Smudger was approaching his turning, he'd calmed himself down to concentrate on getting the better of Scully without risking serious injury to himself. One thing was certain: he couldn't back away from this. The pervert had to pay for what he'd done to Margie.

With time on his side, the guv'nor would have dealt with this and Scully would have begged for mercy. Gregory was gone, though, and it left a bitter taste in Smudger's mouth that he and the man who'd been like an older brother to him had parted badly. In his boss's absence it was down to him to step up and put things right. For everybody's sake, but mostly for Margie's. All the girls had become his friends; for a while he'd had a daft crush on Lily. But since she'd joined the firm, Margie was the one he'd got closest to. In her he'd had a true companion. He could have a laugh with her, and confide in her his feelings for Claudette. She'd always listened without judging. For the first time ever, Margie had ripped into him today, telling him home truths. He was sure she despised him now, and he deserved it. He'd never properly appreciated Margie; she'd just been there, watching his back, sweet and loyal.

He was afraid he'd lost her respect and friendship and it was his own fault for taking her for granted and missing how important she really was to him.

Scully must have lured her into some sort of trap on his own doorstep. Smudger could guess what she'd

250

suffered and the horror of it caused a wail of rage to emerge through his clenched teeth. Immersed in tortured thoughts, Smudger turned the corner, eyes on the ground. An unusual hubbub grabbed his attention first. He glanced up, noticing straight away the street was unusually crowded. He speeded up, craning his neck to see past groups of gossiping people.

'What's going on? What's happened?' he asked a fat woman, staring down the road, arms crossed under her chins. He didn't wait for a reply; he jogged past towards the largest gathering stationed on the cobbles outside the tenement he'd been heading for. A hellish feeling of foreboding was drying his mouth. For a moment he hung about at the back of the knot of people, rubbing a hand on his lower face while his guts twisted and turned and anxiety sheened his forehead with sweat. He suddenly pushed to the front of the huddle. He'd spotted the spinster who lived on the same landing as Claudette, in the lodging opposite. She was a bigmouth who knew everybody's business. She'd certainly know all about anything concerning her immediate neighbours. 'Something bad happened in there, has it?'

'The poor cow has gawn and done it. Ain't surprised. Can't say I blame her, married to him.'

'What?' Smudger turned ashen, sending a sightless stare through the open doorway. 'Who . . . who you talking about? What's gone on?' he jabbered.

'Mrs Scully . . . ' another woman whispered in a hushed voice, crossing herself. 'The gel threw herself down the stairs. A copper's in there taking a statement from her old man. Doctor's turned up 'n' all, to do a certificate.'

'Way they was going at it last night . . . ' The

251

bigmouth took up the story, shaking her head and shooting up her eyebrows. 'Sounded like murders was going on. Hollerin' 'n' bangin' around they was. I won't lie to cover up for the likes of that brute. I'll tell what I know about him, if folk ask.'

'Better watch what you say, Ethel.' Her friend whispered a caution. 'Once he's back to normal, Scully ain't one to take that sort o' talk lightly. He was looking white as a sheet earlier. The man's in shock . . . deserves a bit o' sympathy.'

'He deserves nothing of the sort!' Ethel hissed. 'I heard him riling her, and weren't just empty boasts neither.' She puffed in disgust. 'That lass might've done it to herself, but he's to blame. He might as well have pushed her . . .'

'I'd keep that thought to yourself,' her friend muttered, looking scandalised.

Smudger disguised a despairing sob beneath a cough. He pushed forward to enter the house but Ethel grabbed his sleeve to stop him. 'Don't go in there, son. Nothing to see. They've carried her back upstairs into the room so the doctor could look at her.'

'You heard them fighting and arguing. What was he saying to her?' Smudger shook the woman's arm to hurry her reply.

'Steady on there.' Ethel removed his pinching fingers, clucking her tongue. 'You went after Scully for knocking her about just after they moved in, didn't you? You're a kind-hearted lad, and bound to feel upset.' She patted his arm. 'We all could've done with taking a leaf outta your book, and speaking up for her more. Ain't as though we didn't all know he led her a dog's life. You was brave and did something about

252

it.' Ethel glanced at her friend who looked the other way rather than admit that she'd also failed to help a beaten wife. 'Too late to be crying over spilt milk, though.'

'Was he calling her names and threatening her?' Smudger whipped off his cap to rake a set of shaking fingers through his hair.

'Calling each other names, they were,' Ethel said. 'Nothing new in that. Mostly he was throwing in her face about having a woman in there while she was out.' Ethel wrinkled her nose in disgust. 'I saw the tart standing there, bold as brass, knocking on his door. Then in she went with him.' Ethel shook her head. 'Maybe he feels sorry now he's found his wife dead at the bottom of the stairs. Just glad it weren't me come across her. Would've given me such a turn.'

'Shhh . . . ' The other woman nudged Ethel. 'Somebody's coming.'

The crowd parted to allow through the policeman and a black-suited fellow carrying a doctor's bag. They hurried off down the lane, talking in urgent murmurs. The crowds were dispersing as people slowly drifted back inside their houses. Ethel's friend headed off home, too. But Ethel seemed happy to stay and carry on gossiping.

'Wonder if he'll lay her out or ask the old girl to do it?' Ethel mentioned the handywoman who lived locally. She attended births and deaths for a fee to assist families in seeing their relatives in and out of the world. 'Undertaker could be next to show up.' Ethel turned to Smudger, who was standing motionless and silent, overtaken by shock. 'It'll come as a blow to Claudette's folks. They live over Bermondsey, you know. Met them just the once when they came here to see her. Seemed nice people . . . bit standoffish though.' Aware she wasn't getting much conversation back, Ethel said, 'How about a cup of tea? You look like you've seen a ghost, you do, son. Nice cup o' sweet tea will make you feel better.'

'No . . . thanks . . . gotta get off.' Smudger stumbled backwards. The last thing he wanted was to enter that building and go upstairs. He'd risk coming face to face with Scully. A meeting between them was sure to end in violence; then the whole world would discover his interest in Mrs Scully hadn't been prompted by decency. Perhaps, right at the beginning, his motives had been pure, but the moment she'd signalled she liked him as more than a friend he'd plunged into an affair. She hadn't seduced him to keep him on side, as protection against her sadistic husband. Smudger had wanted Claudette Scully for himself and had gladly got involved. He'd known it was wrong, and he had no right to another man's wife, yet still he'd continued to pursue her, against all good advice and his own reason. He was equally to blame for what had happened here today.

Smudger swiftly headed towards his own lodging further down the street. He pulled at the brim of his cap, shielding his bloodshot eyes and sniffing repeatedly. He managed to get inside his room without looking at, or speaking to, another soul, and sat down behind his locked door and wept.

★ ★ ★

'Don't often see you twice in one day. Oh, you've brought me in some spuds. You're a thoughtful soul, Margie.' Eunice had peeped inside the bag Margie

254

had handed over and beamed at the sight of some King Edwards.

'I only saw Smudger for a few minutes. He was in and out before I had a chance to pass on your message so I thought I'd drop those in myself. There's always a bit of fresh veg stored in the warehouse.'

'Thanks, love. Got a minute for a cuppa and a chat? Something I want to ask you actually.'

Margie started to back off the doorstep. She could see Eunice studying the bruise on her face. ''Fraid not. I'm in a bit of a rush. I promised to help Fanny. She's moving out first thing in the morning.'

'Crikey! That's come round quickly. She did tell me she was off to Islington soon. Hope she'll be happy,' Eunice called out as Margie started to carry on up the road. 'Oh, just a tick, love. There's something I want to ask you about my Bobby. I'm worried about him, see, and I know you and him are pals.' Her son had often brought Margie into a conversation, though never in a romantic way. A number of his old school chums had now joined up and he had few friends left to spend an evening with, apart from this girl.

'A quick cuppa then.' Margie prayed Eunice wasn't about to air her suspicions that her son was knocking about with a married woman. Margie was still feeling fragile and didn't relish the idea of being quizzed about Smudger's love life. But she liked listening to the woman who knew him best, talking about him.

The building was dilapidated, but Eunice didn't live in a slum. Her lodging rooms were clean and tidy with a few plain bits of scrubbed pine furniture, and a small saggy sofa neatly positioned in the living space. A mouth-watering aroma of mince and onion was also a pleasant welcome. Margie was surprised to see

255

an enamel dish containing a shepherd's pie on the table, complete with mashed potato topping. It was ready for baking in the oven.

'You had some spuds after all, then?'

'No, I didn't,' Eunice said, putting the kettle on the hob then turning around to relate a tale. 'I had a feeling I wouldn't be seeing Bobby after I bumped into a friend of mine, so I bought a couple of pounds at the greengrocer's.' She chuckled. 'First time in ages I've had to put me hand in me pocket for veg.' She could see confusion on Margie's face. 'Start at the beginning, shall I?'

Margie smiled that it'd be a good idea.

'I was in the butcher's queue, getting some mutton mince, when I saw a friend in front of me who lives over Bobby's way. She gave me a good idea of why he'd packed up his stall early. Did Smudger mention to you about the to-do down his street?'

Margie shook her head. 'He only said he was finishing early, then went off.'

'A Belgian fell down the stairs just a few doors away from Bobby's place; dead as a doornail, poor cow.' Eunice dramatically widened her eyes. 'Actually, me friend said she'd heard this woman threw herself down the stairs, but I didn't take no notice of that. Could be a wicked lie going round.'

Margie licked her dry lips. 'Belgian woman?'

'Somebody might've said something to Bobby while he was working in the market, and he shot home to find out what's going on. Everybody likes to be on the spot if the Old Bill are poking their noses about in their road. Anyway, that's the reason I ended up buying potatoes and got me pie done early. I'd've waited if I'd known you was bringing me stuff in. Don't matter;

256

spuds only cost a couple of coppers.' Eunice spooned tea into the pot as the kettle boiled. 'Thing is, Margie, I'm glad we're having a chat. I wanted to speak to you about Bobby; he seems different lately. Can't quite put me finger on it. I know you and him are friends . . . you are still friends, aren't you?'

Margie noticed the woman's eyes on her bruises again. She hoped Eunice wasn't wondering if he'd whacked her. "Course we're friends; Smudger's the nicest bloke I know,' Margie gabbled, yet her mind was racing back to pick over what she'd just heard. It couldn't be Claudette, could it? There was sure to be another Belgian woman living in the street. Thousands of refugees had arrived and many had settled in the East End.

Eunice looked relieved; not that she really believed her boy capable of beating a woman. But he'd been like a stranger recently and she didn't want him turning into his father. 'I'm his mum, so I know when he's got something on his mind. Is Bobby thinking of joining up?' Eunice planted her hands on her hips. 'You can give me an honest answer. I won't let on it was you told me. But I have to know. He's me only family, see. I can't lose him, too.'

Eunice looked tearful but her distress went virtually unnoticed by Margie. Her guts had started churning, making her feel nauseated. Smudger hadn't known about a Belgian woman falling down the stairs, Margie would stake her life on it. He'd rushed off to have it out with Scully about her . . . not about Claudette. Margie couldn't fool herself. There had been a disaster involving the Scullys. And by now Smudger would know about it too.

'Has Bobby mentioned enlisting? I'm frantic, see,

257

love . . .'

'No, he's not said a thing. That's the honest truth.' Margie sprang to her feet. 'Sorry, got to go now, Eunice. Can't stop for tea. Just remembered something I need to tell Smudger. About work tomorrow. It's urgent.' Margie scarpered, leaving the older woman drop-jawed, holding the teapot.

Once outside, instead of heading home, Margie ran off in the opposite direction.

* * *

The bunk that Joey had once used had a rumpled blanket on it, as though the lad had just flung it back to jump up and dash off to work. Only days ago, he'd gone home to live with his mum, which was a blessing. Smudger missed the lad's cheeky company, but wouldn't have wanted him here, asking questions and watching while he bawled like a baby.

Smudger longed to go home and get a hug from his mother. She couldn't make this better though, and she mustn't ever know about him and Claudette and all the sordid run-up to this tragedy. Very few people knew that there had been two deaths that day, not one. Smudger had wanted to be a dad; that was something he and Claudette had bickered about . . . along with all the rest.

He'd been thinking of moving away, and he would now there was nothing to keep him here. Claudette had begged him to stay close so she'd feel safe from her husband. And whatever Claudette had wanted, Smudger had done. As far as he could. It hadn't been enough though. He'd failed to protect her and she'd resorted to taking another route out of her hellish life.

He closed the flimsy curtain. It was November, dusk at late afternoon. He was putting a match to a lamp when he heard the tap on his door.

'Smudger? You in there?' The rap came again with a rattle at the handle. 'Let me in, it's Margie.'

Smudger strode over, answering her through the panels. 'What the bloody hell have you come here for?' He rubbed his swollen, bloodshot eyes with the heel of a hand. He didn't want Margie seeing him like this, but what really concerned him was that she'd risked returning to the place where she'd been assaulted. 'Go home!' he ordered. 'You'll end up in more trouble if Scully spots you. Go on, clear off home where you're safe.'

'Let me in. I know what's happened. I know about Claudette.'

Smudger rested his forehead against the wood, letting out a sigh. A moment later he turned the key then trudged back to sit on his mattress.

Margie came in, locking the door after her. 'Is it true? About the accident?' she blurted out. She hadn't really needed to ask. She'd walked past people outside talking in hushed voices. She'd heard the name Scully crop up and it had sent a shiver through her. She'd vowed never to come within a mile of this lane again; Smudger was in need, though, so all bets were off. She'd come to him to offer whatever support he wanted, even if it was just to sit and listen. Moments ago she'd walked past the very doorway that led to Rory Scully's lair. She'd not faltered and had kept her chin high. He didn't frighten her; she loathed and despised him. Smudger frightened her. She'd never seen him look so vulnerable . . . so hollowed out with despair that she felt her own heart breaking. 'Has

Claudette had an accident?' she repeated her question, using the hated name this time.

'Weren't an accident,' he said dully. 'Who told you?'

'Rumours are going round already. After what happened yesterday, I reckoned there could be something in it.' Margie left Eunice out of it; she sat down opposite on Joey's bed. 'I'm sorry she's dead; you probably don't believe that after what I said about her. But it's true. I am. Wouldn't've wished it on anybody.'

He nodded, rubbing at the tension between his brows.

'What a fucking mess.' He was quiet for a moment. 'Know what the worst thing is? If I'd known you was coming over yesterday I would've waited and gone to the pictures with you.'

'Would've liked that,' she answered with pitiable understatement. 'Just our luck, eh? The pair of us might've missed big trouble but for a few minutes. Probably missed a good picture too. *Ivanhoe* was showing.'

Smudger knew she was trying to brighten him up, but he couldn't snap out of it. He held his head in his hands, tormenting himself with regrets. The more he'd thought about things, the more he could see himself as a prize idiot. Claudette had started to demand more than he could give, making him feel inadequate. Then there was the hopelessness of their situation constantly wearing him down. There'd been no need for his boss to point out there was no future in it, only trouble. 'I loved her, Margie, I honestly did. But I couldn't stand it no more. I was ready to throw in the towel and tell her it was over. Only met her last night to give her money and keep that bastard off her back. A commotion started before I even got a chance

260

to give her the four bob she needed.' He covered his face with his hands. 'Useless, I am . . . couldn't even get that right to help her.'

'You're not useless!' Margie said passionately. 'You did your best.' 'Should've walked away from her sooner. For her own good. None of this would've happened then.'

He hung his head close to his knees and Margie was tempted to go and comfort him. She stayed put, instinct telling her he preferred to punishingly grieve.

'Did Scully push her, d'you think?' Margie whispered.

Smudger shook his head. 'Don't reckon so. Ain't yet run into him meself, thank Christ. Neighbours have and are saying he looks to be in real shock.' Smudger closed his heavy eyelids. 'He deserves to burn in hell for how he treated her. She spoke about doing herself in. I thought she was just hysterical. She wanted rid of the baby or she'd kill herself, she said. She asked for money for an abortion.' He suddenly stood up, wandering to and fro. 'I didn't have it.'

'I'd've lent you something, so would the others. If you'd asked!' Margie cried.

Smudger stared out of the window for a few seconds. 'I wanted her to have the baby. Didn't seem right, doing that to my kid.'

Margie frowned. 'Was it yours?'

'She said so. I've lost 'em both now.'

Smudger reflected on what Ethel had said she'd heard and seen last night. He turned back to stare at Margie. 'Did you go and knock on Scully's door? Is that how he caught you?'

Margie was about to lie, keep on denying it, but it didn't seem right to do that any more. 'Yeah . . . dumb in the brain-box, eh? Was sure he'd be out and she'd be in.'

'Why d'you do that, Margie?' In despair he repeatedly knocked a fist against his forehead and came back to slump down on the bunk.

'Wanted to tell her to leave you alone before something dreadful happened.' Margie shrugged in defeat. There was no point stating the obvious, or scoring points. 'I came over yesterday to tear her off a strip, not ask you out. Tried to keep it a secret. Thought you'd go nuts if you found out I'd interfered.' Margie wanted him to know the truth. 'I am really sorry; hope you believe me. Claudette must've been feeling so low, to do what she did.'

'Never knew her to be happy. Don't reckon she meant to kill herself though. It was the baby she wanted to do away with.'

They sat quietly while the lamp flickered, and noise from other rooms hummed through the walls.

'Fancy getting out of here for a while? Have a cup of tea, or something? Find a caff where no one knows us, shall we?' Margie suggested.

'Don't want no tea. I'll walk you back home though. Pitch black outside . . .' Smudger stood up and slanted his eyes to where he'd disturbed the curtains and a sliver of night had been revealed.

'Horrible it is out there; fog's coming down again. Ain't so long to Christmas now . . .' Margie pushed herself to her feet, following him out of the door.

'Be best to take the quiet route,' Smudger said, having emerged into the street and taken a furtive look around. 'Don't want to get nabbed by none of them old biddies.' Through the greyish mist could be seen a knot of gossips back outside, enlightening those returning from work to the excitement they'd missed.

He led Margie down a back alley. A gaslight on an iron bracket was bolted up on the flank wall of the end house. They settled into ambling along towards its miserly halo of light, meandering in between the putrid-smelling dustbins, with a cat dogging their footsteps. The crumbling brick wall to one side was studded with tall gates leading to washhouses and privies at the rear of the tenements. Every so often a crash or bang could be heard coming from an open window, accompanied by raucous raised voices. Margie hated the dark and the enclosed pathway, so narrow in places she could have stretched out her arms to touch masonry either side. But she was with Smudger. For Margie there was nowhere safer to be. She took his arm, hugging into him comfortingly. 'Know you feel rotten now, Smudge, but it'll seem better after a while,' she said tenderly. 'You'll fall in love again . . .'

He didn't comment. Margie wondered if she'd overstepped the mark, and he resented her trivialising his grief and his feelings for Claudette. But he suddenly halted and swore, removing her hand from his sleeve. 'Let's head back,' he muttered, jerking on her arm to hurry her. But it was too late.

Scully had identified his foe too through the foggy atmosphere. And he had no intention of letting him get away. He ran at them, knocking over a dustbin, and crowded Smudger back against a wall.

'D'you know where I've been?' he snarled into Smudger's face, pinning him by the lapels against brickwork. 'Just shelled out to an undertaker. He's coming tomorrow with a coffin so I can get me wife ready for burying.'

263

Smudger tried to shove him off, but Scully wasn't letting go. 'Should be you paying to put her six feet under. It's your fault me wife's got a broken neck. She was an obedient enough gel before you stuck yer oar in, telling her what she should and shouldn't do. Giving her big ideas, wasn't yer, about leavin' me and living with you.'

'I'd stick me oar in again to help her! She shouldn't have had to put up with being knocked about!' Smudger finally broke free of the forearm wedged against his neck. He drew in a rasping breath past his crushed windpipe. 'You made her life a misery, you animal; everybody knows it. Ain't just me heard you layin' into her.' Smudger dragged Margie by the hand, intending to hasten them both towards the mouth of the alley and into the light.

'You ain't getting away with this.' Scully lunged at Smudger, grabbing his jaw in one thick-fingered hand. He whipped out his knife, drawing steel tauntingly against his opponent's cheek. 'I've lost me wife cos of you. Least you deserve is something to remember her by.'

'She's dead cos she couldn't bear the thought of letting you bring up a kid . . . my kid,' Smudger forced out, his eyes swivelling to the blade nicking his skin.

'Your kid? You ain't got a kid in you, sonny.' Scully tightened his spiteful grip on Smudger's face. 'You really don't know, do you? You was nothing to her. That baby weren't yours or mine.' He shoved Smudger away, smiling maliciously. 'Her Belgian bloke promised to take her back home. She owned up last night to what she'd been planning all along. She was going with him as soon as they'd worked out how to pay for a passage back.' He wagged a mocking finger. 'And I told her . . . over my dead body. I told her I'd find her Belgian fancy man and he'd float home, as fish food.'

'Liar! She told me it was my kid.'

'She told everybody it was their kid,' Scully taunted. 'Fuckin' whore she was.'

Smudger lunged forward, punched him in the guts, then backed off quickly. 'C'mon, Margie!' He beckoned frantically for the frightened girl to take his hand before his opponent could get his wind.

Scully straightened up with a sniff, and an elaborate stretch of his shoulders. 'You'll have to do better than that,' he jeered and turned his attention to Margie. 'Couldn't stay away, eh, Li'l Margie? Knew you'd be back for more.' He planted his legs wide apart, dodging to and fro, blocking Smudger's path as the younger man tried to get past and pull Margie to safety. 'You should thank me, mate, for breaking her in for you. Squealing like a stuck pig she were till I give her me fist to chew on.'

Smudger roared and flew at him, arms rotating and lashing, hands gouging and punching.

Margie knew she could escape under cover of the fracas. She'd been so panic-stricken when Scully suddenly burst out of the gloom that she'd wet herself. But she wasn't leaving Smudger behind. She tried to drag him away as he suffered punch after punch from the vicious brute attacking him. Sobbing in terror, she grabbed a dustbin lid and threw it, hoping to break them apart. It caught Smudger on the side of the head, sending him stumbling and making her whimper and groan in despair at what she'd done. Scully landed a kick on him as he started to fall, and was drawing back his boot to do so again when Margie smashed him in the face with another dustbin lid.

She'd used every ounce of her left-handed strength, emitting a feral grunt with the effort. Her assault had given Smudger a moment to push himself upright and wrestle for the knife while Scully was still dazed. Then both men became still, trapped in a savage embrace.

Smudger disentangled himself and stumbled backwards, leaving Scully standing swaying, with both hands clasping the hilt of the knife in his chest. He was trying to speak but blood bubbled from between his lips and he sank slowly onto his knees.

'Quick!' Smudger croaked, anxiously glancing about. 'Margie!' He yanked her away by an arm, shaking the shock out of her until she was able to run with him to the end of the alley. They turned the corner without looking back.

'Is he dead?' Margie pulled away, halting him when they were both out of breath and many dismal streets away.

They stared, wide-eyed, at one another, then their gazes shifted sideways and up and down as they listened for sounds of the alarm being raised. All was quiet. No shouts, no police whistles. But they would come. In time.

Margie urgently shook his sleeve to gain attention. 'Is he dead, d'you think, Smudger?'

'Dunno . . . don't care if he is,' Smudger gasped, pressing his aching ribs which had taken a kicking. 'You can't tell anybody about what just happened. Even Lily mustn't ever know. Understand, Margie?'

She nodded repeatedly. 'I don't care if he's dead either. Just glad you're not.'

'Going down the recruitin' office on Monday, soon as they're open.'

'No!' Margie tried to hold him, stop him saying

that, but he held her at arm's length.

'Got to.' Smudger blinked spontaneous tears from his eyes. 'Could get locked up — or worse — for what happened, Margie.' Smudger knew in his heart that Rory Scully was dead and that he could be branded a murderer.

'Was self-defence! I saw it. And I'll stand up in court and say what he did to me. He raped me.' She'd finally uttered the hateful words.

'No ... don't ever do that.' Smudger solemnly shook his head. 'Keep it to yourself or it'll ruin your life.'

'He would've killed you. I saw it all. Everything. He started it.' Margie's fists tightened in impotent rage.

'Jury might see it different to how it was.' He sounded resigned to injustice. 'This way I'll have a fighting chance. Least me mum wouldn't feel ashamed if I went like that instead of at the end of a noose. Rory Scully ain't worth dying for.'

'Don't want you to go ... ' Margie cried, trying again to embrace him.

He held her away from him though all he wanted was that hug and for them to keep running and find somewhere to hide. 'I know. And I don't want to go,' he said. 'But that's how it is now.' He put an arm about her shoulders, urging her on.

20

'Oh, Margie, thank heavens you're back!' Lily had been in the process of stepping into her skirt but the moment she heard the key in the lock she dropped the garment and dashed out of her bedroom in her underclothes. 'Where have you been? We were worried about you, weren't we, Fanny?' She gave Margie a cuddle.

'Not me; I knew she'd turn up in her own time.' Fanny was clad in her dressing gown, curling rags in her frizzy red hair, sticking out at all angles. She yawned and crossed her arms, clucking her tongue mockingly at the sight of the two girls clinging together.

'Sorry, Lily.' Margie gave her an apologetic peck on the cheek. 'I stayed at Smudger's last night.'

'What d'I tell you?' Fanny trumpeted, giving Margie a wink. 'About time too.'

'Sorry, Lily,' Margie said again and screwed up her face in regret. 'I should've let you know but it was a sort of spur-of-the-moment arrangement.'

'Oh, never mind. S'long as you're safe.' Lily cupped Margie's face, looking searchingly into her eyes. 'You are all right, love, aren't you?'

Fanny had swallowed the yarn about the youngest of her flatmates taking a tumble outside in the icy fog, bruising her face. But Lily knew the truth. Last night, as the hours had worn on, and there'd still been no sign of Margie, she'd started tormenting herself with wild ideas to account for her friend's absence. While Fanny went to bid farewell to some neighbours

268

and tell them she was off early in the morning, Lily had carried on towards the High Street to see if Margie was still at the warehouse for some reason. She wasn't, and there'd been no sign of a disturbance at the premises, or evidence that Rory Scully might've turned up to harass Margie while she was doing the books. Everything had been neatly stowed away as it always was. Lily had painstakingly put all the padlocks back on and quickly returned home as the fog thickened. Searching the streets for Margie would've been a fruitless exercise when it was impossible to see a yard in front of you.

'I said there'd be nothing to worry about,' Fanny explained to Margie. 'I called in to say toodle-oo to Eunice. She told me she'd spoken to you and you'd had to dash off to meet Smudger. Meeting went better than expected, eh, gel?' She gave another slow wink.

Margie played the game, returning her a tantalising smile, shrugging in a way that told Fanny to work the rest out for herself.

Lily wasn't convinced, and continued observing Margie for a sign that there could be a less happy conclusion to be had than the one Fanny had jumped to. It seemed strange Margie would want to sleep with a fellow, even a kind and decent one, so soon after suffering a violent sexual assault. But if she had decided to confide in Smudger about what Scully had done, comfort might have turned into something more passionate. 'You happy now, Margie?' Lily asked quietly, and received a small smile and a nod in response.

'Ruddy ecstatic, more like.' Fanny clapped the youngest girl on the shoulder. 'Right, let's have a cup of tea while it gets light out there. Don't like these dark mornings. You are coming over to Islington,

269

aren't you, Marge? In all your excitement, you haven't forgotten what day today is?'

''Course I haven't.'

Fanny beamed. 'We've done all the hard work, packing up me trunks. Cart's all loaded, ready and waiting out in the shed. All you need to do is help push the bugger.' Fanny went off, humming, to put the kettle on.

'Everything is all right, Margie, isn't it?' Lily asked again when they were on their own. She'd known Margie too long, and grown too close to her, not to sense something in the background.

'Yeah, I'm fine; tell you more about it later,' Margie whispered, and gave Lily a reassuring hug. Oddly she'd meant it . . . about being fine. Catastrophic events might be hemming her in, but she felt content. She would tell Lily about what had happened to Claudette. Rumours were already flying and Lily was sure to find out sooner or later about the Belgian woman taking her own life. The rest Margie would keep to herself. She'd given her word to Smudger and wouldn't break it, even for her best friend.

After the disastrous run-in with Scully last night, she and Smudger had taken a round-about route back to his room through smog-filled lanes. The filthy night had been an ally, allowing them to slip unrecognised past people who were also scurrying along, heads down, eager to reach home. Once inside they had curled up on Smudger's bed and hung on to one another for warmth and reassurance. Little conversation had passed between them as their thudding hearts slowed down. They'd not wept or wailed. Or made love, or even kissed. But they had slept; then before dawn Smudger had woken her. They'd got up, even though it was Sunday and there wasn't any work. There'd still been no sound of alarm outside. They'd realised the body hadn't yet been discovered. When they left the tenement, they'd avoided the dustbin alley, and had walked quickly along the icy black roads, parting outside the warehouse.

Smudger had entered his workplace, saying he'd repair some of the cart wheels, just for something to do. Margie had carried on towards home, with the warmth of his lips branding her cheek in farewell. Smudger was going away to war and she'd miss him and fret about his safety. But she'd calmed down now and understood his logic. He'd no other choice but to distance himself from the area in a way that wouldn't raise suspicion. Rory Scully was dead. If she'd had a glass of port, Margie would have raised it.

Lily rubbed her goose-pimpled arms. 'Better get me clothes on or I'll catch me death.'

'While Fanny's doing tea, I'll make some toast. Fancy some, Lil?' Margie asked, heading towards the kitchen. 'I'm hungry. Didn't get me supper last night.'

'Didn't get no sleep neither, I'll bet,' Fanny said raucously, having heard the comment.

Margie rolled her eyes, picking up the bread knife and sawing slices off a stale loaf. 'Any jam left in the pot?'

Fanny opened the larder and sorted through packets and jars, taking one out. 'Bit of blackberry at the bottom of this.'

Lily came into the kitchen, doing up the buttons on her blouse. Margie handed over the plate of bread she'd cut ready for toasting.

'Would you do the honours, Lil, and make toast while I sluice my face and hands? I'll need my comfortable boots on as we've got a trek in front of us. Then I'll be all set and raring to go after we've had breakfast.'

* * *

Lily didn't agree with the women who traipsed around thrusting white feathers at young men in civvies in the hope of embarrassing them into joining up. She realised a lot of the women were embittered souls who'd lost loved ones in the conflict. But shamelessly prodding somebody else's son or husband to risk his life by implying he was a coward seemed an odd way of easing their own grief.

Fanny was of the same opinion. 'Anybody does that to my Roger while I'm about, I'll have something to say to her. Won't be polite neither.' She glared at the middle-aged woman muffled up in a heavy dun-coloured coat. Moments ago she'd approached a milkman and, when he'd refused to take the feather, had thrown it into his face. Red-cheeked, he'd clambered back onto his cart and had set the horse to a rattling pace before finishing his round.

'You won't get no milk now, silly cow,' Fanny shouted out, gesticulating rudely.

The woman didn't even look up. She was rooting around in her bag.

'Probably got a load more white feathers in there to chuck about,' Margie chipped in as they passed by on a road surface glittering with rime. She'd been sitting on the edge of the cart, swinging her legs while the other two, holding a handle each, pushed the vehicle. 'Your turn for a breather,' she said to Fanny, jumping nimbly down and skidding a bit. 'You should take it easier now you've got a little one on the way.' Margie took over the weight with her good hand and Fanny hitched herself on board.

'I am surprised that Smudger ain't joined up, Margie, now the guv'nor and the others are in France. D'you reckon he will go down the recruitin' office?' Fanny asked.

'He's not said anything to me about it.' Margie immediately replied with a lie. They'd find out soon enough what his plans were. As would his mother. Margie liked Eunice and hoped the woman wouldn't think she'd covered up knowing her son was off to fight. Margie had answered that question with complete truthfulness at the time.

Before Fanny could carry on interrogating her about Smudger, Margie changed the subject. She'd been selfishly tied up in her own problems and had failed to show sympathy to her best friend who'd said goodbye to her fiancé. 'Bet you cried buckets yesterday seeing Greg off, didn't you, Lil? When's he coming home again?'

'Not sure . . . Easter time, I hope.' Lily smiled wistfully. 'Awful it was, watching him getting on the train. Had to walk away in case I made a fool of meself and started howling like a kid.' She reflected on the brave little boy who'd clutched his father's fingers and not wanted to let go. He'd been dry-eyed, but there'd been no mistaking the sadness crumpling his features. 'Anyway, the moment I hear for definite when Greg's back, I'm booking the date for our wedding. It won't be anything fancy. We'll have a bit of a knees-up in the pub though. And you two are still my maids of honour.'

'Long time since I could claim to be anything like

that,' Fanny snorted.

'Have to use our imaginations, won't we?' Lily sounded equally rueful.

'If the pubs were open now, we could have a drink and say proper good luck all round.' Margie raised an imaginary glass. She wasn't a regular drinker and, of all of them, had been least likely to come out with something like that. Her friends exchanged a comically startled look.

'You are in a jolly mood.' Fanny chortled. 'Smudger obviously knows what he's doing between the sheets. No wonder that Claudette had her claws in him. You'll see her off, though, Marge, no problem.'

Margie turned red and looked away, wishing that name hadn't cropped up in the conversation to spoil things. She had been blocking out bad memories and feeling quite relaxed up until now.

'Shush . . . you're making me embarrassed, let alone Margie.' Lily gestured for Fanny to tone it down.

'I could do with a livener as well.' Fanny pulled a Thermos flask from her bag. 'Luckily, we don't need a pub to have a little tiddly.' The flask had been a daily accompaniment when they were working on their street round. It would be filled with tea to be drunk during their dinner break with cheese sandwiches.

'Bit early for me.' Lily looked on with scandalised amusement as Fanny started unscrewing the top of it. 'You've never filled that up with gin, Fanny!'

'No, I haven't. But that's a good idea.' Fanny poured out a stream of steaming tea into the cup. 'Made us a hot drink while you two finished getting ready. I knew it'd be brass monkeys out after that fog last night.' She put down the flask next to her trunks then drew a small bottle of gin from a pocket. 'Medicinal

274

purposes only. Stop us freezing to death.' She tipped a drop into the cup. 'Reckon it's time for a refreshment break, girls.'

The cart was carefully docked by a wall and Lily and Margie eased themselves onto meagre spaces on the handcart's perimeter, hanging half on, half off the vehicle.

'Best of luck and happiness to all of us, and to the people we love,' Lily said after they'd all taken a gulp of doctored tea. She raised the empty cup, thinking of Greg and Davy . . . and her little sister. She wished she didn't have to resume the hunt alone and that Greg was still with her to boost her with suggestions of where else they might try. She wouldn't stop looking. Ever. It would be Christmas soon. The time of year when she and Davy had entered the workhouse with their mother. It was a bittersweet season for dwelling on sad memories and making wishes for the year ahead. Top of most people's lists was that the war would end. But for Lily, finding out what had happened to that little girl, smuggled out of the workhouse under Harriet Fox's cloak, was right up there too.

The girls had fallen quiet, all lost in their own thoughts, as a weak early-morning sun started melting holes in the frost coating the rooftops. Their breaths were clouds in the wintry atmosphere and Lily plunged her stiff fingers into her coat pockets to warm them up. She was wearing gloves but even so the cold had penetrated through to her bones. She let her gaze drift to Margie, watching her friend gazing off into the distance. Something momentous had happened in Margie's life, in addition to Scully's attack. It wasn't anything pleasant, Lily knew that. Margie

275

was keeping a bad secret; Lily recognised the signs because so was she.

'Nearly there now.' Fanny screwed the top back on the flask and jumped down, joining forces with Margie in pushing on the final leg to her new home in Islington.

'I'm gonna miss you, Fanny.' Margie sighed, and linked arms with the older woman.

'Miss you too,' Fanny said. 'Not for long though. I'll be over to the warehouse tomorrow morning, bringing the cart back. Then in the evening I'm doing me first shift as a munitions worker. Fancy that . . . me, Fanny Miller, soldering grenades!'

'Wish this damn war would come to an end. Weren't even our fight to start with!' Margie suddenly burst out with feeling.

'Bloody well is now . . . ' Fanny said flatly. 'And no sign of it being over since Italy's joined in.'

'Well, I've had enough of it,' Margie said. 'Want it done with.'

'Amen to that . . . ' Lily murmured.

* * *

'Got something to tell you, son. You missed some excitement today, while you was at work.'

Smudger was on his way home when he heard his neighbour hissing at him. She was beckoning him from her doorway. He felt dog tired as he'd been on the Chrisp Street stall on his own all day. The wind had been strong, and he'd had a job serving customers at the same time as keeping the awnings from flying off. Lily had been holding the fort in the warehouse while Margie stayed at home, feeling unwell.

276

Smudger guessed that recent events were catching up with Margie. According to Lily, Margie said she'd caught a chill helping Fanny move her stuff in the perishing cold. But Smudger reckoned the girl was feeling sick in heart and mind, more than in body. And little wonder at it, with what she'd been through.

Smudger wasn't in the mood for a natter, especially as he reckoned he knew what excitement Ethel wanted to talk about. She wasn't the only one. All the neighbours had their own theories about the drama that had played out in their road, and were constantly embellishing them with new angles. Ethel was half concealed behind the door frame, but the weak streetlight revealed the scandalised expression on her wrinkly features. She loved a gossip, and by heaven she'd been presented with something to get her teeth into. With an inner sigh, Smudger turned about and went over to her, just in case she'd heard something that he should know about, to put him on his guard. He had done all he could to cover his tracks, and Scully's body hadn't been discovered for two days. But now it was common knowledge that he was dead, and an investigation was under way. This time the death couldn't be put down to an accident, or a suicide, as his wife's had been.

'All right, Ethel? Nippy old night, ain't it?' Smudger rubbed together his palms. He knew it was best to act normally. It'd be odd if he didn't seem agog, considering the commotion surrounding the Scullys was occupying everybody else.

'No . . . I ain't all right. Nearly had a turn earlier when I found out this latest bit o' news about . . . you know who.' She jerked a nod up the stairs, to indicate the deceased couple's vacant room. 'You'll never guess: Rory Scully weren't the only one playing about in that marriage. So was she! Who'd've thought it, timid gel like that?'

Smudger looked suitably surprised, though any mention of Claudette wrenched at his guts. He was glad he'd stopped; he'd been expecting to hear about a murder investigation, or funeral arrangements, not about Claudette's cheating. He leaned an elbow on the door jamb, indicating he was listening.

'While you was at work, Claudette's folks turned up from Bermondsey. None of us round here knew much about 'em. But they'd got wind of what'd gone on and naturally enough come straight over.' Ethel shook her head. 'Well, the mother's gone into hysterics when she found out it's being said Claudette might've done herself in. Apparently, the gel was carrying a baby, though she kept that to herself. She didn't look up the spout, either. But the mother was crying out — in foreign as well as in broken English — that her daughter wouldn't be so wicked as to kill her baby.' Ethel thumped herself on the chest to catch her breath. 'Anyhow, her husband was trying to calm her down and take her back home. She wasn't having it. Then somebody called a copper, cos she was screaming accusations about Scully being to blame.' Ethel sucked her teeth. 'She come straight out with it: her daughter got pushed down the stairs by her husband, and he was beating her. Well, we all knew that. But hang on, there's more: she reckons he did it cos Claudette was leaving him. The gel was knocking about with a sweetheart she knew from back home. This Belgian feller had promised to take her back there, and marry her.' Ethel put her hands on her hips and goggled at Smudger for his opinion.

'Sounds far-fetched,' Smudger said hoarsely, frowning out into the street to keep her from seeing his tormented expression.

'Don't it just! But apparently it's true, and her parents knew all about it. That's why they wanted her to marry Scully. Before they really got to know him, they thought he'd be a better bet than this young Belgian who's been in prison back home.' Ethel leaned closer to whisper. 'You tell me how he was going to take her back there and marry her when she already had a husband? Or perhaps he was prepared to make sure she didn't have a husband.' Ethel gave a significant nod. 'I reckon when Claudette took matters into her own hands, her sweetheart did too, to even up the score. My theory is that he turned up to fight it out with Scully just a bit too late, or Claudette might still be alive.'

Smudger hung his head, rubbing his face as though in contemplation of a tragedy. So it had been true; Claudette had been in love with one of her countrymen. Scully hadn't just been riling him from malice. Despite feeling cheated and foolish, Smudger felt sorry that she'd not got the life she wanted with her sweetheart.

'Coppers have gone over Bermondsey looking for him. So now that's all out in the open, won't need Sherlock Holmes to work out who killed Rory Scully and dumped him in that shed, will we?'

'Seems not . . . ' Smudger thrust his fingers through his hair. 'Right carry-on, ain't it?' he said hoarsely.

'It's that, all right.' Her tale told, Ethel gave his arm a pat. 'Won't keep you. Off you go then and get in the warm.' She clucked her tongue. 'Didn't have a good word for Scully meself, but perhaps it was six of one and half a dozen of the other with those two.'

Smudger gave a noncommittal grunt and walked on. Some of what he'd learned should have cheered him up. The Belgian's involvement with Claudette, his criminal background, had shifted the murder investigation away from the local area. Smudger hoped that the father of Claudette's unborn baby managed to escape back to Belgium. Perhaps, like Smudger, he'd sooner face the Hun than bad memories of the woman they'd both loved.

After he had walked Margie home the morning after the fight with Scully, Smudger had gone into the warehouse. But he hadn't stayed long. While the streets were still dark and empty, he had returned to his neighbourhood. He hadn't wanted Margie to know what he intended to do. She'd suffered enough, yet would have insisted on helping him. He was determined to protect her after what she'd been through in her attempt to protect him.

He'd gone to the dustbin alley. The body had been there, undisturbed. Smudger had known he'd risk questioning if he made out he'd discovered it; to delay the discovery and buy himself a bit more time to get enlisted, he'd half carried, half dragged the stiff corpse into a tumbledown shed in a tenement yard. Then quietly carried on his way, to pay an early visit to his mother.

In the event, the body had still been discovered sooner than he'd hoped. But he had been to the recruiting office now and set the ball rolling on a posting overseas.

280

21

Charlotte could feel her heart beating so fast that it was making her pinafore bodice wobble. She peeped over a shoulder and strained her ears to listen. Certain she could hear a reassuring rumble coming from the parlour, she dragged the chair closer to the wall to stand on. It squeaked on the brick floor and she sprang away from it and crouched down behind the door to hide. Nobody came. She stood up and noiselessly trotted to the parlour doorway. Mrs Jolley was still flopped back against the sofa, snoring with her mouth open.

Charlotte returned to the chair and gave it a push. When it was where she wanted it, she climbed up onto the seat. She'd waited until the babies had quietened down, and Mother was dozing in an armchair after taking her medicine, before silently quitting the back room and coming into the kitchen. Instinctively, the little girl had known she must work as quickly and quietly as possible in the dark so as not to alert her gaoler.

She started to wriggle her small fingers into the gaps either side of the loose brick in the wall, trying to be careful so the brick wouldn't fall and make a noise. Then she'd get really walloped, worse than ever before. The money tin was precious. She understood that from the way Mother stroked it when replacing the lid. She succeeded in moving the brick inch by inch until it was teetering over her fingers. She wasn't expecting its heavy weight and she squeaked in exertion, using all her strength to stop it dropping. Gingerly, crouching on the chair seat, she lowered the dusty brick between her feet then stood up to pull out the treasure. She gazed at it, a smile of wonderment replacing the concentration on her face. She'd done it. She could escape now . . .

'How dare you! Give that to me, you rotten little girl!' Ma Jolley was as astonished as she was outraged to catch her foster daughter in the act of stealing from her.

Charlotte hadn't heard the woman creeping up on her and nearly jumped out of her skin. She jumped down from the chair, letting go of the money box, to ward off the blow she knew was coming from that raised hand. Copper and silver and banknotes were strewn to every corner of the room as tin and lid flew in different directions in a rattling crash.

Ma forgot about punishing the child. With a wail she dropped to her knees, scrabbling to collect the rolling coins before some escaped into the cracks and holes in the floorboards. There was scant light leaking into the kitchen from the parlour's one lamp and she was virtually working blind. Using the chair, she dragged her bulk upright, cursing all the while, to find a candle and strike a match to it.

Charlotte knew she was in terrible trouble; even so, she desperately needed some of that money.

She had known if she was caught she'd never get another chance to have money to run away. Therefore, she had to persevere with this attempt. While her foster mother was shuffling forward on her hands and knees, cursing and moaning, Charlotte swooped on the closest banknote. She'd learned those were better to have than coins. She'd watched Mother flapping the paper in front of her lips, before kissing it as though it were her favourite. With the pound note scrunched in her hand, Charlotte slunk backwards towards the door. Ma Jolley was too intent on thrusting her fingers beneath the skirting board to retrieve a wedged sixpence to notice what the girl was up to next. The woman had the tin, and the candlestick, on the floor beside her, pushing them along so they were ever close by as she beetled to and fro. Every so often she clattered fistfuls of collected cash back into the receptacle, before resuming rummaging between the table legs.

Once out in the hallway, instead of seeking safety in her room, which was no sanctuary at all, Charlotte trotted to the front door. By stretching up on tiptoe she could reach the latch. She quickly opened it, as she had many times before. She slipped outside and yanked on the letter box to pull it to, in the hope Mother would be fooled into thinking she was hiding upstairs instead of making her escape.

Charlotte closed the gate quietly, then hared off as fast as she could. The money was gripped in one set of small fingers, and her pinafore in the other, to keep it from catching beneath her boots and tripping her up.

She knew why Mrs Skipman couldn't let her stay at her house: she was very poor and already had lots of children to feed and put to bed. But now Charlotte had some money to give her, she was sure it would make a difference. She'd seen Annie's brother hand his mother some money and then he'd got soap and washing water and tea to drink. And he had the best bed to sleep on. Charlotte didn't care where she slept if she could just stay and be part of that lovely chaotic family, and have toast and jam and a cup of tea. She wouldn't ask for more than that. And she might be able to go to school again with Annie and her brother and sister. She could remember all of their names; they whirled in her head now as she puffed along through the dusk: Eric was the coalman and George the younger boy. The littlest one was Clare; she had been asleep, making a funny noise breathing with her mouth open.

Charlotte had not seen or spoken to a soul other than Mother since that wonderful afternoon spent with the Skipmans. After being brought home she had been scolded and locked in her room. But she'd not received the beating she'd feared. That was due to Mother fearing Mrs Skipman would come back with a policeman and cause trouble. Charlotte had not been allowed out of her room for a week afterwards. Mother had left her plates of food on the floor by her bed with barely a word or a look her way. Instead of using the privy in the back yard, Charlotte had been made to sit on the po in her bedroom. She hadn't had a proper wash for ages; just a damp flannel flung at her. Her solitary confinement had been spent peeping out into the street from behind the curtain, for a glimpse of Annie passing by. Mother had warned her she'd get a hiding if she didn't stay away from the window. Still Charlotte had gazed out, wishing in vain to see a friendly face.

Mrs Skipman's promises to come back and make sure she was all right hadn't been real. Mother knew that as well and had gone back to her old ways, letting her foster daughter downstairs. The woman's face seemed twitchier though; and something else had changed. Charlotte had been told she was old enough

284

to make herself useful and help with the tots. She had been given a half-filled bottle to hold to feed the little boy, newly arrived. The others had gone while she'd been shut in her room. The new one had been lively and gurgling, as they all were when they first turned up. Charlotte had stroked his soft dark hair as he guzzled his milk, propped up in a corner of the set-tee. When it was all gone he'd wailed. Charlotte had found the milk bottle to tip some more into his feeder to stop him crying. The milk had been snatched away and the brown bottle of medicine used to quieten him down.

After the argument between Mrs Skipman and Mother, Charlotte had waited and waited, longing for somebody to bang on the door to tell off her foster mother for being cruel. But nobody came. Charlotte had lost hope of help arriving. She'd not give up on having her freedom though, now she'd had a taste of it. She had planned her own getaway because she couldn't stand to stay in that place any longer.

As she drew closer to her destination, Charlotte glanced anxiously over her shoulder. She couldn't see, or hear, Mother chasing her along the dimly lit street, but she knew she would come after her and the missing pound note. Charlotte took the turning into the dirty winding lane where Annie lived. Tall buildings stood either side of cobbles that dipped into a central gutter. It was overflowing with rubbish but Charlotte didn't slow down to avoid the mess, she trotted straight through rotting vegetation. Seconds later, though, she did stop running to hesitantly approach Annie's house. Two women were bickering right by the doorway she wanted to use. They took no notice of her and carried on poking at one another

285

and swearing. Charlotte sidled past them onto the step and darted inside. The grim interior was daubed with patches of light from the gas mantle on the landing. The corridor was divided by the stairway, and led in two directions, but Charlotte remembered which way to go to find the Skipmans. She had thought and thought about coming back here, and had dreamt about being welcomed in, and given tea by a smiling lady with brown hair. She wasn't sure who that lady could be; she was much younger and prettier than Mrs Skipman. Charlotte hated waking up from that blissful dream and would squeeze her eyes shut to try to recapture it.

Timidly she used her knuckles on the door and put a small ear close to the panels to listen. It seemed very quiet inside: not at all as she remembered from her last visit, with everybody talking at the same time, and kettles and plates being banged about. She shuffled from foot to foot, fretting that she must have gone the wrong way and chosen the wrong door. A frightening idea dawned on Charlotte: the rooms might be quiet because they were empty. The family might have gone.

Her foster mother was getting ready to leave their house. Charlotte had seen the things being packed away in boxes as they always were just before she was taken somewhere different to live. The looming loneliness had spurred Charlotte on to steal, and run away, before she lost touch with Annie. She hoped the older girl would still be her friend and persuade Mrs Skipman to let her stay, like last time. In a panic Charlotte started whacking at the door, using both flat hands. If Annie wasn't here she'd never find her again, and she couldn't bear that.

'What you doing here, nipper, making all that

racket? Shouldn't you be tucked up in bed?'

Charlotte stopped banging and flattened her back against the door, her heart in her mouth. At first she didn't see anybody, just a moving black shadow, but she recognised the voice belonging to Annie's coalman brother. 'Wanted to see Annie,' she whispered.

Eric bobbed down so his sooty face was level with hers. 'You'd better go home. You don't want to go in there, y'know. You might catch something.'

Charlotte was mesmerised by his eyes; they looked huge and white in his grimy face. 'Don't care about that. Just want to stay here,' she said. She'd no idea what 'catching something' meant, but whatever it was it made no difference. She'd choose this place over home, no matter what.

Two rows of bright teeth were displayed as he smiled. 'You will care, kid, cos what we got ain't nice germs. Me little sister's got took to hospital. You don't want to end up sick like that, do you?'

Charlotte hadn't much idea what being in hospital was like. She was only sure that living with Mother was worse. 'Don't mind hospital,' she said firmly. But she could tell he wasn't going to let her in, so she opened her fist, showing him the pound note. 'Will your mother let me stay now, and have tea?'

Eric took the money in some black fingers and straightened up, giving a whistle. 'Reckon she might at that,' he said. 'Stay there . . . won't be long.'

A few moments after Eric disappeared inside the lodging, the door opened and Annie stepped out.

Immediately Charlotte launched herself at her friend, hugging her. 'Can I stay here with you and your mum?'

Annie untangled the little girl's arms from around

her waist. 'We ain't allowed to touch other people,' she said softly. 'We've got to stay inside cos of diphtheria. Ain't even allowed to go to school. You should go home, Charlie, or you might get ill.'

Charlotte shook her head. 'Not going home. Hate it. Can I go in your bedroom again, and share your toast?'

Annie glanced at the arguing women as they entered the tenement and barged up the stairs still sniping at one another. She knew all the women were on edge now there was a diphtheria epidemic in the locality. Everybody was blaming everybody else, saying their kid was the one that started it. She ushered Charlotte further beneath the stairwell, out of sight. Her mother wanted the Skipmans' business kept quiet in case they got the blame for being the poorest, dirtiest lot. Which was probably true, Annie had to admit. Her mum was worried sick they'd be the family getting evicted for being infectious. Annie had been ordered not to let on that any of the Skipmans were ill with diphtheria. Pol had told the school and the neighbours that Clare had gone to hospital with gastric enteritis. Annie didn't reckon anybody believed that, but she had been banned from talking to nosy neighbours and now they kept themselves to themselves more than usual.

'I brought some money for your mum,' Charlotte persuaded when Annie remained quiet.

'Eric told me.' Annie frowned. 'You've run away, haven't you?'

Charlotte hung her head then gave a single nod.

'Does Ma Jolley know you've taken her money?' Annie tilted up the child's chin and got another nod. If Charlotte was frightened about the consequences, though, she didn't show it.

'Oh, Charlie . . . you won't 'arf be in a bind when Ma finds you.' Annie could feel her lips twitching. She was filled with admiration for what the plucky five year old had done. It wouldn't have been an easy job pulling the wool over that miser's eyes to dip in her purse. 'In you come then, Charlie.' Annie took pity on the little girl although she knew it'd land her in trouble, too. 'But don't go near George cos he's complaining his throat's sore and Mum's worried he's coming down with it, too. I prayed last night that he's not.' Annie demonstrated to her little friend, her hands pressed together in supplication. Charlotte copied the gesture, gladly following Annie inside.

Eric was by the table, stripped to his underclothes and washing himself in the enamel bowl, as he had been the last time Charlotte had been in this room. She could see George lying on the bed, fidgeting, but there was no sign of Mrs Skipman.

'Don't go near George,' Annie reminded, grabbing the child's arm. 'Go into the back room, and I'll put the kettle on.' Annie pushed open her bedroom door, steering Charlotte inside. 'Mum'll be home in a minute. She's out getting some jollop for George. Hope it works.'

Charlotte did as she was told and sank down on the mattress that she remembered Annie slept on. She sat with her knees hugged up to her chin, smiling.

Annie had put the kettle to boil on the hob then had come in and settled down on her knees beside the little girl. 'Bet you thought I'd forgotten about you, didn't you?'

Charlotte nodded.

'Didn't forget you, honest. I had to stay away from

289

all me friends after Clare got really sick. We had to send for the doctor, and he said she'd have to go to hospital or she might not get better.' Annie sniffed back tears. 'He told us all to stay indoors for a while or we'd be in trouble for spreading it. Thing is, Eric has to go to work, and Mum does as well, or we'd have no money, see. Can't stay in all the time. I've been looking after George now he's feeling rotten.'

Charlotte remembered she'd once felt rotten and had simply wanted to stay in bed. She'd had red spots on her chest. Vera had put mittens on her hands to stop her scratching. Charlotte remembered having a horrible headache, and feeling burning hot. Nevertheless, her memories of measles were not bad enough to make her want to go home to avoid getting sick again. 'The doctor might come back and make George well,' she said optimistically.

'Me mum won't let the doctor back in. Can't pay him anyhow, but if he just turns up and sees George like that, he might send us all into quarantine in the infirmary. Then we'll lose this place. Mum said we'll all be trapped in the workhouse for ever and a day if that happens.'

Charlotte put her arms around Annie to comfort her as the older girl snuffled. Charlotte hadn't heard about the workhouse, but if it made Annie cry, it was obviously as bad being there as it was living with Mrs Jolley.

'Mum'll probably go nuts when she finds out you're in here.' Annie leapt to her feet, having heard the door slam and her mother's voice. 'Oh, Gawd . . . she's back already. I'd better go and tell her. Wish there was somewhere to hide you.' She pulled an apologetic face.

Charlotte waited with her knees squeezed tighter to her chest and her big blue eyes fixed on the closed door. Mrs Skipman flung it open and stared at her, open-mouthed, while her daughter peered over her shoulder.

Pol turned and cuffed Annie. 'Ain't we got enough trouble without you bringin' us more?'

'I didn't, honest . . . Charlotte turned up here out of the blue.' Annie cradled her ringing ear.

Charlotte scrambled to her feet, determined to tell the truth to protect her friend. 'I did come on my own. I'm sorry . . .'

'She brung you this for her board and lodging, Mum.' Eric intervened while drying his face on a towel.

Pol gawped at the sight of the banknote swaying between his thumb and forefinger. Pol dealt in copper and silver. It was a long time since she'd even had a ten-bob note.

'G'iss it here then.' Pol beckoned for the cash, and a second after it was handed over, it disappeared into her pocket. But she was dubious as to where it had come from and to how long she might get to keep it.

'Where d'you get that then, Charlotte?' Pol cocked her head at the silent child resting her chin on her chest. 'I see . . . so Ma Jolley'll be next round banging on me door, will she?' Pol sighed on getting no response. 'You can't stay here, love. I'd let you, but ain't fair risking you catching the germs. I could get into as much trouble as you will, if doctor finds out we aren't keeping ourselves to ourselves.'

'The poor kid can have some tea before she goes, can't she?' Eric said as the kettle whistled. 'She must hate it there with that old cow if she's run away to a dump like this.' He started neatening his hair, dipping the comb into the greyish washing water every so often in an attempt to rinse grit from it.

'No harm, I s'pose, in a cup of tea.' Pol grudgingly relented. She had no intention of giving back the money so a cup of tea for a quid was the least she should offer.

Annie smiled. 'Thanks, Mum . . .'

'Don't you thanks Mum, me; you're a bloody nuisance, you are,' Pol grumbled, pulling a bottle of jollop from her bag. 'Me friend swore to me it's just the job for sore throats, and now I owe her for it. So, lucky Charlotte turned up with that pleasant surprise.' Pol thought she'd get that in before any hints were made about treats like fish and chips since she was flush. She started setting out the tea things. 'Nobody's been nosing around, have they, while I was out?' The head-shakes she received didn't calm her worries over neighbours getting wind of another sick child in her lodgings. Cockroaches were dealt with on a daily basis, but disease made people really panic. Her chief anxiety was that Eric would be laid up with it. If he couldn't work, they couldn't pay the rent, and would then most definitely be evicted. The authorities might step in then and quarantine the family in the workhouse infirmary. Pol would sooner thieve to get by, and risk the consequences, than enter one of those gruesome places.

Charlotte sat on the mattress again and allowed Annie to cover her knees with a blanket.

'Gets chilly in here,' Annie said, snuggling her own legs beneath the blanket to keep warm. 'Your mum's being horrid to you, is she?'

Charlotte nodded. 'I've not been back to school

292

either,' she said. 'I wanted to, but not allowed.'

'Not allowed to nick money off your foster mum either, are you?' Eric had come into the room in his socks and pants and closed the door to keep Pol from hearing what he had to say. 'How d'you manage that then, Charlotte? Clever kid, that's what I reckon you are. Ma got lots of them nice banknotes, has she?'

Charlotte hung her head but answered him with a nod. He might praise her but she actually felt rather ashamed of what she'd done, not clever.

'Where's she keep 'em?' Eric crouched down to chuck the little girl under the chin. 'Got 'em hidden, has she?'

His sister knocked his hand away. 'If you're thinking what I think you're thinking, you'd better think again. You're not getting her into more trouble.'

'Ain't thinking nothing . . . other than I'm sick and tired of being stuck in this dump. I wanted to join up and can't now cos of you lot holding me back.' He straightened up and went to pull on some clothes.

'It was bloody selfish of you wanting to do it in the first place. And it ain't any of our fault Clare got sick.' Annie was on her feet to confront him.

'Might've got delayed a bit, but I'm still joining Kitchener's lot, diphtheria epidemic or no diphtheria epidemic,' he retaliated. 'And that's that.'

Eric had been forced to abandon his plan to go to war with his friend. He felt right as rain at the moment, but if it were to come to light at the army medical that he had a raised temperature, the powers that be might take too much interest in the cause. He didn't want people poking about in his background history as it would reveal he was under age. Then he'd never get enlisted as a soldier. He was biding his time, optimistic that if he used his noddle, he would sail through, like his pal, who was a rookie fusilier at just fifteen.

'Here we are then, Charlotte, nice cup o' tea and I expect you'd like a slice of toast, eh?' Pol came into the back room with a smile. The pound note in her pocket had improved her mood.

'Thank you, Mrs Skipman,' Charlotte whispered and took the cup.

'Nice polite kid . . . ' Pol murmured and went off to find the toasting fork.

The moment the coast was clear, the door pushed to, Annie turned to her brother, taking up where she'd left off. 'And you know we can't afford the rent if you don't chip in your wages.'

'Well, I ain't gonna have me job much longer anyhow. Guv'nor didn't take kindly to finding out me and me pal was intending to leave him in the lurch. He said two could play at that game.' Eric looked sullen. 'Don't get no bunce now, and have to do twice the collar for the same pay.'

'Better find another job then.' Annie sounded shocked. She hadn't known that Eric might soon be put off.

'You get a bleedin' job!' he shot back. 'I was working full-time at your age, yer skiver.'

Charlotte had been sipping tea, her eyes batting between the squabbling siblings. But she wasn't alarmed. Though a lonely child, with scant experience of such things, she somehow knew that this was what happened in cosy families. Soon they'd all be drinking tea and finding something to laugh about. She put down her empty cup, hugged her knees and rested her cheek on top, smiling.

22

They'd all heard it. The bang on the door had made everybody freeze and stop what they were doing.

Pol had been in the process of making herself something to eat now the kids were all fed. Even George had managed to swallow a bit of bread and marge and half a cup of tea. She put down the knife and planted her hands on her hips, preparing herself for a ding-dong.

In the back room, Annie had been plaiting Charlotte's long fair hair, having come to an abrupt truce with her brother. Eric had been shrugging into his coat in readiness to get out of the house and mooch about for an hour or two.

'Reckon I know who that is on the warpath.' He jiggled his eyebrows at Charlotte. 'You ain't gonna sit down fer a week, kid.'

'Shut up!' Annie quickly raked her fingers through Charlotte's hair to remove the plaits so the child didn't get into more trouble. Ma Jolley would pick on the girl for any little thing now.

'Right, come in 'ere, Charlotte.' Pol was beckoning from the doorway. 'Shame about you dropping that pound note on the way round here, wasn't it, love?' She tapped her nose and gently gave the girl a significant nudge.

Charlotte nodded, guessing at what she was being asked to do. She'd gladly go along with it. She wanted this family to have the precious pound note. It didn't seem fair that her foster mother had so many and

Annie's mum had none.

Pol smiled at her, brushing the child's cheek with the back of her finger. She was such an adorable kid it was hard not to be smitten. Her blonde hair rippled about her cheeks where Annie had hastily undone the braids. 'Don't you worry, angel,' Pol crooned. 'It's all gonna be just fine.'

Charlotte wasn't so sure about that and cast an apprehensive look at the door. An unmistakable mannish voice was barking to be let in. It sounded as though the unwanted visitor might burst in anyway, judging by the way the handle was being violently rattled.

Pol gave Charlotte a final pat of reassurance. She adopted a defiant expression before opening up to the battle-axe. 'Reckon you've come to find your foster daughter, ain't you, Ma?' she said breezily. 'She's had her tea but I'll fetch her back later if you like. Charlotte's not being a bother to me.'

Ma Jolley shoved past the impudent hussy into the room then hesitated; she'd not expected to have so many pairs of eyes on her. The boy had his head cocked in a belligerent way. The girl was holding the dratted nuisance close to her side, with a protective arm around Charlotte's shoulders.

'She's stolen from me!' Almost incoherent with rage, Ma pointed a finger at her foster daughter. After collecting all her spilled money, the first thing she'd done was empty the tin onto the table to count it. She knew down to the last farthing what she'd amassed in that tin. The moment she realised it was short, and Charlotte was missing, Ma had known where to head. She'd set out to do battle in such a rush she'd not changed out of her slippers. 'The little wretch has taken a pound note. It didn't belong to her, so give it back this instant.' Having burst out with what was uppermost in her mind, Ma thrust a hand, palm up, straight under Pol's nose.

Pol walked away from it, leaving the woman's fingers hanging in mid-air. 'You ain't done that, have you, Charlotte?' Pol was a picture of innocence.

'You know very well she has,' Ma spat. 'Give it back or I'll get the police on you.'

'Go on then,' Pol said. 'And I'll get them on to you right back.'

'I lost it,' Charlotte piped up. 'I was running fast and couldn't find it in the dark.' She knew the game was up and stepped away from Annie to approach her detested foster mother.

Ma immediately yanked the child to her side. 'You'll pay for this,' she snarled close to Charlotte's ear.

Charlotte could see Eric mouthing something at her; she guessed he was telling her to be brave.

'I'm not going back there with you! You're not my proper mum. I hate you! And so do the babies. They're always crying.' Charlotte tried to wriggle from her captive's grip. She almost succeeded. Ma was taken aback by the child's astonishing outburst. Normally Charlotte would restrict her dislike to brooding looks. This family of ruffians were a bad and disturbing influence, drawing the girl too far out of her shell and making her insolent.

'Now, I think we'd better all calm down,' Pol said, wagging a finger. Under other circumstances she would've done more to help the unhappy child. Presently, the way things were, Charlotte would be better off elsewhere for her own good.

Charlotte's big blue eyes filled with tears as she

sensed Pol was abandoning her.

'Mum . . . shouldn't have eaten nuffing. Me froat 'urts . . .' George moaned. 'Feel sick.'

'See to him.' Pol jerked her head at her daughter and Annie rushed to find a basin to hold beneath George's chin.

Ma had been about to again demand the return of her money, but something other than her lost pound note was making her fret. She was always alert to problems that might cause interference in her life. She had noticed the boy fidgeting on the bed. Now he had rolled over she could see he was flushed with fever. She had dealt with enough sickly children to know what serious illness looked like. And when Pol Skipman brought Charlotte home last time she had mentioned diphtheria was going round in local schools.

'Could be diphtheria,' Pol said, having interpreted the workings of the other woman's mind from some of her facial twitches. 'Be best if you don't hang about in here, wouldn't it?' Pol might not want others to know about this, but Ma Jolley was different. Here was a person who'd never rat to the authorities in case they asked her too many questions. In this neighbour-hood lots of people lived in squalor and had underfed kids. Pol knew she fitted that bill better than most. But with Ma things were different. She wasn't hard up. She was mean and she was hiding something nobody must know about. Ma had backed off quickly when her bluff was called over the police being called. Pol realised that sooner or later the fact that diph-theria was in her lodging couldn't be kept a secret. She was just praying that George wouldn't also end up in hospital. He certainly didn't seem as ill as little

298

Clare had been. Pol missed her youngest dreadfully, and she knew the others did too, but Clare was in the right place to make her well.

Ma was boiling up inside. Mrs Skipman had that pound note in her pocket but there was nothing she could do to get it back if the woman wouldn't hand it over. The lad was glowering at her as though raring to get involved in a scuffle. A noisy scene would bring the neighbours running, and that wasn't Ma's style. Neither did she want nurses or doctors nosing around her home. Diphtheria was terribly infectious and, if Charlotte had picked up the germs, the damnable child would need treatment. Beneath her breath Ma cursed all the Skipmans to damnation for having become a thorn in her side.

She marched out into the passage without saying another word, dragging her foster daughter with her. Soon she was gone from the building and was hurrying along towards home. The night air rasped into her nostrils, making her snort with exertion, and she curled her toes to keep the saggy slippers on her feet.

At her side, Charlotte had to trot to keep up with the woman. When they were halfway home the sound of pursuit could be heard. But Ma kept going, though she'd glanced over a shoulder and started cursing to herself.

Eric jogged past then turned about to walk backwards a few yards in front of them. 'I'm watching you,' he said to Ma, giving a slow nod. 'And me mum said to tell you she'll be round to see how the kid's doing in a day or two when George is feeling better.' He kept pace with them for many yards, never taking his narrowed vision off the woman who was growing increasingly agitated by his stalking and veiled threats. Finally he walked past Charlotte, ruffling her hair, then loped across the road.

The little girl cricked her neck, trying to watch him until he disappeared around the corner. Ma jerked on her arm, dragging her along towards their gate, now in sight. Charlotte felt scared of what awaited her when they reached home. At the very least she'd be smacked and locked in her room as punishment. It wouldn't stop her doing it again. The second she managed to escape those beastly watching eyes, she'd be off to Annie's.

Eric had helped her just by being close to her for those few minutes he'd accompanied her home. Charlotte took comfort from knowing she'd more friends in that family than she'd thought.

* * *

The fire was unlit so there was no warmth to be gained from it. Ma Jolley hadn't had her foster daughter's comfort in mind when tugging the hipbath in front of the parlour hearth. While attending to the baby on the settee Ma had wanted to keep a close eye on the mischievous girl now scrubbing herself with a flannel.

The moment they had reached home, Ma had stomped out into the back yard to fetch in the bath from the shed. Then she had started filling it with a copper jug. Just one measure of water had been warmed in the kettle before it was upended into the tub. Charlotte had been ordered to get undressed and to wash herself all over with a bar of gritty, foul-smelling soap that had landed with a splash beside her. She had done as commanded and now sat shivering in the few inches of tepid water. As her foster mother continued to ignore her and feed the baby, she carefully stood up to climb out and use the towel draped over the side.

'Sit down. You're not finished,' Ma snapped. 'Wash all over again and use the carbolic on your hair as well. You filthy little beast, bringing germs into the house from that slum.' Ma put down the feeding bottle and propped up the infant that had been on her lap in the corner of the settee. She came to rest a hand on the side of the tin bath. 'There . . . drowning's what you deserve, you wretched girl.' She scooped up a jugful of bathwater and tipped it over Charlotte's head, making the child cringe and shudder. Ma's palm itched to deliver a slap but she resorted to pulling Charlotte's sopping hair instead. The risk of diphtheria was still present and might yet bring the interference she dreaded to burst open her secret world. 'Little pest. Little thief,' Ma muttered, shuffling away and brooding on the fact she must be increasingly careful on all fronts from now on.

She found the gin on the sideboard and took a nip straight from the bottle. She preferred the solace of laudanum, but it made her sleepy and she knew to keep her wits about her now. She slanted a malevolent glance at Charlotte rubbing the bar of soap onto her wet hair. At five years old she was surprisingly sly and wilful. She blamed that bunch of rogues round the corner for teaching her their tricks.

When Mrs Priest had brought her back months ago, Ma had listened to the accompanying tale of woe and immediately spotted a profit to be had. She'd not allowed her eagerness to show when gladly taking the girl in, despite receiving just a few shillings in payment for her board and lodging this time.

Charlotte's adoptive mother was on her uppers now her sugar daddy was dead, Ma had been told. It had been music to her ears. Secrets and money went hand in hand. As soon as Betsy Finch was off the scene, Ma had reasoned she could profit from the scandal of the major and the strumpet. He might not have actually fathered the bastard, but he'd believed he had, and so had Charlotte, and that was enough. All Ma had to do was track down his family and tell them what she wanted for her silence. It hadn't been as easy as she'd anticipated, and no local searches of directories and newspaper obituaries had turned up a mention of a Major Beresford who fitted the bill. Ma now found herself landed with a child she didn't like, yet couldn't dispose of as easily as she could the tots. Things were getting worse as Charlotte got older; she was turning into trouble with her stealing and absconding. The girl had to go.

No more time could be wasted discreetly searching for the major's widow. Ma was planning to go back to Cheapside where his fancy piece had lived. Mrs Priest had told her she and her mistress were moving away. But a neighbour might be able to help Ma trace the women for questioning. Betsy Finch had been the major's dirty little secret, but she would surely have known her married lover's usual whereabouts when not with her. Ma would need to proceed with caution. If that strumpet cottoned on to what she was up to she'd demand a share in any pay out. Or threaten to expose the truth about Charlotte Finch's parentage from spite. As for Mrs Priest, she had wept when handing the girl over — genuine tears, too. Such sentiment could be an equal problem. The housekeeper couldn't know Ma's plans either.

In future Ma would attend to the infant she still had and not take any new arrivals until her life was clear of hazards and back on an even keel. No more advertisements could be placed offering comfortable upbringings to needy children. No more train trips to fetch home a child and ten pounds. Going to get them was preferable to having a mother come to her, but not always possible. Keeping constantly on the move was the safest way to stay a step ahead of any woman seeking to reclaim a child that had long ago joined the angels in heaven.

Ma would have to keep a close eye on Charlotte in case she'd been infected and began to show signs of disease. The girl must be kept apart from the infant; diphtheria could be fatal, and two dying children would be too much to cope with. Charlotte's disappearance wouldn't go unnoticed by the Skipmans, now that they had become thick as thieves. The immediate neighbours were also sure to pass comment. Quitting the area while the five year old was still looking healthy was of prime importance. Once in a new neighbourhood, Ma knew she could start afresh with new adverts, and new tots. She glanced at the child shivering in the bathwater. She didn't want her catching her death on top of everything else. Besides, there was still a possibility that Charlotte Finch might redeem herself when she was introduced to her daddy's family. Ma came to the side of the bath. 'What do you say to me for such disgraceful behaviour?'

'Sorry, Mother.' Charlotte recited an oft-used, if little-meant, phrase.

'Out you get then, and dry yourself off. Straight to bed for you. Wicked children go without supper. And from now on you will stay in your room until you've learned never to steal from me again.'

Charlotte nodded solemnly at her foster mother. Then turned away and smiled to herself. She didn't want any of her horrible supper anyway. She'd had lovely toast and jam at Annie's. And she had her friends close by. Once George was feeling better, Mrs Skipman and Annie and Eric would come to see her, she was sure of it. And now she'd given them a pound note, they'd let her stay with them for ever.

23

'Oi . . . g'iss a ride on yer handlebars, kid.'

Joey Robley ignored the taunts and carried on pedalling up the hill. The Burdett Road boys kept pace with him on the other side of the road, pushing a barrow loaded with fruit and veg.

'What happened to the other old bike you was riding? Gone off and left yer, has she, the ginger tart?'

Joey still didn't rise to the bait, though inside he was fuming about the insults to Fanny. He turned his crimson face aside and tried with all his might to go faster, though his legs felt like lead weights. The first potato they chucked at him missed, flying past his vision and making him wobble. The next hit its target, knocking off his cap. He put a foot down to steady the bike before he fell off.

That made the aggressors roar with laughter and lob a few more earthy missiles his way. Joey scooped up his cap, trying not to look ridiculous. He knew he was under observation. A horse and cart had stopped up ahead and the fellow unloading it had seen what was going on. The coalman didn't look much older than he was and he didn't like being made a fool of in front of somebody his own age.

He hoped the youth would get on the cart and clear off before he reached him.

Having finished shooting his load into the cellar of a big house, the coalman returned to the vehicle. He was folding up oily sacks when a stray spud thrown by the barrow boys whacked him in the shoulder.

305

'Sorry, mate, weren't meant fer you . . . ' one of the costermongers called out.

'Well, this is meant fer you,' Eric Skipman snarled, and started pelting them with lumps of coal.

Joey got right off the bike to watch, grinning from ear to ear as the Burdett Road boys attempted to return fire but soon gave up. The sooty bombardment was smothering their clothes and ruining their stock, bruising the fruit and shedding black dust over everything. They resorted to shouting abuse then ran the barrow round a corner to escape. Rather than mount his bike now the coast was clear, Joey steered it up to the cart where his ally was prising the lid off a tin of tobacco.

'Thanks . . . ' Joey said. 'They're just a couple of prats.'

'Could see that; know 'em, do you?' Eric continued, rolling himself a smoke.

'Yeah, I know 'em, worst luck. They used to try and poach on my patch. Never let 'em get away with it though. Used to do a barrow round meself, y'see. Worked for Wilding's,' Joey added proudly. 'Best job I ever had.'

'Heard of Wilding's,' Eric said. 'Got a pitch down Chrisp Street, as I recall. Me sister likes the lady who runs the stall, so she buys off Wilding's when she goes to the market.' That was stretching the truth a bit; Eric knew Annie went poncing stuff rather than buying it. Since they'd been keeping to themselves at home, they'd been living on bread and jam and biscuits their mother filched from her client's larder.

'Lily Larkin's the lady your sister means. Lily's running the show. She's the guv'nor's girlfriend and she's a diamond. Wilding's have got the biggest pitch down

Chrisp Street. Guv'nor had a couple of street rounds 'n' all, but that's closed up. Short-staffed, y'see, since Mr Wilding and the lads joined up.' Joey grimaced. 'I had to pack it in. Me mum sorted me out an interview at Hobson's.' Joey sounded glum. In the basket on the front of the bike he had shirts and gloves wrapped up in brown paper and string. Those had to be delivered to opposite ends of Cheapside before he could knock off home.

'No good at Hobson's?' Eric offered the soot-stained roll-up to Joey.

'Ta . . . ' Joey took it while Eric fashioned himself another. 'Hobson's ain't a patch on Wilding's. Go back there in a flash, I would. Used to get extras on top of me wages. Bit of bunce from weighing out short measures . . . ' He rubbed together thumb and fingers, demonstrating making money from scamming. 'And once a week you'd get given a cotchel of fruit and veg, plus a bit o' haddock on a Friday if Smudger — he was me foreman — had done a Billingsgate run that morning.' Joey was about to nudge the boy, but thought better of it. If he got soot on his clothes, his mother would go mad. He made his point by wagging a finger instead. 'Best of all, we got a place to doss, courtesy of the guv'nor. Had some right larks in that lodging.' Joey sighed. 'Worst of it is, there weren't really no need for me to have quit Wilding's in the first place.'

'Why did yer then?'

Joey shrugged. 'Me mum has these bright ideas about me needing better prospects . . . ' was all he said. He liked Fanny too much to talk about her bad reputation behind her back. She'd quit anyway, so couldn't now lead him astray, as his mother had feared. Joey

307

had wanted to beg for his old job back, but his mum had insisted he at least give the Hobson's apprenticeship a try. He'd been there long enough now to know it didn't suit him.

'Well, if you fancy being a coalman instead of a delivery boy, you can have my job. Me guv'nor's building up to sacking me.'

'Been caught fiddlin'?'

'Nah . . . he just don't like me since he found out I was jackin' it in to enlist.'

'You ain't old enough.' Joey peered at the lad's youthful features beneath the smuts.

'Turned fifteen months ago. Me mate got away with it, and he's the same age.'

'I'm fifteen soon,' Joey said, stretching the truth a bit. His birthday wasn't for another six months. 'Not planning on going to war, though. So what's yer name then?' he asked gruffly.

'Eric Skipman. Got a name yourself?'

'Joey Robley.' Self-consciously he stuck out a hand that was given a clumsy shake, then he took out his hanky and wiped his soot-smudged fingers. 'Mr Hobson'll go mad if he thinks I've got black on them packages,' he explained apologetically.

'So, d'you want me to put in a good word for you with me guv'nor? You could do the same for me at Hobson's. We could swap jobs.' Eric had got a sly eyeful of the wrapped parcels in the bike's basket. In his opinion it couldn't be too hard for a savvy delivery lad to lose a couple of those once in a while. He'd appreciate a nice clean job with perks like that.

Joey looked over the filthy youth, peaked cap jauntily askew on his head. 'No, ta . . . reckon having your job would be jumping from the frying pan into the fire.' He realised he'd made a joke and nudged his new pal, making Eric bark a laugh as the pun sank in.

'Yeah, would be at that.' Eric used a grimy finger to rub a mirthful tear from his eye. He lit their cigarettes with a struck match, and watched in amusement as the younger boy got to grips with his first taste of rolling tobacco.

'Usually buy meself Woodbines,' Joey said before he got mocked. In fact he'd only ever had a few crafty smokes out of Smudger's pack when they'd lodged together. Since Joey had been dragged back home, he'd not managed to have a fag under his mother's eagle eye.

'Well, better get on then,' Joey said, stepping on the half-smoked stub then picking it up to stick behind his ear. 'Save it fer later and thanks for . . . you know.' He jerked a nod to the opposite side of the road where his tormentors had scarpered round the corner.

''S'all right, mate . . . any time,' Eric said. 'Might see you around then.' He got back on the cart and set off with a wave.

Eric was heading back to the depot, thinking it would be nice to meet up with Joey Robley again and go out with him to the dogs or to a football match. He missed his pal since he'd joined up. They used to hang about together at the weekend and have a lark. He careered around the corner, clicking his tongue at the horse to giddy up. He had a few more drops to make before the end of the day and had before him the prospect of shovelling up hundredweights of coal into sacks then loading them onto the cart. And not a lump of the black gold could disappear into his pockets for bunce since his guv'nor was watching him like a hawk. Listening to Joey talking about his good times

309

working for Wilding's had made Eric's mouth water. It would've made his mother's mouth water too! Free veg and haddock once a week. And a lodging thrown in. What a job to have! And that idiot Joey Robley had given it up. Eric stopped brooding about it as his attention was caught by somebody he recognised. He eased back on the reins and guided the animal to the kerb to watch the woman on the opposite pavement. He'd never spotted her round these parts before.

Ma Jolley was in the process of knocking on a door. When it was opened she didn't go in but started up a conversation on the step. The two women seemed to be having quite a chinwag too. The housewife had crossed her arms and was shaking her head. Ma was alone, so obviously little Charlotte had been left at home. Annie had told him that the child was often locked in her room while Ma went out. Eric had a soft spot for Charlotte even though she was only a nipper and they were usually beneath his notice. She was a plucky little thing, sweet-natured and pretty. She was bright too, as demonstrated by the way she'd helped herself to the old girl's money then given her lip. Eric had almost burst out laughing and clapping when she did that. Ma had looked set to explode. But he felt sorry for Charlotte, living with a foster mother who bullied her. They'd all seen the bruises on her. She would have earned herself one hell of a clump for pinching that pound note, and it hadn't really been right of Pol to keep it. He and Annie had turned on their mother afterwards for making things worse for the little girl. Pol's argument had been that Ma would go for Charlotte anyhow, simply for taking it in the first place. In fairness, Eric knew that most parents would go berserk if one of their kids stole from them. Poor little Charlotte, in her lonely closed-up world, probably didn't appreciate how bad it was to do something like that.

Eric pulled up his collar against the stiffening breeze. There seemed to be a sinister chill in the air whenever Ma Jolley was close by. Even now, just watching her from a distance, Eric felt a shiver up his spine as though somebody had walked over his grave. It wasn't just that she was ugly and dressed in the same heavy black clothes all the time. She had a nasty slyness. He felt powerless to help Charlotte, and that was depressing. He couldn't even help his own brother and sisters now he was in danger of losing his job. His family deserved somewhere better to live. He'd intended to help find them a nicer home before he volunteered. But since his perks had dried up, instead of adding to his nest egg, he'd been dipping into it, and there wasn't much left.

A few days ago his mother had visited Clare in hospital and returned to tearfully tell them their sister wasn't getting better. And George, though holding his own, wasn't on the mend yet either. Their mother was frantic with worry about what might happen if they all fell ill. And whenever Pol was stressed she used gin to soothe her nerves. The pound note Charlotte had handed over to them had practically disappeared, mostly spent on jollop for George and booze for Pol. Her kids had benefited to the tune of a few ha'porths of chips to share between them at teatime. George, not wanting to miss a treat, had brightened up and tucked in, managing to keep his food down on those occasions.

Eric hadn't given up on plotting to acquire more of Ma Jolley's pound notes, but in a way that wouldn't get Charlotte into any trouble. If he managed to do that, his family could splash out again on some luxuries. Then, when everything was back to normal, he'd treat his mum and the kids to going-away presents from his ill-gotten gains, when he finally got his shipping-out papers.

If he'd known Ma was out this afternoon he would've made a diversion to see if she'd forgotten to lock any of her windows or doors. The woman was suspicious of all the Skipmans now, so he'd need to cover his tracks. A burglary mustn't be traced back to him; it needed to appear that a vagrant had chanced a break-in. The scheme was still a pipe dream and, for now, had to be put on the back burner, for proper consideration later. He was already behind schedule, having stopped for a smoke and a chinwag with his new pal. His boss never needed much of an excuse these days to dock his wages. With that thought spurring him on, Eric set the horse to a trot.

★ ★ ★

'Now you mention it, I did catch sight of her after she moved out of the road. It was ages ago; just the once, in the market.' Betsy Finch's erstwhile neighbour wagged her finger. 'It almost slipped my mind and I know why. I hardly recognised her that day; she didn't look the sort of woman any decent folk would speak to, so I turned my back and pretended not to know her. Painted up to the nines, she was. Probably hoping to hide her shiner under all that powder, but I could see she had a black eye and I expect others could too.' The woman clucked her tongue. 'I remember Betsy Finch when she was a good-looking girl, all classy costumes and curled hair.' The housewife primped her headscarf. ''Course we all knew what she was, and who the major was when he came a-calling. Stanley Beresford, that was his name, but none of the neighbours ever spoke to him, of course. Mostly he'd turn up in the evening and keep very much to himself, as you'd expect.' The woman poked her tongue into her cheek, and raised a scandalised eyebrow.

Ma Jolley's ears pricked up at the mention of the fellow she was interested in. 'Any idea where the major hailed from? A Londoner, was he, Stanley Beresford?'

'Why should I know that?' the chatterbox sharply enquired, looking affronted. 'Anyway, he's long dead . . . in the war. That's why all the trouble started for Betsy, and she went downhill fast.' The woman cocked her head, looking at the ugly frump who'd turned up out of the blue, asking questions. 'So, who exactly are you?'

'Just an acquaintance of Mrs Priest's. We lost touch but I'd like to meet up with her again.' Ma thought it was better to claim that connection rather than seem to have been friends with a trollop.

'I liked Vera. She was a nice woman and seemed very fond of the little girl. I wonder whatever happened to her? 'Course we all knew what she was too. Wasn't her fault, poor little love, born the wrong side of the blanket. Pretty as a picture she was, too. Charlotte . . . that was her name. Charlie, Vera would call her. There was no sign of her with her mother in the market that day.' The woman tapped her chin in consideration. 'Perhaps her father made provision for her to go away to boarding school, while he was still around. Posh man like that would've known his responsibilities, wouldn't you say?'

'Have you an address for Mrs Priest? I'd like to write to her.' Ma quickly got off the subject of the child and the major. The windbag seemed to be heading towards asking some questions of her own.

'All I recall is that Mrs Priest said she was moving to the sticks somewhere. She popped in to say goodbye. She was leaving London for a domestic post in a big country house.' The woman backed off the step into her hallway, having finally realised she was not only being indiscreet but she wasn't sure she believed her uninvited visitor's tale. She couldn't imagine Vera Priest being friendly with such as her. 'Well, I'd better be getting on. Sorry can't be of more help, Mrs . . . ?'

'Jones . . .' lied Ma glibly. It was nothing to her to adopt an alias whenever it suited her. 'Do you have any idea if Betsy Finch is still in the area? She might know Mrs Priest's whereabouts; perhaps she supplied Vera's new employer with a reference.'

'Well, if Betsy did that, it wouldn't be worth the paper it was written on,' the woman scoffed. 'If you want that one you might find her down by the docks, if you know what I mean. The fellow she was with looked like her pimp. Oily sort . . . foreign. If I was you, I wouldn't bother seeking that sort of trouble.' With that she closed her door.

Ma loitered by the gate for a while, wondering whether to try another house, in the hope of receiving a titbit of information to assist her in tracking down Major Beresford's widow. She became aware of the neighbour she'd just spoken to watching her from behind her net curtain, so quickly hurried off along the street. The last thing Ma wanted to do was arouse suspicion.

She returned home from her trip to Cheapside

feeling anxious. She knew she must quickly make a decision on what to do next. She intended to be as far as possible from this neighbourhood in days, so had little time to make further enquiries. Since her second run-in with the confounded Skipman family, and the risk of diphtheria that'd come with it, she had an intuition that trouble was closing in on her. Ma had a nose for it, and had always managed to outrun it in eleven years of illegal baby farming.

She had no intention of trawling dockside taverns, hoping to bump into Betsy Finch. The tart might not sniff money when asked for Major Beresford's details, but her pimp was sure to. Ma wanted no truck with those sorts of people. Once alerted to what she was up to, he'd never be off her back, and might even try to snatch Charlotte Finch if he deduced her to be valuable. Ma hadn't put up with the brat for this length of time, investing time and money in the girl's keep, to lose out on a profit now. If Betsy Finch flaunted Charlotte Finch's birth certificate she could claim the girl.

There was no hope of finding Vera Priest from the information the old tattler in Cheapside had imparted. The housekeeper could be north, south, east or west of London, hundreds of miles away. Vera had brought Charlotte to her almost a year ago now, and Ma had moved from that address virtually straight away, fearing the adoptive mother might have a change of heart and want her back. To Ma it had seemed glaringly obvious that the child was a gold mine but perhaps Betsy Finch had missed that particular trick.

Ma had been striding to and fro, tearing strips off her thumbnail with her teeth. Her perambulation was brought to a halt by the noise coming from the settee.

She'd dosed up the tot to quieten him while she was out, but the laudanum was starting to wear off and his squeaking was starting to grate on her nerves. She picked up the grimy feeding bottle that had been discarded beside him earlier and stuck the teat into his mouth, even though the bottle was empty. But it pacified the little mite and he started sucking. She left the feeder hanging from his frantic little lips and went upstairs. She didn't trust Charlotte now; even a locked door might not thwart the pest in causing mischief. If the girl somehow managed to get out of the room she wouldn't find the savings tin, though. Ma had moved it from the kitchen and hidden it under the stairs.

Having unlocked the bedroom door, Ma stepped inside to find her foster daughter curled up on her side on her bed. 'You can come down now for tea.' Usually the hungry girl would follow her out of the door, but she didn't. Curious as to the reason, Ma went back inside the bedroom.

It was bare of anything that might occupy a child. The toys and books that Vera Priest had brought when handing Charlotte over had all been sold off. So had Charlotte's pretty clothes. She now spent every day in the same faded dress and pinafore. As she'd grown taller the hem had been let down. She wore scuffed boots on her feet that were slightly too big. Anything of value that Ma got hold of from any of the children's mothers — extra clothing and toys or keepsakes that they wanted their precious babies to have — was turned to profit that was dropped into the savings tin. The only thing Charlotte did have to amuse herself with was a pencil. She would take old newspapers to her room — not to read as she'd learned very little — but to spell out her name and write numbers up to ten, as Vera Priest had taught her, in the margins of the *News of the World*.

'I said you can come downstairs now. Are you deaf?' Ma walked closer and stared at the girl, sucking her thumb. 'It's teatime. Do you want some bread and jam, or not?' Ma barked.

Charlotte took the thumb from her mouth and shook her head.

Ma couldn't believe the girl had refused a meal. She was always eager to eat. Ma bent closer, frowning at Charlotte. She noticed her pallor and that she had a sheen of moisture on her forehead. 'Don't you feel well?' she asked in a panic.

'My throat's sore . . . ' Charlotte whispered.

Ma dropped to her knees by the bedside, shaking Charlotte's arm. 'Sit up . . . sit up . . . let me see. Open wide.'

Charlotte struggled to a sitting position and did as she was told, parting her lips.

Ma pinched her cheeks together to get a better view. Having peered at a scarlet throat and swollen tonsils peppered with white spots, she scrambled up, horrified, wiping her fingers on her skirt as though to clear them of taint. 'You must take some medicine to soothe it, then you'll feel better.'

Charlotte slowly sank back down onto the bed.

Ma found the Dr Collis Browne's mixture and a spoon and hurried upstairs, twitching and shaking in alarm. 'Here, it will help you. Drink it down quickly and it will make you better.' In fact she knew it wouldn't do much other than reduce the pain. The mixture was a cure-all as far as Ma was concerned, for everything from toothache to diarrhoea. But an

317

infection such as diphtheria was a different matter. It would have to do though, for now, to boost the child and get her on her feet.

Charlotte could see that the brown bottle trembling in her foster mother's hand was different to the one that sent the babies to sleep. Still, she didn't fancy taking any of the medicine. But she felt too unwell to argue. She opened her mouth and let the woman upend the spoon onto her tongue. Her foster mother soon hurried off and when Charlotte heard the door being closed she parted her lips and let the stuff dribble out onto the pillow.

Ma hastened to fetch the pram from the front parlour. It was a collapsible model that one of the mothers had handed over along with her little daughter at Waterloo Station. The child was long gone to meet her maker but the carriage had been kept and was of immense help to Ma: not that the children were often seen in it, but she would utilise it to cart her belongings from place to place when a hasty move was required. Now though, she used it for its purpose, assembling it with fingers made clumsy by haste, then putting the infant in it. She felt too nervous to immediately dispose of him, although his time had come. She would have to feed him and change him and make him presentable to take outdoors. She found the condensed milk tin and poured what remained in it into the feeding bottle, topping it up with water. Her eyes darted about as she waited for the baby to finish feeding. Already her mind had moved on to assess the essentials that needed to be stowed on the pram.

The house had been rented fully furnished; Ma never put down roots and never had her own fixtures and fittings. Shifting large items would slow her down. In her line of business, it was sensible to keep all her assets in an easily transportable metal box. The moment the boy had emptied the bottle, she took off his dirty nappy and replaced it with a clean rag. Then she pulled the pram blanket over him and went to collect the cashbox from the under-stairs cupboard. It was carefully secreted beneath the pram blanket, then she set about stashing her cartons of belongings on the makeshift rack underneath the coachwork. All the while she worked, she gabbled, congratulating herself on having had the foresight to pack up days ago in readiness for this eventuality. Upstairs she went, to jam her few remaining items of clothing into the carpet bag, forcing it shut. Then it was taken downstairs to join the other chattels beneath the pram.

Charlotte would doubtless feel too ill to walk and would have to sit on the edge of the pram. Ma didn't want the child dragging back on weak legs, slowing her down. Her foster daughter appeared to be in the early stages of diphtheria and was of no more use to her now than was the little boy. But she couldn't leave either of them behind to give the game away. Especially not now Charlotte had found her tongue and had far too much to say for herself. Pol Skipman or one of her brats could turn up at any time, as they'd threatened to do. If they found Charlotte abandoned, they'd relish causing trouble for Ma, reporting her to the authorities. An investigation was sure to bring to light other complaints that had been made about a foster mother who'd subsequently disappeared along with children put into her care. Parents had been on her tail searching for babies they wanted to reclaim from her, but couldn't. Only one had actually caught up with her, offering her money to have her son back.

Ma had assured the woman the absent boy was just holidaying with a relative and that if she returned in a week he would be home and she could take him with her for nothing. But of course Ma couldn't return the child, even if she'd wanted to. It had been too late when he'd already been despatched to join the angels in heaven. Within days Mrs Jolley had disappeared. Just as she must now.

Soon the baby was hemmed in on all sides by tins of condensed milk and other bits and pieces Ma was squirrelling into the pram for the journey. A sewing kit overflowing with a reel of strong braid was last to go in. Sometimes, instead of using that on a tiny neck, Ma would use a pillow . . . . it depended on how her nerves were at the time. And whether she felt up to seeing their little faces in their final minutes.

In less than an hour she intended to be gone from this place for a fresh start under a new name. She stood back and looked about the grim, reeking room. Satisfied she'd not missed anything she might need, she wheeled the pram into the hallway, then started up the stairs. Charlotte Finch was an unwanted burden, like the boy. But for now she had to come along. Somewhere along the line, Ma knew she would rid herself of them both.

24

'How are you, Annie? Haven't seen you for quite a while.' Lily had been serving a customer when she caught sight of Annie Skipman loitering at the back of the queue. The girl acknowledged her with a nod, then hung her scruffy head and shuffled away a yard or so; she'd never scrounge when others were looking. When the housewives had all been served, she came closer.

'How have you been, Annie?' Lily repeated with a frown, looking over the girl's ragged attire. She needed a coat to wear in this freezing December weather, not a shawl that seemed to have more holes than wool in it. Annie appeared scrawnier too, and more downcast.

'We've not been very good, miss,' Annie croaked. 'Me little sister caught diphtheria. She went to hospital . . . but she died.' Annie sorrowfully swung her head and rubbed the heel of her hand on her watering eyes. 'I've hardly been out at all for weeks.'

For a moment Lily was speechless with mingling shock and sympathy. 'Oh, I'm so very sorry to hear that, Annie,' she eventually said, in a voice thrumming with emotion. She reached across the diminished display of apples to squeeze the girl's thin, icy hands. She recalled hearing some of the housewives in the market gossiping about an outbreak of disease at some local schools, and of children being hospitalised. This was the first Lily had heard of a fatality, though.

Annie had started to snuffle and Lily quickly moved from behind the stall to put a comforting arm around

321

her bony shoulders. 'How are the rest of your family?' Lily knew diphtheria was very contagious and deadly. When working as the medical officer's clerk at the workhouse, she'd learned a little about such things. Starved of any novels to read, she'd browse Adam Reeve's reference books instead.

'Was only me younger brother caught a dose of it too. George is much better now though.' She snorted back a sob. 'Clare was only just six. Doctors told Mum if she'd been a bit older and a bit stronger, things might have been different. George is nine, see, and quite a big boy.'

'Your poor mum must be very upset, and so sad,' Lily said through a lump in her throat.

Annie nodded, fiddling with the frayed edges of her shawl. 'She is; she cries all the time.' Annie kept to herself that since the tragedy her mother had rarely been sober enough to know what day it was, or how many kids she had.

'Let's see what I can find for your mum.' Lily hurried back behind the stall to sort out some food for the family. 'I expect you could all do with building up.'

'Thanks, miss . . .' Annie placed her empty shopping bag on the stall, glancing about in the hope that no neighbours would be about to see her. She hated scavenging — poncing, as her brother Eric called it. But pride was a luxury none of the Skipman family could afford. Annie knew they were close to hitting rock bottom now. She took a deep breath to try to pluck up the courage to ask for something else she wanted. 'Can I have a job with you, miss?' she burst out.

Lily stopped tipping potatoes into the bag and gazed at the girl. 'You're too young, Annie,' she gently rebuffed.

'I'm almost thirteen.' Annie tilted her chin and attempted to neaten her straggling hair.

'You'd need to be older for me to take you on and . . . ' Lily looked at the frail girl. She'd lug home a bag weighted down with vegetables, but lifting heavy boxes — day in, day out — and pushing barrows from the crack of dawn, would be beyond her. And so it should be. 'You ought to stay at school and learn as much as you can,' Lily encouraged with a smile. 'I was at school until I was fifteen.' She left it there. She never volunteered information about her childhood spent in the Whitechapel workhouse. She hated bringing it to mind, let alone speaking of it.

'Can't stay at school — Mum says I have to get work. I haven't been to lessons in ages anyway. I've been doing odd jobs to earn money, but I need something better now me brother's lost his job as a coalman. He wants to join up. Keeps going on and on about it, and says he's not waiting any longer.' Annie pressed her lips together to contain the grief welling in her chest.

Eric had been told he was out of work at the end of the week, now his guv'nor had found a lad to replace him. Her eldest brother had been offered a similar job at another depot, but he was so fed up that he'd vowed he was enlisting, even though he knew what a state that would leave his family in. He and Annie were constantly bickering while trying to keep secret from their mother what his plans were.

'I'm sure he'll find other work,' Lily reassured.

'He did. But it pays less and the hours are longer. He wants to be a soldier, like his pal. Don't want him to go and get killed. I'll miss him. Eric's not even sixteen yet.'

That should've surprised Lily but it didn't; her

brother Davy had been just sixteen when he'd shipped out to France. Like Annie, Lily had been devastated by her brother's decision to go. But she had got over it in time, and perhaps Annie would, too. 'What does your mum say about Eric's ideas?'

Annie rolled her bloodshot eyes. 'Eric won't tell her, and when she finds out, we'll all pay. I told him he's selfish, and he'd better not leave me and Mum to hold the fort on our own. I reckon one day he will just disappear, though. Don't know what we'll all do then, when we rely on him so much.'

Lily continued loading potatoes, onions, carrots and a cabbage into the bag, shaking it all down to fill it right to the top with apples. Everybody had troubles, but the Skipman family seemed to be suffering far more than most. Lily liked Annie. She'd often thought she recognised something of herself in the child. Annie seemed keen to hold the family together. But the girl looked as though the stuffing was slowly being knocked out of her now. Lily would love to be in a position to help if she could, but things were changing at Wilding's, and not for the better. She pushed the overflowing bag of produce across the boards.

'Thanks, miss.' Annie dragged the load towards her and finally she dredged up a smile.

'I've got a couple of bruised pears left over . . . d'you want them for your little friend Charlie? I remember you said he liked a pear.' Lily held them out.

Annie's smile faded, but she shoved the fruit into her pockets then pulled her shawl around her, tying the ends in front of her to stop it slipping off her skinny frame. She'd need both hands to lug the bag. 'Charlie's a girl. Can't give them to her; she's gone away. Her horrible foster mother did a flit, just like

324

that. Never even got to say goodbye to Charlie. Don't suppose I'll ever see her again and she was a pretty little thing. Me mum thought she looked like an angel with her blonde hair.' Annie had been stepping backwards while speaking, avoiding a bruiser of a woman who'd barged past to get served.

'How much yer beetroots? Ain't cooked, are they? Like to boil me own so they don't go too soft.'

Lily raised a hand to Annie but she was already heading off home, lugging the vegetables in two hands.

Having shifted the last of the beetroots, Lily was stacking up the empty pallets in the back of the van, thinking of the Skipmans' awful bad luck. For a short while it had stopped her brooding on her own problems. It seemed strange that Annie Skipman had asked for a job when finding a new recruit was constantly occupying Lily's mind. But she didn't regret turning the girl down as she had nothing suitable for her. Profits were being squeezed and that meant staff were at risk of being sacked. Being soft-hearted to Annie was all very well, but generosity, soon withdrawn, was no kindness at all. Lily realised it would be better to stick to helping the family in the way she always had.

Wilding's didn't need an underage apprentice, it needed a foreman, preferably with market experience, now Smudger was leaving them in the lurch. Smudger had enlisted. And Lily reckoned she knew why. But he wasn't giving much away about his reasons, and neither was Margie. Which made Lily even more suspicious that there was more to it. Especially when taken together with the sudden deaths of Mr and Mrs Scully. Lily, along with most other people, had now heard about Claudette's suicide and Rory Scully's murder by a Belgian fellow his wife had

325

intended running away with. The foreigner had disappeared and the consensus of opinion was that, to avoid arrest and the gallows, he'd worked his passage back to his homeland to join the resistance fighters. The gossip had died down now; it was old news and new dramas had emerged to take its place. But Lily hadn't got it out of her head and she knew that neither had Margie nor Smudger.

Lily sighed. She was going to pack up early today though she'd not completely sold out. She felt dog-tired as she'd been running the stall on her own for hours, rushed off her feet. Smudger had finished early as he had army business to attend to this afternoon, concerning his shipping-out dates. Soon he'd be gone. Like Greg and Davy, whose absence was a constant ache in her heart. Lily knew she'd miss Smudger too, as would his doting mother, who had been in bits for days after he broke the news. Lily had experienced the agony of believing she had no family left around her, so honestly knew how Eunice Smith was feeling. Lily had believed her brother dead at one time, and had been overjoyed to discover he'd survived a fire at the Cuckoo School in Hanwell. Then the miracle of her little sister's fate had emerged, making her almost burst with happiness to know that three of Maude Larkin's kids were still alive . . .

Lily's fingers shuddered and she clumsily dropped the empty pallet she was holding onto the floor of the open van. Charlotte . . . Charlie, she could be called. Lily turned about, jaw sagging, then dashed around the stall, but Annie was already lost to view in the crowd of shoppers. Lily hadn't properly heard Annie Skipman's final bit of conversation, as the next customer had been demanding the price of the beetroots.

326

But Lily was sure the girl had said her little friend's name was Charlie and she was a fair-haired foster child.

'Oi, where you off to?' A housewife had approached the stall. 'You gonna serve me or not?'

'Yes . . . What is it you'd like, Mrs Grundy?' Lily said over her shoulder in a distracted way.

'Well, if it ain't too much trouble for you, I'll take a pound of carrots and the same of onions.' The woman sounded narked. 'And I don't want none of the big 'uns. I like the small carrots, and the onions I like to be medium size cos those bake just right with me roast potatoes.'

Lily poured the vegetables off the scoop into Mrs Grundy's bag, then almost forgot to ask for payment she was in such a tizz. She was probably barking up the wrong tree, as she had done many times before, and would end up being disappointed. But she had to know if it was a lead worth following up.

'What're you hoping to find over there?' Mrs Grundy turned about to peer into the distance, as Lily was doing.

'Oh . . . I just wanted to speak to the girl I served a moment ago.'

'Ah, yes, I saw her, that Skipman kid. Always scrounging, that one. You won't get no money out of her if she's skipped off without paying. Might get a mouthful of abuse, though, if she's anything like her mother.'

Lily wasn't going to tell her one of Pol Skipman's children had died to stop the woman finding fault with a grieving mother; no doubt Mrs Grundy would find something horrible to say about the tragedy too. 'Wasn't money I was after,' Lily said. 'Just wondered where the family lived. There's something I want to talk to them about.'

'Oh?' Mrs Grundy perked up, hoping for a gossip.

'Annie's brother's a coalman and I need fuel delivered.' To get rid of the woman, she'd blurted out the first thing that came into her head. She didn't want to lose a regular customer but Mrs Grundy was getting on her nerves.

'You don't want to buy off that tripe-hound, dear!' Mrs Grundy trumpeted a caution. 'You'll regret it if you do. Eric Skipman's a right crafty tyke. He'll palm you off with a load of slack then cream the good stuff off for himself. Old trick, that is. And I heard from one of me neighbours that his mother's got caught pinching again.' Mrs Grundy spat a 'tsk' through her teeth. 'None of that lot living over by Rook Street is a scrap of good. My advice is to stay away and order your coal elsewhere.' With a finger wag, Mrs Grundy departed.

★ ★ ★

Lily pulled up at the kerb, quickly yanking on the handbrake then turning off the headlights. She jumped down from the van, slamming the door with her heart battering against her ribs. Her excitement felt oddly different this time, no doubt in keeping with the direction the hunt for her sister had taken. No orphanage or foundling shelter to enter hereabouts, in the hope of getting answers to her questions. And just as well, she thought, as she stood surveying the dilapidated three-storey buildings that ran off into a blur of stench and shadows. It was almost Christmas and the afternoons short. At four o'clock, twilight had already descended. Lily imagined that she was seeing the Skipmans' neighbourhood at its best, dappled in gaslight. Doubtless it looked even more decrepit during the day. She lived in a rundown area herself, but the maze of lanes leading to her basement flat were impressive in comparison to this slum.

Two women were standing nattering by a lamppost. Lily recognised them as market goers, though they weren't regular customers of hers. Less reputable traders, selling old stock, drew the poorest shoppers. But they didn't give it away for free, so Mrs Skipman sent her daughter to Wilding's, where produce was always top quality and fresh, thus getting the best of all worlds.

Lily approached the women, knowing it'd be best to just ask rather than waste time knocking on doors to find Annie. Drawing attention to herself, and rubbing people up the wrong way in an area such as this wouldn't be wise.

The bystanders had noticed her alighting from the van. Vehicles of any sort were a rarity; the sight of a young woman at the wheel of one was enough to make people stop and stare. The younger of the women cocked her head in a hostile way, taking a couple of drags on a cigarette in quick succession.

'Sorry to bother you but I'm looking for the Skipmans. Know where they live, do you?' Lily politely enquired.

'Could be we do,' the elder of the women drawled. 'But if you're after Pol Skipman, you won't get no sense out of her.'

'Why's that?'

'We saw her coming home a short while ago. Jingling merrily, and it ain't even Christmas yet.' The younger woman puffed smoke and sniggered.

'Pol's usually got a few bottles rattling in her bag,' the older woman explained. 'Poor cow's had some bad luck and likes a drink to settle her nerves.' She looked Lily up and down and, having decided to be obliging, used her thumb to jerk directions over her shoulder. 'That way. Second entrance along and ground floor on the right-hand side, beneath the stairwell.'

'Thanks,' Lily said and made to set off.

'Got any spuds going begging?' the younger woman cheekily called. Wilding's was written on the side of the van but, even if that hadn't been a giveaway, she'd recognised Lily as Chrisp Street's chief costermonger.

'Yeah, a few.' Lily trotted to open up the van's back doors. She pulled out a pallet of wilting greens and a sack of spuds, almost half full, letting them fall to the cobbles. 'Help yourselves,' she said. 'Leave the crate, though. Need it.' She knew that it'd probably disappear to be used as kindling; a bitter-cold evening was on the cards. But she had far more important things on her mind than losing a box. If these women had helped her to take a step closer to finding her sister, she'd give them spuds galore and smash the pallets up herself for firewood.

'Cor, thanks, love . . . ' was chorused in disbelief as the women swooped on the free stuff. They made hammocks of their aprons to carry their booty home.

The noise inside the building came at Lily from all directions: fretful babies, arguing adults, furniture being scraped to and fro. She barely noticed it, though, or the rancid atmosphere. She followed the older woman's instructions and soon stood before a battered old door, no different to any of the others she'd passed. She banged on it, keeping her fingers crossed, almost dancing on the spot as she impatiently waited for somebody to open up. The loudest racket seemed to be coming from within. Pol couldn't be very drunk if she was shouting that loudly. Lily raised her hand to knock again but the door was suddenly opened, making her shoot back a step in surprise.

'What you after then?' Eric hadn't long ago got in from work and was still smothered head to toe in black. And he wasn't in a good mood. His mother had found out from a busybody that he'd been spotted near the recruiting office. He hadn't plucked up the nerve to go in that day, but the damage had been done anyway. The moment he'd stepped indoors she'd blown her top. Eric had been glad of the interruption, but he hadn't expected to open up the door to a stranger. Since the doctor had stopped coming, the only people calling on the Skipmans were rent collectors, tallymen and neighbours making complaints. He could see that this beauty didn't fit the bill on any count. Yet she did seem vaguely familiar.

'I've come to speak to Annie. Is she in?'

Eric stroked his chin and stepped outside, pulling the door to behind him. He and his sister were always at loggerheads these days, but he'd protect his own, just as Annie would watch his back. She hadn't been the one to blab about him wanting to join up, after all. 'What you after me sister for?'

Pol yanked open the door to find out what her eldest was up to. She hadn't finished with him yet, and didn't want him sloping off out. She squinted into the dim passageway, a hand on the frame to steady herself. She was tipsy but nevertheless recognised the attractive young woman. She elbowed her son aside to poke a finger close to Lily's nose. 'Annie said you give her all that fruit 'n' veg, so don'tcha come 'ere causing trouble . . . '

'I haven't . . . I did give it to her.' Lily turned her head to escape the alcoholic fumes wafting off the woman's breath.

Annie's head appeared over her mother's shoulder. When she saw who it was she grinned in delight. 'Have you changed your mind? Can I have a job after all?' She hadn't told the others in her family what she intended to do, thinking she would have little chance of success.

The magic word 'job' was helping Pol to rapidly sober up. She'd been out all afternoon looking for charring work since she'd lost her client. She'd stolen from her lady and been rumbled straight away, before she'd had a chance to pawn the silverware. She'd given it back and the lady had said she'd not report the theft to the police. But she'd refused to give Pol a reference — naturally enough. And she'd sacked her — naturally enough. 'Come in then, miss, if you want to.' Pol sniffed and, propelling her kids in front of her, went back into the room, flapping a hand for the visitor to follow.

Lily was determined not to show any reaction to the dirt and disorder, though it was worse than she'd anticipated. The youngest boy was by the hob grate, stirring a pot, billowing steam. She guessed he must be the lad recovering from diphtheria and, though pale, he thankfully did look well enough. The sooty-faced youth had started unlacing his boots in between slanting her estimating looks.

'We're having potato pie,' Annie said. 'I peeled some potatoes as soon as I got home. Having cabbage and carrots with it. Got it all boiling up, see.' The girl

332

jerked a nod to the rattling pot.

'Smells good . . .' Lily lied. Stewed cabbage, overlaid with the smoky pungency of Eric's clothing, wasn't a pleasant scent.

'Well? How can I help you, miss?' Pol demanded, unsure whether to act belligerent or obsequious. If her daughter had managed to get herself a job with a firm like Wilding's, she'd praise the girl to the skies. This young businesswoman was the sort any mother would be proud to see her daughter turn into. Shiny chestnut-brown hair and deep blue eyes proclaimed the owner to be in the pink. Annie could look that pretty, Pol optimistically told herself, if all it took was a healthy dose of hard work in fresh air, and plenty of fruit and veg to eat.

'Ah . . . just twigged,' Eric said. 'You're from Chrisp Street market.' He chuckled. 'I run into somebody who used to work for you, Lily Larkin. Joey Robley had a very good word to say about you, too.'

'I've always liked him right back. Joey was an excellent worker. I miss him.' Lily wanted to be sociable but she was desperate to move on to the reason for her visit. Yet first she must offer her condolences.

'Annie told me about the diphtheria, Mrs Skipman. I'm so very sorry about your little girl.'

Pol looked away, blinking rapidly. 'Appreciate yer concern,' she said gruffly. 'And fer what you've let Annie have today.' She put up her chin. 'Now, if you're here to speak about giving Annie a job, I'd be pleased to hear about it.'

'I haven't come for that — sorry. Don't need apprentices.' Lily took a deep breath, aware she had everybody's attention now and they weren't looking as welcoming as they had a moment ago.

333

Eric chucked his boots into the corner. He'd been building up to asking for Joey's old job if it was still going, but obviously that'd be a waste of time.

'I came to ask Annie about her friend Charlie, the little girl who likes pears and has a foster mother. Is her name Charlotte and is she five years old?' Lily waited, barely breathing, for her answer.

'What?' Pol barked, unable to hide her disappointment or her confusion.

'I think I might know her,' Lily said urgently. 'I've been trying to find such a girl, you see, to discover if I might be related to her.'

'I called her Charlie, but her name is Charlotte,' Annie piped up. 'And she is five.'

'What's this kid to you then?' Pol was veering between being intrigued and exasperated. She could see the girl looked emotional. But she'd no use for other people's hard-luck stories; she'd enough of her own. And another to contend with now she knew that Eric was intending to abandon ship and enlist.

Suddenly Lily found herself tongue-tied, not knowing where to start to explain about the tangled threads that connected her to her half-sister. 'My late mum had a baby, a little girl with fair hair . . . I've been looking for her to bring her home,' she rattled off. 'I think she was adopted, or fostered, when she was an infant. I've an idea that I'm not the only person looking for her. The name Mrs Priest has cropped up on occasion when I've been to orphanages to ask questions.'

'No, never heard of a Mrs Priest . . . ' Pol declared, shaking her head.

'I have . . . ' Annie had clapped a hand to her mouth. 'Charlotte told me about Mrs Priest. She called her Vera — she liked her.'

'Yes . . . yes, her name is Vera,' said Lily excitedly.

'Well, if she's the Charlotte you're after, I reckon she'd jump at the chance to be with you, rather than with Mrs Jolley,' Pol said. She hadn't been expecting to see tears glistening in their visitor's eyes and was more disposed to be talkative even if no jobs were in the offing. 'We all felt sorry for the kid, fostered by that woman.' She grimaced her disgust.

'Why d'you say it like that?' Lily croaked. 'Isn't Mrs Jolley very nice?'

'That's an understatement . . .' Eric butted in. He'd put off his usual ritual of immediately stripping off and washing. He didn't want to embarrass himself and be seen in his grimy underwear in front of this lovely young woman. Also, he was as interested as the rest of them in listening carefully to the unfolding tale.

'Is Charlotte known as Charlotte Jolley?'

'She's Charlotte Finch, and her dad's dead,' Annie piped up, keen to be of help. 'She told me he was a soldier who got killed in the war.'

'Was your dad a soldier?' Pol asked.

Lily shook her head, mute with bottled-up happiness. The little girl Vera was searching for, and her sister, were one and the same, she was sure. Lily could feel herself to be close to the end of the chase and wanted to hug each and every member of this family in gratitude.

'What makes you think you've hit on the right Charlotte Finch then?' Pol asked, confused as to how this was all going to work out. There seemed to be a lot of different names getting thrown into the pot.

'I can't be sure yet,' said Lily, eyes gleaming. 'But if the Charlotte you know once lived in Cheapside with her parents and has a birthmark on her chest, then it'll be too much of a coincidence . . . ' Lily stopped talking, having noticed Pol rolling her eyes in amazement.

'Gawd-love-us!' the older woman spluttered. 'Charlotte does have a birthmark. On her chest, right here.' Pol patted herself beneath a breast in demonstration. 'I saw it. Remember, Annie? You saw it 'n' all; it was the first time you brought her here cos she said she wanted to live with us. She had toast 'n' jam and spilled her tea down herself and I pulled up her vest to dry her off.'

Annie nodded vigorously. 'Perhaps she is your little sister,' the girl murmured in awe.

Lily covered her face with her hands, overcome with emotion. 'Thank you . . .'

'Ain't done nothing,' Pol said, and sank down onto a chair, looking stunned.

'You've been kind to her, given her tea . . . and she must like you if she wanted to live here with you.'

'Wish I could've done more to help her.' Pol shook her head. 'What a turn-up. Who'd've thought the two of you might be related.'

'Can't be sure it's the same kid; Charlotte Finch ain't that unusual a name.' Eric put a dampener on it, to try to convince himself more than anything that a wonderful chance for the child hadn't been lost. Frustration was knotting his guts. But for a few weeks in it, the little girl might have been rescued, and what a change in fortune for her it would have been. It was too late, though, and it'd be kinder for Lily Larkin to think she was barking up the wrong tree than beat herself up over missing the little girl by a matter of weeks.

Eric had been to Ma Jolley's old place and broken

in, though — just his luck — it had been too late to put his plan of burgling her into action. Nevertheless, he'd taken a look around. There was no trace of the old dragon having left a farthing behind, or anything else of value. But he had seen something that he knew would convince Lily Larkin that Charlotte was probably the child she was after.

'The birthmark and the fair hair and blue eyes make me reckon it must be her.' Annie sounded obstinate. She wanted to believe in this possibility of happiness for Charlotte and she frowned at Eric for being contrary.

'Where does this Mrs Jolley live? Is it close by? I'll go there now.' Lily was agitatedly pacing, wringing her hands.

'She was living just round the corner until about three weeks ago.' Pol brought herself back into the conversation. 'Then Mrs Jolley moved. One minute she was there, next she weren't, and none of us have got the foggiest idea where she might be now.'

Lily bit her lip to stop herself howling. 'Charlotte wasn't happy, was she?'

'No, she wasn't happy,' Pol said flatly. 'But if she's family of your'n, you can feel proud of her.' A wistful smile was tugging at a corner of her lips as she dwelt on the child who'd crept under her tough old skin. 'She got yer heart without saying or doing much, did Charlotte. She'd look at you with them big blue eyes and you'd want to pick her up and cuddle her. Mournful kid though, like a little stray . . . a little angel she was with her sweet face and fair hair.' Pol wasn't often sentimental, and when she was, it didn't last long. Sentiment was a luxury she could ill afford. She stood up as problems returned to plague her. Tracking down a lost sister wasn't the end of the world in her book. She'd lost her daughter and Clare couldn't be found. Pol knew she might've lost her eldest son too unless she could knock some sense into his head.

'Well, I'd best get on, miss. Sorry we can't help no more'n that. Good luck.' Pol went to the door and opened it.

'Thanks . . . ' Lily knew she was being asked to leave. 'Is it all right if I come back another time, just in case you remember something else?'

'Come back if you like, but you might not find us here. Way things are with me selfish son intending to abandon us all . . . ' Pol glared at Eric, making him turn his head away and shuffle uneasily. 'We'll be heading to the workhouse, cos we'll be evicted when the rent ain't paid.'

'Rent will be paid,' Eric snapped in defeat. 'Got another job on the coal, didn't I? And I've said I'll take it. All right?'

Pol breathed a sigh of relief. Bringing that up in front of a stranger had had the right effect and shamed Eric into staying. He wouldn't go back on his word now. 'So, off you go then, miss,' she turned to Lily. 'Sorry, but I ain't got a clue where Ma Jolley headed to. I can tell you straight, though, she didn't tell a soul in her street what she was up to either. I knocked on doors and asked. Secretive she was — kept very much to herself.'

Lily walked slowly back outside, swallowing back sobs that were threatening to choke her. It seemed fantastical that she'd stumbled across a lead that might have reunited her with her sister on this very day. Yet wicked fate had denied her again, taking her straight into a dead end. Unless she caught up with

338

Mrs Jolley or Vera Priest, she'd never know if she were putting her faith in a lost cause.

'Been keeping an eye on yer van, love.' The woman who'd given her directions to the Skipman's lodging was still outside by the lamppost. 'Little toerags round here would've had it stripped down in no time.' She cocked her head. 'You all right?' She could see Lily had been crying. 'I'll have Pol if she's been a cow to you. You've done us a good turn.'

'No, I'm fine,' Lily said, sniffing. 'I like the family. Just heard some sad news, that's all.'

'Oh, yeah; shame what happened to Pol's little 'un. We was all worried sick about one of our own complaining of a sore throat what with the diphtheria spreading like wildfire . . . Oh, look out; one of her kids is after yer.'

'Oi . . . ' Eric shouted as he loped out of the tenement. He gave a short whistle to gain Lily's attention.

'Right, leave you to it then, and much obliged for the veg.' The woman picked up the empty crate she'd planted a foot on to stop it going walkies, and handed it over.

'D'you want to see the house Charlotte used to live in?' Eric said without preamble on reaching Lily's side. 'It's empty, but I'll show you where it is, if you like.'

'Oh, yes, please. I'd love to go there.' Lily brightened up. She opened the door of the van for him to climb aboard, still covered in coal dust. She opened up the back, stowed the crate, then slammed the doors shut again and hurried round to start the motor and set off.

25

'This is it, miss. Pull over there.' Eric jerked a thumb at the short terrace of houses they were approaching. All had drawn curtains patched with lamplight. Apart from the one on the end. 'It's a dump inside. Stinks to high heaven.' He paused, rubbing a finger beneath his nose as Lily steered slowly to a stop. 'If you hold on a moment I'll go in there and fetch something. I spotted it last time I had a nose around; it didn't seem that important then. Reckon it'll interest you, though.' He sounded rather diffident. He hadn't intended letting on to anybody that he'd broken in to Ma Jolley's place. But he'd given the game away now.

'You can get in?' Lily asked expectantly.

'If I want to . . . '

'I'll come,' Lily immediately said. She didn't care if it was breaking and entering. She wanted to go inside the house where the little girl had lived; if she had come agonisingly close to her sister, she wanted to breathe the same air Charlotte Finch had breathed, even if it was fetid.

'Best if you don't do that, miss. I've got to climb over the fence and get in through a window. Too risky to use a torch. Don't want no neighbours spotting comings and goings and reporting it to the coppers, if you know what I mean.' He grinned, a flash of white in his black face. 'Nobody'll clock me. Didn't last time I had a poke around. Ain't many advantages to being a coalman, but there is that one.' He tapped his sooty hooter and one lively eye disappeared as he winked.

Lily smiled acceptance of his logic; with her pale complexion, and dressed in a skirt, she was hardly an able partner in crime. While she waited for his return she studied the other properties. She was tempted to go and knock on doors and question the neighbours about the woman and the child who'd recently moved out. But she had to give Eric time to return first. And he wasn't long about it.

He certainly knew how to creep around unobserved. She hadn't realised he was back until he slipped quietly onto the seat beside her. He took a rolled-up newspaper from under his arm and held it out. 'Take a look . . . just there . . . ' He tapped the edge of the grimy paper.

Lily quickly found the torch on the dashboard and illuminated the margin, free of newsprint. Charlotte Finch was spelled out in childish block capitals and some numbers had been pencilled there as well. She gazed wide-eyed at Eric.

'Hope you find her and she is the right gel,' he said gruffly. 'She was a good kid.' He made to get out of the van. 'I'm off home to get me ears chewed off by me mother, I expect.'

Lily gripped his arm to stop him. It didn't feel right not to give back something in return for this bitter-sweet development in her search for her sister. 'This means so much to me, I can't properly explain it. Even if it leads nowhere, I want you to take a reward for what you've done.' She found her purse and held out some money.

'Glad to help, and don't want nuthin'. Mum was right about the little 'un: she was lovely and I felt sorry for her.'

Eric sounded self-conscious and turned his head

341

from the temptation of the ten-shilling note.

'Annie said you lost your good job and want to enlist.' Lily stuffed the money into her pocket, feeling ashamed for offering it.

'Yeah . . . ' he sounded defeated. 'Weren't that good a job anyhow. Just fed up with dead-end capers and walking around filthy dirty all the time. Be nice to get out of that pigsty where we live, 'n' all. I reckoned digging trenches and getting army rations couldn't be no worse. But it was selfish, thinking of meself instead of them, 'specially after what happened to Clare.' Eric wished he hadn't sounded so whiney and pushed open the door. 'No need to run me back. 'S'only a short walk. G'night, miss.'

'Might be able to help,' Lily said, grabbing his arm again, careless of the muck transferring to her fingers from his oily donkey jacket.

He hesitated and turned his head.

'D'you know how to drive?'

'Been drivin' 'orse 'n' cart since I was twelve.'

'How about a van like this?'

He looked baffled then his gaze quickly roved the van's interior. 'Soon learn . . . '

Lily saw the spark of wonder in his eyes as he closed the van door and turned fully to face her. It was a leap of faith for her, but she was taking it; it felt right. 'I need a foreman. Somebody reliable and trustworthy. Got to be strong, too, and good at bartering with wholesalers. The housewives like a bit of sweet talking . . . a joke and a compliment even when you might not feel like it. Are you up to all of that?'

'I can do all of that,' Eric said hoarsely. 'Swear I can.' He jerked his head in emphasis.

'How about rising at the crack of dawn every day

except Sundays, in the freezing cold and pelting rain and chasing a tarpaulin down the road when the wind whips it off the stall?'

'Ain't a problem for somebody who can't sleep the night through anyhow, and sits on a cart getting drenched, and loses empty sacks when it's blowin' a gale,' he countered, tugging down his cap to shield a glitter of wishful tears.

'In that case, pay's fifteen bob a week to start and I'll give you a two-week trial. To see how it goes.'

Eric blinked in wonder. He got ten bob at present. 'Do I get me cotchel of veg and me haddock and me bunce and me lodgin' thrown in?' he whispered.

Lily chuckled. 'You have been talking to Joey, haven't you?'

He nodded, mute with anticipation as a silence lengthened between them.

'Job's yours then, perks 'n' all.' Lily stuck out a hand and Eric immediately grabbed it and shook it. 'Know where Wilding's depot is, do you?'

He quivered his head, indicating he did.

'Start the Monday after you finish up with your present guv'nor, if that suits?'

He nodded again, and sniffed.

'Our present foreman is joining up. Smudger's nearly nineteen and his boots are going to be hard for anybody to fill, especially for a person who's not a costermonger. Before he sails, he should have some time to show you the ropes: take you round Spitalfields and Billingsgate markets where we buy our stock. He might give you a few driving lessons too, if you play your cards right with him. Listen to everything he says; you won't find a better teacher. I'll help you too, and Margie's the clerk, and a dab hand at paperwork.

She'll let you know what she expects of you in providing daily chitties when you've been out buying. You'll like her.'

'I will . . . I'll like all of you. And I'll learn faster than you think. Fast as I need to. I'll be the best coster-monger ever. Swear on me life. Can I go and tell me mum now?'

'Yeah, go and tell them all,' she said softly. Just as he was about to hop down, Lily stopped him. 'This Mrs Jolley — what does she look like, Eric? Never know, I might just bump into her by chance.'

Eric grimaced. 'You'll know if you do. She's a bit like an undertaker's dummy. Dresses all in black with a black hat pulled down low. Ugly old cow she is. Me mum's nearly forty and Ma Jolley looks at least ten years older than her.'

'Thanks,' Lily said, though it was depressing to think of any child living with such a foster mother. But looks weren't everything. Lily knew she had to cling to some hope that she would find her sister well, if not happy.

She sat quietly for a while after Eric had dashed off. She had her new foreman: just like that. And if anybody had told her he'd be an inexperienced youth who broke into houses, she'd have told them they were nuts.

But she had a good feeling about Eric Skipman, though she'd no idea why. He was fifteen — far too young . . . But she'd been fifteen when she'd started at Wilding's and she'd said more or less the same thing to her new boss, as Eric had just promised her: I'll learn; you watch me make you proud of me. And she had. And every minute of every day she'd loved Gregory Wilding more for putting trust in her, and for the

344

kindness and wisdom he'd lavished on her, even when she'd not recognised those things as such.

She picked up the newspaper Eric had brought out of the house to show her. She read the name again, tracing the misshapen letters with her finger. Then she placed her lips against the childish writing. Mrs Jolley couldn't have been all bad as a foster mother if she'd taught Charlotte to write her name. Her attention was suddenly arrested by a woman opening her front door and letting a cat out to pad away into the shadows. On the spur of the moment, and before the woman had a chance to disappear, Lily jumped down and trotted over.

'Just wondered if you knew where your old neighbour moved to?' she blurted. 'I wanted to speak to Mrs Jolley about something important.'

The woman looked surprised to be suddenly accosted on her doorstep, but did stop to speak to Lily. 'That old girl kept to herself. Never even knew she was moving. Just saw her heading off.' She crossed her arms. 'Landlord didn't know she was going either. He asked me the same question as you; he wanted to speak to her about something important. Seemed she owed him rent. I wouldn't have let on to that old miser, though, even if I'd known where she'd skipped to.'

An idea struck Lily and she blurted, 'Did she hire a removal truck?' If Mrs Jolley had engaged a company, they'd have an address to track her down.

'Her? Ma Jolley?' The woman snorted in derision. 'Likes of her wouldn't part with good money to a removal firm. When I say I saw her heading off, I mean pushing a pram with stuff loaded on it. Good riddance too. Glad to see the back of her. Strange one she was.'

'Was Charlotte — her foster daughter — with her when she left?'

'Yeah . . . little girl was sitting on the pram. Didn't look well, the poor kid. Didn't look well at all. Flushed in the face like she had a fever . . .'

'Shut that bleedin' door, there's a draught cutting me legs off,' bellowed a rough male voice from within the house.

'Sorry, don't know no more than that,' the woman said and went inside, closing the door.

Lily trudged back to the van and got in, her elation evaporating. In a way she wished she'd not spoken to the neighbour and had remained in blissful ignorance of that alarming information. Charlotte Finch had recently been in the home of people infected with diphtheria. Now the child wasn't looking well and was flushed with fever. If she'd picked up diphtheria, Lily prayed to God that she was stronger than Clare Skipman, and would fight the illness and win. Whether her sister or not, she already felt a bond to little Charlotte Finch, and desperately wanted the child to thrive and be happy.

* * *

'How's the new recruit shaping up?'

'Doing all right, I'd say.' Smudger thoughtfully stroked his chin. 'Van might need a new gearbox though, once he's finished crashing around in it. Then if he can stop steering round corners like he's pulling on an 'orse's reins, the kid should be ready to be let loose out there.'

'Ain't doing that bad,' Eric protested with a grin. He knew Smudger was just teasing him. Before

346

they'd entered the warehouse a few minutes ago, he'd received a pat on the back and praise for the way he'd parked up neatly at the kerb. Eric accepted he was still a bit cack-handed, and he did pull back on the steering wheel when braking as though he was reining old Nelly in. Old habits died hard, he supposed. But he was keen to be of use to his new boss, and to show his gratitude for this smashing opportunity. After his work was finished for the day, he stayed on from choice, simply to learn everything he could about his new profession. When Margie had the time to spare, she would get out her files from the cabinet and explain about invoices and order sheets so he'd understand the different accountancy terms and spot if merchants weren't giving him the correct paperwork at the markets. As for Lily, she'd taken him on the Chrisp Street pitch with her, introducing him to regular customers as her new foreman. Eric had swelled up with pride, even when some of the housewives who knew his mother had eyed Lily as though she must be bonkers. Eric had fretted that his boss might regret hiring him over those sorts of reactions, and sack him at the end of his trial period. But she hadn't. She'd let all the snide looks and comments slide, like water off a duck's back; and the customers kept coming back. In dribs and drabs they had stopped loitering in the background until Lily was free and had started to let Eric serve them instead of constantly avoiding his eager eyes. They watched Pol Skipman's son like hawks, though, sometimes demanding he weigh out their veg again, to convince themselves they'd not been diddled. In fact, Eric was so cock-a-hoop with every aspect of his job that getting a bit of bunce on top of his wages was the last thing on his mind. For now.

'We've got time for a cuppa before we close up for the day,' Lily said. She'd been sitting with Margie, going through the day's takings. They were up, as was to be expected, this close to Christmas. Families were buying extra, preserving fruit and making pickles and puddings and cakes for the year's big feast.

'I'll go without me tea. I'll tidy the back of the van before I go home,' Eric said. 'Be off like a whippet in the morning then.'

Lily knew Eric liked to sit behind the wheel and familiarise himself with the instruments and practise on the pedals even when the vehicle wasn't running. He'd sooner do that than have his tea break with the 'adults'. There were only a few years separating them all in age, but Lily understood that there was rather a barrier between the novice and the old-timers.

'Honest opinion, Smudger. D'you reckon Eric'll come up to scratch?' Lily asked after the boy had gone outside and she was putting the kettle on to boil. She thought the lad was doing well. But Smudger was the one supervising him most of the time. Lily valued her foreman's opinion. He was fair and would tell her the truth, and there was nothing about being a coster-monger that he didn't know.

'He's cottoned on to driving quicker than I did when the guv'nor taught me.' Smudger found the biscuit tin on the shelf and put it on Margie's desk where she was finishing up the accounts. He helped himself to a digestive, continuing between chews, 'And he's good at mental arithmetic. He cottoned on straight away to one of the merchants at Spitalfields overcharging us. I did too; the crafty bleeder didn't get away with that one.'

'I've noticed he's very strong,' Margie chipped in.

'He was stacking those iron poles up as though they were made of balsa wood.'

'Comes from humping hundredweights of coal all day long; that ain't easy,' Smudger said. 'Eric could do with a sidekick, though; another youngster to set up the pitch while he's doing the buying and driving.'

'Wish I could drive,' said a wistful Margie, without looking up or losing her place totting up figures.

'No reason why you can't,' Smudger replied. 'You've got enough strength in them hands and elbows of yours to steer and use a gearstick. You need your feet as much as your fingers to drive. Just take it slow and easy. I'll teach you if you like when I'm back on leave.' He took the mug of tea Lily was holding out to him. 'You could take a turn round the compound to start, before we go out on the road.'

Margie was gazing at him with an intensely fond expression. 'Thanks . . . ' she said. 'If anyone can show me, I reckon it's you, Smudge.'

Lily was delighted that Margie was gaining so much in confidence. At one time her friend would have shied away from attempting such a thing, believing it beyond her capabilities. But she was blossoming and Lily knew it was thanks to Smudger's influence rather than hers. She discreetly watched them as their entwined gazes exchanged a depth of trust that surpassed friendship.

Lily's secret bound her to people she barely knew, let alone could count on. But it was in none of their interests to ever disclose what they knew about Harriet Fox's fatal accident.

Since the Scullys had been off the scene, Margie and Smudger had grown closer, yet Claudette's ghost seemed to be a wedge between them, preventing

349

platonic love turning into passion. And that saddened Lily. She knew Margie wanted to be so much more than Smudger's pal; but she didn't want to talk about it. They were still best friends, but Smudger had taken prime spot in Margie's life now. Lily was glad about that . . . relieved too, since Greg had filled her heart to overflowing.

★ ★ ★

'Oi, Skipman. What d'you think you're doing here? You'd better stop messin' around with our van.'

Eric had been in the process of coiling up a rope around his bent arm when he'd heard his name being barked out. He grinned, having recognised Joey Robley by the light of the naphtha flare bracketed on the gate. The younger boy speeded up, striding onto the forecourt swinging his arms, as though to accuse the youth of stealing.

'Could ask you what you're doing here.' Eric lobbed the coil of rope onto the pile he'd already neatened then sauntered over to meet him. 'You finished your bike round early today then?'

'Yeah, I have. What about you? No coal to deliver?' Joey had just twigged that he'd got the wrong end of the stick and the older boy had a right to be here. His hopes withered of getting his job back. That was it then; his chance had gone. It was his own fault, too, for bragging about what a good thing he'd had at Wilding's. This tyke had jumped straight into his empty boots. And who could blame him?

'Packed in me coal round since Lily Larkin offered me the foreman's job. Smudger's joined up and I'm doing me apprenticeship, learning the ropes off him

350

while I've got the chance. He's off soon.' Eric tried not to sound as though he was crowing, but it was difficult. He was still so buoyant about his advancement that he told everybody he could about it. So did his mother and sister. The whole family had benefited, and thus they were all equally scared their good fortune might suddenly disintegrate. His mother appreciated the free veg and the haddock, and without a hint of irony constantly told Eric he'd better keep his fingers out of the till, and work hard, or she'd want to know why.

The extra housekeeping he contributed had started Pol talking about finding better digs, even though they had more room since her eldest had started lodging with Smudger. Now her nerves were more settled, Pol had cut down on her drinking, and was looking presentable enough to apply for charring work. She'd already secured one client but had surprised them all, saying she'd take on another. She was no longer nagging at Annie to quit school either. Eric was fretting that a spoke was about to be put in the works, bringing his world crashing down. The younger lad had turned up with a purpose in mind, and he didn't look at all happy to see Eric settling in, spouting about being top dog.

Joey's jaw was hanging open in astonishment. He hadn't expected promotion himself: getting his old street round back, and the perks that came with it, would have been enough. He felt intensely jealous of Eric but was trying not to show it.

'So what you been up to? Had any more runins with them barrow boys?' Eric attempted to be friendly. He'd liked Joey straight off but he could tell Joey didn't feel the same way about him any more.

'What's it to you? And I already knew that Smudger was quitting to go to war,' Joey spat. 'He was a good pal of mine, so I've come over to wish him good luck.'

'He's all right, is Smudger,' Eric agreed. 'I lodge with him now. Be on me own once he's gone though.' He could see that he was making things worse, so he shut up.

'Bully fer you!' Joey snarled, and pushed past towards the warehouse, unable to hold in his resentment a second longer.

Eric stayed where he was and carried on stacking pallets and neatening tarpaulins, brooding on what was happening inside. Margie and Smudger came out and said their goodnights then carried on up the road together. Eric expected Joey to reappear. But he didn't. Eric closed the van doors and, heavy of heart, went inside to see if he'd been ousted. Joey Robley was an experienced costermonger and Lily Larkin had said she liked him and missed him as an excellent colleague. Eric reckoned the lad's tale about coming to see Smudger was by the by; Joey was really here to get work.

'Thought you'd already gone home, Eric.' Lily glanced at him then continued filling a sack with left-over potatoes brought back from the market.

'Nah, not yet; just locked the van up. Going off now.' He dropped the keys onto the desk.

'Joey was just telling me about that day you helped him out when the gang started on him.'

'Bunch of idiots, they were.' He grinned at Joey but got little response.

Lily handed Joey the bag of potatoes. 'Your mum's welcome to that lot. I would've taken it home for supper but Marge and me said we might treat ourselves to a bit of fish and chips for a change.' Lily could sense an atmosphere between the lads and reckoned she could guess the cause of it. Joey had always been a polite and sociable lad but he hadn't just come to tell Smudger to keep his head down in France. 'How's it going at Hobson's? Last time I came in, I didn't spot you serving behind the counter.'

'Never get to go on the shop floor,' Joey said sourly. 'They've got me on the bike all day long. I'm just a delivery boy, though the boss said it'd be a proper apprenticeship, leading to better things.'

'Nice to be out in the fresh air, though,' Lily suggested.

'Not when the heavens open, it's not, or monkeys are chucking spuds at you,' Joey muttered.

'You used to do your barrow round in all weathers. And that lot have always been a pain in the backside.'

'That was different,' Joey said. 'I liked me job back then . . .' He clammed up, feeling emotional. 'Better get off now. Thanks, miss. Mum'll appreciate the extra spuds.'

'I'm short-staffed . . . what with Fanny and now Smudger deserting me. So if you were thinking of coming back, you'd be doing me a favour. Save me advertising.' That stopped Joey in his tracks. 'Eric's picking things up quickly but he's still new at it and could do with an old hand with him.' Lily watched as the two youths locked eyes, summing up the situation. 'I only need one foreman. Eric's older, and he's well on the way to being able to drive now, and buy at the markets. But he can't do everything. You can have first refusal, Joey, on being his right-hand man. I'd like an answer by the end of the week, if that's all right.'

It wasn't a made-up job, or a sop to keep the peace between two lads she liked. Before Joey had turned up, Lily had been discussing business with Smudger and Margie. Even with the street round out of action, four staff were needed to keep the stall and the warehouse running smoothly. Wilding's still had a few early-morning hire customers, although that side of the business was nothing like it used to be. In its heyday, back when Greg had been in charge, and before the war depleted the amount of men and barrows on the streets, business had been booming. Her first job on the firm had been dealing with navvies at the crack of dawn, filling out their chitties for costermonger equipment, and taking their cash. Recalling those days — when she'd been fresh from the workhouse — always made her feel nostalgic. She'd turn back the clock in an instant to have her brother and Gregory Wilding back here, drinking tea with her as the sun rose, while in the background Smudger and Fred Jenkins argued the toss.

'I'd like to take the job, thanks, miss.' Joey had quickly realised that getting his perks and independence back would compensate for having Eric Skipman lording it over him. Much as he loved his mum and his younger brothers, he was fifteen next birthday. He felt stifled and wanted to go back to sharing digs with a pal so he could have a smoke and a drink and a lark-about. 'Just need to have a word with me mum. But reckon she'll be all right about it. She's been disappointed with the way things turned out at Hobson's. I'll put me notice in. Just got the Cheapside round to do tomorrow . . . '

'I was doing my Cheapside run when I first saw you,' Eric piped up, glad he and Joey seemed to be back on an even keel. More about that particular day infiltrated his mind. 'Gawd!' he exclaimed, and slapped his forehead. 'Just thought of something. I didn't just see Joey that day. When I was heading back to the depot to load up with coal, I spotted Ma Jolley talking to a woman on the doorstep. What with Clare passing away and all the rest going on at home, it completely slipped me mind.' He groaned in regret. 'Sorry, miss, I should've said, cos I know you're keen to find out these things.'

'You've just remembered that you saw Mrs Jolley living in Cheapside?' Lily asked excitedly.

Eric shook his head. 'No . . . this was before she moved out, while she was still living round the corner to us. She was knocking on somebody's door, visiting. A woman opened up and spoke to her on the step. That's all I saw. Didn't take that much notice at the time. But I do know the address of the place cos I'd delivered coke to that house a few months back.' He rushed to the desk and picked up a pencil and paper and started scribbling. 'That's where I saw her.'

26

'I do remember the person you mean, Miss Larkin. She wasn't somebody you could easily forget, you see.' The woman grimaced in distaste.

'You found her unpleasant then?'

'Oh, she was civil enough, but very odd . . . shifty, to my mind. You confused me at first, asking after a Mrs Jolley. She told me her name was Mrs Jones; now you've described her appearance and explained you're seeking Charlotte Finch, I reckon that Jones and Jolley are one and the same. Like you, she was interested in finding out where the people next door had gone.' The woman pursed her lips. 'Individuals who use aliases don't usually have a decent reason for doing so, do they?'

Lily sighed an agreement. The more she learned about Mrs Jolley, the more anxious for Charlotte's wellbeing she became. Why would Charlotte's foster mother want to disguise her identity?

Lily had immediately set out for Cheapside after Eric had given her directions to the house Mrs Jolley had visited. The villa was set in a side road, but people were returning home from work, taking an interest in the conversing women.

There were so many questions to ask that Lily would sooner talk in private, than on the doorstep after dark.

'Might I just come in to talk? It is important that I find the family that lived there.' Lily looked at the attached premises, where a faint glow could be seen in an upstairs window.

'Sorry, but I've things to do.' The woman glanced over her shoulder. 'My mother's an invalid, you see.' She wasn't going to tell a stranger that the woman was gaga and drove her up the wall. 'Oh . . . they don't know anything about their predecessors.' She'd seen the direction of her caller's gaze. 'That Jolley woman knocked there first, to no avail. That house was vacant for months after they moved out. Then the landlord rented it again.'

'Have you any idea where I might find Mrs Jolley? She's Charlotte Finch's foster mother, and it's likely the child is my sister. I've been looking for her for a long while.'

'You're little Charlotte's sister? You're the major's daughter?' The woman goggled in astonishment. 'When I mentioned Charlotte to that Jolley character, she ignored a question about the child's whereabouts. Yet you say she has custody of the girl?' She tutted in disgust. 'Peculiar woman! She didn't leave her address and I wouldn't have wanted it, anyway. I knew she was deceitful.' She turned a speculative look on Lily. 'You've lost your father in the war, then, you poor thing. Such a smart, handsome fellow, Major Beresford . . .'

'He isn't my father. I've no idea who Major Beresford is,' Lily quickly said, before matters got really confused. The woman appeared to be inwardly ruminating on who her mother might be. 'If I am related to Charlotte, we'd be half-sisters. That's what I'm trying to find out, you see.'

'I imagine you're on the right track, dear. Otherwise it's all a very odd coincidence, wouldn't you say? Vera Priest was a nice soul; now I know more about that Jolley woman, I believe she was a liar. Vera wasn't her friend, as she claimed.'

Lily also believed that Mrs Jolley was a liar, but not about having had some sort of relationship to the women. She might have wanted to renew her acquaintance with Betsy Finch and Vera Priest to give the child back to them. A foster mother might resent being burdened with a gravely ill child. The only bright spot Lily had in all of this was knowing pieces of the puzzle were slotting into place; she mustn't let her imaginings about Charlotte's health depress her. She'd made progress, although not enough. A wall was about to spring up ahead to — yet again — thwart her in finding her sister. By the time she had all the information she needed, it might be too late for Charlotte. After all the child had been through, it seemed beyond cruel for her to succumb to disease now.

'Did Major Beresford live next door?' It seemed odd he was known as Charlotte's father rather than a Mr Finch.

'Oh, no. Stanley Beresford didn't live there. He was married and visited Betsy, if you know what I mean.' The woman gave Lily an old-fashioned look. 'And perhaps I've said enough now. Doesn't do to cast aspersions on the memory of a war hero who can't defend himself. After he was killed in France, the women moved out of next door. And that's all I know. The more I hear about it, the more it seems rather a tangle. Perhaps that's why Miss Finch and Mrs Priest kept quiet about where they were off to. None of us neighbours knew they were boarding the child out.'

'So you've no idea where I might find any of them.' Lily sighed glumly.

The woman clucked her tongue in sympathy. She'd

taken to the girl and didn't like to see her looking miserable. She believed Lily Larkin had been completely honest in all she'd said, unlike Jolley. 'All I know is that Betsy Finch was on her uppers after the major stopped coming. To be blunt, she needed another man like him. I'd say she didn't find one. I saw her just once afterwards and she looked a sorry mess.' She cocked her head reflectively. 'Vera was a nicer class of woman, though she was the servant. She went to work as a domestic in a country house out in the sticks. She never said where it was, though.' A crashing sound came from within as though somebody had taken a tumble. 'That's Mother. I'd better get on. She wants her tea.'

'Might I leave my address with you? If you bump into either of them, would you tell them I'm looking for Charlotte Finch?' Lily started talking faster as the woman retreated into her hallway. 'Mrs Priest has searched for Charlotte in the past. I hope she hasn't given up just as Mrs Jolley wants to contact her. It must be about Charlotte. What else would they have in common?'

The woman stretched out a hand for the business card Lily was profferring. 'I don't mind helping, if possible. But don't get your hopes up, dear.' She could see the girl was upset, and gave her a smile before she hurried inside.

'Thank you . . . Merry Christmas for next week,' Lily said to a closed door.

★ ★ ★

Lily had driven back to Poplar to find the two lads were still in the warehouse. They were squatting either

359

side of an upturned crate, used as a card table, and seemed to be good pals once more.

'I thought you'd both be long gone. You can always lock up and take the keys to my lodging, you know. Just leave them with Margie. You don't have to wait if I'm late back.'

'We wasn't in a rush to go,' Eric said. 'Thought we'd just hang on and have a few games of rummy in the meantime.' A sweep of his palm collected the cards then he stood up, idly shuffling them. 'No luck finding out where Ma Jolley's gone, then?' His boss looked fed up and he could guess the reason why. He felt downcast too; he longed for Charlotte to be found and get the better life she deserved.

'No new leads,' Lily confirmed. 'Never mind . . . something will turn up to point me in the right direction eventually.' It was kind of them to hang about for her but she wanted to be on her own to mull it all over and weep a little bit. A new name had been learned from her visit: Major Stanley Beresford. She accepted he couldn't be of much help as he was dead. But any background information was fascinating, helping her build a picture of Charlotte's infancy. 'You two should be on your way. Don't want your mums thinking me a slave-driver.'

Joey pocketed his few coppers in winnings. 'I'm off home to break the good news about me job.'

After the boys had gone, Lily sat at the desk staring into space. She must concentrate on the positive and not get discouraged, or ever give up her search. Determined to cheer up, she helped herself to a digestive biscuit from the tin. In a few minutes she would lock up and head home for a fish-and-chip supper. She'd tell Margie all about her disappointment. She needed her best friend's comforting arms about her, and some pithy advice to stop her wallowing. Then tomorrow Lily knew it would all seem better and she'd be eager to start again with fresh ideas.

She glanced about at the neatly stowed coster-monger's paraphernalia, illuminated by a couple of oil lamps hanging from hooks on timber posts. Each evening everything was cleaned and put back in its place ready for use the following day. They worked efficiently together as a team, even though Greg wasn't around to keep them all on their toes. Lily was proud that standards hadn't slipped in his absence. There was nothing much they could do about tak-ings being on the slide; merchant vessels importing produce were constantly coming under enemy attack and shortages were becoming commonplace. But this warehouse was her little domain . . . more of a sanc-tuary to her than the basement flat. Here, Gregory Wilding was everywhere she looked and touched. His essence seemed to have seeped into the very timbers and the apple-scented atmosphere. She could close her eyes and hear him laugh . . . shout . . . as he often had at the lads, for larking about when they should've been working. At her too, on the occasions they'd crossed swords . . .

Lily heard the door creak and imagined one of the lads had come back, having forgotten something. She carried on daydreaming about the man she loved, and nibbling at the digestive.

'You not got a welcome home for your brother then?'

'Davy!' Lily breathed, too shocked to swallow the biscuit drying on her tongue. She sprang to her feet, gulping it down and choking. 'Oh, Davy . . . '

361

she repeated hoarsely, cupping her face and starting to cry. This excitement on top of her rushed visit to Cheapside was overwhelming.

'Thought you'd be pleased to see me.' He strolled closer and dropped his kitbag to draw her against his uniformed chest. 'I'm back for Christmas, Lil.'

She hugged him tightly, pressing a kiss to his cheek, tasting his salty, stubbly skin and feeling the night air on him chilling her lips.

'Why didn't you write and let me know you'd be home?' she demanded. 'I'd've got a proper welcome ready for you.'

'Didn't know meself till a few days ago. Platoon just got notification we was all getting leave. I wasn't about to argue.' He spun them both round with a whoop. 'It's what we all hope for: passage back to Blighty for Christmas. Lady Luck smiled on me, Lil. How about that!' He let her find her feet and steady herself against the desk while he looked around, grinning. 'Old place doesn't change much, does it?'

She shook her head, still drinking in the sight of him, clinging on to his khaki-clad arm as he would have slipped free. They'd always been two peas in a pod, with their chestnut-brown hair, bluest of eyes and fairest of complexions. But she could see they were less alike now. Her twin looked older than her. His hair was short and spiky, a dark fuzz, his eyes still a deep blue. They were both seventeen, but above his cheekbones were pale creases, radiating towards his temples, where foreign elements had weather-beaten extra years and tiredness into him. He was still handsome, but his youthfulness had vanished.

'Ain't 'arf missed you, Lil,' he said flatly. 'And Smudger. Where is the shirker? Knocked off early?'

'He's joined up . . . soon you'll be seeing more of him than I do.'

''Bout time too,' Davy chortled. 'He would've got his call-ups soon anyhow, way things are going.'

'Don't say that,' Lily pleaded. 'I want you all back for good in the New Year.'

''S'what all of us want 'n' all, now we've had a taste of it over there.' Davy regretted coming out with that. Tommies had it drummed into them that the folks back home mustn't be alarmed with too much truth. He adored his sister and didn't want to worry her. 'Right then . . .' He fondly chucked her under the chin. 'How about a cup of tea? Any biscuits left in that tin? Then later you can take me out and treat me to a nice big slap-up, Lil. Cos I'm brassick, y'know. Spent all me pay before we embarked at Calais . . . in the boulangerie.' He swanked to and fro, twirling an imaginary moustache, for having used a foreign word. 'Cor, they don't 'arf do smashing cakes, them Frenchies. I was bringing you a cream eclair, but me belly never stopped grumbling and I ended up eating it. I've not even got a fag left to me name.' He threw his empty cigarette packet into the wastebin in disgust, then started rummaging in the desk drawers. 'Smudger left any Woodbines in here, has he?'

Lily started to laugh; she laughed and laughed with sheer joy and gratitude for the gift of his company. However mature he looked, he was still her Davy of old. He was scrounging . . . just as he always did. 'Oh, welcome home, Davy.' She flung herself into his surprised embrace, hugging him tightly, the disappointment of her visit to Cheapside already receding from her mind. 'I've so much to tell you. This is going

363

to be such a wonderful Christmas now you're back where you belong.'

Epilogue

February 1916

'Please talk to me and tell me what's up. I want to help you.'

'Nothing's up. I must've eaten a dodgy bit of fish, that's all.' Margie was folded over at the middle as though with bellyache. She straightened her back and put the bowl on her lap down by the side of the bed she was perched on. 'You'll have to tell Eric to stop buying off that merchant. I thought the last lot of bloater tasted off.'

'What about the lot before that? And the lot before that?' Lily stepped closer, her expression grave. She had been making her breakfast when she'd heard her friend vomiting through the closed door. The girl had felt unwell every morning this week.

Margie used a handkerchief on her lips, and a foot to shift the sick bowl further away, out of sight.

Lily sat down beside her white-faced friend, still dressed in her nightie. 'Why won't you tell me you're in the family way, Margie?' she said softly. 'We've been friends all these years and you won't tell me something as important as that.'

'You're wrong, that's why . . .'

Margie made to get up but Lily hung on to her arm, drawing her back down. 'I'm not wrong. Not long ago we were fetching Fanny bowls when she felt queasy first thing. I haven't forgotten it, and I know you haven't either.'

Margie turned her head. 'You'd better get off to work. I'll come in later when me belly's settled.'

'Stay home. I'll do the books when I get back from the market; there's not so much to log these days. It won't take long.' Lily paused. 'But I'm not going anywhere till we sort this out.' Lily had known for over a week now that her friend was pregnant. At first she hadn't twigged that Margie being off-colour was more than tummyache. But she'd clued up now, and made sense of why her best friend was looking fuller in the face and figure. Lily feared she already knew why Margie had been trying to hide her condition, even from her best friend. She couldn't bear to face the truth, or to utter the name of the baby's father.

They'd entered adolescence together as workhouse girls, starved of normal family life, yet dreaming of knights in shining armour giving them wedding rings and children. Now they were women in the real world and knew what all women knew: there was a dark side to desire that made beasts of men. And not all stories had happy endings.

'There's nothing to sort out. And there's nothing for you to worry about.' Margie had taken a deep breath to quell her rolling guts. She wriggled free of Lily's embrace and stood up. Usually she'd take care to disguise her rounded figure but she forgot to do so and the thin cotton of her nightie clung to the small bump.

'It's starting to show, Margie,' Lily said. 'Is it Smudger's?' She couldn't keep a desperately wishful note from her voice.

Margie didn't answer but her bitter expression said it all. She started pulling a brush through her sleep-tangled hair. 'Feel all right now. I'll be fit for

366

work soon. You go on, and I'll catch up.'

'Fancy a cup of tea, or a bit of toast?'

'Not right now . . . bit later p'raps,' Margie said. She dropped the hairbrush and stood still. Suddenly she crouched down at the bowl.

Lily kneeled beside her, holding her long fair hair away from her face. 'When's it due?' she asked when Margie had finished retching.

Margie slowly shook her head. 'Dunno, can't work it out,' she said in defeat. 'Missed two monthlies already.'

'Fanny'll know how to work it out.' Lily helped Margie to her feet. 'We could go over and see how she's doing in Islington at the weekend and —'

'No! She'll ask questions. Ain't telling nobody the truth. Ever.' Margie wiped her mouth again.

'You want to get rid of it?' Lily understood why Margie might want to.

'No . . . I'm keeping it. Always wanted a baby, somebody to love who'd love me back. So that's that, I'm keeping it.'

'You didn't want Rory Scully's baby though, did you?' Lily said quietly.

'Ain't the poor little mite's fault who its father is.'

'I'm so sorry, Margie.' Her friend hadn't needed to utter his name to confirm Lily's worst fears.

'Just my luck, eh? Smudger's never even kissed me properly, yet I'd get into bed with him any time he asked.'

'If you're keeping it, you might be as big as a house by the time he comes back on leave. Can't pretend it's colic then.' Lily paused. 'Will you write and let him know?'

'No!' Margie looked taken aback at the very idea.

'And don't you either!'

'I wouldn't, Marge. But you won't be able to hide it if he turns up unexpectedly, like Davy did at Christmas. Could be Smudger will walk in on you when you're close to your time.'

'Already thought of that. I'll tell him I had a fling with somebody . . . if he wants to know, that is. He might not be interested, if he's found himself a girl over there.'

'Of course he'll ask who's got you pregnant,' Lily exclaimed. 'Anyway, he'll guess, love.'

'Don't care if he does; I'm done with bothering with what he thinks. And I'm done with waiting for him to see me as more than his pal with crippled hands.' Margie put up her chin in defiance. 'Sod everybody, that's what I think. I'll move away from here and raise the baby on me own. I'll say me husband's been killed in the war . . . like all the others do when they get knocked up. Brass curtain ring on me finger and nobody'll be the wiser that it ain't a war baby.'

'You'll know the truth, Margie. So will Smudger. He's not daft — '

'He damn well is!' Margie angrily burst out. 'Oh, yes, he is!' she stormed, to stop Lily defending him. 'He's still mooning over a dead woman who didn't even want him anyway. Claudette was about to run off with the bloke she really loved. And Smudger knows it. She didn't love him; she was a deceitful cow, just using him.'

Lily couldn't deny any of that. She felt tears sting her eyes. Of all the vile, rotten things to happen! Sweet, lovely Margie was carrying her rapist's baby, and she wanted to keep it. Lily didn't blame her for one minute; if she herself were ever in such an awful situation,

368

she'd probably choose the same course of action. She put an arm round Margie to calm her and stop her pacing agitatedly to and fro.

'Come and sit down; you should rest. You'll make yourself throw up again.'

Margie suddenly turned to Lily, seeking comfort. 'It's just a baby, Lil,' she sobbed. 'And I'll love it, no matter what.'

'I know you will; you'll be the best mum ever. Better even than Fanny, you'll see,' Lily crooned.

'Promise you won't tell anybody. It's only you and Greg and Smudger know what that stinking pig did to me.' Margie shook her head. 'Don't want anybody else to know. Can't let anybody guess I'm carrying his child. You will keep it secret, won't you, Lil?' She paused. 'It's still early on. When I was at that cathouse, one of Gladys's girls lost her baby. Gladys said she had a miscarriage . . . so I know it can happen. If it did, nobody would be the wiser.'

'Hush . . . no need to think of that now. And 'course I'll keep quiet. You know you don't need to ask me that.' She planted a kiss on Margie's forehead, using her thumbs to wipe away her friend's tears. 'I'll help in any way I can . . . whatever you decide to do.' She held Margie back from her, to tease, 'You'll need a few roomy clothes before long.' Her friend's blossoming bosom was straining her nightie's buttons.

Margie's lips twitched in a sad smile and she let Lily lead her back to sit on the bed. 'Why's my life such a bloody mess, Lil? Why am I like a magnet for all the bad and horrible things out there?'

'I know it's not fair and damned awful luck, but you'll get over this. Just like you got over what that brute did to you.' Lily sank to her knees in front of

Margie, taking her hands in hers and squeezing them tightly. 'Scully's dead and good riddance. This baby's all yours. He can't ever come and try to interfere. So what if you're not married? You're not on your own . . . that's the thing. You just remember you've got all of us: me 'n' Greg and Fanny and Smudger. He out of all of us will be there for you,' Lily said firmly, having heard Margie's dubious snort. 'We're all here, and got your back, cos we all know that you'll do the same for us when our times get tough.'

'D'you think it will have a hand like this?' Solemnly, Margie examined her deformed fingers.

'Your baby'll be a beauty. And I'll be proud as punch to be the godmother. You will ask me, won't you, Marge?' Lily sounded wistfully serious. 'I know Greg'd like to be godfather, if that's not being too forward of us.'

'I was going to ask Smudger to be godfather,' said Margie with a diffident glance at Lily. 'D'you reckon he'll want to?'

Lily thought about that. 'Well, I reckon Smudger'll have his hands full just being the baby's dad. So better wait and see how things turn out when he gets back home.'

★ ★ ★

Eric was now a capable driver and regularly took the van out on his own. He and Joey were firm pals, growing in confidence, without becoming unbearably cocky. They were sharp enough at mental arithmetic to deal with customers without Lily supervising them. By dinner time she had decided to leave them to it on the Chrisp Street pitch and return to the warehouse to see if Margie was there. Her best friend had been constantly on her mind.

Lily found the premises still locked up, and there was no sign of her friend having been in. Lily hoped Margie was feeling better, in body and mind. Margie had a lot of thinking to do, and perhaps a difficult letter to write.

Waiting until Smudger got back to break the news to him would brew trouble, Lily was sure of that. She'd watched the couple part company on his last day at work. Even a blind man could've seen that Smudger adored Margie. Lily was starting to think that Fanny had been right months ago when saying he needed a kick up the backside to make him acknowledge what was staring him in the face.

Lily opened the desk and got out the ledgers and files she needed. Before settling down to work, she lit the Primus and the paraffin heater to warm the place up. The icy dawn she'd emerged into many hours ago had brightened into a sunny day. But the air was still bitterly cold. She put the kettle on the Primus to boil for tea then held out her hands to the heater, rubbing together her gloved palms to ease the stiffness in her fingers. She'd left the van with the lads and had walked briskly back from the market, stirring from her preoccupation every so often to return hellos and waves to people who'd hailed her in the street.

Christmas spent with her brother and her friends had been magical. All the good food and drink, and the long talks into the night with Davy about family, and her failure to find their sister, seemed a long while ago. She'd not forgotten his disappointment, though, that the lead to Charlotte Finch had petered out when all the signs pointed to the child being related to them.

It had been wonderful to have her twin home, safe and well, but his presence had made her pine for Greg. Waving her brother off at Charing Cross had brought back poignant memories of the last moments she'd spent with her fiancé in that busy place, rattling with noise.

Margie's predicament was uppermost in her mind now. Lily wished she knew more about babies and pregnancies, to be able to advise her friend. Fanny was the person to talk to about such things; there wasn't much about the joy of having babies — or the sadness of losing them — that she didn't know. But Margie was adamant that, for now, nobody must know. There was a possibility nature could intervene. A miscarriage would solve everything. Margie had given it all a great deal of thought and had come up with a sensible approach. In any case, whatever Margie decided, Lily would stick by her friend's decision and never betray Margie's trust.

The girls hadn't met up since Fanny had moved away to Islington, but they'd sent Christmas cards, exchanging news. Lily had been delighted to hear that Fanny was happy with her life, and looking forward to packing up her munitions job to have her baby. The only fly in the ointment seemed to be that Roger's wife had so far refused to give him a divorce.

The kettle whistled and Lily left her warm spot by the heater to make the tea. The biscuit tin was empty: Margie usually did the shopping. But Lily wasn't bothered by the lack, having devoured a newspaper twist of chips earlier. Both the lads had hollow legs and had gobbled up a ha'penny rock eel as well, all washed down with a shared flask of strong, sweet tea.

Lily carried her drink to the desk and was about to sit down when a strip of sunlight and a rush of cold air made her look up. A middle-aged woman, dressed in black, had entered. Instead of stating her business she stopped and stared at Lily.

'Can I help you?' Lily asked politely.

'Are you Lily Larkin?'

'Yes, I am.'

The woman came closer, her eyes fixed on Lily's face. 'I needn't have asked really. You look like your father. I was acquainted with him years ago, you see.' She smiled, holding out her gloved hand. 'I'm Vera Priest. I paid a visit on my old neighbour in Cheapside; she told me you'd tracked your sister that far. I can't tell you how relieved I was to hear that somebody in Charlotte's family was searching for her.'

It took Lily a moment to recover from the shock. She inhaled a long breath and clasped her hands together to stop them shaking. 'I have been looking for my sister. I've been to orphanages and to the Dr Barnardo's home. Along the way I was lucky enough to hear your name mentioned; I hoped you were searching for her too.' Lily suddenly felt overwhelmed with emotion and gave the woman a hug, burying her face into her shoulder. Mrs Priest wasn't at all what Lily had been expecting: a rosy-cheeked, matronly figure, she'd imagined. This woman was small and thin with short, straight iron-grey hair. She appeared rather forbidding — a schoolmarm — but she returned Lily's spontaneous affection, rubbing her back in comfort.

'There, there . . . I should've written to let you know I was coming. I've given you a bad turn, just showing up. I couldn't wait, you see; once I knew where to find you, I just had to come.' She held Lily away from

373

her, cupping one of the girl's wet cheeks with a gloved palm.

'I'm so glad you did,' Lily snuffled, using a hanky on her face. 'I've longed for this moment. I knew if our paths crossed I'd find out if we were looking for the same child.' She distractedly swiped away more tears that had quietly fallen to salt her lips. 'I'm so very pleased to meet you.' She quickly scrubbed her tear-stained fingers on her skirt then held out her hand.

'And I'm overjoyed to meet you, Lily,' Vera Priest returned, taking Lily's hand in both of hers. 'She is your sister. I was there when she was brought into my employer's house as an infant. She wasn't even a full day old when I found out Charles Larkin's wife had given birth in the Whitechapel workhouse.' The woman waited for Lily to stifle a sob before continuing. 'I know that hearing my tale will be a mixed blessing for you. If you want me to continue, I will, and I'll leave nothing out, though I am ashamed of parts of it.'

Lily dragged the chair from behind the desk and gestured for her visitor to sit down, then she perched on the orange box and waited, heart in mouth, for the woman to begin.

When Vera was done relating the tale, she paused for a moment, letting Lily digest the enormity of it all. Then she said, 'I'm so sorry for handing Charlotte back to Mrs Jolley. I desperately wanted to take the child with me to my new position in Hertfordshire, but I couldn't. I've been a widow for over twenty years and have no children. If there had been anybody at all I could have turned to for help, I would have snatched at it to keep Charlotte. By the time I had found a job in Essex that would have allowed me to have a child, it was too late. I went to reclaim Betsy's daughter but Mrs Jolley had disappeared.' Vera sighed. 'In my defence, I thought the woman shifty but had no idea she might be evil or I'd never have left Charlotte with her.'

'Evil?' Lily echoed, dread tightening her guts. The Skipmans didn't like Mrs Jolley either, but they'd not described her as evil.

'I believe she is. When I visited the Foundling Hospital I mentioned Mrs Jolley's name. The woman I spoke to looked shocked that I would have handed a child to her. I said that the foster mother had come recommended — and it is true.

A friend of Betsy's had played the same trick on her sugar daddy and it had ended well. He married her, believing he had a son.'

'Matron didn't mention Mrs Jolley to me.' Lily reflected on that meeting last year. 'But I did get the impression there was something she wasn't telling me.'

'I wish I had spoken to Matron as well. I think I might have got more information about Mrs Jolley. Matron wasn't available, though, and her deputy seemed keen for me to leave. The terms of admission were explained and I understood that Charlotte wouldn't have been accepted as she was four years old.' Vera paused. 'When pressed, the deputy admitted that other visitors were searching for children handed over to the same baby farmer. She suggested I contact the police.' Vera sorrowfully shook her grey head. 'I haven't done so; there would be endless questions about Charlotte's parentage. What a tangle that is to explain. The authorities would want to speak to Charlotte's mother. I have no idea where Betsy Finch

375

is and I doubt she would co-operate, in any case.' Vera gazed kindly at Lily who was gnawing at her wobbly lower lip and from time to time dabbing at her eyes. 'I haven't told you this to upset you. But you should know what you are up against in Mrs Jolley. Oh, to be able to go back and do things differently,' she concluded on a regretful exhalation.

'What else could you have done, though? You had to work or you couldn't have supported the two of you.' Lily's forgiveness emerged in a croak from her throbbing throat. She sniffed back the tears that were threatening. 'I should thank you for giving my sister such happy early years. She thrived with you; she might have died at just days old, without your care.'

'It was no hardship looking after her; she was the dearest child.'

Lily managed a smile. 'Others have told me that. A family living close to Mrs Jolley took a liking to Charlotte and became her friends. She ran away, wanting to stay with them, but was found and taken back home.' Lily only now fully understood the enormity of that lost opportunity.

'I can imagine her running away. She was plucky . . . growing into quite a little tomboy. She'd race around the garden and try to climb the apple tree.' Vera chuckled with the memory. 'Charlie, I called her, and she was bright as a button. She learned her letters and numbers very quickly.'

'*You* taught her to write her name? I saw it, pencilled on a newspaper that had been left behind when they moved away.'

'I did teach her; she picked it up with ease. Your father was a very good solicitor's clerk. Very good with figures. I can even now see him totting up his books

376

in that office.'

Vera Priest had no idea Charlotte was illegitimate. And there seemed no point in bringing it up now. 'Is that how you came to be acquainted with my dad? You were a colleague of his at that place?'

'I just used to make the tea and do the cleaning. I left shortly after your father did. Betsy Finch took me on as her housekeeper.' Vera paused, frowning at her hands, clasped in her lap. 'I was very sorry about what happened to Charles Larkin. I decided I didn't want to stay working at the solicitor's office afterwards. I knew Betsy wasn't respectable, but I accepted her job offer.'

Lily edged forward on the box, anticipating this woman had something of interest to tell about her father's downfall. But Mrs Priest appeared unsure whether to continue.

'What *did* happen?' Lily prodded. 'My twin brother and I were only nine years old then. All we knew was that he got sacked for stealing. He sold our house to stay out of prison. When he died we ended up with our mum in the Whitechapel workhouse.'

Vera screwed up her eyes, shaking her head in despair. 'That it should have come to that . . . I'm so very sorry . . .'

'He changed afterwards, you see. I think he was ashamed of letting us all down. He drank heavily and was always arguing with my mum. I heard a woman mentioned. When I think of it now, being older, I do wonder if he'd been unfaithful and stole the money for a new life with somebody else.'

'I don't believe he was a thief or an adulterer. I was just an underling at that solicitor's office, but I wasn't deaf, blind or stupid. I understood what went on.'

Mrs Priest paused. 'It is hardly my business, and I've no proof of anything. I can only give you my opinion. I think I've a right to air it, and after what you have suffered as a family, you have a right to hear it. Then you can make up your own mind.'

Lily gave an eager nod.

'Your father was a charming man. He often spoke about your mother when I served him his tea and biscuits at his desk. He was never too uppity to pass the time of day with such as me. It was obvious he adored his wife Maude. He was flirtatious though.' Vera paused. 'The boss's wife liked a flirtatious man. She certainly liked Charles Larkin.'

'She went after my dad?' Lily demanded in disbelief.

'She made it clear she liked him. She seemed to visit the office more often than she once had.' Vera was careful choosing her words. 'I believe your father realised he'd been . . . too sociable, and tried to withdraw and be more formal with her. He would busy himself with his books and hardly look up at her.' Vera sighed. 'She didn't like to be ignored. She told her husband that Charles Larkin had been inappropriate with her. That was the beginning of the end for your father . . . after that he had to go.'

Lily mulled over what she'd heard. 'You think my dad was accused of stealing when he'd done nothing, don't you?' She leapt upright, her cheeks a furious red. 'His boss could've framed him to punish him and get rid of him. All Dad had done was flirt with the boss's wife!'

'It's just my opinion. Perhaps I shouldn't have told you. I don't want to distress you, dragging up the past. This water passed under the bridge a long while ago.'

'Doesn't matter to me how long ago it was,' Lily said. 'It's up here all the time, like it happened yesterday.' She tapped her temple. 'Sorry . . . I shouldn't have shouted. I'm very grateful you told me. My brother will be too. We've nobody left to ask about these things, you see.'

Vera got to her feet. 'I understand. Now I really must go. I promised to call in on my elderly brother in Fulham. Then back to work for me. Just another year and I intend to retire.'

'Oh, don't go yet. I'm so sorry . . . I've been rude. I've not even offered you a cup of tea. Please, stay and have some tea.'

'No . . .' Vera gave her a warm smile. 'Thank you, but I must go, or I'll miss my train later and I don't want to take liberties. I was lucky my employer let me have a few days off. I've left my address with my old neighbour in case Jolley returns looking for me. I doubt she will, now she has moved again.' Vera took Lily's hands in her bony grip. 'I'm so glad I called at Cheapside and it led me to you. It's a great relief to know I can hand over the search for Charlotte. I don't manage to get about as easily as I used to. I'll rest easy now we've met and I know I can put my trust in you to carry on.' She gave Lily's hands a fond shake before letting them go. 'You're two lucky girls, having each other. I can see Charlotte in you, in looks and character.'

'You'll keep in touch, though?' Lily sounded alarmed. She didn't want to lose this new and important friend.

'I'd like that. Here, let me give you my address.' Vera took a small notebook and pencil from her bag. She wrote quickly then tore out the page and handed it over. 'If you have any news at all, good or bad, I'd appreciate hearing it. I'll pray nightly for you to find her safe and well.'

Lily accompanied Vera to the door. 'There is something worrying me,' she said. 'Mrs Jolley's neighbour saw them packed up on the day they left the house. She reported Charlotte sitting on the pram, looking very unwell. I'm frightened she might have got diphtheria from a local family. It's been going around in the area and children have died.'

Vera took Lily by the shoulders, turning her to face her. 'Even if your sister were with you, you wouldn't be able to protect her all the time. We're all in the lap of the gods. But if you want my opinion again: that girl's a fighter. She's pulled through some very bad luck. Mrs Jolley, diphtheria, even Betsy Finch, useless mother that she was — none of it will stop Charlotte Finch having the life she deserves now she's made it this far.'

Lily watched the small, slight woman walking off down the street. It had started to drizzle and Vera Priest put up her umbrella, almost disappearing beneath it. She looked older . . . quite stooped, from behind. Lily watched until she'd disappeared from sight. Getting on in years and frail, maybe, but Vera Priest was tough, and wiser than any other woman Lily knew. What a wonderful surrogate mother her little sister had been blessed with, to see her through her infancy.

Lily turned away and returned to the desk. She sat down, staring into her untouched, cold tea, her fears returning. Mrs Jolley was evil . . .

Lily jerked up her chin, eyes a-glitter; so would she be, if she needed to be.

380

Charlotte Finch *was* her sister; Vera Priest was trust-
ing her to find the little girl. And she would. She'd do
whatever it took to bring her back where she belonged.

And that was that.

Acknowledgements

My continuing thanks to Anna Boatman, Sarah Murphy and all the editorial team at Piatkus for their support and enthusiasm for the Workhouse to War series. Also thanks to Penny Isaac for her helpful input. And last but never least, to Juliet Burton, my agent.

Author's Note

Mrs Jolley is a fictional character based upon a very real and wicked person who lived in Victorian times. Amelia Dyer went to the gallows in 1896 after almost three decades of taking money to act as a foster mother, but actually murdering babies for a living.

When finally caught, the public horror and outcry surrounding her Old Bailey trial and subsequent execution wasn't enough to put others off from following in her evil footsteps. More baby farmers were hanged during the Edwardian era.

Back then, attitudes towards unmarried mothers were such that some felt unable to keep their babies. Greedy, immoral people would have seen desperate women and their innocent children as easy pickings. I hope by the outbreak of the Great War in 1914 — the period in which my Workhouse to War series is set — that such characters as Amelia Dyer and my fictional Mrs Jolley no longer existed. But who is to know, when it is probable that not every person involved in this hideous practice was caught and brought to justice.

We do hope that you have enjoyed
reading this large print book.

Did you know that all of our titles
are available for purchase?

We publish a wide range of high
quality large print books including:
**Romances, Mysteries, Classics
General Fiction
Non Fiction and Westerns**

Special interest titles available in
large print are:
**The Little Oxford Dictionary
Music Book, Song Book
Hymn Book, Service Book**

Also available from us courtesy of
Oxford University Press:
**Young Readers' Dictionary
(large print edition)
Young Readers' Thesaurus
(large print edition)**

For further information or a free
brochure, please contact us at:
**Ulverscroft Large Print Books Ltd.,
The Green, Bradgate Road, Anstey,
Leicester, LE7 7FU, England.
Tel:** (00 44) **0116 236 4325
Fax:** (00 44) **0116 234 0205**

Other titles published by Ulverscroft:

THE WAY HOME

Kay Brellend

North London, 1916. When Olivia Bone and Lieutenant Lucas Black share a passionate kiss one summer's evening, it seems as if their love might finally have a chance to bloom. But their brief happiness is cut short when Lucas is sent to fight on the front line, leaving Livvie uncertain if she'll ever see him again. While her friends in London busy themselves with marriage plans and dreams of babies, Livvie returns to France, throwing herself into her work as a war nurse on the Western Front. But when two German prisoners are admitted at the hospital, the dangers of war suddenly feel much closer to home — and Livvie is forced to be braver than she has ever been before... Can Livvie and Lucas find their way to a brighter future before the war tears them apart?

A LONELY HEART

Kay Brellend

Growing up in fear of their cruel, drunken father, Olivia Bone and her siblings haven't had an easy start in life. But when Livvie's fiancé Joe is killed at Ypres and he bequeaths her his house in Islington, it seems like the Bone family might finally escape the worst street in north London. At least Livvie has good friends, and perhaps more than a friend in Lieutenant Lucas Black, her old boss at the Barratt's Sweet Factory. As they grow closer, she decides to enlist as a war nurse, hoping to help brave men like him in fighting for their country. Should Livvie follow her heart, or her head?

A SISTER'S BOND

Kay Brellend

North London, November 1913. After her mother dies, Livvie Bone is left to support her family and protect her younger siblings from their drunken father. But life in Wood Green is hard and full of danger. When the mysterious Joe Hunter steps in to help her, Livvie is drawn to him, despite his reputation.